WHEN THE BOUGH BREAKS

THE EMPIRE'S CORPS: BOOK THREE

CHRISTOPHER G. NUTTALL

The characters and events portrayed in this book are fictitious. Any similarity to real persons, living or dead, is coincidental and not intended by the author.

Text copyright © 2016 Christopher G. Nuttall

All rights reserved.
No part of this book may be reproduced, or stored in a retrieval system, or transmitted in any form or by any means, electronic, mechanical, photocopying, recording, or otherwise, without express written permission of the publisher.

ISBN-13: 9781537637068
ISBN-10: 1537637061

www.chrishanger.net
http://chrishanger.wordpress.com/
http://www.facebook.com/ChristopherGNuttall

All Comments Welcome!

WHEN THE BOUGH BREAKS

Book One: The Empire's Corps
Book Two: No Worse Enemy
Book Three: When The Bough Breaks
Book Four: Semper Fi
Book Five: The Outcast
Book Six: To The Shores
Book Seven: Reality Check
Book Eight: Retreat Hell
Book Nine: The Thin Blue Line
Book Ten: Never Surrender
Book Eleven: First To Fight
Book Twelve: They Shall Not Pass

DEAR READER

While this book is set in the same universe as *The Empire's Corps* and *No Worse Enemy* – and helps lay the groundwork for future developments in the series – I wrote *When The Bough Breaks* to be largely stand-alone. Chronologically speaking, this book starts just after Captain Stalker and his men left Earth in *The Empire's Corps*.

You should be able to read and enjoy it without having read the first two books. However, you can download samples of the first two books – and many others – from my website and then purchase them on Kindle. If you like my books, please review them on Amazon – it helps boost sales and convinces me to write more in certain universes.

As I am not the best editor in the world, I would be grateful if you email me to point out any spelling mistakes, placing them in context. I can offer cameos, redshirt deals and suchlike in return.

Have fun! And if you want a fourth book, let me know…

Christopher Nuttall

DEDICATION

To fight against bureaucracy is like fighting against a slow-moving tidal wave; it can seem an insurmountable foe, utterly impossible to defeat no matter how irrational its thinking. And yet some people have fought and won. In winning, they helped maintain civilisation.

This book is dedicated to those who fought.

For want of a nail the shoe was lost.
For want of a shoe the horse was lost.
For want of a horse the rider was lost.
For want of a rider the message was lost.
For want of a message the battle was lost.
For want of a battle the kingdom was lost.
And all for the want of a horseshoe nail.

- Traditional

CHAPTER ONE

It started on Han, although few recognised what it was without the benefit of hindsight. A single cramped world, divided by political, ethnic, religious and sexual apartheid...tearing itself apart in a rage that threatened to consume an entire planet. Han was the Empire in microcosm...and the Empire's peacekeepers found it impossible to cope with the chaos.

In Han, the death throes of the Empire found an eerie reflection.

— Professor Leo Caesius, *The End of Empire*.

"I think that's him," McQueen said.

Belinda looked up from where she was crouched in the dumpster. This part of New Canton had been abandoned by the forces of law, order and civilisation years ago, leaving it to sink into a state that drove away even the gangsters who existed on the margins of civilised society. The Pathfinders had been lurking in the area for two days and it felt like an eternity. If it hadn't been for the augmentation and bio-enhancement worked into their bodies, she couldn't help thinking that the stench alone would have driven them away hours ago.

"You think it's him," she repeated. "Are you sure?"

"There are no guarantees of anything," McQueen reminded her, as he dropped back down into the dumpster. "But it does very much look like Target One."

Belinda nodded. The Han Civil Guard had managed to identify a handful of the rebel leaders before the shit had hit the fan, but it had been completely incapable of actually *dealing* with them. If they'd been more competent, perhaps Han would never have exploded into chaos... but there was no profit in contemplating what might have been. Right now, nearly a million soldiers and Marines were battling to suppress the insurgency and finding it hard going. Han had been a powder keg waiting to explode for years.

The Pathfinder platoon had been tasked with hunting down what few members of the rebel leaders *had* been identified and taking them alive, if possible. Admiral Valentine, the Imperial Navy officer in overall command of the operation, had been insistent that the rebels had to be taken alive, but Major General Dempsey – the Marine CO – had been more realistic. The Empire never showed mercy to rebels and the rebels knew it. They could be expected to fight to the death. And in New Canton there were too many armed men ready to ambush an Imperial force intent on raiding their territory.

She opened the hatch at the bottom of the dumpster and dropped down into the hidden basement. The other three Pathfinders glanced up from where they were checking their weapons, their hands automatically reaching for the MAG pistols they'd left within easy reach. Missions had been blown before by a sharp-eyed local noticing something out of place and the Pathfinders might have been forced to fight their way out. The rebels had tried to take Imperial bureaucrats hostage to use as bargaining chips, but they wouldn't try to hold Pathfinders prisoner. They'd kill them all once they realised what their prisoners actually *were*.

"Looks like him," Doug grunted, once McQueen had shared the take from his optical implants. They hadn't risked scattering sensors and surveillance bugs near the nondescript house the rebels used as a base, for fear of tipping them off too soon. Han wasn't a particularly high-tech world, but the rebels had managed to import a surprising amount of advanced weapons and armour to support their uprising. "None of the others look familiar, though."

"Everyone on this planet looks alike," Pug grunted. He skimmed through the rest of the recording, before putting it aside. "That's what you get for having a clone population."

Belinda shrugged as she donned the rest of her armour. Han's founders had wanted to boost their population size as quickly as possible, so they'd used cloning tubes as well as volunteer host-mothers and advanced fertility treatments. They'd succeeded beyond their wildest dreams, which was at least partly why Han had a population problem comparable to Earth's – and, for that matter, why there was an eerie uniformity binding the population together. The intrusion of genes from outside the restricted gene pool the founders had deemed acceptable had yet to spread throughout the world.

"Signal the Navy," Doug ordered, once they were all checked out. "I want supporting elements on alert, ready to move, the moment we launch."

"We can handle it," Nathan objected, more for form's sake than anything else. Once they had the rebel leader in their clutches, they would need to get him out of the city – and the quickest way to do that was to have them picked up by a Raptor. Getting him out of the city on foot would be a nightmare. "Really, boss..."

"Get on with it," Doug ordered. "And check everything."

Belinda smiled as she checked her armour and weapons, then allowed McQueen to check hers while she checked his. Pathfinders had access to the best equipment money could buy, but they knew better than to take anything for granted. Everything had to be checked out before they launched the mission, or it might fail – and knowing their luck, it would fail at the worst possible moment. The cloaking field didn't even have to fail completely to alert the enemy that something was wrong.

She donned her helmet and moved over to the door, ready to climb up to the abandoned house they were using as a base. McQueen took point, weapon in hand, and crawled up the ladder, ready for anything. Belinda followed him, her augmented eyes automatically adjusting for the dimming light as the sun vanished beneath the horizon. Han's moons wouldn't rise until much later. She caught sight of a rat scurrying across the floor, chased by a small army of cockroaches, and shook her head. The stench of death and decay seemed much stronger here.

"Activate cloaking fields," Doug ordered. "Move out."

Belinda's first impression of Canton City had been that it was *cramped*. Thousands of buildings had been pressed close together, so close that walkways could be rigged up between them – and had been, as the population struggled to find more living space. There were hundreds of street children eking out an existence at ground level, while the richer part of the population avoided them like the plague. Signs advertising everything from soap powder to prostitutes were plastered everywhere, in both Imperial Standard and the local dialect of Chinese. Belinda had been told that the locals were kept deliberately ignorant of Imperial Standard, making it harder for them to find employment with interstellar corporations or the Empire's military. Looking at the bilingual signs, she could well believe it.

There was nothing distinguishing the rebel base from the rest of the neighbourhood, a wise precaution with the Imperial Navy high overhead, ready to drop KEWs on any rebels unwise enough to announce their presence. A handful of armed guards could be seen in position to intercept anyone who wanted to enter without permission, although *that* wasn't uncommon; anyone who could afford guards hired them. Besides, the rebels had converted a brothel into their headquarters. No one would question furtive-looking men heading into a brothel.

There are innocents inside, Belinda reminded herself, as the Pathfinders took up position. Her upbringing on Greenway hadn't prepared her for the sheer…hopelessness of parts of the Empire. The prostitutes had probably had no choice but to sell their bodies to survive; it was quite possible that some or all of them were actually underage. It was illegal, but what did legality matter when it was a choice between selling one's body or starving to death?

Doug sent a single order over the command network. "Go."

Belinda fired at once, targeting one of the guards and putting a bullet through his head before he even had time to realise that the base was under attack. The rest of the team engaged at the same time, wiping out the guards before they could fire a shot back. Even if they had time to react, they would have found it difficult to return fire; the Pathfinders were hidden behind their cloaking fields. The only real option would have been to spray the entire area with bullets and pray.

"All down," McQueen sent.

"Inside," Doug ordered "Pug, take point."

Pug ran forward and slapped a charge against the heavy wooden door. It exploded a moment later, reducing the door to splinters. Nathan threw a stun grenade through the door, triggering it as soon as it was inside the room. Belinda winced in sympathy as her implants picked up the detonation; anyone without armour or special enhancement would be on the ground, twitching, the moment they were struck by the blast. Pug dived into the room, his implants transmitting what he saw to his teammates. Belinda tracked him even as she moved up behind McQueen, ready to provide support.

"Five guards, none of them listed," Nathan reported. "One dead; I think the poor bastard caught a piece of flying wood. The others are stunned."

"Leave them," Doug ordered. The sound of the breaching charge would have been heard for miles in the still air. They had to assume that the locals knew that they were there. "Search the rest of the complex."

The Pathfinders didn't take chances as they searched the building quickly and efficiently. Everyone they encountered was stunned and left to lie on the ground until they could be recovered, if there was time. Belinda pushed her personal feelings aside as she broke into the whores' living quarters and stunned them, even though it was clear that most of the women were effectively prisoners. There was no sign of the rebel leader, she realised, as they compared notes over the command network. They might have missed him.

She winced as she heard someone opening fire with a machine gun. The rebels were on the top floor and had managed to grab weapons, according to Pug and Nathan. Their leadership was probably making its escape over the rooftops while their guards sacrificed themselves to buy time. The Pathfinders launched high-explosive grenades up the stairs and scrambled up afterwards, determined not to give the rebels any time. Belinda brought up the rear as they burst into the rebel base and followed the ladder up to the upper floor.

"Belinda, McQueen, run SIE," Doug ordered, as he led the other two up onto the roof. "Orbital says that there are mobs forming outside."

"Understood," Belinda said, as she sat down in front of the rebel computers and started tearing them apart, searching for the memory chips. "We're on it."

Organising a rebellion, she'd been amused to discover years ago, required a certain amount of bureaucracy – and a surprising number of rebel leaders had forgotten basic security precautions when it came to gathering data on their recruits. The Marines were experts in getting captured enemy records back to base and using them to locate other targets – or identifying rebels captured in counter-insurgency sweeps. Shaking her head, she dug out the chips and stowed them away in her webbing, under the armour. They'd be safe there – she hoped – until they got back to base.

"Got some too," McQueen reported. "I…"

He broke off as the building shook. "That's the mob," Belinda said. The brothel was almost completely sound-proofed, but audio-discrimination programs in her implants could pick out rebel yells and chants. "Grab everything and get up onto the roof."

McQueen followed her up the ladder and onto the roof. Canton seemed to have come to life suddenly; she could see thousands of people thronging through the streets, shouting and screaming death to the Imperial intruders. She wasn't too surprised that this part of the city would be solidly behind the rebels, but she pushed the thought aside. The team would attempt to avoid engaging the mob, if possible.

"We caught him," Doug sent, from where the other three had followed the rebel leader as he leapt from building to building. "We…"

The signal broke off as a colossal explosion shook the city. Belinda turned to see a giant fireball rising up into the air, shattering several city blocks. The mob howled in pain and anguish as flying debris slashed through the air, cutting through human flesh and bone as though it were made of paper. Belinda felt a burst of pain as three termination signals flashed up in her retina display, informing her that Doug, Pug and Nathan were dead. Even a Pathfinder couldn't survive such an explosion.

Behind them, the mob fought its way up onto the roof. Belinda didn't hesitate; she turned and ran towards the edge of the roof, triggering the boosting implants that had been inserted into her body. There was a rush of energy as she leapt across the chasm between the brothel and the next building; she landed on her feet and kept running, McQueen close behind her. The entire mission had failed spectacularly and all they could do now was break contact and hope that the death of three of their teammates hadn't been *entirely* wasted. But it was hard to imagine that one rebel leader was worth the death of three Pathfinders.

She landed on the third building and realised, instantly, that they'd made a mistake. A settlement of dispossessed workers perched on top of it, the workers throwing bricks and glass bottles towards the two Pathfinders. To her boosted mind, the projectiles appeared to be moving in slow motion, but they were still dangerous. She kept moving, ducking and weaving as best as she could, slamming into one particularly angry worker who tried to block their path physically. Belinda felt his arm snap like a twig as they collided. She left him falling to the rooftop as she jumped to another building, heading towards the city walls. Once they were in clear ground, she *knew* they could outrun any pursuit.

The entire city seemed to have gone crazy. The mobs down on the street below were growing larger, while more and more rooftops were suddenly crammed with people intent on intercepting the two escapees. Belinda exchanged brief messages with McQueen and then started to launch stun grenades towards the next rooftop. The armour and augmentation protected her, but not the locals. She saw a number – including a handful of kids who couldn't be even *entering* their teens – stagger over the edge and plummet to their deaths. But there were so many of them that the stun grenades couldn't stun them all...

She staggered as a local slammed into her, followed rapidly by others, their hands tearing away at her armour. Belinda stumbled and fell to the rooftop, grunting in pain as she struck the hard surface. Grimly, she boosted her strength again and started to lash out, her armoured hands tearing through her would-be captors with ease. Behind her, McQueen made it to his feet, his armour covered in blood. Belinda was no stranger to horror – she'd served on a WARCAT team, back when she'd been looking for a third MOS – but this was something new. It was something they'd done themselves.

Her communications implant buzzed.

"Devils, this is Alpha-Lead," a voice said. "We're inbound on your position."

"Understood," Belinda said, brusquely. They couldn't stay on the rooftop and await rescue, not when the mob was still following them. "Get into position and be ready to fire suppression rounds."

"Ah...strum gas is banned in urban areas," the pilot said. "Orders from Fleet Command, don't you know?"

Not a Marine, Belinda realised, in surprise. The mission briefing had stated that the QRF was composed of Marines, but something had clearly changed between their departure and the actual operation being launched. Only Imperial Navy pilots worried so much about precise Rules of Engagement in the middle of an actual engagement. Even the Civil Guard wasn't that dumb.

"We're the bastards on the ground," McQueen thundered. "Get that gas deployed *now*!"

Belinda leapt to another building, then another. The Raptors were coming in over the city, drawing fire from the ground. She winced, wondering grimly if Intelligence's claims that the rebels didn't have HVMs were about to be proven spectacularly wrong, before returning her attention to their escape. If they could stay ahead of the rest of the mob...

A colossal explosion thundered up behind them as they leapt to the next building. Belinda had no idea *what* had exploded, but the blast caught her and slammed her through a window and into a deserted room. Medical alerts flared up on her retina display as her leg snapped, painkiller drugs automatically entering her system. The armour went rigid, allowing her to try to walk...

"Deploying gas," the pilot said, over the intercom.

Belinda cursed as a fourth termination signal flashed up in her display. McQueen was dead, either killed by the mob or slammed into the ground too hard for his armour to protect him. She could hear the sound of people crashing their way into the building and heading upwards, right towards where she was lying. Desperately, she pulled herself to her feet and limped forward, looking around for something she could use as a crutch. The pilot's cheerful voice in her ear didn't help; the gas was spreading, but not fast enough to help her.

Grimly, she switched her rifle from single-shot to full auto and opened fire as the mob burst into the room. They were thrown backwards as the bullets tore through them, but there were so many more pushing upwards that the dead and wounded were just thrown forwards. Belinda cursed out loud and started to launch her final grenades into the mob, even as new warnings began to flash up in her display. She was pushing herself too far…the grenade exploded, setting fire to the building. Belinda saw the flames starting to spread, heard the mob howling in pain, smelled the stench of burning human flesh…

We failed, she thought, numbly. *And we're all dead.*

And then she blacked out completely.

CHAPTER TWO

For those of us who live after the Fall of Earth and the end of the Empire, there is a sense of inevitability about its collapse. The Empire must fall. And yet, there seemed little reason for its citizens to realise the truth. The Empire had endured for three thousand years. Why should it not endure for three thousand more? To answer that question, we must delve into the history of the Empire itself.

- Professor Leo Caesius, *The End of Empire.*

The glittering towers stretched as far as the eye could see.

Major General Jeremy Damiani, Commandant of the Terran Marine Corps, stood at his office window and stared out over Imperial City. It was an awe-inspiring view; tall skyscrapers punching the sky, massive towers belonging to the Grand Senators and the major interstellar corporations and – in the distance – the hive-like CityBlock structures where countless humans lived and died without ever leaving their blocks. Beyond that, he could see a thin thread reaching up to orbit, one of Earth's six massive orbital towers allowing quick and easy access to low orbit. It was a testament to all that mankind could accomplish on Earth.

"It all looks so safe and tranquil," Hiram Green said. "You would never believe that there was anything wrong."

Jeremy shrugged. Earth's land surface was covered in megacities, each one home to billions of human beings. Centuries of mistreatment had finally pushed the planet beyond salvation; the parts of the land that were not covered with metal were too badly poisoned to support human life. The oceans that had once fed countless humans were now dying, with thousands upon thousands of marine life forms rendered extinct. Even if the Imperial Reclamation Corps had been something other than another boondoggle to extract money from the government, it was hard to see how they could save the planet. Earth was dying.

And yet the population still bred. Officially, Earth's population was listed as forty billion; unofficially, it was at least sixty billion and Jeremy had his suspicions that the true figure was almost certainly much higher. The Undercity warrens were crammed with people, living out their lives in darkness – unless they were deported from the planet or managed to sign up with a colony project. Earth expelled millions of people each month and yet they were only a drop in the bucket of the multitudes swarming over the planet.

There were no visible signs of decay in Imperial City, but Jeremy knew that they were there. The infrastructure built up over centuries to feed the population, to provide light and heat and power, was finally starting to fail completely. There were just too many failure points and too few maintenance crews to fix them, even when the crews weren't diverted to attend to the whims of one Grand Senator or another. Sooner or later, and Jeremy knew in his heart that it would probably be sooner, there would be a cascading series of failures that would finally tip the planet over the edge and into darkness. And then? No one knew for sure, but Jeremy had a feeling that it would make Han look like a pillow fight between teenage children.

His gaze drifted over to the Imperial Palace and, no less grand – the Grand Senate. The Grand Senators had no real understanding of the looming disaster threatening their positions – or they simply didn't care. Imperial City was insulated from the worst of the problems plaguing Earth, but it wouldn't be long before the systems started to fail there too. And then the shit would *really* hit the fan. Jeremy had moved his family from Earth to Safehouse long ago. Countless billions on the planet below didn't have that option.

His communicator buzzed. "Commandant? *Sebastian Cruz* has broken orbit."

"Understood," Jeremy said. He'd left orders that he was to be informed when the transport ship carrying Captain Stalker and his understrength force departed Earth. "Don't interrupt us unless it's something urgent."

He closed the channel and turned away from the window. The Commandant of the Marine Corps was entitled to a large office, if only because the other Joint Chiefs of the Imperial Military had their own large offices. Jeremy hadn't bothered to decorate it, beyond attaching a handful of medals and commendation papers to one wall. The only luxury item in the room was a desk that had been passed down from Commandant to Commandant for thousands of years. Jeremy knew that the Marines were probably the only people in the Empire who remembered where the desk had come from – and what it had once symbolised.

There were two other people in the office, apart from himself and Green. Colonel Chung Myung-Hee served as the *de facto* Marine Intelligence Head of Station on Earth, although the Grand Senate would have been alarmed to discover that Marine Intelligence operated on the homeworld. A tall willowy woman with oval eyes and lightly-tinted skin, few would have believed that she was a Marine on first glance – or that she was one of the smartest people Jeremy had ever met. Beside her, General Gerald Anderson seemed short, stocky and over-muscular. The CO of the First Marine Division had to look the part.

"Report," Jeremy ordered, as he took his seat behind the desk.

"We have been given warning orders for sending three regiments of Marines to Albion," Anderson said, shortly. "They are to be drawn from the First Marine Division."

Jeremy winced. The Grand Senate had been more parsimonious than usual over the last five years, using the Marine Corps as firemen while trying simultaneously to starve the Corps of the resources it needed to carry out its assignments. First Marine Division consisted – officially – of 20,000 Marines, the largest Marine force in the Empire. Unofficially, the division was badly understrength – and had been parcelled out to support the Civil Guard in keeping order on Earth. Losing three regiments would leave him with no more than 4,000 Marines on Earth, all scattered over the planet. There were planets that could be held under control with 4,000 Marines. Earth wasn't one of them.

"The division has duties here," Green pointed out. "They have to know…"

"The Civil Guard has been tasked with keeping Earth under control," Chung said, tonelessly. "Their superiors have every faith in their ability to keep order."

Jeremy didn't bother to hide his disgust. The Civil Guard was notoriously corrupt and incompetent – and most of the units that were neither corrupt nor incompetent developed local ties that made them untrustworthy. One of the reasons the Grand Senate had been pushing for a major deployment of soldiers – and Marines – to Albion was a suspicion that the Albion Civil Guard had grown too close to the population it was supposed to monitor and keep under control. Albion was simply too economically important to be allowed to assert even the local autonomy it was permitted under the Imperial Charter.

"What's more worrying is that the orders weren't sent through Marine HQ," Anderson added. "They came directly to me from the Defence Department."

"I noticed," Jeremy said. The Grand Senate *always* meddled in military operations. It wasn't unknown for them to activate or redeploy certain units without bringing along the supporting elements those units required to be effective. Marine units were meant to be self-sufficient, but the Imperial Army had more logistics officers than it had fighting men. "Luckily, we can use that to delay matters for a few weeks."

Green put their doubts into words. "And then…what?"

"Sir, we cannot go on like this," Anderson said. "Right now, the division is the only thing keeping a lid on a thousand powder kegs. If I have to give up even *one* regiment…"

"I am aware of the dangers," Jeremy said, coldly. He'd been in Anderson's shoes himself, before he'd accepted promotion. "And it is going to get worse."

"It is," Chung confirmed. "We know now who is going to take command of Home Fleet – and effective command of Earth's defences. It's Admiral Valentine."

"Son of a bitch," Anderson exploded. "I..."

"As you were," Jeremy snapped. He found it hard to be truly angry at his subordinate, even if speaking ill of a superior officer was a military offence. Instead, he looked over at Chung. "Why him?"

"Political deals," Chung said, simply. "His patrons are in the Grand Senate itself."

Jeremy nodded, unable to keep a sour expression off his face. The Imperial Navy had been promoting officers on the basis of political connections for thousands of years, pushing competence and dedication aside in favour of political reliability. Admiral Valentine had commanded precisely one major deployment – the operation on Han – and that had been a bloody disaster. By the time the military had restored order, millions of locals had died, either in the chaos or the reprisals that had followed the end of the fighting. If Jeremy had his way, Admiral Valentine would have spent the rest of his career on an asteroid mining station on the far side of the Empire. Instead, he'd been promoted.

"Right," Jeremy said, finally. "What do his patrons have in mind?"

"I don't know," Chung admitted. "The Grand Senate spent months haggling over the position, which suggests that there was some heavy bargaining going on, but we don't know the exact details. All we have is speculation."

"As always," Anderson noted.

Jeremy couldn't help agreeing. Chung, at least, was smart enough to understand the difference between speculation and actual hard fact, unlike some of the other intelligence officers Jeremy had worked with in the past. The disaster that had swept over Han had been so bad partly because the local intelligence services had been thoroughly subverted by the rebels and Imperial Intelligence had dropped the ball completely.

"Leave that for the moment," Jeremy ordered. "The important issue right now is the Childe Roland."

He smiled at their expressions. The Marine Corps was – legally – supposed to provide the guard for the Royal Family, but the Grand Senate had taken advantage of the Childe Roland's minority to edge the Marines out, opening up a whole new field for patronage and political corruption. Jeremy had no idea what his predecessor had been thinking, but it had been a deadly mistake. The Childe Roland – the sixteen-year-old boy who was the Heir to the Empire – was utterly unprepared to rule. He'd been spoilt from birth, given everything he wanted…while being carefully kept away from the reins of power. And once he took the throne, as he would when he turned seventeen, disaster would follow swiftly.

"You plan to insert a bodyguard into his staff," Chung said. "Will they let you?"

"I wasn't planning to ask permission," Jeremy said, mildly. "We still have the legal authority to take command of his protective force – and *all* we're going to be doing is inserting an additional bodyguard."

"They won't like it," Anderson said. "Maybe we should just take him to the Slaughterhouse and make a man of him."

Jeremy snorted. By the time recruits reached the Slaughterhouse, ninety percent of them had failed or had been streamlined into another branch of the Empire's military. The Slaughterhouse filtered out two-thirds of the remainder, assigning them to auxiliary units if they chose to continue working with the Marines. Only the best survived to complete the Crucible and be tabbed as Marines. Putting an unprepared Prince in the training program would be rather like dropping a cat into a blender.

"I don't think we'd be able to do that," he said. He looked over at Green. "And Specialist Lawson?"

Green frowned. "I confess that I would have grave doubts about inserting her back into a combat zone," he admitted. "The physical wounds have healed; we were able to repair and even upgrade her augmentation in the process. But mentally…she has a bad case of survivor's guilt, as well as a burning hatred of intelligence officers. If she had shown the energy to leave the medical centre, I would have been worried for their safety."

Jeremy wasn't surprised. The official enquiry had concluded that the Pathfinders had been the victims of bad intelligence, but Marine Intelligence suspected that the team had been deliberately set up. They'd walked right into a trap that had been designed to kill the entire team. It had been sheer luck that had saved Specialist Belinda Lawson from following the rest of her team into the grave. He couldn't blame her for loathing every intelligence weenie she might encounter in future. But if she assaulted one, it would mean the end of her career.

Lawson's record was impressive, even for the Marines. She'd been born on Greenway, a planet along the frontier where the settlers had been forced to fight to survive. Her father, a retired Marine, had taught her how to hunt and shoot; she'd been winning prizes since she'd been old enough to hold a gun. And then she'd gone into Boot Camp at sixteen, the youngest Marine in her year, and graduated to the Slaughterhouse within two months. Her record there had been remarkable; she'd come first in her class, a rarity for female recruits. The Drill Instructors had said that she would go far.

She'd served as a Rifleman with Potter's Pranksters and seen combat action on several worlds before being offered a chance to return to the Slaughterhouse and qualify as a Pathfinder. Her record made it clear that she'd been pushed right to the limit, like all of the other candidates, but she'd qualified and joined Team Six, under the command of Doug Adams. She'd fitted in well…until Team Six had been effectively wiped out on Han.

Marines were always close to one another – Marines were encouraged to regard one another as brothers and sisters – but Pathfinders were the closest of all. He couldn't blame Specialist Lawson for feeling guilty over having survived when the rest of her team had died. And he knew that they couldn't risk sending her back to the Pathfinders, or even reassigning her to a standard Marine company. But using her as a close-protection operative – a bodyguard, in other words – brought its own risks.

"She does need a new challenge," Green said, as if he were reading his superior's thoughts. "And I don't think that she might go rogue…"

Jeremy grimaced. The media was fond of using rogue Marines as bad guys in countless entertainment flicks with the same plot – and actresses whose clothing was directly proportional to their intelligence – but they were very rare in reality. Marines were tested extensively during their training; those that might break were gently eased out of training or streamlined into a different military branch. Someone who had gone to the Slaughterhouse – even if they hadn't graduated – would do well in the regular military.

"Good," he said, flatly. "She'll be on her own for most of the time. We won't be able to provide her with a proper supporting element."

"Not least because we're moving Marines to Albion," Anderson grumbled. He scowled down at the table, then looked up. "Maybe we can keep a company on QRF near the Summer Palace. There would be no obvious connection between them and your Specialist unless the shit hit the fan, in which case no one would be able to complain..."

Chung coughed. "Have I told you how much I like your optimism?"

Jeremy held up a hand. "See to it," he ordered. Having a company of Marines nearby would be helpful, although they might have to work hard to come up with an excuse for their presence if the Grand Senate asked questions. Securing Imperial City was the responsibility of the Civil Guard. "Maybe we can work it in as a training exercise. God knows we don't run enough joint exercises as it is."

"Yes, sir," Anderson said. His face twitched into a bitter smile. "Of course, they'd find them upsetting and embarrassing. They might even be *discomfited*."

Jeremy scowled. A military unit needed to be training and exercising when it wasn't actually on active deployment – and the Civil Guard barely trained to minimum acceptable standards. It was hard to blame their commanders when every last training exercise required a mountain of paperwork, but it was dangerous. Civil Guardsmen regularly made mistakes that got them killed in the field. Jeremy had once run a Civil Guard battalion through Ambush Alley – a training facility on the Slaughterhouse – and the entire unit had been wiped out. And that had been on the *easy* setting. A full regiment of Marines would have had problems running through the *hard* setting.

"They'll live," he said, finally. He looked over at Chong. Marine Intelligence covered a great many programs that the Grand Senate knew nothing about. It would only have upset the Senators if they knew just how many programs Jeremy had started when he'd realised that the Empire was in serious trouble. "And the preparations for Safehouse?"

"Going ahead, sir," Chong said, unhappily. "I have a full report for you if you want it, but I can't say I'm happy about it. It just feels too much like running away."

"It's a contingency plan," Anderson said. He tapped the desktop, sharply. "We're not going to run away. We are merely preparing fallback positions in case of disaster."

"Right," Chong said sarcastically. "Next time perhaps we could surrender and call it a tactical strike without arms."

Jeremy ignored her. Instead, he looked out towards the looming spires of Earth. Deep inside, he knew that Anderson was likely to be wrong. When Earth exploded into chaos, even the Marines wouldn't be able to keep order. The Nihilist attack that Captain Stalker and his men had defeated was merely the first sign of trouble. It would grow much worse in the future.

For a long moment, he envied Captain Stalker and his men. *They* were well away from the doom looming over Earth. Jeremy and his allies would just have to do what they could to save the planet – or as much as they could of the Empire. If it *could* be saved…

CHAPTER THREE

This is not an easy task. Generations of historians had struggled with the legacy of Imperial propaganda, historical revisionism and outright falsification left behind by the Emperors and the Grand Senate. Indeed, the study of history was discouraged throughout the Empire's existence, with historians who wished to examine pre-Imperial times often denied the funds or access they required to build up a comprehensive picture. The net result was a series of glaring contradictions in the official history that largely passed unnoticed.
- Professor Leo Caesius, *The End of Empire.*

Belinda Lawson lay on her bed and stared up at the ceiling. It was white, but someone had drawn pictures of cartoon animals more suited for a children's ward than a medical centre for recuperating Marines. One of the cartoons – a humanoid rabbit wearing a Marine uniform – had made her smile the first time she'd seen it, but it was hard to feel anything these days. All she could do was lie in bed and wait. But for what?

They were dead. Doug was dead. Nathan was dead. Pug was dead. McQueen was dead. God knew they'd given her a hard time when she'd first been assigned to Team Six, but she couldn't hold that against them. They had to know if the FNG – the Fucking New Girl – could handle the pressure and had mercilessly poured it on until they'd carried out their first combat mission as a team. And then they'd accepted her…

And now they were dead.

The thought tormented her. The medics had repaired her leg and mended the minor wounds she hadn't even noticed during the operation, but they hadn't been able to do anything for her soul. One doctor had tried to tell her that it hadn't been her fault and she'd ordered him out of the room with as much venom as she'd been able to muster. An intelligence scumbag had come by and tried to make excuses for the screw-up that had dropped them into the middle of an armed mob, but he'd fled when Belinda had started to activate her combat implants. She was mildly surprised that he'd been brave enough to face her; intelligence officers, in her experience, preferred to stay well away from danger.

But it wasn't entirely their fault, her mind yammered at her. *She* could have seen the signs, if she'd looked…or maybe they would have realised that they were in trouble earlier, if they'd taken more time. But they hadn't had the time…in the end, all that mattered was that her teammates were dead and she was the sole survivor. And she couldn't even get out of bed.

She reached up and ran her hand through her blonde hair. Like all Pathfinders, she had been allowed to maintain a less-military appearance – Doug had called it *slovenly* – and she'd grown her hair out, although not enough to interfere with the helmet. Now, after six months of lying in bed, it was much longer and utterly unkempt. If it hadn't been for the nurses, she doubted that she would have bothered to wash herself. She couldn't be bothered doing anything. How could she when her teammates were dead?

Bought the farm, she thought, savagely. McQueen's body had been laid to rest on the Slaughterhouse in an unmarked grave, as per tradition for unmarried Marines. His Rifleman's Tab had been transferred to the Crypt, where it would serve as an inspiration to other Marines. The other three bodies hadn't been recovered at all. Belinda blamed herself for that too, even though cold logic told her that they would have been savaged beyond recognition by the blast. At least she could have *tried* to look for them.

There was a knock at the door. Belinda ignored it in the hopes that the visitor would go away, but she was disappointed. The door opened, revealing a young doctor in a white coat carrying a uniform set under his arm. Belinda scowled at him, trying to intimidate the doctor into leaving, but he ignored her. He'd been a medical corpsman as well as a Pathfinder, he'd told her when they'd first met, and it took a great deal to intimidate him.

"You have a visitor," the doctor said. "The Commandant is coming to visit you."

Belinda sat up in surprise, barely heeding her own nakedness. "The Commandant?"

"Yes," the doctor confirmed. He dropped the uniform on the bed and stepped backwards. "I suggest that you get dressed. Reporting to the Commandant naked would not make a good impression."

"Matter of opinion," Belinda snarled at him waspishly. What would the Commandant want with her? Maybe he wanted to give her the discharge papers personally. "Who cares anyway?"

"I do," the doctor said. His voice hardened. "So I suggest that you get dressed or I'll be forced to dress you myself."

Belinda looked at him, decided he probably wasn't bluffing, and stood up. The doctor eyed her for a long moment and then walked away, leaving her to study her reflection in the mirror. Her body hadn't changed much, thanks to the improvements that had been sequenced into her genes, but she still looked absurdly young. Blonde hair framed a heart-shaped face and fell over muscular shoulders and arms. Her legs looked identical; it was impossible to tell that one of them had been broken and healed by the doctors.

Slowly, she reached for the clothes and donned the white panties and bra, then pulled the uniform jacket over her chest, followed rapidly by the trousers. The doctor had given her a standard on-base uniform rather than dress blacks, a message she wasn't sure how to interpret. Her rank badge marked her out as a Specialist, a rank that concealed a great many sins in the Marine Corps. Almost all Pathfinders were Specialists, but outsiders rarely recognised them as being anything special. The rank could mean an officer's driver in the Civil Guard.

She pulled her hair back into a long ponytail and scowled at her reflection. Her blue eyes looked haunted; she couldn't help noticing that her hands were twitching slightly. Absently, she accessed her implants and ran a standard diagnostic, confirming that most of them were still shut down. The doctors had been reluctant to leave her with full control over her implants after she'd threatened the intelligence officer. Still, the augments she had left were enough to get by, at least for the moment.

God alone knew what would happen if the Commandant intended to discharge her from the Corps personally. It wasn't as if all of the implants could be removed.

"Very good," the doctor said. "You clean up nicely."

Belinda glared at him, cursing her own sloppiness in the privacy of her own mind. She'd almost forgotten that he was there, something that could have proven lethal on deployment; how badly had she slipped over the last six months? His mocking smile reminded her of what she'd lost and she silently promised herself that she could get back in shape as quickly as possible. Besides, Doug had always claimed that heavy exercise had cheered him up.

"The Commandant is heading to Room 101," the doctor said. "If you will follow me…"

He marched out of the door before Belinda could reply, so she shrugged and followed him. Outside, the corridors were almost empty – and completely unmarked. Medical staff with the proper implants could find their way around, she reminded herself; patients would be advised to remain in their rooms unless they had an escort. Like most Marine installations, there would be entire sections of the hospital that were inaccessible – and unknown – to most of the residents. She wondered, absently, where they were going, before a door hissed open and revealed a concealed room. Bracing herself, Belinda stepped inside. The Commandant, seated on a chair in the middle of the room, rose to his feet to greet her.

She hadn't seen the Commandant since her graduation from the Slaughterhouse, where he'd worn dress uniform and talked to the newly-minted Marines of the traditions of the Terran Marine Corps. Now, wearing an informal uniform, he looked older – and tired, very tired. Few Marines were ever happy in a desk job and the Commandant, who had to deal with the politics, had to be the unhappiest of all. He looked up as she stopped in front of him and straightened to attention.

"Specialist Belinda Lawson reporting, sir," she said. At least she remembered how to do it. One of the other benefits of being a Pathfinder was even less formality than most Marine units enjoyed. "Team Six – detached duty."

"At ease," the Commandant ordered, tightly. "Be seated."

Belinda relaxed – marginally – and sat down on the nearest seat. *At ease* might mean that she could relax, but it *didn't* mean that she wasn't in trouble. The Commandant certainly hadn't offered her *coffee*. He studied her for a long moment and then leaned forward, his expression unreadable.

"How are you?" He asked, bluntly. "And don't give me any bullshit. I need a honest answer."

"Down," Belinda said, finally. One thing that had been hammered into her head more than once was that you *didn't* lie to a superior officer. "Physically, I am a little out of shape; mentally…"

The Commandant listened as she stumbled through her explanation. "I have a mission that needs someone like you," he said, finally. He held up a hand before she could say a word. "I will outline what we need from you and why. After that, if you want to refuse the mission, you may do so."

Belinda heard what he *didn't* say. If she refused the mission, she would be shipped out to the Slaughterhouse, just in case she felt like sharing information with the media. She found that rather insulting, but she understood the Commandant's concern. The media catching wind of a secret operation could be disastrous. There were plenty of examples throughout history of just what happened if the secret was blown too soon.

"The Childe Roland is in grave danger," the Commandant said. "He needs a close-protection operative right next to him at all times. I would like you to take on that mission."

Belinda asked the first question that came into her head. "Why me?"

"Because you have experience in operating alone," the Commandant explained. "Because you are capable of passing almost unnoticed in Roland's retinue. Because you have experience at working with young men. Because you need something to occupy you."

"Oh," Belinda said. She doubted that the Commandant had assigned her because he cared about her health. It was quite possible that he'd viewed her as a square peg who could be fitted in neatly to a square hole. And then she realised what he'd said. "*Alone?*"

"The security surrounding the young prince is…leaky," the Commandant warned her. "If it were up to me, there would be a small army of Marines guarding the palace, with combat armour and heavy weapons. But it isn't up to me."

Belinda stared at him.

"The external security is provided by the Civil Guard," the Commandant said. His lips twitched into a faint sneer that vanished moments later. "The unit in charge of securing the Summer Palace is one of their best, but the CO has powerful patrons and his XO isn't much better. Marine Intelligence ran an operation against the Guardsmen and pulled out enough information to plan an assassination attempt on Roland's life.

"Internal security is provided by Senate Security – they're more focused around close-protection duties than the Civil Guard. It wouldn't be a bad choice, apart from the fact that they're poorly equipped to deal with a major threat and they have few heavy weapons. A single Marine company could take the Summer Palace from both sets of guards..."

Belinda shook her head in disbelief. "*Two* sets of guards? Who's in charge?"

"There isn't an overall commander," the Commandant admitted. "They are supposed to coordinate with each other, but no one is clearly in charge."

"That's..."

She broke off, astonished. Everyone knew – well, everyone who had been to any military training centre, at least – that a disunited command was asking for trouble. Even with the best will in the world, two chains of command were likely to get tangled at the worst possible moment. A failure to coordinate could mean the Civil Guard firing on Senate Security or vice versa, both sides convinced that the other was actually terrorists. Offhand, she couldn't recall if there had ever been an example of two chains of command working perfectly. She rather doubted it.

"It's *political*," the Commandant said, making the word a curse. "You – if you accept the mission – will be inserted into the Summer Palace, officially as Roland's latest aide. He goes through them very quickly. Unofficially, you will be the last line of defence for the young prince. As his aide, you can be with him at every waking moment. Should he get into trouble..."

"Deal with it," Belinda said. She had to admit that it sounded like a challenge – and also a chance to rebuild her life. Besides, Doug would have kicked her ass if she'd refused. "How many others will know what I am?"

"That's the problem," the Commandant said. "We're going to have to tell both of the security teams that you're there, or your weapons and implants will set off the alarms. And they have to know that you're more than just a decorative piece of fluff. Roland himself…we probably should tell him, even though I don't trust him to keep his mouth shut. He has too many friends who encourage him to be more self-important than he is already."

He scowled down at his hands. "Sergeant Ben Powalski, Civil Guard, will serve as your first point of contact," he added. "Powalski failed the Slaughterhouse and went directly into the Civil Guard. Unlike his two superiors, he's actually competent and can be trusted – he'll do whatever he can to help you. Ideally, we should have some Marines nearby to help if necessary, but getting them into position might prove troublesome."

Belinda could imagine it. Flying Raptors through hostile airspace was one thing, but flying them through an area controlled by at least two different forces – three, if one counted the Imperial Navy's ATC system – was another way to tempt Murphy. One force might not get the word in time and open fire on the Marines, adding to the chaos.

Her implants reported that the Commandant's implants were sending her a file. She accepted it and opened the file, scanning it quickly. It was a complete briefing on the Summer Palace, the men and women who worked there – and a highly-confidential file on Prince Roland. Belinda resolved to read it more thoroughly later, once she had reactivated her implants and run through some exercises to start getting her body back into shape, but what she saw in the summary didn't look promising. Calling Roland a spoilt brat was unkind to spoilt brats.

"This is not going to be easy," the Commandant said. "At seventeen, Roland will be crowned Emperor – and there is no shortage of people who might want him dead before then. Right now, he has little actual power, but that will change once he's crowned. They will try to kill him – and it will be your task to keep him safe."

Belinda frowned. "The security arrangements aren't meant to keep him safe, are they?"

"No," the Commandant said. "We don't think so."

The Slaughterhouse Drill Instructors had taught her never to ascribe to malice what could be ascribed to carelessness, incompetence or stupidity. On the other hand, they'd also taught her that the more unlikely the coincidence, the more unlikely the possibility that it *was* a coincidence. If Belinda had wanted to groom the Empire's Prince for assassination – and she'd had the patience to play the long game – she couldn't think of how she could do it better. And most people looking at it from the outside would see nothing more than another power game...

He was right, she realised. This was *not* going to be easy.

What are you complaining about, thingy? Pug's voice demanded, from out of the past. *The only easy day was yesterday!*

"I accept," she said, simply. "I won't let you down."

"Good," the Commandant said. He stood up. "You have an appointment with the implantation crew in an hour, then another with the protocol officer – I suggest you get a protocol file off him and keep it in primary mode. There are far too many protocols surrounding the Empire's Crown Prince and you will have to bear with them. He will probably suggest clothing as well as everything else."

"Joy," Belinda said. Her father had never worried about what he wore – and neither had any of his children. Their mother had sometimes worried about them, but she'd tolerated it. Besides, it wasn't as if Greenway had a thriving social scene. "I guess I'll just have to cope with it."

The Commandant grinned. "Good luck," he said, as he opened the door. "And *don't* fuck up."

He was gone before Belinda could think of a reply. Shaking her head, she sat back and started to study the file in more detail. Her first impression, she decided reluctantly, had been right. Someone was *definitely* setting Prince Roland up for assassination. And if his file was only half-right, there was a good chance that he deserved it.

It isn't your job to decide who is right or wrong, Doug's voice echoed in her head. He'd told her that when the team had finally accepted her. *Merely yours to serve the Empire.*

The doctor opened the door and nodded politely to her. Pushing aside her doubts, Belinda stood up and allowed him to lead her back into the hospital. It was time to get ready for the mission. Maybe it wasn't a simple combat assignment, but it promised to be just as dangerous.

And besides, for the first time in six months, she felt ready to return to duty.

CHAPTER FOUR

It is not hard to understand why the Empire worked to bury human history. Humanity has a bad habit of looking back to more idyllic times in the past, which would have logically included a time when a specific planet was independent...And that would have encouraged independence movements. It could not be tolerated. However, by suppressing history, the Empire also made it impossible to learn lessons from past experience.
- Professor Leo Caesius, *The End of Empire.*

Belinda sucked in her breath as the Summer Palace came into view. The building sat alone in the midst of a garden, one of the few gardens left on Earth's polluted surface, utterly inaccessible to the public. She felt an odd flicker of homesickness as she took in the greenery and realised that the gardeners just allowed the plants to grow naturally, battling it out for supremacy, before she pushed it aside. The average resident of Earth would never know that the garden even existed. Those who did would only be able to envy Prince Roland from afar.

The Civil Guard maintained a very visible cordon around the edge of the garden, according to the files. Belinda had no difficulty in spotting watchtowers and patrols roving around the walls, although the Guardsmen weren't the main line of defence. Their role was simply to deter anyone who might want to break into the palace; the real lines of defence were hidden weapons concealed within the garden and the palace's walls. It looked to be built of wood and stone, seemingly fragile, but the files stated that it had been constructed of starship hullmetal and then covered in wood and stone. A nuke could go off near the palace and the inhabitants would be relatively safe.

Assuming that they managed to batten down the hatches in time, she told herself as the aircar swooped down towards the landing pad. Her implants reported a series of sensor sweeps, each one more intrusive than the last. If her aircar hadn't had the proper ID codes, she would have been blown out of the air before she flew over the garden, but the Guardsmen weren't taking chances. Obtaining codes that were shared with so many different organisations would be easy, particularly as the codes didn't seem to be changed on a regular basis. On one hand, it made sense; changing the codes made it far too likely that there would be a friendly fire incident, particularly if one group didn't get the word in time. But on the other, it was a major breach in security. The codes could be stolen weeks or months before a planned attack and still be valid.

The aircar settled to the ground and Belinda stepped out, taking a moment to admire the Summer Palace. It reminded her of some of the temples on Han, the buildings that some local factions had used to store ammunition and other supplies in the hope that their protected status would save them from the occupation force. The insurgents had been wrong. The fighting had intensified until the CO had been willing to order extreme measures, destroying any compromised temple.

Her implants reported that they were being interrogated as a handful of Civil Guardsmen appeared at the edge of the landing pad. Belinda studied them carefully, noting that they seemed to be more competent than she'd been led to expect, although they *had* exposed themselves to her. She could boost and take them all out…and be gunned down by the automatic defences built into the palace. Shaking her head, she relaxed and allowed them to check her identity thoroughly. At least they weren't cutting corners here.

"Welcome to the Summer Palace," their leader said, when they had finally completed their checks. The security officers would have received a copy of Belinda's file – suitably edited – but they needed to run their own checks. "I'm Sergeant Powalski."

Belinda shook his hand, taking a moment to study him. He was a tall man with short brown hair, wearing a Palace Guard uniform that had been expertly tailored to allow him to move without restriction. The Sergeant had a reassuring air of competence, although she thought she saw a flicker of envy in his eyes as he studied her. It wasn't uncommon for auxiliaries to resent fully-qualified Marines, she knew; what would someone who had left the Corps altogether think of the Marines?

"Specialist Lawson," she said finally.

"There are other security checks that need to be performed," Powalski said, as they walked into the palace itself. "After that, the two commanders wish to speak with you before you meet the prince."

"Understood," Belinda said. Inside, her implants were reporting more aggressive security sweeps, directed at her and her companions. The Civil Guardsmen followed them as they passed through a solid metal door, their hands never far from their weapons. It wasn't very subtle, but it served its purpose. "How many more checks do you have to perform?"

"We need a complete breakdown of your weapons and implants," Powalski said, flatly. "I'm afraid that the security protocols insist on it."

Belinda nodded, tightly. The security scanners would sound the alert if they detected a weapon being used that hadn't been already cleared with the security officers. It was quite possible that she would be flagged up as an enemy infiltrator if she used a weapon they didn't know she carried. On the other hand, she would have preferred to keep some surprises to herself. The Civil Guard was corrupt and it was quite possible that one or more of the Guardsmen might have been subverted by outside forces.

The security checks were as thorough as she had feared. Some Pathfinder implants were designed to be very hard to detect, but the Palace's scanners picked up almost all of them. Belinda kept one eye on the results as the Guardsmen scanned her again and again, realising that they'd picked up everything apart from one of the neural links. All of her implanted weaponry had been noted and logged. She made a mental note to raise the issue of security with the other Pathfinders when she reported back to the Corps. If this scanner tech became mainstream, Pathfinders might be identified by enemy soldiers before they could go into combat.

Just think of this as another infiltration, she told herself, briskly. *You're here to play a role until you need to fight.*

"I didn't know you could hide a weapon there," one of the Guardsmen said. He didn't realise that Belinda could hear him, even though she had augmented ears as well as eyes. "And to think she looks so *cute*."

Belinda kept her face expressionless. She wore a black jacket and a short skirt that fell down to just above her knees, rather than a military uniform. Everyone looking at her would underestimate her, at least until it was far too late. She allowed herself a brief moment of satisfaction as the scanning finally came to an end. Someone who didn't have access to the scan results wouldn't realise that she was anything other than the Prince's aide. It wasn't as if she was going to carry a weapon openly.

"I need you to seal those records," she said. "No one is to have access to them without being cleared by me personally."

Powalski scowled at her. "We do have to inform Senate Security…"

"Let me worry about that," Belinda said, flatly. "I'm not here to be a visible guard. If those records fall into enemy hands…"

"Right," Powalski replied, tightly. He stood up and motioned for her to follow him. "I'll see to it personally."

Once they were through the security office, the Palace corridors became luxurious. Belinda glanced from side to side, taking in the hundreds of paintings hanging from the walls, each one carefully displayed to best advantage. Tiny nameplates underneath the paintings identified their subjects as heroes of the Empire, although they didn't say what the heroes had actually *done*. Belinda recognised a couple of military figures from her studies on the Slaughterhouse, but the others were a complete mystery. She wondered if the staff knew who they were – they'd have to give tours to the Emperor and his family – before pushing the thought aside. It didn't matter.

"You should have access to the basic housekeeping network," Powalski said. "As you can see, you have clearance to enter every section of the Summer Palace – you have more clearance than me, as a matter of fact. I'm not allowed to enter Senate Security's barracks, for example, any more than they are allowed to enter ours. Everyone in the palace has an implant that determines where they can and cannot go. Those who enter a forbidden zone are rendered comatose until they can be picked up and interrogated."

Belinda made a face. Implants that could be accessed and controlled from outside the carrier's body were rare, not least because they were a security nightmare. But it was one of the requirements for serving in the Summer Palace or another high-security zone, according to the files. The staff had to be supervised at all times.

"The cooks, for example, are restricted to the kitchens and their quarters," Powalski continued. "They are under long-term contracts that keep them within the palace for six months, after which they are released with proper references from the Castellan. If you encounter a cook outside his permitted zone, he's an infiltrator. Grab him."

"Clever," Belinda said. She didn't relax as her implants attempted to link into the security networks. There was a moment's delay as the system checked her ID, then allowed her to draw information from the nodes. "How many different networks do you have in the building?"

"Five," Powalski said. "You should have permission to access four of them. The fifth belongs to the Royal Family. No one else is permitted to access it."

Belinda scowled. She could understand keeping the housekeeping network separate from the security network, but having three other networks struck her as excessive. On the other hand, she told herself, a person who managed to take down one of the networks would still have to reckon with the other four. She tossed ideas around in her head; if she'd wanted to slip into the building, how would she have done it? Maybe the security staff were more competent than she'd assumed.

They stopped outside another door. It appeared to be made of wood, but Belinda would have been surprised if it hadn't been another piece of hullmetal. Powalski knocked once and then waited for a long moment, before the door clicked open. He stepped into the room, nodding for Belinda to follow him. Two men – her implants identified them as Colonel Hicks and Captain Singh – were waiting for her inside the room.

"Specialist Lawson, sir," Powalski said.

Belinda kept her face expressionless as the two men studied her, neither looking very impressed. Hicks was slightly overweight, suggesting that it had been quite some time since he had been on deployment – or a simple lack of concern about his appearance. His dark hair fell down around a face that was too handsome to be real. Cosmetic surgery was technically illegal for soldiers and guardsmen, but Hicks had enough political patrons to make that a non-issue. Beside him, the dark-skinned Singh seemed more competent, although he didn't seem too pleased to see Belinda. Senate Security was normally responsible for close-protection duties and it was possible that he saw Belinda's presence as a unsubtle insult.

"Thank you, Sergeant," Hicks said, finally. His voice was surprisingly light for such a big man. "You may go."

Powalski nodded and left the room.

"For the past fourteen months, we have guarded Prince Roland," Hicks said, as soon as the door closed behind the Sergeant. Belinda's implants reported a counter-surveillance field shimmering into existence. "Why do they suddenly feel that we are not up to the task?"

Belinda could have given him several answers, just by looking at the two officers, but none of them would have been very helpful. Hicks had to be wondering just what had been decided in the Grand Senate about the Prince's future – and just what it meant for him personally. If he hadn't built his career by making himself useful to his political masters, Belinda told herself, he might not have to worry so much about politics. But he probably wouldn't have reached a high rank *without* political support.

"I was not involved in making the decision," Belinda pointed out, instead. She was tempted to argue with them, to attempt to defend the Commandant, but she knew it would be pointless. Giving them the impression that she answered to them would be dangerous. "My responsibility is to be a final line of defence for Prince Roland. As you are no doubt aware, the number of threats against his life has been increasing over the past few months. I am there to ensure that no assassin manages to kill him."

Singh leaned forward. "Your file has been whitewashed," he stated, bluntly. "Are you capable of protecting the young master?"

Belinda silently awarded Singh some points in her head. Her Pathfinder file wouldn't have been given to *anyone* without some careful editing, not when so many details were highly-classified. The file they'd been sent contained little more than the highlights of her pre-Pathfinder career and a list of accomplishments, most of which were uninformative without the context. And *that* had not been supplied.

"I served in a close-protection detail on several worlds," she said, calmly. "That detail should have been included in my file."

"Yes, as part of a team of Marines," Singh pointed out. "How often do Marines operate alone?"

Rarely, Belinda thought. The average Marine platoon was ten men; even Pathfinder teams had five. But then, they had been trained to operate alone if necessary. It just didn't happen very often.

"I have operated undercover in the past," she said, and left them to speculate. The file wouldn't have included *those* details, not when it might have touched on sensitive issues. "Officially, I am here to be Roland's aide. I can play that role as long as necessary."

Hicks snickered. "If you can play that role for longer than three months," he said, "you'll be doing better than most of your predecessors."

Belinda scowled inwardly. The file on Prince Roland had detailed the growth of a spoilt brat, one who hadn't improved as he'd grown older. Several of his aides had quit after he'd made unwelcome advances towards them, even though he had a small harem of pleasure women in the Summer Palace. The file hinted that a number of maids had also been seduced by the young prince, if that counted as seduction. They might not have felt that they had a choice.

"You will be under my command," Singh said, more practically. "I…"

"No," Belinda said.

Singh blinked in surprise. "No?"

"I have been assigned to serve as Prince Roland's bodyguard," Belinda said. "My sole priority is defending him. I am not part of Senate Security, nor am I under your direct command."

They locked eyes for a long moment. Singh looked away first.

"I will expect you to understand precisely how the inner cordon works," Singh said, reluctantly. "And you do not have authority to issue orders to my operatives. I want you to be clear on that detail."

"Of course," Belinda said.

"Now, see here," Hicks blustered, sharply. "You cannot just come in and…"

"Yes, I *can*," Belinda said. There was no point in trying to negotiate with someone like Hicks; give them an inch and they would take a mile.

The only way to deal with them was to make it clear that you couldn't be bullied. "I have been charged with keeping the Prince *safe*. There are *no* other concerns for me. Do you understand?"

Hicks flushed angrily, but he nodded.

"I shall require advance notification of *anything* that might impinge on my duties," Belinda continued. "If someone is visiting the Prince, I want to know about it in advance – and when they enter the palace I want to be alerted. I expect to be the first to hear about any changes in security protocols, or new officers being assigned to the protective detail. And I shall be making recommendations for revising the security arrangements surrounding the Summer Palace."

"Which are *my* responsibility," Hicks said, coldly. "Your task is merely to bodyguard the Prince."

Belinda nodded. "Which is why I need to know about any possible problems," she said, as sweetly as she could. The look Hicks gave her suggested that he wasn't impressed, so she allowed her voice to harden. "There's something that you – both of you – need to understand."

She leaned forward, putting as much determination into her voice as she could. "I am not here to play political games," she added. "I don't have a patron to please. All that matters to me is protecting Prince Roland until he can assume the throne. You can work with me to protect him or you can try to impede me in my duty. And I assure you, if you try that, I will break your careers to the point where you will be lucky merely to be reassigned to Hellhole."

Hicks stared at her. "You can't…"

"I *can*," Belinda snapped. "Work with me or suffer the consequences."

She wanted to smile at their expressions. Hicks, at least, would believe that no one would make such statements unless they could back them up. And if he complained to his patron and word got out, his patron might drop him like a hot rock. Patronage might be the way forward, but the client had to be dependable…and someone who failed so spectacularly was hardly dependable. The political embarrassment of having a client who didn't care for looking after the Prince would be devastating.

"Good," she said. She didn't care if they considered her a bitch, as long as they carried out their duties. "Now, take me to the Prince."

CHAPTER FIVE

What is universally accepted about the decades prior to the Empire is this: humanity arose from Earth, spread out across the galaxy - and promptly fell into war. We lack many of the details of those ancient wars, but we do know that the death toll was in the billions and that a number of planets were rendered lifeless. Eventually, an Earth-based movement began to attempt to unify humanity. It enjoyed wide popular support as the wars had been immensely destructive.
- Professor Leo Caesius, *The End of Empire.*

The Summer Palace grew more luxurious as Belinda walked towards the upper levels, shaking her head at the tacky display of wealth. During the Unification Wars, the first Emperor had collected vast amounts of artwork, a collection that had come to encompass nearly a million pieces by the time he'd died. Copies had been placed in the Imperial Museum; the originals had been used to decorate the Emperor's palaces. Every few meters, there was a pedestal with a piece of art placed on it, along with another nameplate. Belinda stopped to examine a silver and gold-plated BFG-4623 from Heinlein that had been given to the Emperor as a gift, before following the Castellan further into the building.

"The Prince has been up since eleven," the Castellan said, finally. He was a short man, but he somehow managed to look down his nose at Belinda. She hadn't been able to decide if he had the general contempt for the military that had infected the Empire's upper echelons or if he thought that she was too pretty to be a soldier. Too many senior officers had 'aides' who just happened to be beautiful women. "He will receive you now."

"Thank you," Belinda said. "What sort of person is he?"

The Castellan sniffed. His record was one of unbroken servitude to the Royal Family; his family had been bound to the Royal Family for centuries, with a legal right to provide at least five senior officials within the Imperial Household. It gave them a level of patronage that, Belinda was starting to realise, allowed them to produce a power base of their own. At least they didn't *seem* to be moving independently, even in the Childe Roland's minority. It *was* a very small power base, after all.

"His Highness is a Prince of the Royal Blood," the Castellan said. "He is his father's son."

Belinda rolled her eyes. There was little useful that could be pulled from that statement, certainly nothing she hadn't already known. But then, the Castellan knew nothing about her; for all he knew, Belinda might have been sent to spy on his loyalties. Indiscreet conversation could ruin a career, particularly when the speaker served a very powerful family. And if someone happened to be sacked in Imperial City, they tended to fall all the way down to the Undercity. They rarely lasted long in that hellish environment.

They stopped in front of a wooden door, her implants reporting more probes from the security network. She'd been probed every time they passed through a heavy door, marking the transition from one part of the palace to another. As Powalski had promised, the security network had allowed her to pass unmolested, although the probes were becoming annoying. If she'd actually had to work as a maid, Belinda suspected that she would start going mad inside the palace. Walking through the wrong door would mean a harsh interrogation by the security staff, after waking up with a headache.

"Be professional," the Castellan advised. There was a click as the door started to open. "And good luck."

Belinda stepped into the Prince's chambers and looked around, unable to restrain her curiosity. The files hadn't included any details on how Prince Roland had arranged his quarters, an oversight that had puzzled her when she'd realised what was missing. Now, she realised that the file might have been out of date almost as soon as it was produced. The room was vast, luxurious – and crammed. A pile of toys and electronic devices lay on one table, including a set of model starships that actually flew. They'd been a craze for years, Belinda recalled, remembering her brother's attempt to build a collection. Somehow, she doubted that Prince Roland had done any part-time jobs to raise money to buy his toys.

A second table held a small section of drinks and snacks. Belinda glanced at the labels and winced inwardly; the drinks were heavily alcoholic. Prince Roland was the product of a considerable amount of genetic engineering, ensuring that alcohol and drugs wouldn't be able to inflict permanent harm on his body; he'd have to consume a great deal of alcohol before feeling any effects at all. Marines had their own countermeasures spliced into their genes – they couldn't get anything more than a pleasant buzz from alcohol – but then, few Marines had the temperament to become addicted to anything. Roland…might not be so stubborn.

She looked up and snorted as she saw one wall. It was covered in nude paintings of young women, including a handful she recognised from the files on the Grand Senate. The Castellan showed no reaction as Belinda recognised the daughters of several Grand Senators; God alone knew what the Grand Senators would think if they knew that Prince Roland had paintings of their unclothed daughters. Maybe they'd be horrified…or maybe they'd see it as a chance to marry their daughters to the prince. Roland would have to marry one day, just to produce the next Emperor.

The second room was larger, with a comfortable set of sofas perched around a holographic projector and a second table of drinks and snacks. Belinda had no difficulty in recognising the projector as military grade, which raised odd questions about just what Roland was doing with it. A quick probe of the room's processor revealed a vast number of entertainment files, ranging from ancient movies – including many banned by the Grand Senate – to outright pornography. There were so many files that she doubted that Roland could watch them all, even if he devoted his entire lifetime to the task.

She heard the Castellan clear his throat as they entered the third room. "Your Highness," he said. His voice was tightly controlled. "I present to you Belinda Lawson."

Belinda followed him into the third room and saw Prince Roland for the first time. He was lying on a massive four-poster bed, easily large enough to hold five or six people without them being too friendly. Roland looked fit – the enhancements to his body wouldn't allow him to get too far out of shape – but there was an air of slovenliness around him that made him seem unhealthy. His ancestors had engineered themselves so that the Royal Family would have the same basic appearance – hawk-like cheekbones, brilliantly-blond hair and bright blue eyes – but his face had turned puffy through overindulgence. And there was a dull look in the Prince's blue eyes she didn't like at all. It reminded her of the drugged-up insurgents the Marines had fought on several worlds.

She straightened to attention and saluted the Prince. Royal Protocol demanded that he returned the salute, but instead all he did was wave his hand in the air, as if he couldn't be bothered to form a proper salute. Or, she realised, as if he didn't know *how* to salute. The files had all agreed that no one was actually teaching him how to rule.

But that makes sense, she thought, sourly. *The Grand Senators don't want an effective Emperor; they want someone who will sit in his palace and rubber-stamp their decrees…and take all the blame if things go wrong.*

"Specialist Lawson is here to be your bodyguard," the Castellan said, patiently. "You will be escorted by her everywhere, so you should get to know her and…"

The Prince snickered. "Does that include the toilet?"

Belinda scowled at his tone. Prince Roland sounded petulant – and partly drunk. She could smell enough alcohol in the air to suggest that he *had* been drinking; glancing around, she saw a handful of bottles near the bed. How long had he been drinking? And, coming to think of it, *what* had he been drinking? Perhaps she would have to suggest – firmly – that he touched less alcohol in future.

"If necessary," the Castellan said. He bowed deeply. "I shall leave you to get to know her."

Belinda heard the door closing behind him as he left, but she didn't take her eyes off the Prince. Roland stared back at her, his eyes drifting all over her body. She scowled inwardly as a faint smile drifted over his face. The briefing files on the Prince hadn't been anything like detailed enough. And she made a mental note to get her hands on his medical file as quickly as possible. Colonel Hicks would have a copy in his files, she was sure. She would have to ask Sergeant Powalski for access.

"You're my bodyguard," Roland said. "Is mine a body you'd like to guard?"

"You need to get into shape," Belinda said, already feeling tired. She stood up and glanced around the room. "What are you supposed to be doing today?"

"Nothing," the Prince said. His voice dropped, slightly. "I was going to visit the Arena later."

"Not in that state, you're not," Belinda snapped, allowing her irritation to enter her voice. The doctors had tried to interest her in a Drill Instructor post on the Slaughterhouse, but she didn't have the patience to deal with recruits. "Let's see what we can do about that, shall we?"

She walked over to the drinks cabinet and peered inside. The bottles were largely unmarked, suggesting that they were produced in the Summer Palace by the staff, rather than imported from outside. A couple were marked with the thistle and rose of Nova Scotia, identifying them as Scotch from a world that carefully regulated the number of bottles that left the planet every year. Just one of them cost more than most people in Imperial City earned in a year. Behind the bottles, there was a single injector tab containing sober-up. By law, they had to be included in every drinks cabinet on Earth, but she would have been surprised if any of the bureaucrats had dared to inspect the Prince's quarters.

Roland stared at her as she walked back to the bed. "What are you doing with that...?"

"Injecting you," Belinda said, tightly. The Prince started to move away from her, but she caught his arm and held it while she pushed the tab against his neck. There was a faint hiss as it shot the drug into his bloodstream. "That should make you feel better."

"You...you..."

Roland's voice broke off as he started to shake. Sober-up forced alcohol and other drugs out of the body as rapidly as possible. It wasn't a very pleasant process. Belinda helped him to his feet, feeling sweat already trickling down his arm, and escorted him into the massive bathroom. He barely made it to the toilet before he threw up into the bowl.

"Let it all out," Belinda said. "Don't worry, just let it all out."

She'd heard of close-protection details who had ended up effectively serving as nursemaids, but she'd never had to do it until now. Roland didn't just need a bodyguard; he needed a nurse and a personal trainer. What if he'd damaged his brain by drinking so much alcohol? It should have been impossible, but genetic engineering didn't always live up to its promise.

"That was disgusting," Roland protested. He still sounded petulant, but at least the drunken haze was gone from his voice. "I'm going to have you sacked. And fired. And disembarked..."

"I think you mean disbarred," Belinda said. Roland *couldn't* sack her, at least until he was Emperor. He could complain to the Commandant, she supposed, but the Commandant would probably take it as a sign she was doing her job properly. "Besides, you can't both sack and fire me. You can only have one."

Roland glared at her as he tried to work it out. Belinda took advantage of the silence to pour a glass of water from the sink and pass it to the Prince.

"Drink," she ordered. "You need rehydration."

Roland's expression didn't change as he sipped the water. "I'll have you fired," he said, finally. He passed her the empty glass. "And then you won't work again..."

"Believe me, that would be a relief," Belinda said, as she refilled the glass. "Drink again, then we can find you something to eat."

The Prince blinked at her in surprise. "You *want* to be fired?"

"When you are the Emperor, you can fire me and I will happily go into retirement," Belinda told him. "Until then, you will have to put up with me."

She'd given some thought to retiring and going back to Greenway, or another world along the Rim. The corporations that founded colony worlds *loved* to hire retired Marines or experienced soldiers from the

Imperial Army as colony marshals and other law-enforcement agents. She'd even looked at a few of the job offers, although most of them had come from corporations that seemed to specialise in causing problems for the Marines by mistreating their settlers.

Pushing the thought aside, she escorted Roland out of his bathroom, through the bedroom and into the dining room. It was larger than she had expected, easily big enough to allow him to invite over a hundred guests to share his table. The table was massive, but only one place had been set at the near end. A menu had been placed between the knives and forks.

"You need something healthy," Belinda said, plucking up the menu before he could object and skimming through it. She'd been in fancy restaurants with less elaborate menus. Most of the options were unhealthy. Somehow, she doubted that any of the kitchen staff had been encouraged to prepare healthy food for the young man. "Let's see now..."

"I'm not a child," Roland objected, sharply. "I can make my own decisions..."

"Really?" Belinda asked, in the sweetest tone she could muster. "And what are you going to choose for breakfast?"

Roland didn't glance at the menu. "Chocolate toast, half-boiled eggs on toast and fettered cheese," he said. "Very healthy."

"Not even *remotely* healthy," Belinda contradicted. She had to glance at the menu again to find out what fettered cheese actually was. Merely looking at the picture made her arteries feel as if they were clogging up. "We'll compromise. You can have the half-boiled eggs if you also have cereal beforehand."

Roland smirked at her. "I could have cereal afterwards?"

"I've been lied to by experts," Belinda told him, dryly. She accessed the room's processor through her implants and transmitted the order to the kitchens, after adding hot unsweetened coffee to the list. "You can eat the cereal first."

It took only five minutes before the serving maid arrived, carrying a bowl of cereal, a steaming mug of coffee and a small jug of milk. The maid was young – she couldn't have been more than sixteen, perhaps younger – and the way she looked at Roland when she thought no one was watching her told its own story. Belinda eyed the young prince as the maid set the food in front of him, daring him to do anything stupid, but he did nothing. Maybe he'd been in a drunken haze all the other times...or maybe his eyes were doing all the feasting. The maid's outfit left very little to the imagination.

"Put some milk into the coffee," she ordered, once the maid had left. "And then you can start eating."

Roland grimaced as soon as he tasted the coffee. "What sort of shit is this?"

"Finest Arabian blend from Ramadan," Belinda said. Like the Scotch, it had to be imported to Earth and cost more money than anyone outside the nobility could easily afford. "And it will give you an energy boost."

"I want alcohol," Roland insisted, flatly. "Get me a glass of the pink one."

It doesn't have a name? Belinda thought. "No," she said, out loud. "You've drunk far too much already today."

Roland ate his way through the cereal, grumbling all the time. Belinda ignored the grumbles, knowing that hunger – a side-effect of the sober-up – would encourage him to eat. She'd picked the brand carefully; it was reasonably healthy, but it also tasted better than the cereal they'd been fed at Boot Camp, back when she'd first signed up with the Marine Corps. Who knew? Maybe Roland could develop a taste for healthy foodstuffs. Stranger things had happened.

The door opened again, revealing a different maid carrying a plate of sloppy eggs, toast and several tiny bottles of sauce. Unlike the first maid, this one seemed eager to attract Roland's attention, as if it was almost welcome. Belinda puzzled over it for a long moment before realising that if Roland kept her in his quarters, her superiors could hardly complain. Besides, if she *did* start a long-term affair with the Prince, it might lead to social promotion for her. Several minor noble families had started with someone who had been the Emperor's mistress for a time.

Belinda motioned for the maid to leave before anything could happen and watched with mild disgust as Roland slurped the eggs. His table manners were worse than those of raw recruits, even though as Emperor he would be hosting formal dinners. Clearly, no one had even bothered to teach him how to be a good little puppet. Sooner or later, someone would realise that they didn't *need* Roland at all.

"I'll have to get you an etiquette tutor," she said once Roland had finished. She'd been briefed on fitting into society on Han and a couple of other worlds, but Imperial City was a universe unto itself. "For the moment, you have a lot of work to do."

The Prince looked appalled. "Bitch," he muttered.

"Quite right," Belinda agreed. "But it's Drill Sergeant Nasty Bitch to you."

Chapter Six

Thus began the Unification Wars, which pitted the newborn Empire against much of the settled galaxy. We lack many details of what happened in the wars, but we do know that the Empire scored many successes - and that each success made it stronger. Further, those planetary systems that submitted quickly were allowed a degree of internal autonomy, as long as they did not seek to regain their independence.

- Professor Leo Caesius, The End of Empire.

"Mandy would have loved this, you know?"

"Don't mention her name here," Jacqueline advised. "You never know who might be listening."

Amethyst Winston shot her best friend a sharp look. Mandy Caesius had been her friend – had been *their* friend – until her father, a professor at Imperial University, had been fired under mysterious circumstances. Since then, she hadn't heard anything from Mandy – and rumour had it that she'd been banished completely from the planet. What had her father done?

She dismissed the thought as she caught sight of a pair of handsome boys from Social Studies class and smiled at them. They smiled back, clearly impressed with the amount of effort Amethyst had put into her appearance; her long brown hair drew attention to the shape of her body and the tight shirt she wore over her chest. Her mother wouldn't have approved of her decision to leave the apartment without a bra, but it had definitely paid off. If only she'd been able to convince Jacqueline to follow suit. Both of the boys were definitely hunks and members of a particular society she wanted to join.

"I'll have the beefy one," she muttered, keeping her eyes on the boys. "You can have the other one."

"You wish," Jacqueline said. She ran a dark hand through her white hair. "He's clearly paying more attention to me."

A dull gong sounded in the distance, drawing their attention towards the man standing on the podium. Imperial University was a hotbed of student dissent, at least partly because the tutors encouraged the students to join protests to boost their grades. Amethyst liked to think that *she* was there because she had considered the issues personally and decided where best to place her political support. The planned deployment to Albion was going to be stunningly expensive and that money could be better spent on Earth. Imperial University was permanently short of funds. Why, some of the students had actually had to withdraw because they couldn't keep up the payments on their student loans.

"They plan to deploy our fighting men to Albion, where they will loot, rape and murder their way through the population," the man bellowed. Loudspeakers picked up his words and rebroadcast them over the throng, drowning out the chatter from thousands of throats. "Not content with laying waste to Han, they intend to do the same to Albion. Do we want to tolerate it?"

"*NO*," the crowd roared back.

Amethyst couldn't disagree. She had never met a single soldier in her life – it wasn't a respectable career for someone from Imperial City – but she *had* watched the news reports from Han, particularly the ones that they'd been warned not to watch without permission from their parents. The reports had been gruesome; by the time the fighting had ended, millions of people were dead, wounded or displaced from their homes. Wouldn't it have been easier to simply let them go? It would certainly have been cheaper.

"They tell us that this is for the good of the Empire," the speaker bellowed. "But it is really for the good of the interstellar corporations! Who else benefited from Han? Who will benefit when Albion is ground into the dirt, its men killed, its women raped, its children rendered homeless? Who benefits? The corporations!"

This time, the shouting was even louder. Many of the students had read the illicit pamphlets passed around by some of their tutors and student body organisers, all lambasting the planned deployment to Albion. Amethyst couldn't disagree with their conclusions either. Albion merely wanted to exist without having to pay back impossible levels of debt to interstellar corporations. The deployment was intended to force them to pay. But Han had been hammered into the ground, leaving it even more incapable of paying its debts. Who had *really* benefited from the war? Even the corporations hadn't really gained anything, beyond displaying their willingness to send in the troops if their victims refused to pay.

"That guy is definitely interested in me," Jacqueline muttered, as the protesters finally started to march. "Look! They're coming over to us!"

Amethyst primped her hair quickly as the two boys joined them. Up close, they were definitely hunky, although the shorter one had the telltale signs of cosmetic surgery. It was commonplace in Imperial University, paid for out of university funds to boost student self-esteem; there were very few students who *hadn't* taken advantage of it.

"Hey," the unenhanced boy said. "Didn't you used to be Mandy's friends?"

Amethyst blinked in surprise. She hadn't expected them to ask about *Mandy*. The unenhanced boy might have been one of her boyfriends... but if he was, surely he would have been given her call-code. But Mandy was gone.

"Yeah," Jacqueline said. "Who are you?"

"Very rude boys," the enhanced boy said. He chuckled and, after a moment, the others joined in. "I'm Tom. This is Richard."

"Pleased to meet you," Amethyst said, holding Richard's hand just long enough to convey interest. "How do you know Mandy?"

"Now, that's a long story," Richard said. "How much of it do you want to hear?"

The press of the crowd forced them to start walking, following the rest of the protesters towards the Imperial Palace and the Grand Senate. Someone at the front started a chant and the protesters took it up, bellowing their horror at the thought of more fighting towards the politicians in the government buildings. Outside the protest lines, crowds were forming to watch as they marched by.

"All of it," Amethyst said. She had to shout to be heard over the racket of the crowd. "What happened?"

"I used to study under her father," Richard said. "And then he was given the sack."

"That isn't a very long story," Amethyst objected. "What else is there?"

"Think about it," Richard urged her. "How many professors do you know who have been given the sack without a public reason?"

Amethyst blinked in surprise. She'd been a student at the university for three years – she was midway through her final term – and several professors had been fired, but always for reasons that had been publically admitted. At least three professors had been sacked for demanding sexual favours from their students and one more had been sacked for embezzling money from university funds…yet none of them had had tenure before they left. And they'd all deserved to go. Everyone had agreed on that, even the students who had earned better grades on their knees rather than at their computer terminals.

So why had Professor Caesius been fired?

Amethyst had never attended any of his lectures, but she had met him when she'd visited Mandy's apartment and he'd seemed a nice guy, if somewhat henpecked by his wife and elder daughter. She couldn't recall any of the students complaining about him, apart from the standard complaints that they were actually expected to turn in essays on time – and most students could obtain an extension if they actually filed the request before hitting the deadline. But if he had done something wrong, why hadn't it been discussed?

"I know the answer to that," Richard told her. He reached into his pocket and produced a strip of paper, displaying the name of a nightclub near the university, only a few kilometres from the apartment she shared with Jacqueline and four others. Beneath the name, there was a time and a date. "If you come tonight, you will hear all about it."

"Oh," Amethyst said, looking down at the strip of paper. It looked like a standard advertisement for a nightclub, apart from the absence of any special offers for students. She knew the club, but she'd never been there. Still, it was in a safe part of Imperial City. "I suppose we could come."

Richard gave her a smile that turned her legs to jelly and then walked off, out of the protest march. Amethyst watched him go and then turned to give her friend the thumbs up as the protestors finally reached the gate to the Grand Senate Hall. A handful of students were already advancing past the line drawn by the Civil Guard, ready to be arrested by prior arrangement. Nothing bad actually happened to them, Amethyst had been told, but it played well in the student papers. She watched a handful of young men and women being cuffed and led off towards a hover-wagon and then relaxed as more speakers appeared in front of the Senate Hall. They were Junior Senators, looking for re-election, ready to speak to the crowd if it would garner them a few more votes. Amethyst didn't bother to wait to hear what they had to say. Instead, she slipped out of the crowd and started to walk back towards the university. She was just in time to see the arrested protestors being released and given a gentle push towards the university.

"Frauds," Jacqueline muttered. She looked up at Amethyst. "Are you going to go to the nightclub?"

"I guess so," Amethyst said. Richard *had* been handsome – and he'd piqued her curiosity by talking about Mandy and her father. "Come on. We'll get something to eat and then go study in the library for a few hours. It isn't *that* long until seven o'clock."

Night was falling over Imperial City as they reached the nightclub. It had apparently been booked by a private party, but Amethyst showed the slip to the guard and he pointed the two girls towards a narrow staircase leading up to a higher floor. When they reached the top, Amethyst was surprised to see a large room filled with sound equipment – and a dozen other students, standing in a line in front of a set of lockers.

"Hi," Richard said, coming over to greet them. "If you have any electronic devices at all, take them off and drop them in the lockers. Anything at all – handcoms, locators, computers, recorders…take them off and put them in the lockers."

Amethyst blinked in surprise. "Why?"

"Security," Richard said, which explained nothing. "Or you can go, if you don't want to comply. There isn't a choice, I'm afraid."

Amethyst exchanged a long look with Jacqueline and then obeyed, removing her handcom from her belt and dropping it into the locker. Thankfully, her parents had decided that she was old enough not to have to wear a personal locator bracelet any longer. It had made her feel such a dork when she'd been a first-year student, unable to go to any of the more risqué nightclubs because she'd known that her parents would be instantly informed of their daughter's activities. Jacqueline had been much luckier. She'd been legally emancipated from her parents since she'd turned fourteen.

They finished filling the locker and closed it. Amethyst took the key and pocketed it, feeling oddly naked without the handcom. She didn't have the slightest idea how it worked beyond a few generalities, but she could use it to call her parents – or anyone else – in the solar system, even if there *was* a time delay if she wanted to call someone on Mars. Without it, she was isolated in a city with millions of residents, completely alone.

"In here," Richard called, waving them through a door. "Don't worry. Everything in the lockers will be safe."

Inside, there was more sound equipment – she could feel a faint vibration from the dance hall below through the floor – and a man she didn't recognise, carrying a silver wand in his hand. He waved it over Amethyst's body before she could object, then motioned for her to pass into the room. Everyone was checked, she realised, before the door was closed and locked. A moment later, Richard touched a button and she heard a faint sound in her inner ear. Judging from the number of people rubbing their ears, she wasn't the only one to hear the maddeningly faint sound.

"The sound you hear is a modified anti-surveillance system," Richard said, as he sat down on top of a giant speaker. "It isn't quite perfect, but anyone who tries to spy on our meeting will have some problems listening to us. We can speak freely here."

"We can speak freely," a male student Amethyst didn't recognise said. "Just what the fuck is going on, dickhead?"

"I'd like to make one other thing clear before we continue," Richard continued, ignoring the interruption. "You may want to go no further with this after we explain – and we will allow you to leave – but you have to keep your mouths shut. If you decide to tell anyone without our express permission, you will be killed."

Amethyst gasped. She wasn't the only one.

"This is deadly serious," Richard said. His voice echoed around the silent room. "Our lives are at stake. So is everything else. If you want to leave, you *can* leave – but if you breathe one word of it to anyone, you will die."

He smiled, thinly. "If anyone wants to leave now," he concluded, "the door is over there."

There was a long pause.

"No one, then," Richard said. "Good."

He stood up and clasped his hands together. "You all knew Professor Caesius or his daughter Mandy," he said. "You should also know that the Professor was sacked from the University and then exiled from Earth to the Rim. What you will *not* know is why the Professor was sacked – or, for that matter, why Cindy Jefferson was expelled from the University on grounds of drug abuse and returned to her homeworld."

Amethyst gritted her teeth. Drug abuse was technically an offense against university regulations, but if the staff had expelled every student who had experimented with drugs – or become an addict – they wouldn't have had anyone left to teach. Expelling someone for that was almost unheard of. She'd never met Cindy Jefferson – had never even *heard* of her until the meeting – but she felt a moment of pity for the girl.

"The question you should really ask," Richard continued, "is what connects the two departures from the university."

He paused to allow them to wonder. "Cindy Jefferson asked the Professor a set of awkward questions about the Empire," he said. "He discovered that he couldn't answer them. Instead of referring her to the computer files, he started to conduct his own independent research program, intent on writing a book himself. That book was submitted nine months ago – and both of them were expelled two weeks afterwards.

"The poor girl – Cindy Jackson – comes from Montana, a very strait-laced planet in the Edo Sector. A charge of drug abuse would be enough to blight her life after returning from Earth in disgrace. Certainly, no one would pay close attention to her – which is what the university staff wanted. Professor Caesius, on the other hand...he was harder for them to deal with. Eventually, they arranged his exile. The question we must now ask is *why*. Why did they go to all this trouble?"

He paced over to a cupboard and opened it, revealing a small stack of loosely-bound books. "The interesting thing about the planetary datanet is that the controllers can erase almost anything from the files," he said, as he picked up the books. "If you happened to have a copy of a banned book on your private terminal, it would be erased after you hooked it into the datanet. But they can't erase a printed book unless they destroy every copy in existence."

Amethyst took the copy he passed her automatically. "This is what destroyed my tutor's career," Richard said, flatly. "Cindy Jefferson asked him about the true state of the Empire; Professor Caesius researched it and decided that the situation was far worse than we were led to believe. He wrote this book...and his career was destroyed. And if any of you are caught with the book, your career as students will be over. At best, you will be expelled; at worst, you will be transported to a new colony world as an indentured colonist – a slave, in all but name."

"I..." Jacqueline coughed and started again. "I've only got a few months of study left. I don't want to be expelled."

"I don't think that Cindy Jefferson wanted to be expelled either," Richard replied, dryly. "But tell me something. What are you going to be when you grow up?"

Jacqueline scowled at him. "A sociologist," she said, proudly. "My tutors say that I have real promise..."

"I bet they do," Richard said. He tapped the book. "Have you looked at the employment figures – I mean, have you *really* looked at them?"

He pressed on before Jacqueline could answer. "The figures have been carefully massaged," he said. "The average employment rate for newly-qualified students is roughly five percent – that's your chance of getting employed in *any* career. Even shitty jobs like working in bars and night-clubs – or even prostitution – are on the decline. And if you get lucky and you *do* get a job, you'll lose eighty percent of what you earn in taxes and paying back your loan."

One of the other students interrupted. "And what if we don't get a job?"

"You sit in a shitty apartment eating shitty food and trying to die young," Richard said. "And *that's* the lucky outcome."

He looked around the room. "Take the books with you and read them," he said. "Read it all; I'm afraid that there are no summaries, pre-written answers or any other shortcuts for *this* book." There were some nervous chuckles. "There's a note in the back for how to leave us a message if you're interested in joining us. If not…well, no harm done, as long as you keep your mouths shut."

Amethyst felt her head spinning as they were gently urged out of the room. She wasn't sure what she'd expected, but it hadn't been what they'd received. Richard had made his speech, given them the book and then…left them to decide what to do on their own. *That* wasn't common at Imperial University.

There was only one thing for it, she decided, as she shoved the book into her bag. She'd have to read it for herself.

Chapter
Seven

It might have remained stable indefinitely if the first Emperor hadn't made a dangerous mistake. Elections to the Senate were determined by population size: Earth, with a population in the billions, was entitled to elect no less than 100 Senators and 10 Grand Senators. Many of the other long-settled worlds were heavily populated themselves. The newer colony worlds, however, rarely qualified to have a Senator, let alone a Grand Senator. This left them at a major disadvantage in the political arena.

- Professor Leo Caesius, *The End of Empire.*

"Remind me," Colonel Chung Myung-Hee said, as she stepped up behind Jeremy. "Why are we supposed to defend these people again?"

Jeremy gave her an icy look. Marines – and other military officers and men – couldn't question their responsibilities. Their duty was to defend the Empire and that included the ignorant young students thronging through the streets below, protesting the military's planned deployment to Albion. It was clear from their own statements that they knew almost nothing about what was *really* going on, although their narrative did have the advantage of being simpler than the truth. Blaming everything on evil interstellar corporations seemed to make more sense than the fact that if Albion left the Empire, other protective parts of the interstellar economy would leave as well.

The irony would have been amusing, if it hadn't been so sad. *He* didn't want to send Marines to Albion, but for different reasons. And the negotiations with the Grand Senate had not been productive.

"They have a right to protest," he answered, finally. But did they, really? All protests had to be cleared in advance with the Civil Guard and a protest that touched on a truly sensitive issue would never be allowed to get off the ground. If the protesters had started raging about the Grand Senate's political leadership being firmly entrenched, with elections nothing more than a joke, he doubted it would have been long before the Civil Guard was ordered to move in and crush the protestors, exiling them to a newly-settled world as indents. Let them protest thousands of light-years from Earth.

"I'd be more impressed if they actually spent their time in university *learning*," Chung said tartly. "How many of those students down there are failing remedial arithmetic?"

Jeremy shrugged. The Empire handed out handcoms and pocket terminals to its children, without seeming to demand anything in return. But using the devices left them ignorant of the basics of mathematics or handwriting – or, for that matter, how the devices actually *worked*. They were never taught how to produce their own, or even to repair them if they broke down. The students were kept in ignorance without ever truly realising it. Their tutors didn't help. If they couldn't find the answers in a computer file, the answers might as well not exist.

He wasn't being completely fair to the tutors, he knew, or to the students. Some of them *did* manage a fairly good education, if they had kept the drive to learn by the time they reached university. Most students were content to absorb their tutors' words without bothering to actually think about them, or anything else. If the protestors down below had been capable of thinking critically, they might have noticed that their list of demands was contradictory and their own narrative was confusing as well as inaccurate.

"I would hate to guess," he replied, and turned away from the window. The remainder of his inner council were already seated in front of his desk. "I was negotiating with the Grand Senate about the planned deployment."

"You poor bastard," Colonel Gerald Anderson said. "What did they have to say for themselves?"

Jeremy scowled at him. It was hard to blame anyone for speaking disrespectfully of the Grand Senate, but it was a bad habit as well as being bad for discipline. The Grand Senate *were* the lords and masters of the Empire, no matter how self-serving and grasping they were. And the Marine Corps was sworn to uphold the Empire.

"They've agreed to cut the number of Marines redeployed from Earth to Albion," Jeremy said. He couldn't help smiling at the look of relief on Anderson's face. "However, they have insisted on making up the numbers by stripping Marine platoons out of Home Fleet and redeploying them to the expeditionary force."

There was a long pause as that sank in. One of their duties was to provide troops for capital starships who could serve as a boarding and internal security force – and a police force, if the shit hit the fan and the crew mutinied against their commander. Ideally, a platoon of Marines should be deployed to any ship heavier than a light cruiser, but there just weren't enough Marines to go around. Home Fleet had over two thousand Marines scattered over five hundred starships. Other fleets and tasks forces had to make do with fewer Marines, if they had any at all.

"That might not be a bad idea," Anderson said, reluctantly. "It isn't as if Home Fleet is expected to go into battle any time soon."

Jeremy nodded. Home Fleet *wasn't* expected to do more than look intimidating – which was fortunate, as the fleet wasn't in good shape. The starships had been allowed to decay, while crewmen had been reassigned to other units – or encouraged not to waste money on basic maintenance. Officially, there was nothing wrong with Home Fleet and it was ready for deployment at a moment's notice; unofficially, Jeremy would have been surprised if the fleet could have been redeployed in less than five years. The starship hulls were intact, but everything else had been allowed to wear down until it was no longer reliable.

"But the crews are not happy," Chung said, into the silence. "They're spending half their time drunk, or cursing the payment delays – when their superiors haven't stolen their salaries outright. The fleet may need the Marines to help keep order."

"Civil Guard units will be redeployed to pick up the slack," Jeremy said. "Or so I have been told."

Anderson barked a harsh humourless laugh. The Civil Guard provided military police units when troops and spacers were on shore leave, but they were very unpopular and tended to suffer accidents when no senior officers were looking. Even Marines sometimes joined in the contest to see how many helmets they could steal off the Civil Guardsmen who were supposed to be supervising them. And *that* was on the ground or a large orbital station. Putting the Civil Guard on starships was asking for trouble.

Jeremy had been a Major during a deployment where Civil Guard units from one world had been rushed to another to provide additional numbers to keep the peace. The experience had been hellish; the Civil Guardsmen hadn't been trained for operations in space and several managed to kill themselves by accident. He still had nightmares about the officer who had proposed, in all seriousness, that opening both airlock doors at once would make disembarking much easier – and started directing engineering teams to do just that before Jeremy caught him. And *that* had been on a troopship. Who knew what would happen to the Civil Guard when they were deployed to a battleship?

If there isn't a mutiny planned already, he thought, *one will be planned once the crews realise that the Guardsmen are likely to get them all killed.*

Anderson put his thoughts into words. "How many crews are they prepared to lose?"

"Apparently, the Guardsmen will be intensely supervised," Jeremy admitted. He wouldn't have put money on it succeeding. Civil Guard officers tended to treat everyone else as the enemy, even people who were trying to help them. "However, that isn't our problem."

"We need more Marines," Anderson said. "Can we not launch another recruiting drive?"

"We don't have the funds," Jeremy reminded him. Even if they *had* the funds, it wouldn't have been simple to expand the yearly intake of new recruits. Marine Boot Camps were the harshest in the Empire, deliberately so, and plenty of prospective candidates were weeded out before they were assigned to the Slaughterhouse. "And besides, we'd have to drop our standards to bring more recruits to the Slaughterhouse."

Anderson made a face. The Civil Guard's standards were so low that they might as well not exist. Marine Intelligence had once conducted a survey and discovered that at least ten percent of Civil Guard recruits in any given year had criminal records, some of them quite serious. At least that wasn't a problem on Earth, where almost all criminals were exiled to a new colony world as soon as they were caught. Other recruits had drug problems, or medical conditions…only a handful could really be considered decent recruits.

The Imperial Navy and Army had the same problem. They were so desperate for recruits that standards had been allowed to slip. At least the Army had a hard core of NCOs who were capable of bashing young recruits into shape, if they were allowed to do their job. Failure to push enough recruits through the training camps would reflect badly on them and their superiors, who were little more than bureaucratic beancounters, wouldn't understand their position. How could they?

"It is going to get worse," he continued. "From what they were saying, both the Trafalgar and Midway fleet bases are going to be shut down within the next six months. The Empire will effectively abandon its authority over at least three sectors, simply because we don't have the funds to maintain the bases."

"They want to preserve the more developed worlds," Chung said. "I don't think it will work."

Jeremy couldn't disagree. The Core Worlds weren't in much better shape than Earth, while the Inner Worlds deeply resented the Grand Senate's economic dominance. Indeed, the underground economy was far more efficient than the official economy – and people were noticing. Marine Intelligence suggested that several entire sectors were slowly slipping out of the Grand Senate's control. No wonder they were so determined to make an example out of Albion. Failure to keep one sector in the Empire would result in others slipping out of their grasp and forming their own economic alliances.

And if the price for maintaining control over the productive worlds was abandoning the colonies along the Rim, well…you couldn't make an omelette without breaking a few eggs.

Jeremy could imagine the chaos spreading across the Rim as the Empire withdrew its remaining ships and men. HE3 supplies would come to a halt, forcing the colonists back on more primitive sources of power. Some of the luckier worlds would be able to set up their own cloudscoops, while others would have no choice but to become farming worlds. They'd survive – the standard settlement procedure was to ensure that each new colony could feed itself without needing food from outside – but life would become much harder for a very long time. Few colony worlds would be able to return to space in the lifetimes of anyone who remembered the Empire.

But there would be other dangers. The Empire had driven thousands of discontented factions out of settled space, out beyond the Rim. Those factions would start probing back into the abandoned sectors, rapidly discovering that there was nothing left that could oppose them. They'd have a chance to build empires of their own…

He shook his head, pushing the thought aside. "I'll have to send a message – and a promotion – to Captain Stalker," he said, bitterly. "They didn't want to send a ship to Avalon."

"Sir…" Anderson started to protest. "We don't leave men behind!"

"I know," Jeremy said. Marines *didn't* leave their own behind – and if a Marine died on the battlefield, his brethren would do everything in their power to recover his body and transport it to the Slaughterhouse for burial. Abandoning an entire unit on a distant colony world went against everything the Marines stood for, but there was no choice. There wouldn't be any recovery mission to Avalon. Or any of the other worlds where small units were going to be isolated indefinitely.

"Surely we could just send one ship," Green said. "It wouldn't even have to be a long mission…"

"Apparently not," Jeremy said. He slapped the table before anyone else could speak. "I am aware of the…betrayal and I have argued as strongly as I could with the planners. They are not going to arrange a starship to pick up Stalker's Stalkers and that is *final*."

There were other considerations, he knew. Captain Stalker – he'd have to put the paperwork through to promote him to Colonel – had enough supplies to build Avalon into a first-rank world…given enough time without interference. They'd have to beat the insurgents on Avalon first, but Jeremy had read the file carefully and concluded that at least half of the insurgency would be willing to come to an agreement with the Marines. Ironically, the Empire's decision to abandon the sector would work in Stalker's favour. The insurgents wouldn't find it so easy to blame their woes on distant Earth when the Grand Senate had washed its hands of them.

"I think that we should re-examine the decision to pull Marines off the capital ships and away from Earth," Chung said, changing the subject. "Marine Intelligence has been unable to follow all of the convoluted bargaining in the Senate, but it seems likely that *some* kind of deal was struck."

"Undoubtedly," Jeremy said. He'd puzzled over that himself. Logically, the last place the Grand Senate should want any kind of major explosion was Earth. "But then, they do want to win quickly on Albion – if it comes down to a fight."

"It will," Anderson predicted, grimly. "They have the choice between fighting or submitting to crushing economic demands from Earth, as well as rendering themselves helpless in the future. I think they'll fight. And their Civil Guard is untrustworthy."

"You mean it may be loyal to Albion rather than to the Empire," Chung said. She looked over at Jeremy. "Intelligence tends to agree, sir. The Albion Civil Guard will be on the opposite side, as will the planet's defences. I don't think that the deployment force will be allowed to land peacefully."

Jeremy nodded. Marines were hard to kill on the ground, but they were as vulnerable as anyone else on starships and assault shuttles. An entire platoon could be wiped out by a HVM that took out their shuttle, unless they managed to bail out in time. God knew that enough brave Marines had died during the hastily-improvised attack on Nova Taipei on Han, when there had been no time to soften up the enemy's defences. Albion might not have the population of Han, but it did have the technology to be an order of magnitude worse for the newcomers. The *invaders*, as the locals would see them.

Albion was required, like all of the Inner Worlds, to pay for its own defences and Civil Guard. Unsurprisingly, the planet's defenders were loyal to the planet rather than the Empire – and why not, when the Empire had been draining their planet's resources ever since day one? The Grand Senate's persistent 'clarifications' of Imperial Law had made millions of enemies in the Inner Worlds, particularly when they blatantly overrode rights granted to the Inner Worlds by the First Emperor. Jeremy knew that the Grand Senate had sacrificed long-term stability in favour of short-term gain. He didn't know if the Grand Senate knew it too.

"It is unlikely," he agreed, finally. "And if the fighting does spread out of control, we might see other uprisings in the Inner Worlds. There just aren't enough military units to run around on fireman duty."

He scowled as he looked down at the ancient desk. It was a simple rule of insurgency and counter-insurgency warfare that the longer it took to respond to an insurgency, the harder it was to put the insurgency down. The insurgents would have time to strengthen their position, recruit openly and link up with others who had the same complaints against the occupying power. If Albion inspired other Inner Worlds to rebel, the Empire would take months to respond…and by then it might be too late. On paper, the Inner Worlds wouldn't stand a chance; they would be massively outgunned. In practice…

…The fighting might tear the Empire apart.

"Maybe they should redeploy Home Fleet," Anderson suggested. "A few units in each of the Inner World systems might cool their tempers."

"Or it might push them into open revolt," Chung countered. "Besides, how long would it take to redeploy Home Fleet?"

Jeremy nodded. "That isn't our problem at the moment," he said, standing up. "All we can do is try to keep the lid on and pray."

He watched them leave his office, then turned and walked back to the window. The protesters below were finally dispersing, having made their point – a point that Jeremy knew would be ignored. The Empire couldn't avoid responding to the crisis on Albion, no matter what the protesters thought. Besides, what did the Grand Senate care about the opinion of a bunch of ignorant students?

Perhaps we should have recruited more on campus, he thought, sourly. It had certainly been proposed, years ago, but there was a ban on the military attempting to recruit students. They were allowed to walk into the recruiting offices and sign up, if they knew that the recruiting office even existed, yet they had to discover it on their own. The Marines weren't allowed to help them locate the office, let alone try to convince them that there was a genuine career in the military waiting for anyone with the determination to seize it.

But it wasn't too surprising. After all, the Grand Senate didn't want the Civil Guard having *too* many connections to the students. One day, the Guard might have to crush them...and they wouldn't want sentiment getting in the way.

Bastards, Jeremy thought, as he walked towards the door. His next appointment was in ninety minutes, just long enough for him to work off some frustration in the shooting range. Maybe then he'd feel better...

...But the true condition of the Empire wouldn't just go away.

CHAPTER EIGHT

This combined with another major mistake to produce a highly dangerous situation. In order to fund the war, the Emperor had to make deals with various interstellar corporations, granting them future concessions that would be redeemed after the end of the war. These corporations allied with the Core Worlds and used their voting blocs to push through legislation that benefited them – and exploited the newer colonies.

- Professor Leo Caesius, *The End of Empire.*

"This is torture," Roland protested. "I'll have you flogged! And then I'll have you…"

Belinda rolled her eyes at the young prince as he lay on the examination table. A quick check had revealed that the medical staff assigned to the Summer Palace were not expected to do anything more than basic treatment, so she'd had to call in a specialist from the Marine Corps infirmary to examine Roland's condition. It had taken days to convince Hicks and Singh to allow Doctor Thorn to enter the Summer Palace; both of them, for different reasons, had been reluctant to allow another outsider into their domain. Belinda had finally resorted to threatening to bring the whole matter to the attention of the Grand Senate, which had convinced them to change their minds.

"You should see what young recruits go through," she said, although – to be fair – the examination procedure for new recruits was fairly basic. Boot Camp took everyone who met the minimum requirements and then put them through hell. Those who were overweight were streamlined into sections where they would lose weight and bulk up their muscles before rejoining the other recruits. "This isn't so bad."

Roland's face twisted unpleasantly. "You could at least hold my hand," he whined, crossly. "I can *feel* the machines inside me."

"I highly doubt it, young man," Doctor Thorn said. He had been one of the finest medical corpsmen in the Marine Corps before he'd suffered a nasty injury that had taken him out of the front lines for good. Serving on Earth just wasn't the same, even if he *was* helping to develop the next generation of military medical facilities. "The nanites are so tiny that they can pass through the cells of your body without resistance."

"I can feel them," Roland insisted. He sounded as though he were on the edge of panic. "They're *there*!"

Belinda wasn't too surprised. Other Marines had reported the same sensation, at least when they'd *known* that there were nanites pervading their bodies. It was psychosomatic, according to the headshrinkers, but that didn't stop it seeming real. Besides, her augmentation was designed to pick up on and counter unwanted intruders in her body.

"Don't worry about it," she said, reaching out to squeeze his hand. In many ways, Roland was still an immature child, someone who needed a father figure in his life. But all he had were the Grand Senators, who wanted to use him, and servants who had to do as he said. It wasn't a healthy combination. "Besides, it will all be over soon."

Thorn held a scanner against Roland's head for a long moment, then moved it down his chest, over the groin and down between his legs. "The procedure is nearly complete," he assured the young prince. "And the rest of it won't hurt at all."

"Good," Roland said. "Can I sit up now?"

"Just a few more moments," Thorn said. "Let me recover the nanites first."

Belinda used her implants to call a maid and order a glass of orange juice for the prince as Thorn removed the nanomachines, then the sensors he had affixed to Roland's body. The prince really didn't know how lucky he was, she considered. On the Slaughterhouse, the medical examinations were much more intrusive – and the process for inserting Pathfinder implants better left forgotten. Some recruits never woke up after the procedure, or so she had been told. It was quite possible that they'd been streamlined into units that the rest of the Corps didn't know existed.

"All done," Thorn said, cheerfully snapping a glove. "You can sit up now."

"And drink this," Belinda said, passing Roland the glass of orange juice. "You may feel somewhat dehydrated."

Surprisingly, Roland sipped it quickly.

"I'll process the results now," Thorn said. He'd been warned that everything he needed to do would have to be done inside the Summer Palace. The complete medical records for the prince could not be allowed to become public. "I should have a breakdown for you in an hour."

"Good," Belinda said. She took the glass back from Roland and placed it on a table for the maid to recover later. "Come on, Your Highness. You need a nap after that tiring experience."

Roland gave her a sharp look, probably suspecting – correctly – that he was being mocked, then stood up and followed her out of the medical centre. A handful of staff outside bowed low as soon as they saw him and remained that way until he had walked past them, something that made Belinda feel an eerie chill running down the back of her neck. What sort of person would Roland become if everyone prostrated themselves in front of him? She looked at the prince's back and suspected that she knew the answer.

His quarters had been cleaned by the maids in their absence, following orders that Belinda had given to them personally. The alcoholic drinks and drugged snacks had been removed and replaced by fresh juice and healthier energy snacks. Roland would no doubt complain about Slaughterhouse Chocolate – as the Marines called the energy bar – but he'd learn to like it. After all, the new recruits learned to like it too. The maids had also vacuumed the floor, scrubbed the walls and filtered the air. It no longer stank of drugged smoke.

It can't be good for anyone breathing in that muck, she thought, as she watched Roland carefully. Would he even notice? Her own augmentations filtered out the smoke, but others wouldn't be so lucky. Even Roland wasn't immune to long-term exposure. *We need to move him to a chamber with proper air circulation...*

Roland yawned as soon as Belinda closed the door. "You're right," he said, as he walked over to the bedroom. "I do need a nap. Would you care to join me?"

Belinda was only surprised that it had taken him so long to make the pass – and that it wasn't particularly crude. But she couldn't go to bed with him, even if she had *wanted* to. If she was to do anything for him, she had to be his tutor as well as his bodyguard – and sex would destroy that relationship. And besides, she simply didn't find Roland attractive.

"No," she said, firmly. "You need to actually sleep."

"But you could at least tuck me in," Roland whined mischievously. "I'm only sixteen…"

"But mentally three," Belinda said. She followed him into the bedroom and watched without surprise as he threw himself on the bed without bothering to undress. *That* was something else that would have to be cured, given time. Roland *definitely* needed an etiquette tutor if he was to start hosting dinners after his coronation. "Close your eyes and go to sleep."

She'd watched over her younger brother when he'd had trouble sleeping and, in some ways, Roland reminded her of her brother. But then, Grey had learned to take care of himself rapidly, just like the rest of her family. Farming, hunting, shooting, even basic education…they'd learned it from their father. Roland had never had a real father figure in his life.

Roland tossed and turned for several minutes before finally falling asleep. Belinda listened carefully to his breathing until she was convinced that he would remain sleeping for several hours – she'd had to crawl through occupied bedrooms in the past, back before Han – and then stood up, walking soundlessly out of the room. The Prince's suite was completely soundproof, she'd discovered while reviewing the files. She carefully closed the door behind her, ordered the local processor to inform her if there were any problems, then started to walk back down towards the medical centre. Thorn was waiting for her there.

"The good news," he said, as soon as the door was locked and a counter-surveillance field was in place, "is that there isn't any permanent damage. The bad news is that he will have to work hard to reinvigorate his body."

Belinda sat down. "Give me the basics," she said. She'd learned more about battlefield medicine than she'd ever wanted to know, but Roland's condition was more subtle than bullet wounds and lost limbs. "What is happening to him?"

"His bloodline was genetically enhanced from very early on," Thorn said. "That was far from uncommon in the early days of the Empire; everyone who could afford it spliced basic improvements into their DNA, particularly the improved disease resistance that saved countless lives on various colony worlds. Much of the early work was hackwork by our standards, but it proved remarkably stable. And what didn't prove stable was easily handled by later geneticists."

Belinda nodded. Genetic engineering tended to cause unintended consequences that manifested several generations down the line, no matter how much care was put into developing the procedure. There were always surprises when modified DNA interacted with unmodified DNA or DNA that had been modified in a different way. But most issues could be nipped in the bud before they caused real problems – or so she had been assured. Some planets were still suffering from unintended consequences that had gone too far to be stopped easily.

"However, he really has been pushing his body too far," Thorn continued. "Any unenhanced person who had drunk as much alcohol as him would be dead by now, probably of liver failure. That doesn't include the drugs, which would probably have had a similar effect. Overall, he's damn lucky to have had such limited side-effects. Right now, my very strong advice would be to prevent him from drinking alcohol or taking any more drugs at all, even for…medical purposes."

Belinda narrowed her eyes. "Medical purposes?"

"I found traces of Long Pole and Never End in his bloodstream," Thorn said. "He overdosed on them too."

"Crap," Belinda said. "Who prescribed them for him?"

"His medical files are poorly maintained," Thorn said. "I intend to have a few words with the doctors here, but for the moment I just don't know."

Belinda cursed out loud, drawing up words she'd learned from the Drill Instructors who'd berated her and the other recruits on her first day.

Long Pole and Never End were both designed to prolong and increase orgasm in men; as such, they were immensely popular, but also heavily restricted. Using them too often could produce nasty side effects, even assuming that the medicine had been produced properly. Earth's productive facilities, she had been warned, had developed the habit of cutting corners where possible. God alone knew what was in some of the vials that were handed out to Earth's citizens. Even the Grand Senators had to be careful – or import their medical supplies from off-world.

"But he did make a pass at me," she said, finally. "Erectile dysfunction doesn't seem to be one of his problems."

"It will be, if he keeps abusing the drugs," Thorn told her, bluntly. "And it is quite possible that they will have affected his fertility. He may not be able to have children, at least not naturally. That…will cause him problems when he is crowned Emperor."

"Yeah," Belinda said. "It will."

There was no reason why the Empress – whoever she ended up being – couldn't transfer her child from her womb to an artificial birthing matrix, or even having the child conceived without ever having to have sex with the Emperor…apart from tradition. The Crown Prince had *always* been grown in his mother's womb. It was tradition and could therefore not be gainsaid by mere mortals. Belinda suspected that many of the upper-class girls who might have been considered suitable candidates for becoming Empress would become reluctant to marry Roland if they realised that they would be expected to carry their child to term personally. After all, that was what *lower-class* women did.

And what would happen if the Emperor was impotent? Science could provide a solution, but would it be accepted by the Empire? Tradition was important, particularly when *not* adhering to tradition would give the Grand Senate an excuse to refuse to recognise the new son as Crown Prince. Had any other Emperors been impotent? Belinda couldn't remember, but suspected that the records would never have admitted the truth. The Royal Family wouldn't want anything to occur that called the legitimacy of their children into question.

"Apart from that, most of his muscles have decayed to some extent," Thorn said. "Thankfully, his enhancements prevented it from becoming too dangerous, but he will require a long program of physical exercise to get him back into an acceptable state of health. Right now, he gets tired easily and has problems concentrating on anything for more than a few minutes. Notice how quick he was to demand to be allowed to sit up."

Belinda sighed. "What about his state of mind?"

"Spoilt brat," Thorn said, shortly. "I'm surprised you needed me to tell you that."

He shrugged. "We generally find that Boot Camp sorts the men out from the boys," he added, as Belinda scowled at him. "But in the Prince's case, expelling him from the camp isn't an option. There *isn't* another heir, is there?"

Belinda shook her head. The Empire had run into problems when there were two competing princes who both wanted to be crowned Emperor. Eventually, the Royal Family had stopped having sons after the Crown Prince was born, although as women were not eligible for the throne there was no shortage of royal daughters – and their descendants. Right now, she had no idea who had the best claim to the throne after Roland – and the blood claim would probably be overridden by the Grand Senate when it chose the next candidate. It made her head hurt just thinking of it.

"Overall, give him firm treatment and see how he responds," Thorn advised. "If there's something worth saving inside, he should respond well to common sense and discipline. If it's too late to save him from the effects of his mistreatment, you might want to consider deserting and fleeing to the Rim."

Belinda snorted, rudely.

"Health-wise, make sure he eats properly and gets plenty of exercise," he continued. "You can probably encourage him to go onto the playing courts if you tried; most young men are intensely competitive if they think they can win. You'll have to step down a level or two, but don't just *let* him win."

"True," Belinda said. If she couldn't beat Roland at any physical game, all of her expensive augmentation would have been thoroughly wasted. But Thorn was right. Roland would learn nothing from her steamrolling him into the ground every time they played tennis or badminton. She'd have to hold back without making it obvious that she was holding back. "Anything else?"

"I'd recommend him having physical examinations at least once a month," Thorn said. "I don't think that he's physically addicted to anything, but his system may have built up a need for the drugs anyway. If he shows anything more than very basic withdrawal symptoms, call me at once and make sure the guards know to let me through the perimeter at once."

"I'd prefer to keep you here," Belinda admitted.

"A fate worse than death," Thorn countered. "Although I do want to have a few words with the doctors here…and perhaps meet them out back with a baseball bat. Call themselves doctors? Ha!"

"Have fun," Belinda said. She could understand the doctors being reluctant to take responsibility for Roland's welfare, not least because of all the drugs and alcohol, but it was their damn job. "If you have any other suggestions, feel free to send them to me."

"Watch your back," Thorn advised. "I have a feeling that you've put quite a few noses out of joint already."

Belinda shrugged and stood up. "Send me a copy of your complete report," she ordered finally. "And make sure that no other copies leave the building."

"Then don't give it to the Civil Guard," Thorn said. "If you do, we might as well upload it to the datanet and save time."

Shaking her head, Belinda left the medical centre and walked back to the Prince's suite, letting herself into the main room. A quick glance through the security sensors in the bedroom revealed that Roland was still asleep, although he had moved since she'd left. Sleeping so irregularly wasn't good for anyone, she reminded herself, even though *she'd* slept irregularly when she'd been on active duty.

Silly girl, she thought she heard Doug say. *You ARE on active duty and don't you forget it.*

Sitting down in the chair, Belinda closed her eyes and started to access the security network, checking it out section by section. It seemed to have been programmed to keep out anyone without the proper codes, but it didn't take her long to find a handful of unlocked nodes, allowing someone to slip inside. Carelessness…or malice? There was no way to know. At least there didn't seem to be any outside connections at all, even to the planetary datanet. An intruder would have to be *inside* the palace before he could use the unlocked nodes.

They'll have to be closed, she thought, and made a mental note to have the Civil Guard see to it. And then to check it herself, just in case. Hicks might decide to be obstructive. Again.

Accessing the housekeeping part of the network, she started to issue orders. By the time Roland woke up, she would be ready for him. He wouldn't know what had hit him until it was too late to object.

I'll make a man of you yet, she thought, and settled down to rest.

CHAPTER NINE

Such a development should not have been surprising. Running for election on Earth was expensive. Corporations had the cash to buy prospective candidates – and, to a very large extent, controlled the media in the Core Worlds. Over hundreds of years, the political and corporate class merged together, creating a power and patronage bloc that was impossible to unseat legally. Independent candidates were mocked, pressured and had their private lives torn apart and used as ammunition. Those who were selected by the machine were cosseted and propelled into office. The true surprise is that a handful of independents did succeed in being elected.

- Professor Leo Caesius, The End of Empire.

Roland woke up four hours after going to sleep, his fancy suit looking crumpled and worn after he'd slept in it. Belinda, alerted by the security sensors, was at his bedside before he was fully awake. If he believed that she'd been there all the time, so much the better.

"What…what time is it?"

"Four o'clock in the afternoon," Belinda said, patiently. "The maids have already prepared your lunch."

"I must have overslept," Roland said.

Belinda snorted in amusement and helped him to his feet, then followed him out of the bedroom into the dining room. Four sealed containers had been placed in front of the sole chair, which Belinda opened as Roland sat down. It had taken some arguing to convince the cooks to produce an extremely healthy as well as tasty meal, but she'd finally succeeded by threatening to bring in cooks from the Boot Camp on Mars. Boot Camp cooks had a reputation for having the hardest MOS in the Empire. It must be; no one had ever passed the test at the end. Or so the Marines joked.

"Oh," Roland said. "What is it?"

"Food," Belinda said, dryly. The smell was better than she'd expected, reminding her that she hadn't eaten for hours herself. Her augmentation could keep her going for days without food and drink, but that was never a very pleasant experience. "And an energy drink to build up your strength."

"You know you're going to hate it when they won't tell you what it is," Roland grumbled, as he lifted his fork and picked up some of the rice. "I thought the chefs knew what I liked to eat."

"And I told them to cook what you *needed* to eat," Belinda asserted, bluntly. Honestly, it *was* like talking to a five-year-old kid. "Besides, you should try it before you throw it back in disgust."

She watched in some amusement as Roland took a bite – and then started shovelling it into his mouth as quickly as possible. The food was not only tasty, but laced with appetite enhancers to encourage the eaters to take as much as possible. She'd learned at Boot Camp that you could eat more food and like it – even if you normally hated it – as long as you were hungry enough. The food was also laced with supplements to help his body repair itself.

"More juice," he grumbled, as he opened the sealed bottle. "What happened to the glasses?"

"I had no idea when you were going to wake up," Belinda said. "So I *ordered*" – she stressed the word deliberately – "the cooks to prepare the meal and then leave it here for you to wake. And the juice is good for you too."

"I need a drink," Roland said. He meant alcohol. "I *really* need a drink."

"You don't need alcohol at all," Belinda stated, flatly. "Your health is *not* in a good state right now."

Roland glared at her. "And you know this because?"

Belinda ticked off points on her fingers as she spoke. "First, you're about twenty to thirty percent underweight for your size and age, which is worrying," she said. "Second, you have been damaging your internal organs through excessive alcohol and drug use. Third, you have developed eating habits that have been utterly unhealthy for you. Fourth..."

She broke off and smiled at him. "Is there any need to go on?"

"I'm going to be the Emperor," Roland said. The absolute confidence in his voice was disturbing, even if it was partly justified. "Do I *need* to be healthy?"

"Yes," Belinda said, flatly. "As Emperor, you will be the number one target for every terrorist group in the entire Empire. I checked the records; hundreds of assassination plots have been stopped before they even penetrated the secure perimeter protecting you, but there were *millions* of threats. Your life is in danger – it started from the moment you were born."

"But I have you to look after me," Roland whined. "And I have the guards..."

"I may be killed first," Belinda said. "Or they may contrive to separate us. Besides, a healthy body will improve your life in other respects. You won't need the Long Pole any longer."

Roland looked sullen. "How did you know about that?"

"It showed up on the medical exam," Belinda deadpanned, sarcastically. "And if you're taking it in such quantities, you're putting your life in danger. Live healthier and you won't need it at your age."

She watched as he finished eating his food. The cooks had advised her that Roland rarely ate his plate clean, no matter how much food was wasted, but this time he'd finished everything, even the plain rice. He looked surprised at his own appetite, just like many other recruits, the ones who had to be taught to be careful how much they ate. Eating too much before physical exercise could be dangerous.

"Come on," she said, and led the way back into the bedroom, picking up the clothes the maids had produced as she passed through the living room. "You need to get dressed; I'll get changed outside."

Roland stared at her. "What are we going to do?"

"I believe that your family has a long tradition of playing tennis," Belinda said. She'd looked it up and Roland's great-great-great grandfather had actually rewarded anyone who could beat him with a thousand credits. He hadn't had to pay out very often; the files had stated that he could have played professionally, if he hadn't been Emperor. "You're going to start playing with me."

"But..."

"No buts," Belinda said, firmly. "It's time to take some exercise."

She walked out of the door, leaving the prince to get dressed. Her own shorts and shirt were waiting for her – the maids had produced them at her request – and she donned them quickly. She'd ordered something modest, she realised as she glanced in the mirror, but Imperial City's definition of modest was clearly different to Greenway's. Her shirt was alarmingly tight around her breasts and her shorts showed off too much of her legs.

Maybe it will encourage him, she thought sourly.

Roland's eyes went wide when she tapped on the door and let herself back into his bedroom. He'd changed quicker than she'd expected, she was relieved to see, although it was alarmingly clear that he wasn't healthy at all. His skin was alarmingly pale and his arms looked flaccid, with hardly any muscle tone at all. He was going to have to work hard to develop his potential, she reminded herself. *She* would have to keep pushing him until he developed the self-discipline to do it for himself.

"You...you're *beautiful*," he stammered.

Belinda ignored him. "You know the way to the gardens," she said. Unsurprisingly, the Prince had his own private passageway down to the gardens. "Lead the way."

She followed Roland down the passageway, carefully checking the security precautions as they passed. None of them seemed insecure, but the absence of live guards worried her, if only because she knew that a prepared infiltration team could spoof them, given enough advance preparation. On the other hand, live guards could be bribed or simply killed...

Maybe we should see if we could move Roland to the Slaughterhouse, she though, grimly. *We have complete control there.*

But she knew that the Grand Senate would never agree.

Bright sunlight struck her as they reached the end of the passageway and stepped out onto the grounds. A large tennis court, surprisingly simple even though it belonged to the Emperor, lay right in front of them, surrounded by trees that had been preserved even as the rest of Earth slowly died. Earth's biosphere had proven stronger than almost every alien biosphere in the Empire, displacing or exterminating the natives on most settled worlds, but it was losing the fight to survive on Earth. Humanity's carelessness had destroyed its own homeworld.

"I used to look at that needle," Roland said. For once, he didn't sound whiny or irritated. "I used to think that I could climb up it and escape."

Belinda nodded as she followed his gaze. The orbital tower was hundreds of miles away, visible only as a silvery thread that caught and reflected the light pouring down from high overhead. It was easy to forget that it was massive, nearly five kilometres in diameter, easily the largest engineering project in humanity's history. No other world in the Empire boasted anything more complex than a space elevator or a skyhook.

"Millions of people live there," she said, softly. The lower levels were just like the megacities, she knew from experience, although they were considered to be better accommodation than anywhere outside Imperial City. After all, unlike the megacities, they *were* heavily policed by the Civil Guard. The Empire couldn't risk terrorists gaining control of one of the towers. "And millions more go up every day to escape Earth."

Roland gave her an oddly wistful look. "Do you think I could go, one day?"

"I think so," Belinda said, although she had her doubts. The last time an Emperor had left the solar system had been centuries ago. Roland's ancestors had rarely gone anywhere further than Luna or Mars. The furthest any of them had gone had been Pluto, after it had been reconfirmed as a planet for the nineteenth time. "We can certainly try to arrange it."

She led the way over to the tennis court and found the rackets where the maids had left them at her request. They'd offered rackets fit for an Emperor that cost more than she made in a year, but she'd turned them down and ordered rackets that could be broken without breaking her credit account. Roland blinked in surprise as she passed him a racket and motioned for him to take one side of the court, then walked over and took up a stance that suggested that he was out of practice. Belinda wasn't surprised.

"We will forget about the rules," she said, as she took up position on the other side of the net. Marines rarely played tennis; Boot Camp and the Slaughterhouse had taught games that were intended to encourage young recruits to work together, like football, rugby and Slaughterhouse Jousting. She wondered what Roland would make of the latter, before pushing the thought aside. There were *Marines* who weren't prepared for jousting. "Just concentrate on trying to score against me."

Roland eyed her, his eyes clearly not on her face. "And what do I get if I win?"

"Victory?" Belinda asked, dryly. She thought about reminding him of the health benefits, then decided against it. Too much nagging wasn't good for a young man – or prince. "You get to go to the Arena this Sunday. I hear they brought in a creature from Ripley."

"And then the Arena staff had to put it down before it could break out," Roland said. His face twisted into a grin. "I *love* going to the Arena…"

"You win and you get to go," Belinda said. She tossed the ball in the air and knocked it over the net as lightly as she could. "You lose and you get to try to beat me again tomorrow."

Roland lunged forward and managed to serve the ball back at her, just lightly enough so that it barely missed snagging in the net. Belinda had to hold herself back; her training insisted that she should boost, just to ensure that she actually won. Instead, she allowed the ball to hit the ground and twisted her face into a disappointed expression. Let Roland think he'd won the first round easily.

"You can't stop me from going," Roland said, as she prepared to launch the ball towards him again. "I have a Royal Box in the Arena and…"

"And I am your bodyguard with absolute authority over where we can and cannot go," Belinda reminded him. She could understand Roland's feelings – she doubted he was allowed to go more than a few places outside the Summer Palace – but she needed to make him work for his reward. "Besides, I need to have the Arena checked out before you can be allowed to go there."

She launched the ball at him before he could respond, pushing it – according to her tactical implants – into a trajectory that he could intercept, if he worked at it. Roland moved forward and barely managed to serve it back at her, but it was aimed right at her position and she had no difficulty launching it back towards him. The prince managed to hit it, yet it went right into the net and fell down.

"I've been to the Arena hundreds of times," Roland protested. His face was already shining with sweat. "I never had a problem."

"There's always a first time," Belinda said. She'd heard that there were a number of retired Marines working for the Arena staff, if only to ensure that there was absolutely no cheating. The gladiators who fought for the amusement of the crowds had to win fairly or not at all. "And besides, security precautions have to be checked and rethought from time to time, or someone will find a way through the holes."

"It's the *Arena*," Roland said, in horror. "Who would want to cheat?"

Belinda grinned. "Everyone who has money on one of the gladiators?" She asked. "Now…stop wasting time and serve the ball at me."

Roland flushed, but obeyed. Belinda tossed it back at him effortlessly and watched as he ran to intercept it, barely succeeding before the ball hit the ground. She held herself back and allowed the ball to land in her side of the court, giving Roland another point. Grinning to herself, she picked the ball up and launched it towards him. Roland had to run again to catch it before it was too late.

The game lasted for nearly forty minutes before Belinda called a halt and pointed out, regretfully, that Roland had been beaten by five points. The prince seemed to want to keep playing, which was a good sign, even though he was clearly aching in pain. She remembered her own pain as she struggled through Boot Camp, pushing herself a little further every day, and felt an odd flash of sympathy. Roland wasn't entirely to blame for his own condition, she reminded herself. He'd been allowed to atrophy away while the Grand Senate ran the Empire.

"Not too bad," she said, as she held out her hand for Roland to shake. The prince seemed bemused at first, then realised what he had to do and shook her hand. "We'll play again tomorrow?"

"I'll defeat you tomorrow," Roland promised her. He hesitated, then asked the obvious question. "What happens if you beat me on the following day?"

Belinda pretended to consider it. "You still get to go to the Arena, but you have to beat me again before you can go the following week," she said, cheerfully. "And it will get harder, I'm afraid."

Roland ran his hand through his glistening hair. "Why don't you sweat?"

"Enhancement," Belinda said, deadpan. She couldn't tell him that he hadn't pushed her very hard at all. Facing a fellow Pathfinder at tennis would be much more interesting, if alarming for anyone else who had to watch. "You'll need to work harder in future."

"I…ache," Roland admitted. Now that he had stopped playing, he seemed to be having trouble walking. "I think I sprained something."

"You just pushed your muscles a little further," Belinda reassured him. She smiled as she recalled one of her first Drill Instructor's favourite sayings. "Pain is weakness leaving the body."

Roland scowled at her. "Can't I get an enhanced body from the body-shop?"

"You'd still have to work to make it yours," Belinda pointed out. Besides, body-shops were notoriously unreliable, although the Crown Prince could probably hire the best, and long-term results depended on the user keeping up with his exercise routines. If someone was prepared to go to all that effort, it would probably be cheaper to build up his natural body anyway. "And I think it wouldn't be good for you either."

She picked up a towel, tossed it to Roland and watched as he wiped the sweat off his brow.

"You can have a soak in the bath, then a massage that will help work some of the kinks out of your muscles, and then you can eat," she continued. "After that, you will be ready for bed."

"It's only six o'clock," Roland said, and then yawned. "It's way too early to sleep."

Belinda grinned. "See how you feel after a bath and a meal," she said. "Besides, you have to beat me tomorrow if you want to go to the Arena."

She allowed her smile to widen as Roland started to walk back towards the passageway. Maybe she *would* let him win tomorrow, once she'd checked out the Arena and contacted the guards. He *did* need to get out of the Summer Palace, after all. And by then, she had a feeling that she would be glad of the diversion too. She just had to be careful not to forget her mission – and make sure that Senate Security didn't forget it too.

After all, people *died* at the Arena.

CHAPTER TEN

Why did the Senate allow it? Put simply, they needed money for one reason: they wanted re-election. In order to gain re-election - and to keep Earth's population under control – it was necessary to provide an endless supply of bread and circuses. Looting the colonies provided the funds they needed to keep themselves in power. They believed that they could do so indefinitely.
- Professor Leo Caesius, *The End of Empire.*

Amethyst couldn't help a sense of relief as she returned to her apartment and threw her bag down on the bed. Art classes were tedious at the best of times, even though some of her fellow students saw them as an easy grade, as long as they could bullshit the teachers into believing that they had made a new breakthrough in art and design. Normally, she would have agreed with them, but now? She wondered just what the point of even *trying* was while she was at the university.

She hadn't taken everything Richard had told her on faith, but it had taken several days to actually research his statements. Neither she nor Jacqueline had realised that they had never been taught how to do research properly, even though they were meant to carry out an investigation of their own for their final grade. All they'd been taught to do was look up the information in the computer files and regurgitate it for themselves, rather than doing something completely original. In hindsight, it made her wonder just how brilliant some of her earlier work had actually been. Should she have really been charged with plagiarism?

The official figures stated that seventy percent of graduated students found jobs. It had been suspiciously difficult to draw specifics out of the university files, forcing her to resort to other methods – and what she'd found had been alarming. Very few graduated students found work suited to their degrees – and the remainder tended to have jobs that, at best, led nowhere. The official figures didn't seem to include the students who just went into their own apartments and vegetated, which made her wonder just how many other official figures she had been taking for granted. How much of what she had been told was a lie?

Parsing out the other official statistics had been complicated and she wasn't at all sure that she'd succeeded. Most of their coursework came with handy answers for them – to prevent the students from thinking for themselves, she recognised now. She couldn't ask a tutor to look over her results and tell her if she was on the right track, not unless she wanted to be expelled from the university. Back in her parents' apartment block, she'd known girls who were grandmothers at thirty. She'd told herself that going to Imperial University was a way out of that trap. In hindsight, perhaps she should have wondered a little more about why those girls became caught in the first place.

I was a fool, she thought, savagely. The tiny apartment seemed to be closing in around her, just as her own life was being constrained. She was in a cage and she'd never even seen the bars! Angrily, she paced over to the small fridge, opened it up and removed a bottle Jacqueline had brought home from one of the local nightclubs. It smelled suspiciously like paint-stripper, but she took a swig anyway. What did it matter what it did to her? Her life was already over and yet it would never end.

Shaking her head, she put the bottle back in the fridge and sat down on the bed. It was a simple bed, but special – because it was hers. Or was it, really? She'd rented the apartment from the university and she knew that it would go to another student after she left, but she'd taken it as a sign of her independence from her parents. But her independence – and that of all the other students – was a joke. Over the last few days, she had looked – really looked – at her fellow students. Very few of them could have survived in the university without the tutors doing much of their work for them. How would they get on outside the academic world?

She reached under the bed and produced a secure box. By law, all children had to have at least one place where they could store things they didn't want their parents to see – it was a human right – but she rather doubted that it was as secure as the manufacturers claimed. Who knew how easy it would be for the university staff to open it – or simply demand that she open it for them? But she hadn't had anywhere else to store Professor Caesius' book, not when discovery might mean expulsion from the university. Opening it to a random page, she started to read the text. She'd read part of the book every night since meeting Richard.

Professor Caesius didn't seem to have a very organised mind, she'd decided on the first night. The text jumped around, as if it had never had the services of an editor – or as if the writer hadn't wanted to look too closely at what he was writing. He also seemed to have had a man-crush on the Terran Marine Corps, although Amethyst wasn't sure why. She'd never met a Marine, or seen one outside the gory entertainment flicks that kept the boys amused when they weren't trying to get tickets to the Arena. Who knew if they were really as noble, brave and just plain superhuman as the Professor painted them? On the other hand, they *were* being compared to bureaucrats and Amethyst had enough experience with *them* to know that almost anyone else would be preferable.

One section leapt out at her and she read it more carefully, slowly figuring out the difficult words.

> *Student activists on Earth and the Core Worlds often partake in political protests, directed at influencing the Empire's government. Such protests provide nothing more than a safety valve to prevent the students from realising that they have almost no say in what the Empire actually does. The protests are planned by university staff, cleared with the Civil Guard and kept under firm control. Most student protesters never truly realise that their protest marches are little more than a way to blow off steam, at best.*
>
> *A quick survey of protest marches on Earth only confirms this. There were no less than seventy major protest marches against the fighting on Han, yet the Empire continued rushing troops to the planet with the avowed intent of putting down the rebellion. The*

only student protest march that can be said to have succeeded was a march demanding an increase in the Student Living Allowance, which won an official raise of seven percent. However, owing to the steadily-rising level of inflation, this was a rather dubious victory at best. The actual buying power of the SLA remained relatively stable.

Unfortunately, most students are utterly ignorant of the true state of affairs. The protestors against the war on Han were unaware of the mass slaughter being perpetrated by almost all of the rebel factions, let alone what would happen to the Empire's economy if the rebels were allowed to succeed. As such, the Grand Senate simply ignored them, confident that the students could do nothing to interfere with their operations. Their confidence was well justified.

Amethyst ground her teeth together as she closed the book. She'd marched against Han too, when the first reports had started to come in – and it had all been for nothing. They'd been told that their marches could influence the government, perhaps even convince a few Senators to vote against the war, but from what she'd read it was easy to see that it simply wouldn't matter what the lower-ranking Senators did. The Grand Senate held all the power and it could afford to ignore public opinion.

Desperately, she reopened the book and flicked through a handful of other pages, looking for something hopeful. But there was nothing. The Professor had concluded that the Empire was doomed as long as the Grand Senate kept control over the reins of power. It had to be brought down before the entire structure collapsed. But how? She looked back at the paragraph and shuddered.

The Empire is being strangled by the level of control exerted by the Grand Senate and the bureaucracy it has created. Put simply, the cost of doing business is skyrocketing because of the need to cope with the vast amount of red tape the bureaucrats use to justify their own existence. Because of this, the actual amount of tax revenue available to the Empire is shrinking rapidly, which forces it to increase the demands on the remaining sources of tax – which adds to their burden until they break. Right now, the only way to save the Empire would be to restructure the economy completely – and that would mean forcing the Grand Senate to give up its power. It is unlikely that they will peacefully accept oblivion.

"So what," Amethyst asked out loud, "can we do?"

She reached for her handcom and fired off a message to the number Richard had given her, then placed the book back in her secure box. Normally, she would have gone to one of the eating places outside the apartment block, but she didn't feel like eating. Besides, she didn't really know where the money in her credit account really came from. The Professor had quite a few things to say about the credit system in his book as well as everything else.

Her handcom vibrated a moment later, announcing the arrival of a new message. She glanced at it, noted the address and time – another nightclub, two hours later – and stood up, pulling off her clothes. There would be time to get dressed properly before she went to meet Richard. Maybe *he* had some idea of what they could do about the whole ungodly mess.

Jacqueline hadn't returned by the time she had finished dressing – she'd chosen a long shirt and tight black trousers, which suited her mood perfectly – so she left a note for her roommate and walked out into the corridor, heading down towards the exit. She had lived in the apartment block for years, but she had never really realised just how many students were crammed into the massive construction – or just how many citizens lived in the megacities that covered much of Earth's surface. The book had suggested that there were *billions* of unregistered humans on Earth, draining the planet's once-considerable resources. Anyone who wanted to eat anything other than algae-based rations had to buy expensive imports from the orbital farms, or the Inner Worlds.

The streets were thronging with students, most of them chattering about the upcoming gladiator duel in the Arena. Amethyst hated them all at that moment – how *could* they witter on about nothing when the Empire was slowly falling apart? But she'd been just as ignorant only a few short days ago. She looked back at the naive girl she'd been and cursed herself. In hindsight, the clues had been right in front of her nose and she hadn't seen them; she hadn't even *looked* for them. She'd been a fool.

Imperial City was meant to be brightly illuminated, day and night. Looking around, she could see that a number of the street lamps had failed, without anyone trying to repair them. It was a minor sign, but a worrying one nonetheless; the book had warned that the Empire's infrastructure was decaying so rapidly because there were so few people available to work on repairing it. She looked up towards the aircars flying overhead and wondered what would happen if the traffic control system failed, as it had on other parts of Earth. The results would be disastrous.

Richard met her outside the nightclub. He smiled as he saw her, then motioned for her to follow him into an alleyway and then into a metal door set in the wall. Amethyst took a breath – she'd heard horror stories of what could happen in parts of the lower city – and stepped inside, wincing as the door slammed shut with a hideous *clang*. Richard motioned for her to take off her electronic devices, swept her body with a security sensor and then invited her into the next room. Feeling oddly isolated, Amethyst obeyed.

There were seven others inside the room; three of them wearing masks and robes that concealed their features completely. Amethyst couldn't help noticing that they even wore gloves, presumably to prevent them from leaving fingerprints for the Civil Guard to find. A chill ran down her spine as she realised that this was deathly serious. If they were caught together, who knew *what* would happen?

"Welcome," Richard said, as he closed the door. "This room is secure. We can talk freely."

He nodded to the masked men. "The Civil Guard has authority to do whatever it feels necessary to get information that might lead to the arrest of our senior leadership," he added. "Accordingly, they're wearing masks to prevent you from knowing their identities. What you don't know you can't betray."

"I wouldn't betray anyone," a young male student said, hotly.

"It is astonishing how easily someone can be convinced to talk," one of the masked men said. His voice was flat, completely atonal. "There are drugs that will have you giving up everything you know, right down to your girlfriend's bra size – if they feel like being sophisticated. They might just hook you up to a lie detector and beat you with sticks every time you told a lie. People break."

"Quite right," Richard said. "It's a simple precaution."

But they know who we are, Amethyst thought. She didn't say it out loud.

"You've all read the book, I assume," Richard said. "You know by now that nothing short of direct action is going to convince the Grand Senate to change its ways before it is too late. We intend to take that direct action. If any of you are not committed to the cause, if you do not feel that it is necessary, walk out that door" – he pointed – "and don't come back."

Amethyst hesitated. She hadn't been told what would happen when she attended the meeting and there was no time to think about it, but… she *had* read the book. And she couldn't disagree with Richard, even if she hadn't been so angry about so much of her life being wasted in useless studies. She'd looked at the requirements for leaving Earth completely and discovered that the only way someone as unqualified as her would be able to go would be through signing up with a colony corporation. She might as well have been an indent.

"You are all welcome," Richard said. No one had left. "Understand; from now on, you keep your mouths shut outside the secure rooms. If you talk to *anyone*, you will be killed. Some of you will have friends you will want to bring into the group. Do not bring them inside without my permission. We have to check out all possible recruits before accepting them into the brotherhood."

He sat down on a chair and motioned for the others to sit down too. "I will be providing you all with some training, but we don't have much time before we have to take direct action," he added. "For the moment…"

He reached under the chair and produced a box, which he opened by pressing his thumb against a sensor. It clicked open, revealing a gun. Amethyst felt her heartbeat starting to race as she stared at it, unable to look away. She'd rarely seen guns outside the ones carried by Civil Guardsmen – and she'd certainly never been allowed to touch one. Guns just weren't available on Earth, at least not in Imperial City. The book she'd been given had suggested that Earth actually had the largest number of illegal guns in the Empire, but she didn't have the slightest idea where to find one. Maybe in the Undercity, she assumed…

"They say that political power comes out of the barrel of a gun," Richard said. His voice was very calm, very controlled. "And yet the population of Earth is largely disarmed. I wonder why that is?"

It was a rhetorical question, Amethyst realised. The gun was almost hypnotic; she found herself reaching for it before she could stop herself. Richard smiled as her hand closed around the barrel and lifted it out of the case. It was heavier than she'd expected, forcing her to grab it with her other hand just to hold it safely. She reached for the trigger and then stopped. What if she fired the gun by accident? All of the flicks she'd seen had included scenes where a gun had been triggered by a mere touch…

…And yet she felt a strange excitement just from touching the weapon. If the Civil Guard caught her, she'd be indentured for sure…and yet she was excited.

"It's unloaded," Richard said. He seemed amused at her reaction. The masked men leaned forward to peer at her, although she couldn't tell if they were amused or merely interested in her thoughts. "Most of what you have been told about guns is nonsense, I'm afraid."

He took it back from her and passed it to the next recruit, who handled it with the same mixture of awe and fear that Amethyst had felt. Her palms were sweaty; she wiped them on her trousers, unable to understand her own feelings. The gun was power…wasn't it? Her heartbeat was still racing in her chest…

"We will be learning how to use these weapons over the next few days," Richard said, softly. "Whatever the flicks say, you can learn to use most of these weapons easily – you don't need years of training to fire a gun safely. And then we will start teaching the Grand Senate that they can no longer push us around."

CHAPTER
ELEVEN

This naturally led to the growth of the Empire's bureaucracy. Administering the vast new territories and enforcing the Senate's laws required an equally vast army of civil servants, who would carry out orders from appointed governors. Naturally, this civil service grew stronger and stronger as the years went by, a trend encouraged by senior managers, governors and even Senators. Once embedded, the civil servants could not be removed...
- Professor Leo Caesius, *The End of Empire.*

"See?" Roland said. "The Arena is fantastic!"

Belinda shrugged as the aircar convoy descended towards the complex. Roland definitely deserved a treat – and she had made him *work* for it. It had only been yesterday that he'd finally managed to beat her at tennis, although it had been a matter of losing to him convincingly rather than actually being beaten. But he was getting better as his body repaired itself under the new treatment Belinda was enforcing. Given time, he would definitely return to full health.

The Arena was over a hundred square miles of land to the south of Imperial City, surrounded by a massive wall that ensured that only people who'd bought tickets were allowed to enter. According to the retired Marines she'd contacted, the security guards were permitted to use jangle-pulses on anyone stupid enough to try to climb over the wall, just to ensure that the monopoly on tickets remained intact. The crowds down at the main gates were being heckled by touts, some of whom were offering tickets at grossly-inflated prices. Belinda wasn't too surprised. The Arena was the greatest attraction on Earth.

Six massive domes dominated the heart of the complex. One of them was specifically for matches between different wild animals, captured on far-off worlds and brought to Earth to fight and die for the entertainment of the crowds. The remaining domes were for the gladiators, volunteers willing to fight publicly and soak up the cheers of the audience. There was no shortage of volunteers – *anyone* could walk into the Arena and start fighting – despite the short lifespan of a gladiator. Those who survived long enough to reach the top hundred were feted as celebrities, at least as long as they survived. Belinda had heard that a dead gladiator had no fans. The merchandise was thrown out and replaced by something else.

"I have a box in all six domes," Roland said. "And I have even ordered a chair for you!"

It was a status symbol; there were only a limited number of private boxes and most of them belonged to the richest and most powerful families in the Empire. The few that went on the market every decade were fought over savagely by everyone who wanted another sign of wealth and power. Belinda's contacts had told her that the Imperial Navy could buy a whole new cruiser for the cost of a simple box in the Arena. It wasn't difficult to believe.

"Thank you," Belinda said. Did that mean Roland was learning to think of other people as more than servants or that he was trying to put her in debt to him? It was unlikely that she'd ever be able to afford the better seating in the Arena on her salary. "Still, stay in the aircar until we have checked out the security arrangements."

The Arena had a good reputation for security, she'd been relieved to discover; most of the staff were retired military and the complex itself was largely sealed from the outside world. Most of the gladiators lived in tiny rooms buried below the ground, unless they happened to be famous enough to deserve one of the apartments at the edge of the complex. All of the animals, particularly the man-killers, were held in secure compounds, trapped in holographic representations of their homeworlds. The entire system was remarkably secure, or so she had been informed. No one could even walk through the Arena without a ticket bracelet strapped to their wrist – and if they took it off, the alarms would sound.

She braced herself as the aircar dropped to the ground. If there *was* an ambush waiting for them it would be sprung now. Roland was inside a heavily-armoured aircar, but a single direct hit with an HVM would blow it to atoms, along with his bodyguard. She watched as the Senate Security staff spread out of their aircars and checked the area quickly, before sending the all-clear back to Belinda. The aircar door hissed open at her command and they stepped out onto the landing pad.

There was a faint scent of blood in the air, something that brought back unhappy memories from Han and a dozen other worlds. She glanced at Roland and saw, to her alarm, that he seemed almost excited by the smell, as if the air was slightly drugged. Her implants ran a quick analysis, but found nothing apart from the scent itself. She dragged her attention away from him as a gorgeously-robed man appeared at one edge of the pad and bowed low to Roland.

"Your Highness," he said. "Your Royal Box awaits your presence."

"We are pleased," Roland said, in a rather high-pitched tone. "Lead us to the box."

Belinda scowled inwardly as the man turned and led the way into the dome, down a long flight of stairs. The plans she'd downloaded into her implants revealed that the Royal Box was actually quite small, barely large enough for five or six people, something that puzzled her until she realised just how limited space in the Arena actually was. She heard the noise of the crowd cheering in the distance, even through the hullmetal walls, and shook her head. The Arena might have enjoyed real blood and guts, but it was not war. No one who had seen Han could have seen the Arena as anything more than a travesty.

They walked through a set of wooden doors and into the Royal Box. As Roland had promised, there were two chairs, both set up so the spectators could use binoculars if necessary. Belinda was surprised that they didn't use magnifying fields, but apparently the binoculars were part of the experience. Besides, it was tradition, like so much else. Roland took his seat and smiled as he stared out over the sands. Two gladiators were bashing away at each other with swords and little else.

"I shall have your regular drinks brought to your box," the guide said.

"No," Belinda said, quickly. She accessed the box's processor, skimmed through a menu and placed her own orders. "Bring juice and biscuits, but nothing else."

The guide stared at her, then at Roland, then back at her, clearly puzzled over what was going on. Belinda's eyes never left his and, eventually, he bowed and headed off to carry out his orders. She expected Roland to argue, but he seemed captivated by the gladiators on the field below. Belinda was much less impressed; sword fights were hardly part of modern military training, but it was evident that the gladiators didn't have the slightest idea of what they were doing. She could have beaten both of them with one hand tied behind her back. Or both hands, given how careless they were. It would have been simple to manipulate them into killing each other.

She accessed the processor and downloaded a copy of the programme. Unsurprisingly, the warm-up acts consisted of complete amateurs, men and women who had walked into the Arena's office and signed up to fight. Most of them wouldn't last the week, she decided, but those that did would start the long crawl up towards superstardom. But if there were thousands of newcomers and only a hundred gladiators allowed to stay at the top…she pushed the thought aside, tiredly, as one of the gladiators finally managed to stab the other properly. His victim staggered and fell forward, tearing the blade from his opponent's hands as he hit the ground. If there had been a third gladiator, Belinda decided, both of the others would have been killed.

The crowd showed no enthusiasm as the victor held up his hands, clearly expecting cheers and rewards. He looked rather downcast as the cleaning crew came onto the field, picked up the dead body and carried it and the weapons over to the exit, leaving the blood behind to stain the sand. Belinda rolled her eyes; the crowd, clearly jaded, didn't care about the first battles. The only people who were applauding were the blood junkies in the first row.

She stood up and spun around as someone new entered the box. A young man carrying a tray of drinks blinked at her in surprise, then retreated the moment she took the tray from him and put it down on the small table. Roland had been complaining less about the healthier drinks she'd been serving him, suggesting that he was slowly coming to like the more natural juices. Or maybe he'd just realised that bitching wasn't going to get him anywhere.

Belinda shook her head as she surveyed the crowd. Everyone who considered themselves important had splashed out thousands of credits for a seat in the upper or middle section of the Arena, where they were seated in their gaudy clothes, watching the fighting. The lower section was assigned to citizens from outside the higher families, although it wasn't uncommon for the buyers to then sell them onwards to people willing to pay through their nose for a seat, even if it was among the commoners. None of them looked very happy to be seated there, but the alternative was not going to the Arena at all.

Rolling her eyes, she looked up at the other boxes. A handful of Grand Senators and their families sat in their boxes, although she was surprised to see that several boxes were actually empty. Another way of showing their wealth and power, she decided, as she saw several Senators looking back at her. The Grand Senators could afford to purchase a box at the Arena and then leave it empty. Anyone who owned a box could have reclaimed the expense just by hiring it out to someone else. Leaving it empty was more than *mere* conspicuous consumption.

"Ladies and gentlemen," a voice boomed, silencing the chattering crowd. "Put your hands together for the Female Furies!"

The crowd suddenly roared with delight as the doors opened and the next set of gladiators marched into the pit. There were nine of them, all women wearing nothing more than chainmail briefs around their thighs, their breasts bouncing free as they walked forward. Their skin glistened under the spotlights as they reached the centre of the sands and raised their swords in salute to the crowds. Roland leaned forward, pressing his binoculars to his eyes, as the women lined up, ready for their first bout.

"And their opponents," the voice bellowed. "The Barbarians!"

Belinda's eyes widened as a second door opened, revealing four men carrying whips. They wore leather loincloths to conceal their groins and nothing else, suggesting warrior barbarians from one of the colony worlds that had lost all technology during the first expansion from Earth and slipped back into barbarism. The crowds cheered even louder as the men swaggered forwards, cracking their whips towards the women, who sneered at them. Belinda watched them carefully, recognising the discipline half-masked by their absurd postures. Having proven that they were killers in the early bouts, the gladiators would have been snapped up by talent spotters and offered proper training...and a chance to fight as part of a team.

The two sides glared at one another as the crowd's cheers slowly faded away, replaced by an intense anticipation that made Belinda feel uncomfortable. Roland seemed unable to take his eyes off the women, who were brandishing their swords towards the men. Belinda couldn't help feeling that the women, despite carrying the better weapons, were outmatched. They didn't seem to have the same level of training as the men.

A whistle blew...and the women lunged forward, swords in hand. The men cracked out with their whips, aiming for eyes – or for the weapons the women were carrying. One woman stumbled backwards, only to be kicked to the ground by her opponent; another lost her sword, only to have it snatched up by the man and used to behead her. The women looked good, Belinda realised, but not much else. All four of the men were working as a team.

One of the men was stabbed by a woman and sent falling to the ground, but the other three rapidly overcame the other women. Once they had acquired the upper hand, they used fists and whips rather than the captured swords, lashing the women and driving them back towards the exit. The crowds went wild as blood glittered on their skins where they'd been cut by the whip, howling obscene suggestions towards the male gladiators. Belinda watched as the surviving women were beaten out of sight, their male opponents winning the match, then looked at Roland. There was a thoroughly unpleasant look on his face, his mouth twisted into a sickening leer.

The roar only grew louder as the staff walked back onto the sands, picked up the bodies and carried them towards the exit. Belinda had no difficulty in imagining just what they thought the male gladiators would do to the female gladiators. Who knew – maybe it wouldn't be long before the whole act, from start to finish, took place under the spotlights. Or perhaps it didn't; having the women taken away allowed the crowd to assume that they had been raped. It would be comforting to believe that was true.

Depraved, she thought, and shuddered again. What did it say about Earth's current state that mass slaughter constituted entertainment?

The next set of matches were more even, she realised, as she sat back in her chair and tried to watch, splitting her attention between the arena and the crowd. Most of the gladiators seemed to have equal levels of training and equipment, although a couple of the pairings had the gladiators wielding very different sets of weaponry against each other. A large holographic scoreboard appeared at the side of the Royal Box, allowing her to track each gladiator as they climbed upwards in the rankings towards the top hundred. She honestly couldn't understand why most of the gladiators fought. The rewards were vast, true, but they were very hard to reach. Statistically, she estimated, the odds were massively against *anyone* reaching the top.

She looked over at Roland and asked a question. "Can the gladiators retire?"

"Of course," Roland said. "But they never do."

Belinda considered checking that, before deciding that it wasn't her concern. It would be simple enough for a new gladiator, all flushed from winning his first fight, to get into debt with a backer and then discover that he had to keep fighting until he'd paid back his loan. Perpetual debt was an old way of controlling people – it was a favourite trick of corporations operating along the Rim – and there was no reason why it couldn't be used against a gladiator. Weapons and training were grossly expensive, particularly on Earth.

The crowd roared again as a woman wearing a long red dress and carrying a sword strode into the pit, raising her sword to the Royal Box. Belinda found herself staring at the woman, seeing the easy confidence with which she carried her sword. Another warrior, she realised, even if the woman did have a china-doll face that made her look childlike. Her opponent, another swordsman, appeared at the far end of the pit and advanced towards her. Sparks flew as their swords clashed together, before they separated and circled each other, probing for weaknesses.

Roland leaned forward in glee as the two gladiators clashed again and again, his face displaying naked excitement. Belinda silently studied the two gladiators and realised that her first impressions had been right. Both of them had some proper training and plenty of experience. The red dress didn't seem to hamper the woman at all as she lunged forward, only to be stabbed in the side by her opponent. For a long moment, Belinda thought that the woman had lost, before she pulled herself along the blade and swung her sword, beheading her opponent with a single stroke. She'd seen Marines show similar pain tolerance in the field, but they had augmentation to help. The Arena's rules banned any form of tech enhancement.

"She won," Roland yelled, his voice lost in the cheers from the crowd. "She always wins!"

"Impressive," Belinda conceded.

The woman had slumped to the ground as the medical team raced towards her. She had to be someone important, she decided, or a good investment for her backers; no one else had received the attention of a medical team on the field. Maybe she'd recover without problems, Belinda told herself. Medical science could heal almost any wound as long as it wasn't fatal.

Roland elbowed her. "Could *you* do that?"

Belinda hesitated, then nodded slowly. In fact, if she'd used boosting implants, she would have been able to best both of the gladiators without being touched herself. But if she had been unenhanced…it would have been an ugly fight, she decided. It wasn't something she wanted to try.

She checked the programme and discovered that the woman was called the Scarlet Witch and, apparently, had never been defeated in her field. Injuries were common, it seemed, but she'd been back on the sands within weeks at most. Belinda wondered if she'd had some bio-enhancement, before deciding that it didn't matter. The Arena was still a mockery of war.

"See," Roland said. "I told you that you would enjoy it."

"Yeah," Belinda growled, deciding not to argue. There was another two hours of blood and guts and death to go before they could go back to the Summer Palace. "But you're going to have to beat me again to come next week."

"I will," Roland assured her.

You won't, Belinda thought quietly. *You shouldn't be here at all.*

CHAPTER TWELVE

...But the effects were disastrous. Each civil servant cost very little, but there were millions of them. Their pay alone ate up a staggering portion of the Empire's budget. So too, less directly, did the other costs they imposed. Put simply, the endless regulations they invented to justify their existence. The smaller businesses couldn't afford to keep up with them and went out of business. This, unsurprisingly, ate away at the Empire's tax base. The big corporations, naturally, had already written themselves exemptions, or simply paid fines that would have destroyed their smaller competitors.

- Professor Leo Caesius, *The End of Empire.*

The next few days passed very slowly. Belinda kept Roland working at his physical education program and watched as he slowly grew healthier. Every day, they played tennis until Roland was pushed to the limit, although Belinda didn't let him win again. She knew that he found it frustrating to push so close, but never to actually win – but there was no choice. He had to keep flexing his muscles to widen his limits.

Retaining an etiquette teacher hadn't been easy. No one would have accused the average marine of having High Society etiquette and the handful that had come from the Grand Senate families had been deployed well away from Earth, separating them from those who might seek to curry favour with them. Eventually, she'd had to kick the question upstairs to the Commandant, who had selected someone who owed him and the Marine Corps a favour or two. Belinda was sure that there was a story in there somewhere, but there was no time to ask questions. Her mornings were spent learning the finer points of etiquette.

"I don't see why I have to do this," Roland protested, one morning. "I'm the Crown Prince!"

"You have to make people think that you care about them," Belinda pointed out, as Mr. Harris – the only name she'd been given for the tutor – organised the dining table. "Think of it as a disguise."

"I could pretend to be a very rude prince," Roland said, with a faint smile. "That would be easy."

"You have to convince them that you are *not* a very rude prince," Belinda countered. "That's a little harder." She grinned at him. "But think of all the time you can spend laughing at them without them knowing it."

Roland listened as she told him about some of her experiences as a Pathfinder. Standard Marines wore uniforms and fought as part of a team; Pathfinders were often expected to go undercover on enemy worlds, wearing enemy uniforms and blending in with their surroundings. Belinda herself had been a peasant woman on Han – that hadn't been a pleasant experience – and a trader queen with her own starship, both roles that were very different to her everyday life. Pretending to be someone else was challenging, particularly when dealing with sexist pigs and bureaucracy, but it had also been fun. Roland, she suspected, would appreciate it.

"So I can pretend to like someone," Roland said, "and laugh afterwards. I can do that."

"Glad to hear it," Mr. Harris said. His voice was calm, the product of impeccable breeding or intensive study. "Now, young sir, you are going to greet the daughter of a Grand Senator when she walks through the door."

He motioned for Belinda to take up position behind him, then step forward with a grand expression on her face. A Grand Senator's daughter, even one far enough down the family tree to miss out in inheriting anything important, would still have a sense of entitlement larger than a planet. She would lack for nothing; she would have few restraints on her behaviour, as long as she didn't call the family's position into question. Belinda summoned the right mindset – snooty, arrogant and demanding – and stepped forward. On cue, Roland rose to his feet.

"Lady Acosta," he said, taking her hand and kissing it lightly. "It is a great pleasure to see you."

Belinda curtseyed, then stepped past him.

"Good," Mr. Harris said. "You will be expected to greet all of the senior personages at your coronation. Should you miss a step, they will remember and it will be used against you later."

Roland rubbed his forehead. "Why can't I have a memory implant and a live feed from the network?"

"Because live feeds have been known to jam," Mr. Harris reminded him. "It isn't uncommon for someone to deliberately try to jam the local communications links just to see if the victim can still remember the names of all of those you have to greet. Consider yourself fortunate; there are none who are socially superior to the Emperor. A Senator would have to bow to you, but accept a bow from a Guildmaster."

"Oh," Roland said. "And what if one of those daughters wants to spend more time with me?"

"She won't say so, of course," Mr. Harris replied. "You will never meet a potential marriage partner alone, young sir. Her mother will always be present in the room. Should her mother have passed on, her closest female relation will be expected to carry out the duty. However, the decision on whom you marry will not be made by yourself."

Belinda felt a flicker of sympathy as Roland scowled. The Grand Senate would approve the Princess Consort – and then the Empress – and just about every family with a daughter in the right age bracket would want to put her name forward. There would be years of horse-trading before a suitable candidate was placed into Roland's bed. He'd be expected to take lovers, of course, but none of them could become his bride. Or, for that matter, bear his children.

"This is all stupid," Roland grumbled. "Who cares what fork I use to eat with?"

"Your throne is based largely on your personal prestige," Mr. Harris said. "You will strengthen or weaken it with every move you make. In this case" – he tapped the table – "you are showing that you are one of them by sharing their manners. Suggesting that you are *not* one of them will have consequences down the line."

"Right," Roland growled. "But I don't have any prestige, do I?"

He stood up and ran for the bedroom door. Belinda started forward, but she was too late to catch him before he slammed the door closed and locked it. A moment later, the security network sounded an alert as he opened the passageway leading down to the grounds and ran down outside the palace. Cursing under her breath, Belinda motioned for Mr. Harris to stay where he was and headed out of the other door. There was no point in trying to break into the Prince's room without heavy weapons or cutting tools. The designers of the palace had even built the doors out of hullmetal.

Obsessive paranoid bastards, she thought as she ran. *What the fuck is he doing now?*

Her implants reported pings from the Senate Security staff as she ran through the main doors and out into the gardens, but she ignored them. They knew who she was, even if they didn't know just what she was doing. She ran around the building, drawing on boosted speed, and reached the tennis court. There was no sign of Roland. Cursing again, Belinda drew on tracking skills she hadn't had to use for years and saw a faint trail leading into the thickly-packed part of the garden. Belinda followed him, realising that Roland hadn't been really trying to hide – or perhaps he simply wasn't very good at it. There were too many places where his passage had snapped branches off plants and crushed small flowers under his feet.

The gardeners hadn't done any proper gardening in this part of the gardens, according to the guidebook she'd been given; they'd merely dropped countless seeds from thousands of worlds and waited to see which ones would win the ensuring contest. They'd produced a tangle of plants as Earth-native fauna fought with imported fauna, creating an environment that smelled almost alien. Belinda ignored the scent as best as she could as she tracked Roland, finally locating a treehouse hidden in the midst of the greenery. On her homeworld, her family had built one using their own hands and manual tools. Here, it was obvious that technology had been used to build and steady the treehouse.

She heard Roland sobbing as she climbed up the ladder and peered through the hatch. The Prince was curled up in the far corner, pretending to be unaware that she was there. Belinda sighed inwardly and pulled herself all the way into the treehouse, then stepped over to him and reached out to take his shoulder. He shook his head angrily and tried to crawl away.

Idiot, Belinda thought. No one would act like that on the Slaughterhouse. Boot Camp perhaps...but a recruit who discovered that the military life wasn't for him could always just request dismissal from the camp. Roland couldn't run away from his position unless he was prepared to abdicate completely – and it was possible that the Grand Senate wouldn't even allow him to do that. If he'd been one of her brothers, failing to carry out his household chores, her father would have given him a good strapping. Absently, she wondered if that would be a good idea before pushing it aside for the moment. There were other things she could try first.

"You shouldn't have run," she said, pulling him towards her. He'd put on weight, thanks to the course of appetite enhancers and supplements she'd ordered for him, but he was still alarmingly slim. "It hasn't made it easy to protect you."

"I don't want your protection," Roland howled, tears streaming down his face. "I wish I was *dead*."

"Death is permanent," Belinda said, unsure of how seriously to take him. A couple of the brats she'd babysat while trying to make some money as a teenager had said the same thing, although they hadn't really meant it. "Do you really want to die?"

"I don't have a life," Roland said, pushing at her as he tried to pull free. "I'm just...just a puppet!"

Belinda frowned. That showed more self-awareness than she'd realised, although Roland hadn't really been shielded from the truth behind his position. Or one of his few friends had pointed it out during a drinking session. Or maybe one of the servants had told him...there were too many possibilities, none of them good.

"The Grand Senators want me to look good, marry one of their bitches and bless all their laws," Roland said. "You want to control my life! You say it is for my own good, but you control me and control me and control me..."

Belinda shook her head, tiredly. Perhaps she had come on too strong, but there had been no choice. Not that she could really explain it to

Roland, at least not yet. Teenage boys lacked any sense of long-term planning, particularly when they'd been raised to get more or less whatever they wanted whenever they wanted it. The more drink and drugs he took, the harder it would be for his body to repair itself afterwards. Maybe she should have removed the drugs first, then banished the alcohol later.

"They all laugh at me," Roland screamed. "They call me a child! I'm sixteen and they call me a child!"

"You are growing up," Belinda said, as reassuringly as she could. None of her brothers had acted like Roland – but then, none of them had been raised to think that the world was their oyster. "You're doing much better on the tennis court…"

"It's not good enough," Roland said. "It's *never* good enough."

"You should see some of my failures," Belinda said. She'd known that she was good when she went to Boot Camp, but the Drill Instructors had been masters at showing her just how little she really knew. "You're getting much better."

"But for what?" Roland demanded. "What do I have to live for?"

Belinda hesitated. In truth, Roland was right; the best he could hope for in life would be to wind up as a constitutional monarch, rubber-stamping bills the Grand Senate had passed after endless debate and political horse-trading. And Roland would get the blame for everything that went wrong with the Empire…she'd wondered why the Grand Senate hadn't taken advantage of the situation, before realising that having someone to blame could be very useful for them. Most of the Empire's population didn't understand politics at all, even without the Grand Senate muddying the waters. All they'd grasp was that someone called the Emperor was at the top.

"See," Roland demanded. "I *don't* have anything to live for."

He lashed out at her, his fist cracking into her jaw. Belinda moved on instinct and avoided the worst of the blow, although she'd had worse during basic training. Her implants automatically adjusted and compensated for the pain, leaving her feeling nothing more than a faint numbness that quickly faded away to nothing. She caught his hand before he could do that again and pulled him around to face her.

"You don't know what's going to happen next," she said, remembering how she'd talked to the children she'd babysat. Most of them hadn't thought past the night either. "You're going to be Emperor. Whatever the Grand Senate may say, you will have some formidable emergency powers. With a little time and patience – and determination – you will have a chance to carve out a place for yourself where you can operate independently."

Roland stared at her. "The Grand Senate would never allow it," he protested. "They don't want me..."

Belinda sighed and spoke over him. "The Grand Senate is itself divided," she pointed out, dryly. "You could do all sorts of things with a little care and forethought."

She sighed again, louder this time. "The Grand Senate has been arranging for you to stay here and drink yourself to death," she added. "Why do you *think* they haven't stopped you from destroying your own life? They want you to sit in the Imperial Palace, keep blasting your brain into the next dimension and maybe sign one or two papers for them."

"They won't let you keep working on me," Roland said, after a long moment. "If you're making me healthy..."

"They can't sack me," Belinda said. She grinned at him, inviting the prince to share the joke. "The Marine Corps has responsibility for your safety, at least on paper. They couldn't sack me; they'd have to pressure my superiors and my superiors are feeling stubborn. You could sack me, once you were Emperor, but they couldn't make you sack me."

Roland laughed. It came out as a choking sound. Belinda patted his back and then pulled him into a hug. "Listen to me," she said, before he could start sobbing again. "You can make something of your life if you try. I can help you get healthy and get ready to become Emperor, if you let me. Or you can go back to drinking and injecting yourself with drugs and waste away day by day. The choice is yours."

She leaned forward until her lips were almost touching his ears. "Do you really want to let the bastards win?"

"No," Roland said, slowly. He looked up at her through tearstained eyes. "Are you going to be with me?"

"I'll be with you as long as you need me," Belinda promised. Absently, she wondered just how long that would be. She'd always assumed that it wouldn't last after the Coronation. "I..."

"I looked it up," Roland said, before she could continue. "I can have oath-sworn liegemen, if I take their oaths personally. Even a Crown Prince can have liegemen. Will you swear to me?"

Belinda hesitated, just long enough to think quickly. Marines weren't supposed to swear to anyone personally, only the Empire itself. It created a conflict of interest that might be impossible to resolve. By swearing to be Roland's liegeman, she would be opening up a whole new can of worms, both for her career and the young prince. At the very least, it was unlikely that she would ever be able to go back to active duty. Offhand, she couldn't recall any Marines who'd been oath-sworn to anyone.

But if it meant that he trusted her, that he would be willing to listen to her, it would be worth it…

Still, she told herself, *I can always go out to the Rim and retire there.*

She should have run it past the Commandant first, but she knew that Roland needed an immediate answer. Anything else would destroy his fragile trust in her.

"I will," she said, and meant it. She took his hands in hers and tried to remember the words. They'd been mentioned in a briefing on military protocol, but she'd long-since buried them at the back of her mind. "I, Belinda Lawson, swear loyalty to Crown Prince Roland for as long as I live…"

She stumbled through the rest of the words and then pulled the Prince to his feet. "Come on," she said, seriously. "You have to clean up and then face me on the tennis court again."

"I can order you to lose now," Roland pointed out dryly.

Belinda snorted. "And what would you actually learn from that?"

Surprisingly, Roland didn't argue any further. Having an ally made him feel better, Belinda decided; it wasn't an uncommon pattern among young men who'd been abused. And the way Roland had been brought up had *been* abuse, even if it hadn't been physical torture. Having everything he wanted from an early age would have left different scars on his soul.

Shaking her head, she allowed him to lead her down the ladder and back towards the palace, where he could get a shower and change his clothes. After that, they could get back to work.

CHAPTER THIRTEEN

Humans being humans, this oppression bred discontent and resistance. Unfortunately, the resistance was insufficient to change the Empire before it was too late or force it to evolve with its very existence on the line. Planets that tried to declare independence often found themselves attacked by the Imperial Navy and bombarded back into submission. Once suppressed, they would find themselves indebted to the Empire – and paying off debts that bound them for generations.

- Professor Leo Caesius, The End of Empire.

They were going to take his ship.

Captain – although he wasn't going to be a Captain much longer, was he? – Absalom Wyss stared down at the message on the display. They'd timed it perfectly, the bastards. *Sunny Jim* was on her final approach to Earth, well inside the Phase Limit. If the message had reached him while he was still on the edge of the solar system, he could have reversed course and re-crossed the Phase Limit, jumping out of the solar system before the revenue cutters could catch up with him. But it was too late to escape. There was no way he could get out of range now.

The message was blunt, coming straight to the point. His debts to the banks were being called in – and if he couldn't pay, his ship would be repossessed by the bailiffs. They'd promised him a year to scrape up the money to repay his loans, but the promise had been broken, the bankers citing an emergency statute that meant nothing to him. He didn't have the credits he needed to pay off the bankers, not in the current economic climate. All of the independent shippers were having similar problems. There just wasn't enough work to go around, not for the independents. The big corporations worked hard to lock them out of most shipping jobs and all that was left was semi-legal smuggling. And now even that was gone.

He loved his ship, for it had given him a life less ordinary. He'd loved having his wife and children as his crew, even if there was a small forest worth of paperwork to fill in and submit to gain the necessary permissions. He couldn't bear the thought of having to live in a tiny apartment on Earth, his children exposed to the lawlessness of the megacities or the schools that specialised in turning young children's brains into mush. And yet, what could he do? They were going to board his ship and evict them, by force if necessary. Everyone in the trading community had heard about crews being stunned and waking up in hospital, where they'd been hit with the bill for removing them from their ships. It wasn't going to happen to him...

Of course it is, he thought grimly, as he stared at the message. They would have armed bailiffs waiting for the ship to dock, whereupon they would swarm onboard and drag the crew off the ship. He could just imagine the scene...he turned his head and stared at the massive station orbiting Earth. Once, the sight had awed him, convincing him that there was still wonder in the universe. The boxy structure orbiting Earth was humanity's work, the product of a society that had spent centuries in space. Now, it represented the end of the line.

He knew he should talk to his wife, or even to his daughters, but what could he say? Absolute despair gripped him as he realised that he had lost everything and ruined their lives. The kids didn't have the paperwork qualifications to work on other starships, so they'd have to live on Earth... and there was no shortage of other qualified spacers looking for work. He and his wife would have to go on the dole on Earth, sinking into the same stupor that gripped most of the planet's inhabitants...for someone used to travelling between the stars, it was a fate worse than death.

His console chimed as he received permission to approach from Orbit Station Seven. Even now, there were still thousands of starships docking and undocking at Earth every day, most of them transporting food and drink to the wealthier natives. He gritted his teeth in rage as he thought of the Grand Senate and the bureaucracy it had spawned, devoted to keeping the independent shippers – and all of those who wanted to lead independent lives – down and out. How much of his time had he wasted filling in their damned paperwork? He'd tried to lead a honest life and what had it gained him? Nothing, but taxes, paperwork…and now they were taking his ship.

Damn them all, he thought, as he keyed a command into the drive system. He couldn't bear to see his wife waste away in a megacity block, or his daughters sucked into what passed for society down on Earth. There were enough horror stories – theft, rape, murder – to convince him that anything would be preferable. Hell, he'd once met a woman from Earth who had been raped twice – and considered it perfectly normal. He was *not* going to let his daughters live there.

The ship shuddered to life as the drive system engaged. Like most freighters, *Sunny Jim* had a very low acceleration rate, but he could risk overloading the drive one final time. He smiled grimly as the ship started to pick up speed, aimed directly at Orbit Station Seven. If he could have, he would have aimed the ship at the Imperial City, but it was on the other side of the planet. The Orbit Station would have to do.

He reached for his wristcom to call his family, then stopped himself. It was better they died unknowing. They would never have to know that he'd failed them.

Millicent Wycliffe was not having a good day.

Managing the thousands of starships, spacecraft and orbital stations in the Earth-Luna conjoined system was not an easy task at the best of times. Earth's orbit was crammed with everything from orbital defence stations to transhipment hubs, each one requiring its own brand of attention from System Control. Home Fleet's anchorage in Luna orbit had to be kept isolated from commercial shipping, while the freighters bringing foodstuffs and other supplies to Earth had to be steered in and out as quickly as possible. Keeping track of it all wouldn't have been simple even if the systems hadn't kept threatening to break down. Merely monitoring the relatively small area of space under Orbit Station Seven's control was a nightmare.

Her supervisor had been trying to convince *his* superiors that they needed a chance to shut down and do some repairs, but he'd been unable to convince them to give System Control the time it needed. Millicent could understand why – Earth depended on the constant stream of goods from out-system – yet she knew that the tiny problems and near-disasters would eventually catch up with them. Hell, there *were* little disasters all the time. God alone knew what would happen if the system actually came under attack.

An alarm sounded and she rolled her eyes. The security network was hyper-sensitive, designed by some fool with only the barest grasp of theoretical knowledge – and absolutely no practical experience. He'd convinced whoever was in charge of procurement – countless levels above Millicent's position – that having a system that sounded the alarm whenever *anything* happened was a good idea, but Millicent could have told them better. There were so many false alarms that the staff were completely desensitized to them. Response times were poor and grew worse as the day progressed.

They really should give us more leave, she thought, as she looked over at the display. It had been months since her last vacation in Luna City, where she'd found a few new friends and partied with them for several days. The memory of a nine-person orgy made her smile as she glanced at the display…and froze. A freighter was picking up speed, heading directly towards Orbit Station Seven, right towards her. For a moment, all of the emergency procedures simply flew out of her head. The freighter was going to *ram* the station! There was no way that it could be an accident, or even a freighter commander trying to get in and out quickly before the bankers caught up with him. This was deliberate…

She licked her suddenly-dry lips and hit the emergency button, praying that it worked perfectly for once. There had been so many false alarms that her supervisor had installed a secondary emergency network for *real* emergencies, but he'd had to go outside the bureaucratic system to obtain it and it hadn't been properly integrated with the rest of the network. *Dear*

God, she realised. They were under attack! For all she knew, this was the first blow in an all-out invasion of Earth.

A loud klaxon rang through the station as the alert sounded, followed rapidly by the noise of panic from her co-workers. They'd seen the danger, finally. Her communicator buzzed a moment later.

"Report," her supervisor barked.

Millicent pushed aside the old resentment at his habit of staying in his quarters and allowing his crew to do the work – at least he was better than her *last* supervisor, who had been fond of hinting just how much he would enjoy bedding her – and snapped out a report.

"One freighter on an impact trajectory," she said. Training sent her hand reaching for her shipsuit helmet, only to find nothing. After days of wearing the hot garment – without anything ever happening to justify wearing it – she'd stopped donning it. The simple uniform she wore was comfortable, but it would provide no protection at all if the hull was breached. "I..."

She thought fast, trying to think of something – anything – that she could do. But there was nothing, apart from firing on the freighter. And that required permission from her supervisor.

"Sir," she said, formally, "I request permission to engage the incoming ship."

Her supervisor hesitated, just long enough for the freighter to pick up more speed. Millicent winced in disbelief; he might be reluctant to take responsibility for destroying the freighter, but the freighter would destroy *them* if it rammed the station! Surely no one would hold it against him... she shook her head, tiredly. She'd worked in System Control long enough to know that any decision, no matter how rational, could be held against the person who made it – or the scapegoat, if an unscrupulous manager decided it was better to shovel shit downhill. And *someone* had probably purchased the cargo on the freighter. They'd sue for compensation if it was destroyed...

"Granted," he replied, finally.

Millicent hit the arming key and the weapons slid out of their storage blisters, too late. Orbit Station Seven and its twins had been denied missiles, leaving them with energy weapons alone – and it was too little, too late. The weapons started to fire, just as the freighter closed in…she closed her eyes as the freighter rammed the station and a colossal impact shook the entire structure.

The gravity field vanished a moment later. Millicent opened her eyes, just in time to see the power surge – causing several consoles to explode – and then fail. The lighting went out, followed rapidly by the remaining consoles, even though they were supposed to have their own independent power sources. She could hear an unholy sound echoing throughout the entire station, a hint of tearing metal…moments later, she heard the faint sound of escaping air. System Control was located well above the docking bay, but the entire structure had been decaying for years. God alone knew how many of the safety precautions had failed under the impact. The emergency lighting should have come on at once, but it seemed to have failed completely.

There was a snapping sound in the darkness, followed by a pulse of light as one of her co-workers found a flashlight and shone it around. Millicent saw several bodies drifting through the air, although she couldn't tell if they were injured or merely unable to catch hold of something to pull themselves back to the ground. One of them was definitely dead, she realised as she saw blood spewing out of a nasty wound in her chest. She had to swallow hard to keep from throwing up. Tiny globules of blood flowing through the air were bad enough, but vomit would be worse. Still, she couldn't help feeling queasy. It had been years since she'd done anything in zero-g.

Another dull explosion echoed through the structure and she shivered. At least the freighter hadn't been loaded with explosives or they would have been vaporised when it hit – or so she thought. No one had ever rammed an orbital station with a freighter before. Maybe the emergency procedures had worked better than she thought. But she could still hear the sound of escaping air…two more flashlights appeared as her co-workers found the emergency lockers and passed them out, although several of the flashlights didn't seem to work. They'd grown lax with their emergency supplies too.

We should have kept our fucking shipsuits on, she thought, too late. There was no point in wasting time on what might have been, if they'd bothered to take safety precautions seriously. *And maybe kept a closer eye on what the hell was going on outside.*

She cleared her throat. No one had taken charge – they hadn't been trained to take command, at least until they were formally promoted – but *someone* had to do it. And she had the makings of a plan. "We need to get out of here," she said. She could hear other sounds echoing through the structure now, suggesting that the entire station was slowly ripping itself apart. "If we stay here, we will suffocate."

"But they'll know where to find us here," one of the other workers said. She was young; it was common knowledge on the station that the only reason she'd been promoted was that she'd put out for the last supervisor, who'd since abandoned her to carry out a job she was ill-prepared to handle. Her co-workers ignored her where possible, knowing that she was looking for another sugar daddy to take care of her. "They'll be looking for us, right?"

"In theory," Millicent snapped. In practice…she wasn't so sure. The SAR teams would be on their way, she was sure, but they'd have no idea what they were getting into. For all she knew, it might look as through the station had been completely depressurised from the outside. "What happens if we're falling towards Earth?"

She saw their expressions in the gloom and smiled, grimly. Orbit Station Seven was massive, even if most of its mass was storage bays for goods awaiting shipment to the orbital towers and down to Earth. If it happened to fall out of orbit, it was large enough to survive a fall through the atmosphere and strike the planet's surface. The results would be devastating *wherever* the station fell. She knew what the planet's defences would do if it looked like the station was going to fall; they'd blow the station to atoms to prevent a greater catastrophe. And even if the entire crew was still alive, their deaths would be nothing compared to the billions on Earth who would be at risk if the station fell.

"We're going to have to get up to the upper shuttlebay," she said, now that she had their complete attention. The freighter had struck the lower half of the station; logically, the upper levels shouldn't have suffered so much damage. "That's probably our best bet to get out. If necessary, we put on spacesuits and turn into Dutchmen. They'll be able to pick us up from the outside."

She felt the air moving as soon as they got out of the command centre, suggesting that the internal airlocks had failed completely. Maybe she'd been wrong, she thought, feeling curiously light-headed as she led the way towards the internal transit tubes. The hull breach might be closer to the command centre than she had assumed. Or maybe something else had broken under the force of the impact…she pushed the thought aside as the rush of air grew stronger. How long would it take the entire station to completely depressurise?

One of the emergency lockers was dead ahead. Millicent breathed a sigh of relief as she realised that it was still sealed and pulled herself towards it, silently grateful that the designers hadn't insisted on using electronic locks. Instead, she opened it with her hands and started to pass out oxygen masks. It was starting to become hard to breathe, she realised, as she pressed the mask against her face. She had no idea how long she could survive in vacuum, but if she had a mask she might just have a chance to be rescued before it was too late…

She took a breath…and recoiled. The air inside the mask's compressed supply *stank*. This time, she couldn't help throwing up; she barely managed to pull the mask off before she threw up everything she'd eaten before going on duty. They hadn't changed the masks, she realised in horror, as she saw others having the same problem. The staff had been warned that the masks had to be replaced regularly, something else they'd dismissed as bureaucratic nonsense, but now she knew why. But it was too late.

Millicent struggled for breath, even risking pushing the mask back against her face, but found nothing. The atmosphere inside the station was almost gone; the masks were useless. She looked back at her co-workers and saw her own horror reflected in their eyes. The safety procedures had failed through lack of maintenance…and they were all going to die.

The world went dark around her and Millicent knew no more.

CHAPTER FOURTEEN

Unsurprisingly, this constant state of unrest granted special prominence to the Imperial Navy. Corruption spread rapidly, with everyone from the leading admirals to junior officers and chiefs being on the take. This trend blurred with Grand Senatorial attempts to expand their patronage networks and divided the Navy into factions, each one unthinkingly hostile to the others. It is quite likely that the Navy would have broken if faced with a serious challenge from an outside force. However, such a force failed to materialise.
- Professor Leo Caesius, *The End of Empire.*

"We," Grand Senator Stephen Onge muttered, "are victims of our own success."

"Pardon?"

"Nothing, Lindy," Stephen said. Lindy's family might have served the Onge family for generations, but there were some matters best kept private. After all, who could *really* be trusted completely? "Do you have a final report?"

"Orbit Station Seven disintegrated completely nineteen minutes after the impact," Lindy said. She looked young, barely old enough to be considered an adult, but her mind was sharp even without the benefit of memory implants. And besides, others tended to see a beautiful girl beside the Grand Senator and underestimate both of them. "All five hundred crewmen were killed, either in the impact or the disintegration. Three hundred and twelve bodies have been recovered so far."

"Never mind the dead," Stephen snapped. "What about the physical destruction?"

"Everything stored on Orbit Station Seven is gone," Lindy replied, briskly. "That's upwards of seventy *billion* credits worth of foodstuffs from the Inner Worlds and forty-two million credits worth of technical equipment for Earth. As yet, we are still computing the exact total of the loss; it is unfortunately possible that insurance will not be able to make up the shortfall for several corporations.

"Furthermore, thousands of pieces of debris were spewed into orbit by the impact," she continued. "So far, there have been several secondary impacts – and an alarming amount of material has fallen into Earth's atmosphere. The Imperial Navy is vaporising anything large enough to prove a threat to the orbital towers or the planet's surface; orbital defences are sweeping anything that might damage other installations out of space."

Stephen nodded, tiredly. Losing Orbit Station Seven was going to hurt – and not just financially. Billions of credits had been tied up in the destroyed foodstuffs and technical supplies, but billions more had been wrapped up in the futures market – and with a missing orbital station, it was going to be harder to bring supplies down to Earth. The economic knock-on effects could be disastrous.

He activated his implants and reviewed the economic model of the Empire his staffers had prepared, using information that was rarely available to people without the right clearance and the intelligence to ask the right questions. Several medium-sized corporations were going to take a nasty hit in the pocketbook, right up to the point where they might fold over and collapse. Even the bigger interstellar corporations were going to be in trouble, he realised, even the ones that were tied to the Grand Senate. They might be able to convince the Senators to help preserve them, but the Senate might not be able to afford it. And even if they could, it would require more political horse-trading that would eat up time and energy.

"In addition, nineteen freighters – seven of them independents – were destroyed in the blast," Lindy informed him. "The remainder belonged to various corporations and will represent another drain on the insurance companies, particularly the corporations based in the Inner Worlds…"

Stephen scowled. Albion and most of its sector were already teetering on the brink of declaring independence – and the rest of the Inner Worlds would follow, if they thought they could get away with it. A major crisis on Earth might prompt them to do just that, particularly if the economic shitstorm took down most of the Empire's economy. If the Inner World corporations threw their not-inconsiderable power behind the secessionist movements, the Empire would be in big trouble.

He stood up and paced over to the window, staring down at Earth's teeming megacities far below. All of the Senatorial families had residences in Imperial City, but only the very richest of families could afford a tower so close to the Imperial Palace. Stephen's family had been close to the centre of power since the Unification Wars, so tightly enmeshed within the Empire that they had regularly provided wives and mistresses for the Emperors. But now the Empire seemed to be finally winding down to an end.

Professor Caesius had been right. God alone knew how he'd gotten his hands on restricted data – Stephen had his suspicions about Marine involvement in the whole affair – but he'd drawn the correct conclusions. The Empire's economy had been warped for generations and the bills were finally coming due, just as large parts of the most productive parts of the system were either grinding to a halt or trying to get out of the system. How could he blame them? But in the end, it didn't matter. Stephen's duty was to the family he headed, not the Empire as a whole. What did it gain him if he sacrificed his family to save the Empire?

Centuries ago, his ancestors had made a deal with the First Emperor. They would provide support for his bid to unify the human race and, in exchange, they would have the opportunity to expand their economic and commercial power. And they'd capitalised on it magnificently. His family controlled over ten percent of the Empire's entire economy, with trillions of humans working directly or indirectly for them – and it had interests everywhere. There was hardly a colony world that hadn't taken out a long-term loan from his family, or a smaller corporation that wasn't indebted to them...

...But if the Empire's economy started to collapse, it would take his family with it.

It had been a simple matter to intermesh the family with the first Grand Senators, and then to create a political class – an aristocracy in all but name – that would control the reins of power. Indeed, Stephen suspected, from reading between the lines of the family's private records, that it would have happened with or without deliberate intent. Control over both politics and the economy gave the Grand Senate awesome power to offer patronage, placing their own people into vital positions. It would have been very difficult for anyone to break their stranglehold on power. But now the very foundations of their power were weakening and threatening to collapse.

"Tell me something," he said, looking over at his personal assistant. "Do you think we made a mistake locking out the talented but unconnected?"

It shouldn't have been surprising, he knew. The political class had become an aristocracy – and birth had become more important than talent. Why allow someone from the outside to marry their children and join the families when there were so many candidates who brought family connections and patronage opportunities to the marriage? And besides, any outsider would be shunned by the rest of the quality, no matter how talented.

But that might have been a mistake.

He silently remembered his own struggle to find roles for some of his relatives, men and women so stupid that he doubted they could count to eleven without taking off their socks. If the geneticists hadn't kept a close eye on the family genetics, he would have wondered if they were suffering the effects of too much inbreeding. But he'd *had* to find them roles suited to their status…there had been times when he'd seriously considered holding a cull instead, after looking at some of the disasters they'd caused. The third cousin who had been murdered by a man he'd dragged into his bed had only managed to cause the family some embarrassment. Most of the others had been worse.

"It isn't my place to say," Lindy said.

Stephen scowled as he stared down at the city below. Of *course* it wasn't her place to say; she was only a bloody personal assistant, someone who could be removed, memory-wiped and dumped among the Undercity's denizens on a whim. She wouldn't risk angering him, even if her family's entire position hadn't depended on keeping him sweet. How easy it was, he knew, to hear what he wanted to hear – or what people *thought* he wanted to hear. But that wasn't the same as being told what he *needed* to hear.

"The Grand Senate has called an emergency meeting to discuss the crisis," Lindy added, a moment later. "Will you be attending?"

"I suppose I must," Stephen growled. There was only one Grand Senator per family, thankfully, and no nonsense about elections. The Junior Senators *did* have to worry about elections, which tended to make them insistent that all the so-called social security provided to Earth's teeming poor was left untouched. But then, keeping Earth's population sweet was vitally important. "What will this do to Earth's food supply?"

Lindy didn't show any surprise when he changed the subject. "On the face of it, costs for imported foodstuffs will skyrocket over the next four weeks," she said. "Algae-based foodstuffs will probably not be affected. However, many in the middle classes will find themselves unable to afford imported foods. There may be trouble."

Stephen nodded, unsurprised. Algae-based food was healthy, but tended to taste terrible, no matter what flavourings were added. For the poor in the Undercity, there was literally nothing else to eat; Earth's farming industry had long since stopped producing anything but algae. The middle classes, on the other hand, had been accustomed to putting better meals on the table. That certainty was suddenly under threat.

"There *will* be trouble," he grunted. He turned to face her, admiring – once again – the perfection of her body, the result of months in the cosmetic body shop. But all he ever did was admire her. Power was so much more rewarding than sex. "You can go and inform Senate Security that I will attend the session, naturally. And send in Bode as you go."

He watched Lindy's swaying hips as she left his office and closed the door behind her, then turned back to the window. Once, Imperial City had been the richest city in the Empire – and the safest. Now…Stephen knew that a rising tide of anarchy threatened to overwhelm civilisation – and Earth itself. And where would the Grand Senate be then?

The door opened, revealing Bode. Like Lindy, his family had been trusted retainers for generations, but the tall muscular man's expertise lay in a very different arena. Bode had served in the Imperial Army's Special Forces before returning to the family and taking control of their private security force. Lately, however, Stephen had been using him for a different purpose.

"I heard the news, boss," Bode said. Unlike Lindy, he was almost always informal. "It's going to be bad on the surface."

Stephen nodded, turning to look at his retainer. Bode had done dirty work for the family before – everything from nerve gassing colonists who had been reluctant to move to hunting down and assassinating several rebel leaders – and could be trusted, at least to some degree. The psychologists who'd examined him had called Bode a certifiable sociopath, someone who would do anything, no matter how appalling, as long as he got paid. He was a tool, Stephen knew, but one who could easily turn in the hand that held him.

"You were in the city," Stephen said, flatly. "Just how bad is it going to be?"

"May take a few days for it to sink in, then they'll be eating algae and farting in tune," Bode said. He smirked, as if it was amusing. "And then I dare say that things will start getting worse for the poor dears. You'll have riots on your hands."

"No doubt," Stephen said, tightly. Useful or not, there was only so much of Bode he could stand before he felt the urge to throw him out of his office. "And your agitator cells?"

"Coming along nicely," Bode informed him, cheerfully. "God bless those ignorant student dears. They're so ignorant that it never occurred to them to ask where I got the weapons and equipment, let alone the training. You can't get that on Earth, not outside the military. Stupid bastards."

He made a show of licking his lips. "But the girls...*they're* fun."

"Just remember that you cannot afford to alienate them too soon," Stephen reminded him. "None of your *games*, not yet."

He'd read the sealed reports on Bode when he'd taken the man back into his service and, reading between the lines, Bode had managed to make even the hardened commanding officers of the Imperial Army sick.

The Imperial Army was not unused to committing atrocities, which made the achievement rather remarkable – and alarming. If Bode hadn't had political connections, he would probably have been dishonourably discharged and then dropped on Hellhole.

A dangerous tool, Stephen reminded himself.

"Get the cells ready for operations soon," he ordered, out loud. "But make sure you keep them under control until the time is right. We don't want to act too soon."

Bode straightened up, tossed him a mocking salute and walked out of the door without waiting for permission. Stephen watched him go, cursing the day he needed to resort to such tools. Bode had several security implants in his head, including one that would terminate him if he turned into a threat or someone tried to force him to talk, but Stephen disliked relying on them. Such implants were not always reliable.

But Bode was the best person for the job. Later, when he'd outlived his usefulness, the implant could be triggered. And that would be the end of him.

Shaking his head, Stephen activated the holographic display and brought up the latest from his intelligence staff. They were primarily focused on watching the rest of the wealthy families, but he'd insisted that they keep a sharp eye on the Marines. The Marines didn't know it – he thought – yet they posed the greatest threat to his plans in the solar system. So far, their Commandant didn't seem to have realised that the 'compromise' the Grand Senate had offered him played into Stephen's hands, but it was only a matter of time. No matter how often he played the bluff soldier, uninterested in politics, Stephen knew that there was a sharp political mind under the facade.

But he'd have some problems finding a reason to object to pulling the Marines off Home Fleet. Or, for that matter, opposing the change in command.

If there was one upside to the disaster in Earth orbit, it was a chance to have Admiral Valentine brought in ahead of schedule. With such a disaster taking place on his watch, the current CO could be unceremoniously fired and Valentine could take his place. Once the newcomer was in position, the next stage of the plan could be moved forward swiftly – and it would *have* to move swiftly. No one had predicted the Orbital Station Seven disaster, but it had already caused problems for his final gamble. Who knew what else would happen as the repercussions of the disaster started to spin out of control?

The Empire needed a strong and ruthless hand to save it from total disaster, but Stephen knew better than to think that anyone else would be suitable for such a role. There was no way that Prince Roland could provide leadership for the Empire, even if he hadn't had the Grand Senate subtly sabotaging his upbringing. Besides, anyone apart from Stephen might seriously consider crushing Stephen's family to promote their own interests. No, he had to take power himself for the good of his family. And the Empire, of course.

A new note blinked up in his implants, transmitted by one of his clients in logistics. The Marines had been requisitioning more supplies than normal – and, in fact, they'd been doing it for months. Marines often wanted more supplies than the book said they needed, but this was odd; they were ordering supplies on a far larger scale, working carefully to make it harder for someone to put the pieces of the puzzle together. Why?

Stephen thought about it for a long moment, then pushed the matter aside. It could be contemplated later.

Standing up, he deactivated the display and called for his maids. They entered, carrying the formal robes that were traditionally worn by Grand Senators to emergency meetings. It had often irritated Stephen that he, for all of his power, couldn't order the robes replaced by something more practical. Tradition had a power – and inertia – all of its own, he'd discovered. The Grand Senators were not only the victims of their own success, but prisoners too. If he'd wanted to flee Earth, he would have had to leave most of his power and resources behind. He *did* have contingency plans for that…using them might mean complete destruction. It would certainly shatter his family's reputation.

Accessing his implants, he checked the latest security updates. The media had yet to tell the public what had happened to Orbit Station Seven, but there had been no mistaking the debris falling through the planet's atmosphere. Once the news got out…even without it, the first traces of panic could be seen in a dozen megacities. No doubt they thought that

Earth was under attack. Stephen had wondered that too, until it became clear that no battle fleet lurked just outside detection range, ready to engage Home Fleet. Maybe the whole issue of the Empire's future would have been decided there and then if one had.

He stepped outside his office and headed towards his private aircar, a small army of security specialists falling into step around him. The rewards of power were vast, but they came with risks; the tools he was hoping to use for his own purposes could easily turn in his hand, or lash out at the Grand Senator without ever knowing that he was their patron. But the game was worth playing. He had to believe that.

The alternative was surrendering to entropy and allowing the Empire to die.

CHAPTER FIFTEEN

This grew worse as competent officers were sidelined by those with strong political connections. The professional officers were forced into subordination, the proud officers simply resigned...And the ambitious officers contemplated rebellion. Why should they have any respect for the Empire when they were treated so badly? As the Empire started to break apart, discontented officers started to set themselves up as warlords. Forces that might have saved the core of the Empire were thus lost to it.

- Professor Leo Caesius, *The End of Empire.*

It took four days for the Imperial Navy to clear Earth's orbit of debris, during which time thousands of tiny pieces – the remains of Orbit Station Seven – rained down on the planet below. None of them were large enough to survive their passage through the atmosphere, but the population looked up and wondered. Belinda watched the security monitors as riots broke out in parts of the megacities and the Undercity – and discontent spread through Imperial City itself.

She hadn't really realised just how comprehensive the planetary datanet actually was, or just how much her new status as Prince Roland's liegeman allowed her to access. The network itself was ancient, dating all the way back to the times before the Unification Wars; no one, not even the Grand Senate, could have hoped to control it all. No other world had a computer network like Earth's. She watched as dispassionately as she could as the Civil Guard slowly brought the rioting under control, knowing that it was just the first explosion. There would be more to come.

The Grand Senate kept the media under total control, but rumours were spreading rapidly, not helped by Admiral Van Houghton's removal from command and dismissal from the Imperial Navy on charges of gross incompetence. Belinda would have found that amusing – Van Houghton might have proved inadequate when tested, but few others would have done any better – if she hadn't known who was going to succeed him. Try as she might, she couldn't imagine Admiral Valentine serving the Empire, or anyone other than his patrons. The same patrons who had proven so eager to fight the war on Han.

She sat in Roland's dressing room and watched as the maids dressed him, piece by piece, until he actually *looked* like a Prince. By tradition, the newly-appointed CO of Earth's defences had to receive his commission from the Emperor – and the Grand Senate, for whatever reason, had insisted that Admiral Valentine receive it from Prince Roland directly. Belinda had puzzled over their motives for hours before reluctantly deciding that they were probably trying to suggest that they were upholding tradition and nothing else, unless they also wanted Roland to get the blame for Admiral Valentine's appointment. Given the disaster he'd caused on Han, Belinda suspected that the Grand Senate could not have made a worse choice for Earth.

"Ready," Roland said, finally. He sounded irritated at having to wear an outfit that made him look rather like a peacock, complete with feathers in his cap. "Is the Admiral here?"

"You will be meeting him in the receiving room," Mr. Harris said, patiently. He never seemed to get angry with Roland, but then – he *had* been training young children for years in how to conduct themselves in high society. "Your liegeman will escort him in."

Belinda took her cue, winked at Roland when the maids weren't looking at her and then turned to walk out of the room. The maids would see to it that he moved to the receiving room, while she had to greet the Admiral personally. As she walked, she accessed the palace network and realised that the Admiral hadn't been given a proper search by the close-protection detail. His uniform and pass from the Grand Senate had been enough to let him into the Summer Palace. Gritting her teeth, Belinda walked into the waiting room. This was *not* going to be pleasant.

Admiral Valentine didn't recognise her, unsurprisingly. The last time they'd met, she'd worn a helmet and a full urban combat uniform, her hair cropped so close to her skull that she might as well have been bald. He certainly hadn't been to visit her in hospital, even if his staff had been the ones responsible for the false intelligence that had wiped out Team Six. But she remembered him; short, overweight, with more political patrons than brain cells…

That wouldn't be very many brain cells, she thought, wryly.

"On your feet," she snapped, producing a sensor rod from her belt and activating it. The Admiral started to his feet and opened his mouth, but Belinda ran the wand over his head and down his uniform tunic, monitoring the feed through her implants. He had command-level implants, she noted, although she would have been surprised if he ever used them properly. He'd never commanded a real fleet action in his entire career.

"Stretch out your arms and spread your legs," she barked. "Now!"

The Admiral was too stunned to do anything, but obey. Belinda concealed a smile and finished sweeping his legs, holding the rod near his bottom just long enough to worry him. The rod revealed a standard terminal, a Navy-issue pistol – that should have been removed – and a pair of datachips. One of them carried the Grand Senate's insignia, the other was unmarked.

"This is outrageous," the Admiral finally managed to say, as she confiscated his pistol and removed the single clip of bullets. Like most Navy officers, he didn't bother to carry spares unless he had some reason to think he was going to need them. "I am an Admiral in the Imperial Navy…"

"And I am a liegeman to Prince Roland, Crown Prince and Heir to the Throne," Belinda snapped back. "Do you know that you could be arrested for trying to bring a weapon into the Summer Palace?"

She dropped the pistol and terminal in a secure box and transmitted an instruction to Senate Security, ordering them to give the box back to the Admiral when he left. The datachips would have to be inserted in a terminal designed specifically for the Summer Palace but isolated from the network, just in case someone was trying to be clever. A sealed network could still be brought down if someone inserted a chip carrying a virus or a subversion program.

"I have orders from the Grand Senate," the Admiral stammered. "I…"

"They cannot order you to take weapons into the Prince's chambers," Belinda informed him. It would have been an illegal order, although she had a feeling that the Admiral wouldn't have recognised an illegal order if one had bitten him on the rear end. "Now, with your permission, I will escort you to meet with the Prince."

The Admiral glared at her as she turned to lead him through the corridor. "I should be greeted by the proper servant," he grated, "not just a bodyguard."

"As a liegeman, I outrank the other servants," Belinda assured him, sweetly. "Not being met by me would be an insult in itself."

She kept her expression under control as she led the way into the receiving room. The Commandant hadn't replied to her short report informing him that she was now a sworn liegeman, although the crisis in orbit had probably distracted him from dealing with her. She wasn't looking forward to that conversation…or the row she'd get when the Admiral had finished complaining about her to the Commandant. Or should he be screaming to the Prince instead? Did her status as a liegeman override her status as a Marine? There was no precedent, as far as she knew. They were in uncharted waters.

Roland's receiving room hadn't been used since his father had inhabited the Summer Palace, but the maids had done an excellent job cleaning it up, bringing out new tapestries to hang along the walls and preparing Roland's throne. As Crown Prince, he was entitled to a smaller throne than the Emperor – the Imperial Throne itself was in the Imperial Palace, hidden behind a curtain when the Grand Senate used the throne room as a debating chamber – but it was perched on a dais, allowing him to loom over the Admiral. Belinda opened the door, waved the Admiral through and then took up position behind him.

Admiral Valentine seemed to hesitate before advancing towards Roland and going down on one knee, just before the dais. Roland studied him for a long moment and then nodded and stood up. Admiral Valentine clasped his hands, then stood up himself. Roland sat down on the throne and waited.

"Crown Prince," Admiral Valentine said. His voice was flatter than Belinda remembered, but the last time she'd met him he'd been barking orders to his social and military inferiors. She'd never seen him with a social superior. "I seek your confirmation of my position as Commander of Earth's defence force."

Roland pretended to consider. In truth, Belinda knew that his confirmation would be meaningless. The Grand Senate had already decided on the person it wanted to take the post and Roland's confirmation would be nothing more than a rubber stamp. Even if he didn't confirm Valentine, Belinda suspected that the media would simply say that he had – and produce faked footage to back up the claim. The thought made her wonder why they were bothering to insist that the meeting took place at all…

"We are concerned with recent events, Admiral," Roland said, as grandly as he could. He had taken to pretence, once he'd gotten the idea, like a duck to water. "The rioting on Earth has caused many problems for Our loyal subjects."

Valentine looked surprised – and then tried to hide it. "The rioters will be dealt with, Your Highness," he said, reassuringly. "Those who try to test our patience will be crushed and then exiled."

That was true enough, Belinda knew. For most of the riots, the Civil Guard had moved in with stunners and stunned the ones who didn't manage to run away fast enough. Once they'd restored order, the captured rioters had been transported to the orbital towers, where they were waiting in holding pens for the next starship heading out of the system. They would never see Earth again.

"But there are others who will suffer as a result of the recent disaster," Roland said. "How long will it be until you restore food supplies to Our world?"

The Admiral hesitated, then attempted to answer. For someone who had insisted on countless briefings, often pulling officers away from vital duties just so they could brief him, he hadn't come very well briefed. Belinda guessed that he'd expected – or had been told – that Roland would do nothing more than give Valentine his blessing and then let him go. He hadn't taken the Prince seriously at all. Belinda, on the other hand, had prepared Roland carefully.

"My office believes that we can restore a full supply of foodstuffs within two weeks," the Admiral hazarded, finally. "We are, however, working on ways to ensure that the disaster never happens again..."

"Such security precautions will mean more delays," Roland pointed out. He quirked an eyebrow at the Admiral. "Will they not?"

Belinda felt a flicker of pride. She hadn't pointed *that* out to Roland. He'd thought of it for himself.

"It may, Your Highness," the Admiral conceded. "However, we must prevent another disaster and that means additional security precautions."

He was understating the case, Belinda said. The investigation had barely gotten underway, but she'd downloaded the preliminary report, which had suggested that a freighter captain had simply rammed his freighter into the orbital station. Reading between the lines, it was clear that the captain had been about to lose his ship. An emotional reaction upon discovering that was about to happen was not uncommon. Often, repossessing bureaucrats took the ship, only to discover that the ship's computer had been wiped, rendering it useless. It had been a random act, utterly unpredictable, that had pushed the Empire one step closer to the abyss.

It was going to get worse. There had been ten orbital transhipment stations in Earth orbit; now there were nine, with a huge backlog of freighters to deal with. System Control would have to deal with delays under the best of circumstances, during which time many freighters carrying perishable goods would discover that their cargo was rapidly becoming unsellable. They'd be hit with penalty clauses in their contracts, which would probably start them heading down the road to bankruptcy...

Belinda shook her head. Every independent shipper was one bad cargo away from bankruptcy.

But even if that wasn't a problem, the nine remaining orbital stations had no slack left; they couldn't start absorbing the flow that should have gone to Orbital Station Seven. It was possible, she suspected, that one of the other orbital stations could be adapted to replace Seven, at least for a few months or years, but eventually the station would have to be replaced. Technically, the freighters *could* dock at the orbital towers, but she doubted that the Grand Senate would permit it. Losing an orbital tower would be far worse than losing any of the orbital stations. The thought of a tower collapsing onto Earth…the entire planet would be rendered uninhabitable.

"We shall hope that your precautions work, Admiral," Roland said. "Lawson, if you please?"

Belinda unhooked the palace terminal from her belt, inserted the Grand Senate's datachip and watched as the Admiral's commission appeared on the screen.

"Your Highness," she said, passing it to Roland. At least the Prince could read, although he had problems with some of the longer words. "It appears to be in order."

Roland read it slowly. "You will assume command of every military force in the solar system," he said to the Admiral. "Are you sure that you are up to the challenge?"

Belinda realised, in a moment of horror, just what the Grand Senate had intended all along. Every military force in the solar system would include the Marine Corps, which was allowed to operate quasi-independently as long as Roland was in his minority. Roland's confirmation would give the Grand Senate's chosen Admiral command over the Marines, at least the ones deployed in the solar system, or an excuse to bring heavy pressure to bear against the Commandant. She needed time to think – and bring it to the attention of her superiors – but there was no time. Roland couldn't avoid signing the orders.

"Yes, Your Highness," Valentine said. He sounded confident, at least. Belinda would have been more reassured if she hadn't known that Valentine was a military incompetent. To think that competent officers were pushed out of the service while incompetent officers with powerful patrons were allowed to remain in high positions…she shook her head in disgust. Was the Empire even *worth* saving? "I will save your world."

"Then I grant you my confirmation," Roland said, and pressed his thumb against the sensor. It automatically scanned his thumbprint and took a tiny sample of his DNA, confirming his identity. "See to it that food supplies are restored as quickly as possible, Admiral. Our citizens need their daily bread."

Belinda escorted the Admiral out of the receiving room and down to where the Senate Security team was waiting for him. She watched the Admiral climb into his aircar and depart, then gave the officer in charge a thorough chewing out for allowing the Admiral to keep his pistol. The officer looked rather surprised at her tirade, but promised to do better next time. Belinda gave him a detailed description of precisely what *she* would do to him – or anyone else – if it happened again and then stormed off, back to Roland's bedroom. The Prince had already managed to shuck his regal clothes and get into something more comfortable.

"I could *feel* his tongue on my ass," he said, after the maids had been waved out. "He was disgusting."

"That's a mental image I didn't need," Belinda said, tightly. She needed to contact the Commandant and warn him about the Grand Senate's trick. Who knew *how* many other plans the Grand Senate had in mind? "What did you make of him, apart from being oily?"

"He smiled too much," Roland said. "I wanted to kick him right in the face."

"An understandable impulse," Belinda said. *She* would have given her hind teeth to have a chance to meet Admiral Valentine in a dark alleyway. So many soldiers and Marines had died under his command – as well as innumerable citizens of Han, caught in the middle of the war he'd commanded – that it would have been a pleasure. "Get into your tennis outfit. A game of tennis will make you feel better."

Roland snorted, but nodded as Belinda withdrew to the room she'd taken over for herself. It was very simple, despite the offers of fantastic luxury from the maids, who seemed to credit her with Roland's reformation. Once inside, she composed a report with her implants while undressing and changing into her tennis outfit, then transmitted it to the Commandant's personal communications code. He'd have to see what he could do to head the Grand Senate's plan off at the pass.

"You look great," Roland said, when she returned to his bedroom. His eyes flitted over her and then looked away. At least he'd stopped making crude passes. "When do we start learning to fight?"

"Soon," Belinda said. The last medical report had said that Roland was improving, but he really needed two more weeks of intensive treatment before starting anything more strenuous. He really had no idea just how lucky he was. A person without the genetic enhancements spliced into his bloodline would have killed himself by now, or spent years recovering – if permanent damage was avoided. "But once you start learning, you'll also start suffering."

"Pain is weakness leaving the body," Roland parroted back.

Belinda couldn't help herself. She laughed.

CHAPTER SIXTEEN

Once order was restored, the task of policing the suppressed worlds was handed over to the Civil Guard. These were, at least on paper, local defence forces that could nip future trouble in the bud. In reality, most Civil Guardsmen were recruited from the dregs of society and tended to be grossly abusive to the local population. (A handful were better trained and led, but they were very much the exception.) Unsurprisingly, the Civil Guards actually encouraged future rebellions – and also proved unable to cope when the explosion finally came. On Han, for example, no Civil Guard unit remained in existence three days after the uprising began.

- Professor Leo Caesius, *The End of Empire.*

"What happened to our food?"

Amethyst heard the question echoing through the university as the students discussed the fall of Orbit Station Seven. It said something about how shocking the disaster was – and the sudden rise in food prices – that few seemed to believe the official story. The government claimed that it had been a terrible accident, but that seemed unlikely, not when food prices had already started to rise. Matters hadn't been helped by the story changing several times, moving from blaming the disaster on Nihilist terrorists to insisting that it was nothing more than an accident. The inability to agree on a story made it easy for rumours to spread, each one more outrageous than the last.

Like all students, Amethyst was entitled to a Basic Living Allowance, a stipend from the government that allowed her to broaden her diet – or spend on drugs and alcohol, if she saw fit. She'd often used hers to buy imported food, sharing the costs with several other students so they could enjoy proper meals. They'd had to pay the cooks too; the university's safety rules forbade them to cook for themselves, even in hired apartments. Apparently, it was a health risk for students to cook without proper supervision. But her last visit to a food superstore had revealed that prices for almost everything had doubled or tripled. Buying a single chicken breast, imported from the farms on Terra Nova, would consume a third of her BLA.

The students might have been ignorant – it still shocked her to realise how little she had known about the Empire, or how carefully she and the others had been prevented from learning anything useful – but they could do the maths. If prices continued to skyrocket, they wouldn't be able to eat anything, apart from algae bars. And *that* assumed that the prices for algae bars wouldn't start rising too. The government had officially banned hoarding – and there were limits to how much one could buy with a credit chip – but somehow she doubted that many people were going to listen. There were other ways to buy food.

But the students were *angry* – and they weren't alone. Amethyst walked through her classes and listened to the grumbling from other students, all firm in the belief that they should still have access to cheap food. Someone had started a rumour that Orbit Station Seven hadn't been destroyed at all; the corporations had decided to raise food prices and had invented the story about the station's destruction to provide justification. Another student had pointed out that they'd all seen pieces of debris falling through the atmosphere, but he'd been shouted down; those pieces of debris could be anything from litter to lunar rock brought in to create the impression that something had been destroyed.

Amethyst rolled her eyes as she heard one young female student bragging about what she'd done to secure food supplies – apparently, she'd offered her body to the storekeeper in exchange for some off-the-record supplies – and headed out of the main building. It was clear that there would be no learning today, just like yesterday and every other day since Orbit Station Seven had been destroyed. The entire student body was, for the first time, worried about its future.

She couldn't help noticing that there were more university cops on the streets as she walked back to her apartment block. The cops were normally only there to provide directions and deal with students who were too drunk to stagger home, but there were more of them now. Absently, she wondered what that meant, before pushing the issue aside. There were other problems to deal with. As soon as she got home, she checked her home terminal and discovered a message from her parents, asking if she was alright. She sighed – her parents never seemed to quite realise that she was a grown woman – and briefly composed a reply, informing them that she was fine.

Her handcom buzzed. Hooking it off her belt, Amethyst glanced at it and saw a message inviting her to visit yet another nightclub. It looked just like one of the thousands of spam messages that floated through the datanet – apparently, blocking them was illegal – but she'd been warned to keep an eye out for any messages from this particular source. Richard wanted a meeting within the hour. Grinning, Amethyst changed into something a little more suitable for clubbing – she had to look as if she was just a normal student – and headed out of the door. She couldn't help looking forward to seeing Richard again.

The university cops tossed her odd, unreadable glances as she walked past them into the nightclub district. Amethyst frowned, puzzled; she knew what it was like to attract the admiring gaze of male admirers and it didn't feel like that. Instead, the stares felt almost *hostile*. Certainly, she knew better than to trust the Civil Guard – her parents had hammered that lesson into her head – but the university cops had almost seemed friendly. Feeling their gazes following her, she hurried into the nightclub and found the stairs leading up to Richard's latest meeting place. By now, she knew to put all of her electronic devices in a sealed box before entering the meeting room. Richard still ran the scanner over her before relaxing slightly and motioning for her to join the others.

"The nightclub is desperate to attract newcomers," he said, as soon as the door was closed and locked. "They've actually started bringing in alcohol from the Undercity so be careful what you drink. And, for that matter, be careful what they ask in return."

Amethyst frowned. The Undercity dwellers had their own ways of producing alcohol, but the single glass she'd tasted had been thoroughly awful – and strong enough to leave her feeling dizzy after a few sips. Who would want to drink it when they could get proper drinks from the nightclubs? But if food prices continued to skyrocket, would the price of alcoholic drinks *also* go upwards? The Professor's book certainly seemed to imply that they would.

"I hate that stuff," one of the others said. "What do they want in return?"

"Everything from trade goods to sex," Richard said. He shrugged, then smiled grimly. "And, believe it or not, there is a point to me bringing it up. How long do you think it will be before food prices return to normal?"

No one answered.

"They won't return to normal," Richard said. "Right now, they are discovering that they can increase prices without facing any backlash from the population. Even after they build a replacement for Orbit Station Seven, they are still going to keep the prices high. Why should they not?"

Amethyst shuddered at the thought of spending the rest of her life eating nothing but algae bars. They might have been healthy, yet they also tasted awful, unless one spent extra on flavourings. The price of flavourings was probably also going to go up, she guessed. They were imported from off-world too.

"But there are two other issues that should be of equally great concern," Richard continued. "Do you know why the disaster in orbit was so bad?"

"No," Amethyst said. She knew nothing about space technology, apart from what she'd seen on entertainment flicks. Watching starships explode was fun, but it didn't actually tell her anything useful. "What happened?"

Richard shrugged. "The short version of the story is that a freighter rammed the orbital station," he said. "That's true, as far as I can tell. He was desperate, you see; his debts had overwhelmed him to the point where he chose to lash out rather than accept defeat and a return to the megacities. How many other people have debts that they can never pay off?"

Amethyst considered it. She'd taken out a student loan, of course, when she'd gone to the university. There had been no choice; her parents couldn't have paid for her to go without it, nor could she have earned the money to go on her own. She'd assumed that she would have no trouble finding a job afterwards that would have allowed her to pay off the debt quickly, but there were few jobs to be had. The debt would just keep mounting up until she spent the rest of her life paying it off, if she was lucky. If not…it would haunt her children and grandchildren.

There were millions of students on Earth. How many of them were in the same boat?

"But even that isn't the worst of it," Richard added. "Why did the loss of the orbital station cause food prices to rise?"

"Because supplies on the station were destroyed?" One of the others guessed. "Or because shipping them to Earth was suddenly more expensive?"

"Both of those," Richard said. "And more. You see, the distribution companies invested money in the destroyed foodstuffs. Because they were destroyed, the companies cannot pay their debts by selling the foodstuffs onwards to consumers. Food prices are going up because the supply is suddenly more limited, but also because those companies need to raise money quickly to pay off their debts before their creditors catch up with them. But those creditors are going to need money themselves, so they will demand it from everyone who owes them money…"

He shook his head. "I'll spare you the full details, but we – my superiors – believe that a number of smaller corporations and businesses are going to collapse within the month," he concluded. "They have debts that simply can't be paid. When they can't pay, they will be forced to fold…"

One of the girls leaned forward. "So what?" She demanded. "Those… pigs overcharge for everything, anyway!"

Richard scowled at her. "Think about it," he said. "Each of those businesses employs thousands of workers, who will suddenly be unemployed. The job market, already awash with people in desperate need of employment, will suddenly become saturated. In the meantime, those suddenly-unemployed workers will be unable to pay *their* debts. Their creditors will find themselves in serious trouble."

Amethyst had a sudden vision of a series of dominos falling, one after the other, until the entire economic structure underpinning the Empire lay in ruins. The Professor's book had warned about the debt crisis and what it was doing to the economy, but she hadn't really understood what he meant until now. It had only taken a random accident to start the dominos falling...and God alone knew where it would end.

She grimaced as she put two and two together – and realised that they had barely scratched the surface of the looming disaster. "How long can they afford to keep handing out the BLA for us students?"

Richard winked at her, leaving her feeling oddly pleased with herself. "Good question," he said. "How many people does the government give money to?"

Amethyst did the maths. Giving a single person money – even at the highest rate of BLA – would barely be noticed in the sheer immensity of the government's funds. But it would mount up rapidly as more and more people were added to the scheme. Officially, if she recalled correctly, nearly two-thirds of Earth's population were entitled to claim the BLA. A hundred credits for a student became...maths weren't her strong point, but she thought it was somewhere around three hundred billion credits, a sum so vast that she couldn't even begin to comprehend it. And *that* assumed that there were no other expenses.

But there *were* other expenses. The government had to spend money on maintaining the basic infrastructure on Earth, paying the army of bureaucrats who kept the whole system running, paying the military who defended the Empire and imposed the Grand Senate's will on rebellious planets...the costs would just skyrocket. And if millions more were suddenly forced to claim the BLA...

"Shit," she said, numbly.

"I do love lectures on basic economics," one of the others said. He had a thin nasal voice; Amethyst wouldn't have given him a second glance if she'd met him anywhere else. "But you promised us direct action. What are we going to do?"

"One final question," Richard said, holding up a hand. "How many of you have heard of the Protest Coordinating Committee?"

Amethyst blinked in surprise, but nodded. The PCC was responsible for organising protest marches and coordinating them with the Civil Guard. She'd sometimes thought about trying to run for election to the committee, although it had really seemed too much like hard work. Besides, the committee had to work closely with the university staff and she knew that she would have disliked that.

"They wanted to run a protest march against the rise in food prices," Richard said, "so they filed a formal request through their liaison officer. You do know that the Civil Guard has to approve protests, right?" They nodded. "Permission was *not* granted. The PCC was so surprised – apparently, they thought the whole getting permission thing was just a formality – that they made the mistake of protesting loudly."

He scowled. "The entire PCC was expelled from the university yesterday," he concluded. "They're gone."

Amethyst stared at him. "They can't do that..."

"They can and they did," Richard said. "Do you know that the university contracts you all signed give them blanket authority to expel you at any moment?"

"...No," Amethyst said. The contract had been over four hundred pages – or would have been, if it had been printed out. There had been so many clauses that her eyes had glazed over and she'd signed it without reading it through. That, clearly, had been a mistake. "But surely there will be protests..."

"They were escorted off the campus by the Civil Guard and taken directly to a holding pen," Richard told her. "By now, they may be on their way to a Rim colony world as indentured colonists. Their families may also have been exiled."

He tapped the table. "Do you understand just how far they will go to preserve their power now?"

Amethyst nodded, mutely.

"What the government doesn't know is that there is going to be a protest march anyway," Richard said. "A handful of agitators have been organising one to take place in two days, a protest demanding a freeze in food prices and immediate debt relief. The PCC may be gone, but there are others willing to take its place. You may already have heard whispers that *something* has been planned."

He looked from face to face. "But the government is likely to simply ignore a peaceful protest," he continued. "We have to show them that they can no longer take us for granted. The protest has to be...violent."

"Good," one of the others said. "That's why you've been giving us weapons training, right?"

"Right," Richard said. "The day before the protest march begins, you will be issued with weapons and a handful of devices that might come in handy. Several protest organisers are going to be handing out makeshift weapons too. When the Civil Guard comes to push the protesters back into the university, they will be greeted with live weapons. We will show the government that we will no longer remain quiet as they drive the Empire towards destruction."

Amethyst felt an odd flash of excitement spreading through her body. She'd known that she would be called upon to do something ever since they'd started training with live weapons, but this was the first true call to action. She could finally do something effective – and if the government realise that their population was prepared to demand something, they might just give in and grant debt relief. And lower food prices and everything else the protesters wanted.

"This is what we have been preparing for," Richard warned them. "It will be dangerous – if you are caught with a weapon, you will certainly be exiled from Earth, after they've made you talk. But it's too late to back out now."

I know, Amethyst thought. The thought of being interrogated scared her – on the entertainment flicks a person could be injected with truth drugs and they'd start giving up everything they knew – but she told herself that she could live with it. Besides, she knew very little; she didn't even know the names of her comrades. Richard had told them that they would eventually take on codenames, but they hadn't been assigned yet.

"We won't let you down," Amethyst said. "I'm looking forward to it."

The others echoed her sentiment.

"Good," Richard said. He pointed to three of the girls, including Amethyst. "I want you three to stay behind so I can brief you on your part of the operation. The rest of you will be called in tomorrow, where you will get your briefing. Operational security has to be maintained."

Amethyst nodded. He'd told them that right at the start and she'd taken it to heart. She hadn't even told Jacqueline where she was going when she met the rest of the team, allowing her roommate to assume that she'd met a new boyfriend. There had been a time when that would have been true...

But now she had much more serious concerns.

"All right," Richard said, as soon as the others had gone. "Here is what I want you to do."

CHAPTER
SEVENTEEN

What this meant, in practice, was that the Civil Guard was poorly trained to deal with problems that required anything other than a very firm hand. The concept of protecting the local people was alien to the Guardsmen, at least partly because it was not a major concern of the Empire. All that mattered to the Grand Senate was keeping them under control.

- Professor Leo Caesius, *The End of Empire.*

"You'd think that they could find someplace better for us," Private Theodore Lowell muttered. "I *hate* Earth."

Sergeant Yang snorted, rudely. The Mars-born found Earth's vast cities to be smelly, overpopulated and claustrophobic. Mars had been terraformed long ago and the planet's government had managed to prevent much of the surface from being covered in cities – or, for that matter, the kind of pollution that had killed Earth. In many ways, Mars was a paradise, although it was colder on average than the homeworld. Yang himself didn't know what the fuss was about. He'd grown up in Earth's Undercity.

415th Battalion (Civil Guard) had been assigned to Earth for centuries, but this was the first time in living memory that it had been deployed to Imperial City. Yang and his men were used to East-Meg Two, where the megacity's population spent most of their lives in their apartments, eating slop and watching entertainment on their display screens. There had been little trouble there, apart from the ever-present trouble in the Undercity. Yang was silently grateful that he'd been offered the chance to join the Civil Guard, rather than simply being exiled when they'd caught him with the shipment of illegal nanites. It had given him a life out of the dull hopelessness that pervaded the Undercity.

But now they were in Imperial City. The destruction of the orbital station – Yang didn't know the truth about just what had happened, but he could see food prices going up with his own eyes – had caused rioting in dozens of cities, including East-Meg Two…but they'd been sent to Imperial City. None of his men were familiar with the city, or the more restrictive rules of engagement governing the Civil Guard's actions. And they'd been dumped in a half-converted warehouse because the regular Civil Guard barracks were crammed full of other Guardsmen.

Imperial City was…*strange*. Parts of it were bright and open in ways East-Meg Two was not and could never be. Many of the people seemed happier than the easterners, although others looked as if they were running forward, too scared to look over their shoulder for fear of seeing their approaching doom. The students, in particular, seemed happy, despite the food shortages. Yang felt cold envy pervading his mind whenever he looked at them. They just didn't know how lucky they were to live in Imperial City.

The Undercity had been hellish. Yang had no idea who his father had been – and his mother, a prostitute, had been knifed to death when her son had been five. He'd grown up scavenging in the lower levels of the grimy CityBlock structures that made up East-Meg Two, struggling to survive against all odds. The price he'd paid to become a rat runner for one of the gangs still haunted his dreams, as did the moment he'd been struck by a jangler and sent falling to the ground when the Civil Guard had caught him. If they hadn't recruited him…no, the students definitely didn't know how lucky they were.

His wristcom buzzed. "Alert," the dispatcher said, tonelessly. "All units, alert. Unauthorised protest march forming along the Avenue of Good Hope. Unit designations and orders follow…"

"Grab your gear," Yang barked.

The Civil Guardsmen had been poorly trained when he'd assumed effective command of the unit; their Captain, the one who was nominally in command, had gone on leave and hadn't returned. Yang had insisted on going through everything they needed to know, even though he'd had to invent most of the procedure for himself. Earth's Civil Guard received very limited training in the camps before being unleashed on the population. The Guardsmen had also argued with him at first, before he'd beaten the crap out of two of them to make his point. They could hate him as much as they liked, as long as they feared him too.

He donned his body armour and tied the straps, silently cursing the procurement division under his breath. No specially-tailored armour for the Civil Guard, no matter how many small injuries it would prevent; his armour had been handed down from someone who had died in the line of duty years ago. He'd done his best to get a set as close to his size as possible, but it wasn't perfect. At least he'd managed to do the same for most of his men.

As soon as they were ready, he led them into the armoury and started passing out weapons. It had been harder to convince the clerks that paperwork was a waste of time – threatening them with violence merely made them cry – but he'd finally managed it. Normally, he would have had to sign for every stunner, shockrod and jangler his men took out onto the streets. The elite of his unit were also allowed to carry assault rifles too, just in case. There was so much paperwork involved in taking out lethal weapons that most units simply left them behind.

The command network updated itself automatically as he pulled his helmet down over his head. Students were protesting – without permission. The protesters were to be boxed in and pushed back to Imperial City as gently as possible. Yang rolled his eyes at the ass-covering from someone with no experience on the streets. Stopping a protest was *not* easy at the best of times, nor was it bloodless. People *always* got hurt.

But these are students, he thought, as he led his men out of the building. *They deserve to get hurt.*

Amethyst had to admit that she was impressed with whoever had organised the protest. They'd managed to get most of the popular students on their side without giving many clues to anyone who might have alerted the authorities. A number of events had also been scheduled at the same time, just to allow the crowds to gather without raising suspicions. Finally, a leader had appeared, made a brief and stirring speech and led the way towards the edge of the university campus. The other organisers had followed, dragging the rest of the crowd in their wake. Word spread quickly through student handcoms and the datanet, inviting others to join. The more, the merrier – and the harder it would be to single out and expel the guilty.

They can't expel the entire university, she thought, as she walked at the front of the crowd. Like the other girls, she'd deliberately worn something that showed off her chest – and a mask that half-concealed her face. The ever-present cameras would be scanning the crowd now, looking for people who seemed to be in leadership positions, but Richard had told her how to fool them. From what he'd said, even something as simple as a hat could obscure her identity. The protest organisers had clearly learned the same lesson. They'd had students handing out multicoloured hats as the protesters marched past them and out onto the streets.

The organisers started a chant demanding debt relief and the students joined in, creating a deafening sound that echoed through the streets and towering city blocks. Amethyst had read more of the Professor's book while waiting for the protest to begin and knew that debt relief was something that would appeal to almost everyone, even the highly-paid professionals who lived in the middle districts of Imperial City. She'd envied them when she'd started trying to choose a career – they seemed to have no problems at all in their lives – but she knew now that they were just as indebted as everyone else. Debt relief was a cause that *everyone* could get behind.

She'd been told that the plan was to march all the way up to the Imperial Palace and the Senate Hall, demonstrating outside both buildings. Richard had warned her that they would almost certainly not be allowed to get that far. She couldn't help feeling a shiver of fear as she thought about the Civil Guard's reaction to the protest. They'd have to show the students that they couldn't mount a protest without permission or they'd have more protests on their hands than they could handle. She glanced back at the crowd following her, noting the handful of onlookers who had joined the march. The more, the merrier.

A set of police drones flew overhead as the marchers reached the corner and turned onto the Avenue of Imperial Supremacy, the road leading up to the Imperial Palace. The Civil Guard was waiting for them.

―――

Yang felt his mouth drop open as he saw the protesters for the first time. He'd never seen a student protest before, not in East-Meg Two. Students went to Imperial City if they qualified, Brit-Cit or Hondo City if their qualifications were less stellar. And they rarely returned to East-Meg Two afterwards. He couldn't quite believe his eyes; the students looked healthy, without a care in the world, and yet they were protesting…?

"I'd like to show that girl what's what," one of his men muttered. "Look at her!"

It was hard to blame him for staring. The front row of protesters was composed of girls – it was hard to think of them as young women – and most of them were topless, their breasts bouncing as they walked forward towards the Civil Guard. He wasn't a stranger to women – in East-Meg Two, women would often trade sex for favours from the Civil Guard – but this was something different. The women in his home city were… reluctant to show more than necessary, even when spreading their legs for him and his men. But the students…they didn't seem to have a care in the world.

"Concentrate on your duties," he snapped, tearing his gaze away from one particularly nice set of breasts that bounced invitingly. The girl was beautiful, studying so that she could earn qualifications that would get her a job in the corporate universe; what the hell was she protesting for? "Mount shields and stand at the ready!"

The network kept updating as other Civil Guard units moved into position. Some would block off side-streets, others would reinforce the picket line if necessary, or stand ready to pick up the stunned if the protest turned *really* nasty. Yang found himself hoping that the protesters wouldn't turn around and go home, even though he knew that any confrontation would lead to a bloodbath. The smug faces the students were showing to the world made him burn with envy and contempt. There were people in the Undercity who would sell their souls for half of what the students took for granted and yet the students were not content with their lot! What would he have made of himself if he'd been born outside the Undercity?

There was a dull series of clicks as the riot shields linked together, forming a wall that the protesters should find impassable. Yang had once spent a punishment duty beating his fists against the plastic shields, discovering that it took an astonishing amount of force to break them down. Rioters in East-Meg Two generally carried improvised weapons when they confronted the Civil Guard, but the student protesters didn't seem to have thought of it. If the girls wanted to press their breasts against the transparent plastic, that was fine by him. Their deafening chant sounded intimidating, but he knew better than to be scared. After what he'd done to earn his place in the gang, little else could actually bother him.

The protesters didn't slow; they just kept coming. And coming.

Amethyst swallowed hard as she walked towards the Civil Guard barricade, feeling the pressure from the thousands upon thousands of students and local citizens behind her. She couldn't stop now, even if she had *wanted* to. They would keep pushing her onwards until she hit the wall and was crushed against it. People had been killed in protests before, she'd been warned, particularly when they turned violent.

Part of her mind wondered if Richard had planned it that way. Either she carried out her part of the plan or she was crushed against the barricade, the massed force of thousands of students knocking it down. But he'd told her that it would be dangerous and she'd accepted it, partly to impress him and partly because she was angry. Who knew what would happen when the debts were called in and she couldn't pay? She'd never heard of anyone being sentenced to involuntary transportation, even indenture, for failure to pay debts, but Richard had assured her that it did happen. Colony development corporations *loved* indentured colonists. They didn't have to be given political rights to settle on the new worlds.

The weapon Richard had given her didn't *look* like a weapon, nothing like the pistol or assault rifles they'd practiced with during training sessions. It looked more like a heavy drumstick than anything more lethal, only really dangerous if it was rammed into someone's eye. Richard had explained that it was an assassination weapon, intended to remain unnoticed until it was far too late. It carried three bullets, all of which could be fired in quick succession, after which it could simply be dropped on the ground. Bracing herself, Amethyst pointed the stick at the Civil Guard barricade and pushed down on the trigger.

She winced in pain as the weapon jerked in her hand, firing three shots towards the barricade. A moment later, the other girls fired as well, sending several Civil Guardsmen staggering backwards. The barricade started to fall apart, the plastic shields falling to the ground like a row of dominoes. For a long moment, the students seemed to come to a halt before the pressure from the rear pushed them onwards towards the suddenly undefended Civil Guardsmen. Cursing her own hesitation, Amethyst dropped the weapon – she didn't think that anyone had realised what had happened, but Richard had warned her not to keep it after she'd fired it – and started to scramble towards the edge of the crowd. She had to get out as quickly as possible.

Yang barely registered the shots before two of his men staggered backwards. One of them had been hit in the mouth, the bullet – or whatever it was – almost certainly killing him. The other had been hit in the leg, his body armour deflecting most of the impact. Even so, he might well be out of the fight for the moment. The ill-fitting body armour was far from perfect.

They fired on us, he thought, shocked. How had the students gotten weapons? Hell, *why* had the students obtained weapons? Did they really think that a handful of guns would be enough to push through the Civil Guard? But they might have been right; the barricade was shattered and the crowd was moving forward with incredible force, advancing right towards the unprotected Guardsmen.

"Whips," he barked. Regulations demanded that he request permission from higher up the food chain, but his superiors weren't the ones whose lives were on the line. He'd spent months training his unit and he wasn't going to see it wasted. Besides, handing out a thrashing to the students would be a good thing in itself. "Now!"

He pulled the neural whip off his belt and cracked it threateningly towards the bare-breasted girls. They looked alarmed, but the protesters behind them were still pushing them onwards, even if they *had* thought better of it. Yang leered at them as his men formed up, then lashed out with the neural whip. The beauty of the device was that it caused brief intensive pain, enough to put *anyone* off trying to force the issue, without causing any real damage – at least unless the victims were lashed time and time again. Yang had seen hardened Civil Guardsmen dropping to the ground and begging for mercy after a single touch. He doubted that any students could endure even a second of such pain.

"Fall back," he ordered, "and strike!"

The Guardsmen formed a ragged line as they lashed out with their whips. At least they were still obeying orders, Yang told himself, as students began to scream. Some Civil Guard units had fragmented into panicky masses when confronted by unexpected situations. His men were probably more scared of him than they were of the students. Besides, it was hard to take bare-breasted opponents seriously.

He lashed out again and saw several girls crumpling to the ground, screaming in pain. The ones behind them were still coming forward; they trampled over their friends before they could stop themselves. Yang felt little pity as the next row were whipped and sent staggering backwards. They'd fired on his men and now they were going to pay the price. He knew precisely what they would do to the girls afterwards. His men would want to extract their pound of flesh and *he* wasn't going to stop them. Hell, he wanted some payback himself.

There was a dull roar from the crowd and a number of young male students charged forward. Several were lashed and sent howling to their knees, but their sacrifice shielded their companions, who crashed into the Civil Guardsmen. Yang stumbled backwards as a student slammed into his armour, knocking him to the ground before he could react. Hands clawed at the weapons on his belt, pulling them free. He tried to lift his hand, only to have someone jump on him and break every bone in his arm. Yang felt them all break before someone else started to stamp on his body armour, then slammed his foot down on Yang's face.

There was a moment of blinding pain…and then nothing.

CHAPTER EIGHTEEN

The one exception to the general corruption of the Empire's military and civil services was the Terran Marine Corps. This should not have been surprising. To serve within the Corps, a Marine had to undergo two years of intensive training. And if he or she wanted to be a senior officer, the prospective candidate had to have at least two more years on active duty and pass muster with the Corps NCOs. The Corps was not entirely free of officers with powerful patrons, but they did tend to be intensively loyal to the Corps. After all, they were Marines too.

- Professor Leo Caesius, *The End of Empire.*

"What the hell is going on?"

"Emergency alert from the Civil Guard," the dispatcher reported, as Jeremy burst into the command and control centre. "An unscheduled protest march in Imperial City has turned into a major riot. At least nine Civil Guardsmen are dead…"

"Show me the live feed," Jeremy ordered. He'd been expecting the shit to hit the fan ever since Orbit Station Seven had been destroyed, but an unscheduled protest march in Imperial City…? Normally, the students were very well behaved when it came to civil disobedience. "And pass the alert down the chain. I want every Marine unit on the planet ready to move to Imperial City if necessary."

"Aye, sir," the dispatcher said. "Live feed coming online now."

Jeremy swore out loud as he saw the feed from the Civil Guard drones. The first barricades had been overrun; the students rampaging out of control. Dozens of bodies lay on the ground, several wearing body armour. Their weapons had been stripped from the Guardsmen, he noted. *Someone* had been thinking ahead.

He quickly ran through the forces available to the Marines. The Grand Senate's insistence that the force earmarked for Albion be dispatched as soon as possible had paid off – and backfired spectacularly. Jeremy barely had four thousand Marines to call on, most of whom were parcelled out over the planet. It would take hours, at least, to get them to Imperial City; all he had on hand were two companies, one of which normally served as a guard force for Marine HQ. The other had been preparing to return to the Slaughterhouse for a mandatory training cycle.

"Admiral Valentine has declared a full state of emergency," the dispatcher said suddenly. "The Civil Guard is moving up additional reinforcements, the Grand Senators are evacuating the Imperial Palace and Senate Hall…"

Jeremy stared at the display, putting it together. The rioters were in a position to threaten the very heart of the Empire, although he doubted they could actually storm the buildings. They were all built out of hull-metal, naturally; the rioters could hammer on the walls to their hearts' content without actually getting anywhere. Unless they had some heavy weapons, of course…the panicky uploads from the Civil Guard suggested that the rioters *did* have some weapons, mainly small pistols. The reports could be wrong – Jeremy would have insisted on checking everything the Civil Guard sent to the Marines – but the dead Civil Guardsmen argued otherwise. How many weapons did the rioters have?

"The guard company is to seal the building, but remain on alert," Jeremy ordered. If they were lucky, the rioters would ravage the grounds without doing any permanent damage. "Grey's Greys are to armour up for riot control and then prepare for deployment."

"Sir," the dispatcher said, "Admiral Valentine has not asked us to intervene."

"I don't care," Jeremy snapped. Cold anger raged up within him, only to be forced down. "What do you think will happen when the Civil Guard reinforcements arrive?"

He sat down in front of one of the consoles and placed a call to Admiral Valentine. If they were lucky, the Admiral would be looking for something to cover his ass; he'd just taken control of the system, only to watch helplessly as the Senators fled Imperial City. He should grasp at any straw, even sending in the Marines rather than the Civil Guard...

Jeremy gritted his teeth as he waited. Whatever happened, one thing was clear. The coming hours were going to be bloody.

Amethyst had thrown herself to the ground as soon as the Civil Guardsmen started lashing the crowd with neural whips, but they'd still managed to catch her for a microsecond. The pain had seared along her back, convincing her that they'd set her on fire before she realised what had actually happened; the pain had been so intense that she had come close to collapsing altogether. But she couldn't risk it, she knew; somehow, she managed to crawl to the edge of the crowd as angry students poured through the hole in the barricade and threw themselves on the Civil Guard.

Richard had been clear; as soon as she'd fired her shots, she was to get the hell out of the riot and leave the protesters to attack the Civil Guard. She staggered forward, bleeding from her left arm – she had no idea when she'd been cut – barely able to process what she was seeing. The entire street seemed to have turned into a nightmare; protesters were rampaging everywhere, smashing windows and throwing rocks as they advanced upwards towards the Imperial Palace and the Senate Hall. Bodies lay everywhere, some of them bleeding onto the street…she choked back a sob as she saw one of the protest organisers lying on the ground. Her head had been crushed like an eggshell. The only way Amethyst could recognise her was through the outfit she'd been wearing.

She reached an alleyway and stumbled down it, only to run right into a minor barricade. The four Civil Guardsmen manning it looked as terrified as Amethyst felt, although they were clearly not terrified of her. Thankfully, she had resisted the suggestion that she too should go topless; if she'd come at them with her bare breasts hanging out, they would have *known* that she was one of the organisers, or at least knew who the organisers *were*. The Guardsmen looked at her for a long moment and then clearly decided that she was harmless. One of them pulled a shield out of the way to allow her to pass.

He caught her shaking her arm before she could leave them behind. "Don't stay here," he hissed, right in her ear. "Get back to your apartment and *stay there*."

Amethyst, who had expected worse, simply nodded and started to walk. The sound of rioting was only growing louder; she turned and saw a great plume of smoke rising up towards the pale sky. She saw aircars racing away from the direction of the Senate Hall and wondered how many Senators were fleeing for their lives. Richard had been right; the Senators *hadn't* expected to hear about their population's displeasure so loudly.

But how many people were going to die because of what they'd done?

"The Civil Guard cannot handle this," Jeremy snapped. He'd finally managed to get through to Admiral Valentine, but the Admiral seemed to be vacillating between absolute panic and a jingoism that Jeremy found shocking. "You have to let us deal with it."

"I cannot put Marines on the streets," the Admiral protested. "I…"

"Marines have operated on Earth before," Jeremy snapped. "Admiral, right now, the Senate Hall itself is under threat. The Civil Guard is disorganised. Let my Marines deal with the crisis before it gets out of hand. Your men can back us up."

The Admiral stared at him. "Very well," he said, finally. His face twisted into a sneer. "But you'd damn well better not fuck it up."

Jeremy closed the channel before he said something he'd regret. "Contact Captain Grey," he ordered, bluntly. "The word is given. The streets are to be cleared."

Captain Tamera Grey cursed under her breath as the commandeered helicopters swooped low over Imperial City. Her company had been enjoying a little Intercourse and Intoxication at Earth's premier spaceport before being shipped back to the Slaughterhouse and – naturally – their Raptors had already been assigned to a different unit. If their equipment had been gone as well, they might have wound up borrowing weapons off the Civil Guard as well as transport. Marines were expected to master all weapons, but using ill-maintained Civil Guard equipment would have been risky. The helicopter ride was bad enough.

"Put us down in the Square of Honour," she ordered the pilot, who was eyeing the crowds nervously. "Just hover a few meters above the ground and we'll rappel down."

She would have preferred to put one of her Marines in the cockpit, but she couldn't spare a single Marine. Even so, it was going to be tough. One full company – one hundred Marines – was hardly enough to impose order on an area as vast as Imperial City. All she could do was hope and pray that the Civil Guard was feeling unusually competent, although the reports she was picking up through the Marine network suggested that wasn't going to happen. The Civil Guardsmen who had been first on the scene had been scattered and most of their reinforcements were trying to set up a cordon on the edge of the city. It hadn't escaped Tamera's attention that their cordon included most of the city, including the government buildings they were supposed to protect. As always, the Marines were expected to pick up the slack.

The Square of Honour was massive, filled with towering statues, each one modelled after a great military leader who had helped build the Empire. There had been no new statues in generations, Tamera had been told; the Grand Senate committee that was supposed to approve proposals for new statues had been gridlocked for generations. Apparently, newcomers to the committee just kept on filibustering until everyone else had forgotten the military leaders the statues were supposed to honour. The rioters seemed to have largely ignored the square, apart from a handful of students who were spray-painting obscene slogans on the shorter statues. Tamera stood up, caught the rope as the jumpmaster started to lower it and swung herself down to the ground. Her armour absorbed the force of her impact as she landed.

"DROP THE CANS AND RAISE YOUR HANDS," she ordered the painters, as the remainder of the Marines followed her to the ground. The painters stared at them, unable to decide what to do. Tamera had seen that reaction before; the Marines just looked *deadlier* than the university cops or Civil Guardsmen. "NOW!"

The painters offered no resistance as the Marines pushed them to the ground and secured their hands with plastic ties. They could be picked up later, Tamera knew; they weren't the real problem. As soon as all of her Marines were on the ground, she barked out orders over the command network and led the way out of the Square, onto the Avenue of Imperial Supremacy. She winced as soon as she saw the bodies on the ground. Most of them looked to have been trampled to death, rather than anything else

"ATTENTION," she bellowed, activating her suit's megaphone. "STOP WHAT YOU ARE DOING AND RAISE YOUR HANDS! THIS IS YOUR ONLY WARNING!"

The rioters turned to stare at the Marines. Tamera hoped that they looked intimidating enough to stop the riot in its tracks. If not…it was going to get bloody. The Marine body armour should protect them against improvised weapons, but no one knew for sure what the rioters had…

For a long moment, she thought that they would obey. Several students dropped sticks and captured weapons and raised their hands…

…And then an emergency alert popped up in her display.

Too late.

Joachim had been delighted with the trust Richard had placed in him. His mission wasn't to start the riot, but to wait on the sidelines until the Marines arrived. The black-armoured figures were as intimidating as he had been warned – their armour would deflect blows, bullets and even small bombs easily – yet there *were* weapons that would hurt them. And Richard had given him one of them.

His orders had been very clear. He was not to activate the weapon until the Marines arrived – the energy signature could be detected – and he was not to hesitate. The Marines would instantly recognise the threat and move to counter it. Quickly, he lifted the heavy pistol and fired the first pulse of energy towards the Marines.

Tamera swore out loud as the plasma pulse burned through one of her men. Plasma pistols were rare in the Empire; like their larger counterparts, they had a nasty habit of overheating and exploding if fired too rapidly. In fact, she'd never heard of one that could fire more than four shots without starting to overheat. They were almost never used outside of training exercises.

But the rioters had one…

Several Marines fired as one, blasting the gunman down; his weapon hit the ground and exploded in a sheet of white fire. Tamera swore again as the rioters started to panic and flee, or throw heavy objects towards the Marines. Most of them were harmless, but it made it harder for the Marines to avoid harming the rioters. The gunman's body would be so badly burned that it would be impossible to identify him and track down whoever had sold him the weapon. But where had it even come from? The Civil Guard didn't normally use *any* kind of plasma weapon.

"Marine down," the medic snapped. "Captain, they killed Kenny!"

"Switch stunners to rapid fire," Tamera ordered. "Take them down as quickly as you can!"

There was no longer any time to try to take prisoners the proper way, she knew. All they could do was stun everyone and let the courts sort them out. If they *could* sort them out. The latest estimate had stated that half of the university students in Imperial City had joined the protest, at least before it had turned violent. They couldn't *all* be indentured and shipped to a colony world.

Sticks and stones rattled off her armour as the Marines broke down into fire teams, searching for targets. Most rioters scattered in front of them, or fled into the nearest buildings and tried to hide. The Marines just didn't have the manpower to search them all, let alone sort out the guilty from the innocent. Tamera had fought on Han, where it could be difficult to distinguish the insurgents from the local population, but that had been easier to handle. It was amazing how few people realised that firing a gun left residue that a basic sniffer could detect. Here, very few of the students would have guns.

She glanced into an alleyway and saw a pair of Civil Guardsmen – having deserted their posts – raping a young girl. Tamera stepped forward, yanked the rapist back and slammed him into the wall with augmented strength. The rapist screamed as his legs shattered and he crumpled to the ground. His friend tried to run, only to be brought down by a stun pulse that struck his neck. He hit the ground hard enough to break his jaw.

"Leave them here," Tamera ordered. Their victim was still bent over the dustbin, so badly shocked that she didn't seem to be aware of where she was or what had happened to her. Tamera hesitated, then pressed her hand against the girl's neck and injected a sedative into her bloodstream. The medics could take her to the nearest hospital as soon as the city was secure. "Take their DNA. I'm going to want to file charges."

None of the Marines argued.

An hour passed slowly before the streets were finally clear. Thousands of prisoners lay on the ground, their hands tied behind their backs with plastic cuffs. Marines and Civil Guardsmen kept a wary eye on them, unsure of just what to do with so many prisoners. The medics had arrived in force and started transporting the wounded to the nearest hospital. Going by the updates, the closest medical centres were already overrun...

"Dear God," Tamera muttered. Han had been bad, but this was *Earth*! Such things weren't meant to happen on humanity's homeworld, certainly not in Imperial City. "Is this how it's going to be like from now on?"

Bode hadn't been able to resist the chance to watch his handiwork from a safe distance. It had been really pathetically easy to hack into the Civil Guard network and watch through the drones that had monitored the entire riot from start to finish, a security hole that no one had ever tried to fix. But then, Earth's Civil Guard had never really been tested, apart from the Nihilist attacks. Other Civil Guards learned the hard way – or died.

Using the plasma pistol had been a risk, but it had paid off handsomely. The Marines would know that *someone* had been behind the riots, yet they'd never be able to trace the pistol back to its source. He'd taken care of that personally. It would have been nice to laugh in their faces, to rub in just how thoroughly they'd been played, but there was no need for it. Besides, his master would never have let him gloat. It would have given the game away far too soon.

Overall, he decided, it had been a good day's work. Hundreds of students had died, but the rest had been shocked – and radicalised. The Senators had been forced to flee the Senate Hall, made to look like cowards in front of the planet's population. Plenty of Civil Guardsmen had been killed, or had their confidence shaken; even the Marines had been bloodied and shocked. The rest of the planet would watch on their displays as armoured Marines wiped the rioters off the streets and grow to fear them. Humanity's faith in the Empire and its government had died in one bloody day.

And he wondered, as he poured himself a glass of imported Scotch, if anyone would ever realise that it had been murdered?

CHAPTER
NINETEEN

This worried the Grand Senate and they did what they could to limit the Marines and prevent them from becoming a threat. Funding was cut, starships were withdrawn and direct cooperation between the Marines and the Imperial Navy was hampered by officers with strong political connections. A number of the more noticeable Marine officers were exiled to the edge of the Empire, never to return to Earth.
- Professor Leo Caesius, *The End of Empire.*

Roland stared in horror at the images on the display.

Belinda divided her attention between him, the media display and the constant updates coming in through the Marine network. The media seemed to have decided that the whole catastrophe was the fault of the Marines; the talking heads were raging about the decision to allow armed Marines onto the streets of Imperial City. None of them seemed interested in mentioning the shots fired from the protest march, or the Civil Guardsmen who had been killed in the student rampage. The whole affair seemed designed to blacken the name of the Marine Corps.

That might have been the point, she thought, sourly. The average citizen of Imperial City wouldn't have the slightest idea where to get a standard projectile weapon, let alone a plasma pistol. She had a feeling that attempts to track down the source of the weapon that had killed an armoured Marine would prove futile. Someone in the Imperial Army had probably taken a large bribe to report it lost, or accidentally destroyed. So much material passed through the logistics department that quite a few weapons could vanish without anyone being any the wiser.

She listened to the updates coming through the Marine network and shuddered. The Civil Guard had arrived in force, allowing the handful of Marines a chance to concentrate on moving the wounded to the nearest hospitals. They'd commandeered every civilian aircar in the city – something else the media commenters were bitching about – but it wouldn't be enough to save every life. Most of the nearest hospitals were already overloaded; the wounded were having to be rushed to makeshift locations or tended on the streets. More would die, Belinda realised, simply through not having proper medical attention in time.

God alone knew what they were going to do with the prisoners. Upwards of eight *thousand* students had been arrested, either by the Marines or the Civil Guard. The holding pens that would be required to keep them prisoner simply didn't exist, not in Imperial City. For the moment, the Civil Guard had secured a number of warehouses and turned them into makeshift prison camps, but that was a very short-term solution. These were *students* who were under arrest, not criminals from the Undercity. She doubted that they could all be exiled from the planet…

And if they were, she asked herself, *what would the others do*?

There were over a million students in Imperial University alone, living in Imperial City, and many more in the lesser educational establishments. What would happen if they *all* turned radical? Keeping control over Imperial City might prove impossible unless the Civil Guard resorted to deadly force. The thought of the carnage that might result was horrific, but it couldn't be avoided. What would happen to Earth if her streets were drenched in more blood than Han?

Roland's voice distracted her from her thoughts. "What…what happened to them?"

"I wish I knew," Belinda said. The general consensus on the Marine network seemed to be that someone had deliberately planned a student march that had become a riot. It wasn't something she could argue with, not when the protesters had not only had live weapons, but a workable plan. Whoever had carried out the planning had known precisely what they were doing. "There was a riot."

She'd seen riots before, on several different worlds, and they were always terrifying. A *person*, Drill Instructor Kay had warned her, was smart, but *people* were dumb, panicky animals who were barely as smart as the stupidest person in the group. The students who'd rampaged through the city might have been smart enough to think better of it if they'd been alone, yet they'd been part of a mob, sucked into a collective rage that had overpowered common sense. They had been so caught up in the collective entity that even neural whips couldn't dissuade them from rampaging forward, trampling over their fallen comrades.

"I have to do something," Roland said. He looked down at his hands. "What can I do?"

"I don't think that there is anything you *can* do," Belinda admitted.

She racked her brains, but nothing came to mind. Roland simply didn't have the prestige needed to convince maddened crowds to go home, thanks to the rumours about his conduct that had been slipping out for years. By now, the students would have good reason to believe that Roland had *ordered* the violent response to their violence. The fact that they had started the violence would pass them by.

But she doubted that most of the protesters had *known* that violence was going to break out. Whoever had planned it would have been alert to the possibility of betrayal; they wouldn't have told anyone who didn't have a need-to-know. The students would be convinced – and they would be right, from their point of view – that the whole affair was someone else's fault, that they had been exercising their right to protest when the Civil Guard had met them with neural whips. Belinda gritted her teeth as the truth sank in. Thanks to the media, they would be convinced that Marine Corps had *caused* the disaster.

"There must be something," Roland protested.

"You can exercise with me," Belinda said, firmly. At least she'd managed to get Roland onto some exercises that would develop his muscles, as well as preparing him to fight. The genetic potential was there, thanks to his ancestors; he just needed time to develop it. Belinda had a nasty feeling that he wouldn't *have* the time. "And then we can play tennis."

She frowned as the next set of media updates blinked up on the screen. The Arena Corporation had announced that their next performance would be a charity one, in honour of those who had fallen on the Avenue of Imperial Supremacy. In the meantime, the Arena's medical chambers were being thrown open to the wounded students – but not to Civil Guardsmen. Belinda had no idea if that was even legal – by law, most medical centres had to take everyone who turned up in need of help – but it would be a great media soundbite. The students would receive help – and the nasty mean Civil Guardsmen would be left in the cold to die. It might have been amusing if it hadn't been so serious.

"All right," Roland said, as he stood up. "Can I at least make a donation?"

Belinda lifted an eyebrow. "To whom?"

"So tell me," Richard said. "How do you *feel*?"

Amethyst hesitated, trying to put her thoughts and feelings into words. Part of her was shocked at the nightmare they'd created – and she couldn't escape the awareness that it *was* a nightmare. The media was claiming that millions of students had been injured or killed…she knew that the media lied regularly, but she couldn't avoid believing that there had been thousands of injuries or deaths. She'd seen enough bodies lying on the ground to believe it.

And the rest of her was excited. They'd *caused* the whole affair, from beginning to end. It was something *significant*, something that had shaken the Empire…and they'd done it! How could anyone call her an insignificant student now, when she'd helped cause a crisis that had made the Senators flee Senate Hall and shaken the foundations of the Empire's power? The government would know that they could no longer take the students for granted now.

She eyed Richard as he lay beside her on the bed, admiring his superbly-toned body. Most male students used the body-shops or cosmetic surgery to improve their appearance in line with the dictates of fashion, or merely to avoid having to exercise. Richard, on the other hand, seemed too toned to be anything other than the product of heavy exercise, as if he'd spent part of his life working for a living. She'd studiously avoided asking questions – the less they knew about each other, the better – but she did wonder. What had Richard been doing before he'd come to Imperial University?

He'd called her to his apartment – a simple rented room barely large enough to swing a cat, if she'd been willing to spend credits on a pet licence – before she could return to the apartment she shared with Jacqueline. The excitement had been still blazing through her, intensified by how close she'd come to being captured by the Civil Guardsmen, and she'd seduced him, pushing him onto the bed and locking her lips to his as Imperial City burned. It had been years since she'd lost her virginity – like most students, she'd spent plenty of time pursuing the holy orgasm – but fucking Richard had been different. But then, she'd never been involved in starting a riot before. The excitement seemed almost unholy.

"I feel *great*," she admitted. They might be caught and arrested at any moment, but she found it hard to care. Even watching on the display as hundreds of students were hauled off to god-knows-where failed to blunt her excitement. They'd achieved something great, whatever the cost. And the rest of the students would no longer doubt the identity of their true enemy. "What are we going to do next?"

"I have a few ideas," Richard said, touching his groin.

"*Men*," Amethyst protested. "I meant…what are we going to do next?"

"I think we will be lying low for a few days," Richard said. He quirked an eyebrow at her. "There isn't anything to connect this apartment to us, you know. You could stay here for as long as you liked."

Amethyst shrugged. "Maybe," she said. Richard *had* been good in bed, after all. The old reluctance to share her life fully with a man no longer seemed to apply, not after all they'd done together. And yet…part of her knew that being too close to him would only give the Civil Guard a chance to scoop them both up. "How do you know all this?"

Richard lifted an eyebrow. "I beg your pardon?"

"You told us how to hide, you taught us how to use weapons…" Amethyst shook her head. "I wouldn't know *anything* without your help. How do you know these things?"

"Well, if you insist on knowing…" Richard began. He winked at her. "You do realise that most of the information I know – the stuff I taught you – is available in the computer databases? If you actually learned how to search the system, instead of only looking at the files your tutors suggested, you'd be able to find out much of it for yourself."

"Really?" Amethyst asked. "It's that simple?"

"Oh, yes," Richard assured her. "Earth's computer network is unique, babe. Even the WebHeads who play with it have no idea how deep it truly goes. There are computer cores connected to the network that date all the way back to the time before the Empire…plenty of them are hidden treasures for archivists. Others are crammed with porn."

Amethyst had to laugh, before realising just what he'd said. The students hadn't been taught to consider that there had been a time before the Empire, any more than they had been taught that the Empire might be in danger of coming apart. Her tutors had given her the impression that the Empire had always existed, or that there was no such thing as history, that the entire universe existed in a stasis that had lasted for thousands of years. It was obvious nonsense, when she considered it critically, but the students had been discouraged from any form of critical thinking. Who knew *what* the universe had been like before the Empire?

"There are history files there?" She asked. After she'd read the Professor's book, she'd gone back to the university library and studied the history files in the databases. Most of them, she saw now, had been deliberately written to conceal the truth. "Real ones?"

"Yep," Richard said. "And much more besides."

He grinned as he reached out and pulled her towards him. "If you read carefully, you can learn a great deal about how the Empire maintains its power," he said. "I was able to learn how the security systems work – and how the Civil Guard monitors the local environment. And, through doing that, I was able to work out how to subvert it. If you take a few precautions…"

Amethyst gasped as his fingers started exploring her breasts.

"If you take a few precautions," he repeated, whispering the words in her ear, "you can avoid being noticed for *years*. You can get away with *anything*."

She felt his hard cock pressing against her leg and shivered, feeling excitement welling through her body again. There were more questions she wanted to ask, but they were swept away in a wave of pleasure as he lowered her onto him, his hardness pushing into her. All that mattered was enjoying herself before they went back out and caused more chaos.

It wasn't until much later that she realised that he'd never really answered her question.

It was a simple fact of galactic economics that the price of any given item, whatever it was, tended to depend on a number of factors. The distance from source to destination, for one; the available supply…and yet such basic facts were lost on the sheep below. Stephen sipped a glass of Firewater from Mountbatten – a world several thousand light years from Earth – and smiled at the images on the display. The students, none of whom could have afforded Firewater if they'd saved their last credit, just didn't understand the true factors governing the Empire, or even the law of supply and demand. If they had truly understood, they would have emigrated to a new colony world.

Orbit Station Seven's destruction had been a nasty shock – and all the more so for being completely unexpected - but he'd managed to turn it to his advantage. The unthinking students below had played right into his hands. He skimmed through the preliminary report again and allowed his smile to widen. There was no media distortion in the reports reaching the Grand Senate, although there was probably a sizable amount of ass-covering. But Stephen had been a Grand Senator long enough to make allowances for such little details – and to learn how to read between the lines. The truth could always be found if one looked hard enough.

So far, nearly two thousand students, Civil Guardsmen and civilians were dead – and one Marine, of course. The bodies had been removed, but it would take weeks to clean up the mess, let alone repair the damage to the various buildings and statues attacked by the protestors. Several thousand more had also been injured, some critically; the report's writer stated that the full death toll was not yet known. Some of the wounded might slip away, no matter what medical care they received. If, indeed, they received *any* medical care.

Stephen took one last look at that section, then dismissed it. There was no shortage of students on Earth, most of whom were completely useless to him – or anyone else, for that matter. Most of them had no idea how the universe actually worked; they thought that their degrees gave them a right to be employed, when in truth they were ill-prepared to do anything beyond grunt labour. It *was* possible to get a decent education on Earth, Stephen knew, but the students had to motivate themselves. The tutors weren't there to encourage them to develop their talents.

The real question was just how much damage the protesters had caused – and *that* was significant. Once again, the writer had hedged his bets…but it was clear that billions of credits worth of damage had been done to Imperial City. Orbit Station Seven's fall had been bad enough – insurance companies were scrambling desperately to come up with good reasons why they shouldn't pay out, as it would ruin them if they had to pay all of the losses – yet this was going to be worse. How could they avoid paying, even though it would ruin them? The Senators connected to the insurance companies would want action…

…And the Senators had been forced to flee. They'd been attacked in their own stronghold and forced to run for their lives. Cold logic pointed out that the student rioters wouldn't have been able to do much damage to the Senate Hall, but cold logic had been missing, particularly after the Civil Guard had been forced to retreat. The Senators had been made to look like cowards and they wouldn't forget it in a hurry. They'd want a little revenge.

His wristcom buzzed. "Sir," Lindy said, "you asked to be informed when the Royal Committee reached a decision. They've done so. Prince Roland *will* visit the university campus."

Stephen smiled. He had never been elected to the Royal Committee… but what did that matter when he controlled three of its members? It allowed him a chance to deny any involvement in their deliberations, if necessary.

"Good," he said. "Thank you."

He closed the channel, thinking rapidly. Bode would have to be informed, of course; the plan had to move ahead. There was no longer a chance to climb off the tiger they were riding…

Stephen took a final swig of his Firewater and grinned to himself. Whatever else had happened, he could hardly have hoped for a better outcome to the student protest. It suited his plans perfectly.

CHAPTER TWENTY

By the time of Avalon's settlement, therefore, the Empire was staggering under its own weight. The upper classes controlled the wealth and power, the middle classes enjoyed themselves and the lower classes suffered. In Earth's Undercity, countless millions of humans lived and died, struggling to survive on the scraps that filtered down from the upper levels. Their resentment and hatred was almost palpable.
- Professor Leo Caesius, *The End of Empire.*

This, Belinda thought for the thousandth time, *is a completely insane risk.*

But she hadn't been given a choice, any more than Roland himself had been given a choice. The Grand Senate's Royal Committee, scrambling to respond to the crisis in Imperial City's streets, had ordained that Roland was to visit the hospitals and Imperial University, apparently in hopes that a show of concern would help mitigate the tensions running through the city. It hadn't taken long for Belinda to realise that their hopes were not going to bear any fruit. The hospital staff might have genuflected in front of Prince Roland, but the students – and even some of the civilians – were mutely hostile. None of them seemed very impressed by the Prince.

Belinda tailed Roland through the hospital, splitting her attention between the Prince and monitoring the local security situation. The Civil Guard was on the streets in force, while Senate Security had reinforced the close-protection detail assigned to Prince Roland. Even so, Belinda couldn't help feeling naked and vulnerable. Most of the standard security precautions were being neglected; few, if any, of the patients had been searched. She worried as she walked, trying to take in everything at once. If there was the slightest hint of a real threat, she'd privately resolved, she would shove Roland to the ground and lay down enough fire to cover their escape.

She'd seen horror – but most of the citizens of Imperial City had lived in a paradise, certainly when compared to Han or one of the other worlds that was caught up in simmering ethnic or religious warfare. The hospital had only been designed to take a few hundred patients at best; now, there were wounded lying in the corridors or sharing beds with their fellow wounded. A handful of medical corpsmen from the military had been added to the staff, but there weren't enough of them to make a real difference. Belinda hated to think just how unhealthy the entire scene was becoming. Her Drill Instructor would have roasted the recruits if they'd made their living space so unhealthy.

Roland stopped in front of a bed, staring at the young woman lying under the sheets. She had been pretty once, but now half of her face had been scarred so badly that she would need cosmetic surgery to fix it. One of her eyes was covered with a medical patch, flakes of dried blood surrounding it. Belinda briefly accessed the room's processor and scanned the girl's medical files. Someone had gouged out her eye and left her for dead. Normally, it would take months – and thousands of credits – to replace a missing eye. Now, with so much demand for medical services, it might be years before she was truly healed.

Another girl, sitting next to her, looked up at the Prince. "Why?" She demanded. "Why did this even happen?"

Belinda could have answered the question, but she kept her mouth shut. None of the students had really appreciated their own ignorance, or how easy it was for someone with bad intentions to manipulate them into starting a riot. The latest update from the Civil Guard – who had taken the lead in the post-riot investigation – had stated that no one connected to the terrorists who had started the riot had been caught. They *had* arrested a handful of organisers, but the people who had backed them had been careful to avoid giving names or contact details. Belinda wasn't too surprised. Whoever had started the riot was too smart and knowledgeable to be caught easily.

"Laura was going to be a model," the girl added. "Now look at her!"

"She will be healed," Roland said, quietly. "The facilities are overstressed right now, but she isn't in any immediate danger..."

The girl didn't look impressed and Belinda, if she were forced to be honest, found it hard to blame her. She and her fellow students had been sheltered from the harsh realities of life for so long that they had no idea what it was really like out there. The protesters who screamed their outrage at military deployments – to Han, to Albion, to countless other worlds across the Empire – had no awareness of the chaos that might overwhelm the Empire if brushfire wars weren't stopped as quickly as possible.

They see the little evils that are committed in their name and are rightly repulsed by them, Doug's voice seemed to whisper in her mind. *But they do not see the greater evils committed against them and so they do not exist in their universe.*

They moved on through the ward, seeing an endless series of horror. One boy had been trampled so badly that the medics had put him in a stasis field, knowing that he would die quickly unless he was brought out in a properly-prepared operating theatre. Another had had both of his legs broken, something he loudly blamed on the Civil Guardsmen who'd attempted to drive the students off the streets. Several girls had been raped, including one who had a broken arm; they should have been in a separate ward, but there was simply no space for them. They seemed terrified of the world, even flinching away from other women.

Belinda urged Roland past them – there was no point in trying to talk to the rape victims – and into the next ward. It too was crammed with patients and a handful of medical staff trying to cope with them. Belinda winced when she saw the bloodstains on the floor, knowing that – sooner or later – someone would slip on the blood and break their neck. And it was unhygienic...but there was no choice. The planet's supply of painkillers, to say nothing of more advanced medical treatments, was running out. Belinda had picked up a note on the Marine datanet that half of the medical supplies stored for the Marines had been rushed to Imperial City. She assumed that the Civil Guard storehouses were also being looted.

A security alert popped up in her retina display and she tensed, before realising that the outside media had finally realised that Prince

Roland was visiting the injured. A small army of reporters had been in the hospital, but Senate Security had – at Belinda's request – asserted their authority to prevent them from sending any messages out of the building until after Roland had left. Even so, she wasn't surprised to discover that the cat was finally out of the bag. The Grand Senate wanted some good press and pictures of Roland consoling the sick might just help them. Or, perhaps, allow them to shift the blame onto the powerless prince.

She caught Roland's attention as he stepped away from yet another wounded student. "The media is here," she said, softly. "It's time to move to the university."

Roland nodded, grimly. He seemed to have aged overnight, much like Army officers who had graduated from Sandhurst or West Point Mars without ever having seen combat – and then looked the elephant in the eye. Belinda had once wondered why the other services didn't copy the Marine practice of insisting that every officer served in the ranks first, before she'd made the mistake of asking her first platoon sergeant. He'd explained that there was no shortage of opportunity for patronage in a system that put qualifications before experience and everyone who might have been able to change the system benefited from it. And then they wondered why the Imperial Army – and the Civil Guard – was a bizarre assortment of competent and incompetent units.

More alerts popped up in front of her as the reporters – aware that the secret was now out – started uploading reports to the media networks. It was rare for anything to go out live – after all, a live show was inherently unpredictable – but Roland's visit would probably be an exception. She gritted her teeth as Roland led the way out of the hospital, checking in with the Senate Security officers outside the building. The new reporters were, thankfully, on the other side of a small barricade.

It didn't stop them from shouting questions at the Prince. "Will you condemn the slaughter? Will you have medical expenses paid for the wounded? Will you strip the Marines of their Royal Charter?" The questions started to blur together into a mass of words, bombarding Roland and everyone standing near him. Surprisingly, Roland seemed unaffected by the racket, even if he didn't try to answer the questions. Belinda felt a moment of pride as he climbed into the Royal Aircar and sat down. As soon as Belinda joined him, the doors hissed closed and the aircar rose into the air, heading towards Imperial University.

"This isn't going to be pleasant," Belinda warned.

"No," Roland said. Now the reporters couldn't see them, he looked nervous. "I have never spoken in public before."

Belinda nodded, ruefully. If she'd thought of it, she would have hired one of the oratory tutors from the House of Cicero, the business that supplied training to young men seeking to stand for election. But even if she had, the speech Roland had been ordered to give had been written by the Royal Committee. Whoever had said that a camel was a horse designed by committee had never had to deal with the Grand Senate. The Royal Committee's speech wasn't even a camel!

"You'll have to start now," she warned. The Grand Senate had kept Roland isolated to allow rumours to go unchecked. Now, though, they wanted him to take on a public role. "Just remember to try to sound as if you believe what you're saying."

She looked down through the transparent windows as Imperial University came into view. It looked impressive, she had to admit; the walls seemed to be made of solid white marble, even though she knew that they were composed of the same composites that made up most of Earth's buildings. The material was solid; it didn't erode away over generations, something that might have been the only thing keeping parts of the city intact. Imperial City was built on the remains of other cities, which might have themselves been built over even older cities…few saw the Undercity, or the unregistered population lurking there. It was rarely factored into their calculations.

The aircar dropped down and landed neatly on the landing pad. It was surrounded by Civil Guardsmen, Belinda was relieved to see; the reports from the university had suggested that the whole campus was simmering with rage. If anything, she realised as she followed Roland out of the aircar, the reports had been understated. The sullen hatred from the students gathered to hear Roland speak hit her like a physical blow. If Roland had been more sensitive, he might have turned and fled. Belinda would have found it hard to blame him.

Every Marine knew the theory of counterinsurgency warfare. If the occupying power happened to use too much force, they created new enemies; if they used too little force, they convinced the population that the occupying force was not prepared to take risks to defend them. Or, for that matter, that a few bloody noses could cause them to retreat. Now, looking at the students, Belinda realised that the Civil Guard – and the Marine Corps – had made hundreds of thousands of new enemies. Few of the students had really understood the realities of their world. They understood now.

A handful of students could be expelled and few would notice, she thought, grimly. There were so many students on campus that no one could hope to know them all. *Hurt thousands of them and they will take note…*

She gritted her teeth again as Roland stepped onto the podium. The Civil Guard had searched the area, including the students themselves, but Roland was still a big target in plain view. A sniper several miles away, lying on the roof one of the massive CityBlocks, could have shot him – and no one would have known he was there until it was too late. Belinda would have been happier if Roland had been in a suit of Marine Combat Armour, but it took months to produce one customised for an individual user and months of training to learn how to use it properly. Besides, it would have suggested to the watching students that Roland was *scared* of them. Who knew what they could do with *that* impression?

Traditionally, the university band would play the Empire's anthem – *The Power of the Unified Human Race is Beyond Compare* – and the students would sing the five principal verses, but the organisers had decided to skip that step. Belinda was privately relieved, even though she knew that it might be taken as a sign of weakness; even when sung by the best singers, the anthem was more than a little tedious. The Marines had joked that the lyrics had been written by some Grand Senator's idiot cousin who fancied himself a composer, then approved by the rest of the Senate after huge bribes had been passed out by his uncle. It was as good an explanation as any for why it had been chosen, Belinda had thought at the time. Now, though, the words would have sounded like a bad joke...

She wrinkled her nose as the wind changed, blowing the scent of burning fabric towards the podium. The students had burned hundreds of Imperial Flags over the past two days, even though it was technically a form of treason. They'd also burned the personal banners of the Grand Senatorial families and several Marine Corps flags. The disrespect made her want to show those students precisely what threats the Marines faced, just to keep them safe. But she pushed the rage aside as Roland started to speak. He had barely gotten through the first line before the students started to howl their fury.

Belinda braced herself, ready to leap up to the podium and yank Roland away if the crowd surged forward, just before the sound died away. Someone was *coordinating* the whole display, she realised; someone bright enough to figure out a way to do it without alerting the Civil Guard. Roland hesitated, preparing to restart, just as a figure pushed his way out of the crowd and stepped forward.

"Your Highness," he said, his voice booming over the campus. He was using a voder, Belinda realised; somehow, he'd slipped it past the guards. All it would have taken, the cynical side of her mind realised, was a large bribe. A voder wasn't a weapon, after all. No doubt the Civil Guardsman had rationalised taking the bribe that way. "We have demands."

Roland hesitated, clearly surprised. "You have demands?"

"Yes," the student said. "I, Maxim J. Freeman, have demands."

"I see," Roland said, finally. "And who do you speak for?"

"I speak for the entire student body," Freeman said. "If our demands are not met, we shall take action."

Belinda thought fast. Freeman was in the midst of a massive crowd of students – and attempting to arrest him could prove disastrous. And he also seemed to have enough control to start or stop a riot. They couldn't let themselves be dictated to, but they didn't seem to have any alternative. Roland seemed to have come to the same conclusion.

"And what," he asked, "are your demands?"

Freeman produced a sheet of paper from under his shirt. "One; the Marines are to be withdrawn from Imperial City and the Civil Guard is to be withdrawn from the university campus. Two; there is to be a full and open investigation into the mass slaughter of peaceful protestors by the Marines and Civil Guardsmen. Three; all food prices are to be frozen at the level they held prior to the deliberate sabotage of Orbit Station Seven. Four; all debts are to be written off without further ado. Fifth…"

Belinda shook her head in disbelief as the series of demands, eleven in all, rolled out of Freeman's mouth. Each demand was more outrageous than the last; did they really believe that the Grand Senate would give up its power so easily? Or, for that matter, that all debts could be written off without consequences? Or that the Senate could legislate new food deliveries into existence? And as for the demand that the students had a say in running Imperial University? They'd had that say for years. It explained a great deal about the current state of the establishment. No doubt new recruits to the military would vote to make the training easier, if they had a choice. Real life would punish them for *that* piece of stupidity.

"The Grand Senate will consider your demands," Roland said. His lips twitched. "Seeing that my speech appears to have been ruined, I will take your demands instead."

The crowd of students gave him a good-natured cheer. Freeman – Belinda had a feeling that wasn't the student's real name – vanished into their ranks as Roland climbed down and walked back towards the aircar. Belinda took one last glance at the students, who were congratulating each other as if they had won a great victory, then followed Roland into the vehicle. It was a relief when the door hissed closed.

"I don't believe it," Roland said, as he looked down at the scrawled list of demands. "He has to be insane!"

"Or crazy like a fox," Belinda muttered. The car was passing over the massive residency blocks on the edge of Imperial City, heading back towards the Summer Palace. "Maybe they're just nailing their colours to the mast. Or looking to put forward demands they know the Senate won't grant…"

The alarms sounded, jerking Belinda back to the here-and-now. "Brace yourself," she snapped. "We're under attack!"

CHAPTER TWENTY-ONE

Worse, the middle classes were becoming infected with poisonous political ideals. At one extreme, there was a belief that they had an intrinsic right to free food, drink and entertainment. At the other, there was nihilism - the belief that life was worthless and the Empire needed to be destroyed. In between, there were countless billions seeking pleasure – as if they knew, on some level, that the good times were coming to an end.
- Professor Leo Caesius, *The End of Empire.*

Amethyst hadn't been in a residency block for years, ever since she'd gone to Imperial University. Walking up the endless floors of Block 173 in Imperial City had reminded her of everything she'd tried to forget, from the ever-present smell of urine to the failing infrastructure that rendered the structure unsafe. A handful of young men loafed around, their eyes searching for possible targets; if she'd been alone, she feared that they would have come after her. Even with Richard and several others with her, she didn't feel safe at all.

The rooftop had been locked, but Richard had obtained a code-breaker from somewhere and used it to get out onto the roof. She'd been told that the air pollution in the upper levels of Imperial City was minimal, compared to some parts of the planet, yet the wind still stank as it blew across her face. There were no barriers to prevent someone from falling to their deaths if the winds grew much stronger; she couldn't help shivering as she took the weapon Richard offered her. It was a sign of his trust in her, she told herself, that she got to fire one of the shots that would echo around the entire galaxy.

She looked over at Richard as he peered into the distance, using a pair of binoculars to sweep the sky. He looked even more handsome since they'd been sleeping together, she decided, or maybe it was the shared excitement and danger. The Civil Guard normally didn't bother to patrol the upper levels of residency blocks – hence the growth of gangs and protection rackets – but that was about to change. Richard had warned them, in no uncertain terms, that they couldn't stay around to watch the show. The moment they opened fire, the entire planetary defence network would be alerted. Troops would be rushed to their position as quickly as they could board helicopters or assault shuttles.

"Tell me," she said. "How do you know the Prince will fly this way?"

"Simple," Richard said. "If you draw a line between Imperial University and the Summer Palace, that line passes over this building."

He grinned at her, then resumed peering through the binoculars. "Keep the power blocks ready to slip into place, but don't insert them until I give the command," he reminded them, grimly. "If the sensor heads activate too soon, the security officers escorting the Prince will be alerted."

Amethyst nodded and waited. She found it hard to feel any concern for Prince Roland; the rumours she'd heard had made the Prince out to be a depraved monster, a man who sucked on the Empire's teat while millions of students and their families went hungry. No one would be making *him* eat algae bars, she knew; the best of the imported foodstuffs were reserved for the wealthy and powerful. She'd show them just how their subjects felt about how their lords and masters treated them. The death of Prince Roland would shock the entire establishment.

"Ah," Richard said, softly. "Here they come; three targets. The one we want is the one in the middle; the other two are gunships. We have to take them all down or we're in deep shit."

Amethyst held the power block over the slot and waited. Smog was drifting through the sky, but she could see the three aircraft as they came into view, heading northwards. Two of them were bristling with weapons; the third seemed unarmed. Richard barked a command and she slammed the power block in and hefted the launcher. It was already bleeping as its sensor head picked up its targets.

"Fire," Richard snapped.

Amethyst pulled the trigger. There was a wave of heat as the high-velocity missile blasted away from its launcher, heading towards its target. She wasn't quite sure which of the aircraft it had locked onto, but it hardly mattered. There were five missiles in the air and, by the law of averages, at least one of them would go after the Prince. And, at such short range, the countermeasures should have no time to work.

"Drop the tubes and go," Richard ordered. "Hurry!"

Amethyst obeyed, dropping back down the hatch into the block's interior. So far, none of the residents knew what had happened, but that was about to change. They had to be well away from the rooftop by then…

Belinda swore out loud as she linked into the aircar's command network. Five missiles, heading towards the aircraft at several times the speed of sound. HVMs, part of her mind identified them; they were moving too quickly to be stopped. One of the gunships started to drop flares and other sensor decoys, but it was far too late. Two missiles slammed into its airframe and it vanished in a colossal fireball.

"Hang on," she barked, as their aircar lurched. She'd been impressed by the heavy armour the designers had added, along with the active defences – but then, the active defences had just failed. "One of the missiles is coming right for us!"

The missile crew hadn't been very well trained, she realised, as the aircar attempted to evade the incoming threat. If they had been trained, they would have made certain of their targets; as it was, both of the gunships were larger targets and the seeker heads had gone after them, rather than Roland's aircar. But one missile was still coming in…time seemed to slow down, just before the missile slammed into the aircar's prow.

She heard Roland cry out in shock as the aircar lurched violently, flipping over and spinning through the air. They'd been lucky, she realised; if the missile had struck another meter to the right, the warhead would have punched through the doors and detonated inside the cabin, killing them both instantly. As it was, they were going down, yet they were still alive.

The pilot was wounded, but he was still trying to put them down as gently as he could.

An alert flashed up in front of her as the second gunship vanished in a fireball. One of the crewmen had managed to bail out in time, she noted; she hoped that he would manage to land safely, even though they were above the outer edge of Imperial City. By now, assault shuttles and rescue craft should be being scrambled, but she added her own alert to the Marine network, just in case. It was far too possible that someone in the Civil Guard had been bribed to hamper the recovery effort.

The aircar lurched again as one of the engines failed. For a long moment, it seemed to hang in the air, before falling down towards one of the rooftops. Belinda reached out and took Roland's hand, seeing his terror reflected in his eyes, a moment before they hit the rooftop. There was a thunderous crash, then silence.

"Get up," Belinda barked. The door was jammed, unsurprisingly, but she boosted her strength and pushed it open wide enough to allow her to crawl out. Roland followed her, grimacing at the stench in the air. Belinda didn't have the heart to tell him that it was far worse only a few hundred miles from Imperial City. He'd rarely breathed unfiltered air in his life.

She glanced around, scanning for possible threats. Her implants reported energy fluctuations in the aircar's surviving antigravity generator – it might explode at any moment – but nothing else immediately threatening. The absence of any rescue mission, on the other hand, was worrying. She ran around the aircar and glanced into the cab, but knew at once that there was no point in trying to recover the pilot. The force of their landing had killed him.

"Get over there," she ordered, pointing towards a small structure in the middle of the rooftop. Some CityBlocks had gardens on the roof for children to play, but this one was clearly too poor to afford it. There was nothing on the metal apart from scratches where something heavy might have stood, once upon a time. "Hurry!"

She took a final look at the aircar as Roland obeyed, then stuck her hand into the pilot's cabin and recovered the emergency pack. Roland could run swiftly – she'd helped him to learn by chasing him around the gardens in the Summer Palace – and he was already at the structure.

Belinda swung the pack over her shoulder and raced towards him, leaving the aircar behind. If it was about to explode, they didn't dare stay on the roof.

The door leading down into the CityBlock was locked. Belinda, still drawing on the boosting drug in her bloodstream, kicked it as hard as she could. The lock shattered, allowing them to tumble downstairs into the semi darkness. It would have to serve as a rudimentary form of shelter. She heard Roland gasp at the stench – it was far worse inside the block – but ignored him. There *had* to be a rescue mission on the way, so where *were* they?

She reached inside the emergency pack and found the locator beacon. The pilot, thankfully, had been reassuringly competent; the beacon had clicked on automatically the moment he'd declared an in-flight emergency. Her implants tested it, confirmed that it was sending out a signal, then linked into the Marine network. It seemed that there was a great deal of confusion over what had happened to Prince Roland. Half of the reports seemed to suggest that he was dead...

"We're not dead," Belinda snapped. At least the Marine network was working properly. "Get a recovery team here now..."

The ceiling seemed to shake as the aircar finally exploded. Belinda braced herself, half-expecting the rooftop to cave in, but the metal sheathing of the CityBlock held up under the blast. At least *that* didn't need constant maintenance. She put her head up and peered back at where the aircar had been. There was a nasty scar on the metal, but little else.

"This place stinks," Roland said, crossly. "Do people actually *live* here?"

"Yes," Belinda said. She was in no mood to shield the Prince from the lives of the less fortunate. They were supposed to be his subjects, after all. "The lucky ones live here."

She recalled the last report she'd seen, back when her former company had operated briefly on Earth, and hit him with the details. "There are CityBlock units that are completely controlled by criminals, where the Civil Guard never venture," she said. "Those unfortunate enough to live there are completely at their mercy. Men are press-ganged into small armies and forced to fight wars with the other gangs. Women are forced into prostitution, selling their bodies to survive. By the time they turn thirty, they will already have had children and started to burn themselves out. Very few people live longer than forty years in those blocks.

"Other places seem to be more civilised," she added. "There's a Civil Guard presence; outright gangsters keep their heads down. But life is still no bed of roses. If you'd been born there, the best you could hope for is a cheap apartment, shared with your family, where you could eat ration bars and watch bad entertainment programs until the day you died. I remember meeting girls who had grown up in such places. They felt that being raped was commonplace, that it was nothing to complain about – and if they did, who would listen? And who cared if they carried their attacker's baby or not?"

Roland stared at her. "But it can't be that bad…?"

"Of course it is," Belinda snapped. "I could show you scenes of horror, worse than any of your porn, taking place only a few miles from the Summer Palace."

Her IR implants caught the flush on Roland's face. She'd scanned his private collection of porn a few days after she'd first met him…and she'd been lucky that she hadn't looked at it *before* meeting him. Collecting dominance porn was often a sign that someone *knew* that they had very little power in their lives, but if she hadn't known Roland first she might have given up on him completely, right at the start. His collection had been thoroughly disgusting.

"Those students are luckier than they know," she added, tartly. "They come from the better class of residency blocks, places where the worst to fear is boredom. There, they speak in whispers of the Undercity, if they speak of it at all. They think that they can better themselves through whining and demanding more and more from the Empire. But in truth the Empire has nothing more to give. How long will it be before the bough breaks and the cradle falls? How long will it be before the Empire destroys itself?"

She saw the Marine shuttle flying through the air and climbed out onto the roof. "Come on," she said, softening her voice. "It's time to get you home."

Roland scrambled up beside her, his fine clothes smeared with dust and filth. Belinda's implants provided a few suggestions of what had happened in the upper levels, but she knew to keep them to herself. The Prince almost certainly didn't want to know. Instead, he looked grim, almost broken, reminding her of more than a few recruits who had made it through Boot Camp – only to discover that the worst was yet to come.

Her implant buzzed. "Specialist, the Civil Guard is attempting to secure the CityBlock the assassins used as a base," the dispatcher reported. "Do you have any visuals?"

Belinda shook her head, although the dispatcher couldn't see her. "No," she said, out loud. Something might have been recorded by the aircar's defences, or the gunships, but they were all gone. Twelve men had died, unable to do more than watch their doom racing towards them. "I don't have anything."

It was unlikely that the Civil Guard would find anything either, she knew. The CityBlock was a towering edifice with thousands of rooms and passageways, inhabited by people who cared little for the forces of law and order. And there were dozens of ways *out* of the maze…she would have been surprised if the Civil Guard caught *anyone*. The terrorists might well have made their escape good before the Civil Guard arrived in force. Even if they hadn't, half of the residents of the block would be unregistered. Finding and identifying the terrorists might prove difficult.

The Marine shuttle touched down and two armoured Marines stepped out, intending to provide covering fire. "Get in," she ordered Roland quietly. "We'll go straight back to the Palace."

Roland said nothing as they flew back towards the Summer Palace. Belinda was privately impressed; she'd expected him to start complaining about the stench. Marines often smelled bad after several days of uninterrupted fighting – Belinda was used to it; besides, there was no point in bitching about it – but whatever they'd trodden on while they'd been inside the block was truly awful. She couldn't help feeling sorry for the inhabitants. God alone knew what happened inside the massive building.

Or, for that matter, what was going on inside Roland's head.

"Well, *pooh*," Richard said.

Amethyst glanced over at him in surprise. As he'd promised, their escape from the CityBlock had been almost pathetically easy. They'd been outside the cordon long before the Civil Guard had arrived in force and started to clash with outraged residents, who might not give two rusty credits for the Prince, but hated the Civil Guardsmen with a white-hot passion. Several other nearby blocks had started to shed people too, advancing towards the Guardsmen with grim intent. It had looked as though another riot was about to break out by the time they left the scene.

"The Prince survived," Richard elaborated. "It seems that his pilot was very lucky or very skilled."

"Oh," Amethyst said. The excitement was fading away, leaving her with the dull awareness that they'd killed a number of men – and yet they'd missed their target. "There will be another chance, won't there?"

"I'm sure of it," Richard said.

He said nothing else as they made their way back towards the safe apartment he'd hired under an assumed name. Amethyst had been surprised at his paranoia, but he'd told her that staying too long in one place could be disastrous. Thankfully, a number of students had fled the university after the riots, providing a convenient excuse so that no one would miss her. She'd told Jacqueline that she was staying with her new boyfriend, but nothing else.

"We'll lie low for a few days," he said, as he dismissed the others. They had their own safe apartments, presumably in other blocks. Amethyst hadn't been told where they were hiding themselves and, she assumed, they didn't know precisely where Richard and her were staying. "And maybe we can enjoy ourselves too."

"I don't know," Amethyst admitted, as soon as they were inside the apartment. "How many innocent men did we kill?"

Richard caught her shoulder and spun her around so he could look into her eyes. "They're not innocent," he said, flatly. "Every one of those men was working to uphold the Empire – and keep people such as you and I down. They willingly *chose* to serve the Grand Senate, knowing just how corrupt it had become. I will shed no tears for them."

His eyes hardened. "Or are you no longer willing to fight for the right to be free?"

"I am," Amethyst protested. The look in his eye scared her; she wanted to run, but she'd gone too far. Attacking the Crown Prince was probably treason. "I will fight."

"Good," Richard said. "Now, go get into the shower. I'll join you in a few moments."

Shaking, Amethyst obeyed.

CHAPTER TWENTY-TWO

Defining nihilism is not an easy task. At their core, they were effectively death-worshippers, believing that mass slaughter was a holy act. Their fanatics would seek self-destruction, committing terrorist attacks intended to kill as many civilians as possible. They did not seek death, but they did not avoid it either. For the Empire, the nihilists made a bad situation worse.

- Professor Leo Caesius, *The End of Empire.*

"And why are you wasting water? There are entire *planets* suffering from drought!"

Belinda snorted as she heard the voice of her first Drill Instructor echoing in her memory. The recruits had been expected to shower quickly, to be in and out of the shower in two minutes, no matter how much mud they'd waded through on the exercise field. Now, she could afford to take as long as she wanted to wash, but habit drove her out of the shower after barely five minutes. Besides, she didn't want to share the shower with Roland for any longer than necessary.

But there had been no choice. Judging by the faces the maids had pulled as soon as they'd returned to the Summer Palace, they both stank terribly, worse than raw recruits at Boot Camp. Their clothes would probably have to be burned or, more practically, dropped into a molecular disintegrator. Roland still looked pale, Belinda decided, as she watched him washing himself desperately. It would be a long time before the memory of the smell faded from his mind. He hadn't even been able to stare at her, even though she'd been naked.

Belinda grinned briefly at the thought as she stepped out of the shower and started to dry herself with a long white towel. The Prince was holding up better than she would have expected, although it was possible that he simply didn't appreciate just how close he'd come to death. Belinda did; a few seconds either way and they would both have been blown to atoms. Pathfinders weren't unafraid to die, but they knew how to put their feelings aside and carry out their missions. The Prince had no such training.

Once she was dry, she reached for a dressing robe and pulled it on, before stepping outside and accessing the Marine network. It seemed that the Civil Guard and Senate Security were having a political tussle over who got to take the lead on the investigation – or, reading between the lines, who *didn't* have to put themselves forward as the prime investigator. That made a certain kind of sense, Belinda knew; the organisation that got the blame for exposing Roland to danger might be punished by the Grand Senate. The leadership would have preferred to ensure that they avoided all blame, rather than learning from the experience…

Someone was quite incompetent, she thought. The aircars had flown back to the Summer Palace in a straight line, the shortest distance between two points – but also an extremely predictable path. All the assassins had needed to do was lie in wait along that line and open fire when the Prince's aircar came into view. Roland – and Belinda – had been spared by the incompetence of their enemies, something she knew better than to count on in future. Besides, twelve good men had died to save Roland's life. It wasn't something she took lightly.

Absently, she checked the palace's security network and relaxed slightly when she realised that it was still in place. One advantage of being the Prince's liegeman was that she had near-complete access to the third security network, the one intended for the Royal Family and its closest servants. She had been astonished to discover that there were more hidden passageways and rooms in the Summer Palace than she'd seen on the original set of plans she'd downloaded, all very well hidden from prying eyes. She'd wondered how they'd remained unknown even to most of the security staff, before deciding that the original designers and builders had probably been quietly memory-wiped – or murdered – after they'd completed their work.

She looked up as Roland stepped out of the bathroom, a towel wrapped around his waist. "I feel strange," he said, shaking his head. "Excited and fearful at the same time. Is that normal?"

"It can be," Belinda replied. Survivors of disasters often found themselves feeling horny, she knew; it was something to do with the thrill of remaining alive when others had died. "Under the circumstances, why don't you go for a massage?"

Roland grinned, brilliantly. The girl who provided massages to the Prince specialised in working kinks out of the body, yet she also provided erotic massages and outright sex. Belinda had stopped Roland playing with the maids – it was a dangerous habit, she'd told him – but she hadn't done anything about the massages. Roland needed some relaxation after everything he'd been through...and besides, it would keep him out of trouble for thirty minutes or thereabouts. Just long enough, Belinda decided, for her to visit the two commanding officers.

"You should come with me," Roland said. "Miss Yang is very good."

Belinda chuckled. She'd watched the woman working her way over Roland's body and had to admit that she knew her stuff. But then, she *should* have known what she was doing; whatever she looked like, she had over fifty years of experience in her field. It was astonishing just how *young* a person could look with the right application of rejuvenation treatments. She wondered if Roland knew – he did have access to the files – before deciding that it didn't matter. All that mattered was the woman being competent and trustworthy.

"I have something else to do," she said. "Besides, too much luxury and I will go soft."

"So you keep saying," Roland said. He donned a dressing gown, then headed towards the door. "I'll see you in my suite."

Belinda watched him go, then logged onto the network and issued an order for Colonel Hicks and Captain Singh to meet her in the guardroom. Both officers had been conspicuously silent ever since Prince Roland had returned to the Summer Palace, as if they were busy getting their stories straight before the Grand Senate appointed an investigating committee. After all, the assassins had come alarmingly close to murdering the Crown

Prince; they couldn't assume that it would be business as usual in Imperial City. And *someone* was going to have to take the blame.

Shaking her head grimly, she walked out of the room and down towards the guardroom, part of her mind following the progress of the investigation. The Civil Guard had searched a quarter of the CityBlock so far, turning up plenty of evidence of illegal activity but finding nothing that seemingly related to the assassins. So far, they'd captured over two hundred illegal weapons, mostly makeshift devices built by the gangs for their petty wars; there had been some excitement, the report noted, until it was pointed out that the assassins had had access to military-grade weapons. A ramshackle pistol that was likely to explode in its user's hand wasn't in quite the same league.

Maybe they'll scare a few people straight, she thought, although she knew that it was unlikely. *Or maybe they will just make themselves even more unpopular.*

The security alerts on the Marine network were far from reassuring. Imperial University seemed to be simmering with resentment, even though there had been no response to the student demands; the Civil Guard had searched for the elusive Freeman, but failed to find him. Outside, there were small confrontations between the Civil Guard and the city's residents, each one threatening to blossom into another riot before slowly fading away into nothingness. The parents of the arrested students were demanding their freedom – and, as so many students had fled and dropped off the grid, many of them didn't *know* what had happened to their children. Most of them seemed happy to assume the worst.

No one even seemed to know what should happen to the arrested students. Standard procedure was to exile them, just as almost every other criminal arrested on Earth was exiled to one of the colony worlds. They certainly wouldn't be given a trial – but with so many people under arrest, how could the Grand Senate *avoid* giving them a trial? Earth's Grand Senators had been secure in their power and positions for generations, with elections little more than a joke, yet now they felt the ground shifting beneath their feet. Who knew *what* would happen if a mass movement arose to challenge their position? Earth was one of the few worlds where upheaval could make the whole Empire shiver.

And what would the Grand Senators do in response?

Belinda scowled as she stepped into the guardroom and discovered that she was the first one there. Angrily, she took a seat and forced herself to wait, even though she wanted to send demands for the two COs to present themselves to her at once. It took nearly seven minutes before Singh arrived, looking harried, and took a seat facing her. Hicks arrived five minutes after him, his face expressionless until he saw Belinda. He glared at her, as if the whole affair was her fault.

"I have work to do," Hicks said, shortly. "The cordon around the Summer Palace…"

"Sit down," Belinda said, putting as much command into her voice as she could. She might not have been a Captain, but she knew how to take command. Besides, a Pathfinder 'Specialist' outranked anyone below a Major, if they saw fit to assert themselves. "We have much to discuss."

"This is outrageous," Hicks snapped. "I…"

"Sit down," Belinda repeated. She met Hicks' eyes and held them, daring him to look away. "I will not ask again."

The Colonel sat down sullenly.

"Good," Belinda said. She looked over at Singh. "Do you want to make any objections too or can we proceed?"

Singh scowled at her, but said nothing. He, at least, had been doing something relatively useful before she'd summoned him, although there was very little of his close-protection team to recover. Both gunship aircars had been blown into atoms. Still, Senate Security had done better than the Civil Guard……

"There was a massive security breach," Belinda stated, flatly. She held up her thumb and forefinger, holding them close together. "Prince Roland came *this* close to death. And if he had died, we would have a succession crisis at the worst possible moment."

She saw them grimace, although she doubted that the succession crisis was their prime concern. Even if they had been personally blameless, their careers would have died with the Prince; their superiors would have ensured that they took the blame. Not that they would have been completely blameless, Belinda had decided; a quick scan of the records had confirmed that Roland's aircar had *always* followed a predictable path on his few journeys outside the Summer Palace. She was mildly surprised that the assassination attempt hadn't taken place as Roland flew to or from the Arena.

But I stopped him going twice, she thought, in the privacy of her own head. Roland hadn't *always* managed to beat her at tennis – or, rather, she hadn't wanted him to get used to winning. *They might have felt that they couldn't have counted on him going to the Arena on a specific weekend.*

But the implications of *that* were worrying.

"Let me be clear on this," Belinda said. "The decision to have the Prince visit the hospitals and Imperial University was made barely a day before he actually went. *In that time,* an assassination team found out what was going to happen, got into position with military-grade weapons – and fired missiles towards the Crown Prince's aircar. We had a massive security breach and our charge came very close to death."

She wondered if either of them would dispute it. Roland's schedule should have been a closely-guarded secret, but too many people had known *something,* enough to put together the rest of the details. It was highly unlikely that the assassination team had acted on the spur of the moment. Belinda had carried out assassination missions herself and knew just how hard it could be to get a team into position at the right time. No, they'd had at least a day's warning to plan their operation, prepare lines of retreat and then get into position.

The investigation team was trying to locate the source of the HVMs in the hope that would lead to the assassins, but Belinda didn't hold out much hope. Chances were that they'd been stolen from a Civil Guard or Imperial Army weapons dump; so many weapons went missing that it was unlikely that the loss would ever be noticed. Hell, there was so much paperwork involved with securing weapons and ammunition that the army bureaucrats might just have allowed them to slip through the cracks. The whole system sounded insane to Belinda, but it was astonishing how logical illogical thinking could sound when done by a committee.

"I am the Prince's liegeman, charged with his safety," she added. "I will not tolerate another security breach on such a scale."

Hicks went purple. "And who are you to talk to us in such a manner?"

Belinda smiled. "The Prince's liegeman," she said, simply.

She watched their faces closely, wondering if they knew what that really meant. It was quite possible they didn't; Belinda herself hadn't known until she'd researched the issue, *after* Roland had accepted her oath of loyalty. Technically, as his oath-sworn liegeman, she outranked both of them. Even if they swore their own oaths of loyalty, she would still have precedence. Roland – deliberately or otherwise – had given her a weapon she could use against them.

"I will spare you the details," she said, calmly. She accessed her implants and transmitted a brief outline of her position – and the legal precedents from prior Emperors – to the two men. "Suffice it to say that I am assuming control over the palace's security. Any attempt to obstruct me will be considered a *de facto* attempt at threatening the Prince's safety – and thus treason. I have included a *précis* of legal cases for your edification in the datadump."

Hicks started to splutter. "But..."

"But nothing," Belinda said. "You may wish to refer to the case of *Travis V. Establishment* or *Jalap V. Establishment*. In both cases, the precedence of the Emperor's liegemen was upheld by the Grand Senate."

She had to smile. Lawyers all over the Empire specialised in digging up precedents from the past – and there were so many precedents that they could point in any direction, depending on which particular precedents were exhumed. And the Emperor's powers had been chipped away over the generations...and Roland was the Crown Prince, not yet crowned Emperor...but would they dare to oppose her? If they tried and failed, their careers would be over.

"In any case, I also have authority to take more...*direct* measures if you appear to threaten the Prince's safety," she added. "There are precedents that allow for the summary execution of known traitors."

Hicks went pale. Legally, starship commanders and military commanders did have authority to execute their subordinates if they believed they had cause, even though it was rarely used in the field. A CO who *did* execute one of his subordinates would certainly face a hostile Board of Inquiry at the very least, as well as a lawsuit from the dead soldier's relatives – and most of the officers who deserved execution had powerful families or patrons. Belinda might not get away with executing Hicks, but that would be no consolation to the pitiful man.

"I see where this is going," Singh said. "You are asserting control over the entire security edifice."

"That is correct," Belinda said. If she had the authority, she was going to damn well use it to carry out her primary mission. "I will be bringing in outsiders who will bring a fresh approach to the task of protecting the prince. Until then, you will cooperate and coordinate your operations. I understand that both of you have secrets you wish to protect – and I don't give a damn. Your task is protecting the Prince. If either of you wish to resign now…"

"You cannot force us to resign," Hicks protested.

"Actually, I can," Belinda told him. She cut off a renewed protest with a glare. "And *you* will not be issuing *any* more orders. You will remain in your quarters and not interfere with my operations. Your second can serve as my deputy."

She looked over at Singh. "You've done marginally better than Colonel Hicks," she added. "Cooperate – or be relieved too."

"I will cooperate," Singh said. He hesitated. "But who do you intend to bring into the security team?"

"People I can trust to know what they're doing and work together," Belinda said. She wondered if she could convince Singh to transfer to the Civil Guard – Senate Security's team could be dismissed, but she needed the Civil Guard to man the perimeter – before deciding that it was probably unlikely. "And that will be *my* decision."

She scowled at Hicks. "Go directly to your quarters and stay there," she ordered. "You will remain in nominal command of the Civil Guard detachment, but I will issue instructions that any orders from you are to be disregarded. If I hear that you have been attempting to interfere with my operation, I will execute you on the spot. Do you understand me?"

Hicks lowered his eyes.

"Yes," he said, so quietly that Belinda barely heard him.

Ass, Belinda thought, coldly. If he'd done his job properly, right from the start, she wouldn't have had to break him. But he'd left her no choice.

"Go," she said.

She watched Hicks shuffling out of the room and down towards the living quarters for the security staff. He had a small apartment suite to himself, thankfully. It would serve to keep him out of trouble, at least until she could have him transferred to a different unit.

Good, she told herself. *Now all I have to do is find a few good men.*

CHAPTER TWENTY-THREE

...But they were not the only ones. Countless other radical groups arose on Earth. Some of them believed that the only way to mend the Empire was to force the Grand Senate to impose changes, even if those changes happened to be profoundly against the Grand Senate's interests. Others just wanted power for themselves...and still others were puppets of shadowy factions that thrived on chaos. And still others were centred upon apocalyptic religions that were growing up in the Undercity. All of them made demands that the Empire could not meet.

- Professor Leo Caesius, *The End of Empire.*

The Imperial Palace had been designed as more than just the Emperor's residence, back when the Empire was young. It was intended to serve as the nerve centre of Empire, playing host to the officials who translated the Emperor's instructions into action. Now, Jeremy knew, the Grand Senate used it as a meeting point, rather than the Senate Hall. Their control over the Imperial Palace was an unsubtle reminder of their control over the Empire.

When he'd first visited the Imperial Palace, he had been impressed by the colossal pyramid that made up the base of the Palace. Now, he couldn't help thinking that the Palace was not only ugly, but a metaphor for the Empire itself. The base held a small army of bureaucrats who were not allowed to do anything – particularly thinking – without direct orders from higher up, while the upper levels held the Emperor and his immediate family. Or they would have done, if there *was* an Emperor. Roland would not take up residence in the Imperial Palace until he was crowned Emperor. Until then, the Grand Senate had free use of the structure.

His aircar drifted down towards the landing pad. The summons had probably been meant as a surprise, but he'd been expecting it ever since the unauthorised protest march had turned into a riot. Media coverage had been very hostile to the Marines – and that, Jeremy knew, would only have happened with the express permission of the Grand Senate. There was no such thing as an independent media in the Empire, except on a very small scale. The big media corporations were all owned by the Grand Senators. Untangling the network of shell companies and hidden bank accounts was tricky, but doable – if one cared to look. Most citizens sucked in the news without wondering who benefited from pushing a particular viewpoint while burying others.

There was a faint bump as the aircar touched down, followed rapidly by a hiss as the door opened. Jeremy climbed out, feeling as if he was walking towards his own execution. The politicians who had summoned him ruled the Empire, their positions effectively unassailable – and yet they knew nothing of honour, or loyalty. Jeremy was ruefully aware that he'd spent much of his career cleaning up messes the Grand Senate had – directly or indirectly – caused, but none of the battles he'd fought had been more than short-term victories. The factors that caused the rebellions often remained in place, ensuring that the war would be refought at some later date.

He shook his head as a trio of armoured guards greeted him, ran sensors over his body and removed his pistol and spare clips of ammunition. At least the Grand Senate was taking its own security seriously, although it didn't seem to stop them weakening their own long-term position by backing the Empire's population into a corner. How many planets would have become productive parts of the Empire if the Grand Senate's rules hadn't crippled them? For what was, to all intents and purposes, an aristocracy, they seemed to have little sense of the long term.

But maybe that wasn't too surprising, he considered, as the guards escorted him down the corridor and into the secure room. It had only been a few decades since Grand Senator Medici had died. The official report had said that it had been an accident, but Jeremy rather doubted it;

the Grand Senator had been pushing some very minor reforms when he died. If he'd succeeded…but he hadn't succeeded – and other would-be reformers had taken note. A Grand Senator had died – who else could feel safe?

He kept his face under control as he was escorted into the Chamber of Government. Traditionally, the Grand Senators would assemble in the chamber to hear the Emperor's yearly speech to his government – but the tradition hadn't been honoured for centuries, ever since the Grand Senate had taken the levers of power away from the Emperor. Instead, it served as a secure meeting place for the Grand Senators, a place where they could debate matters to their heart's content. And, for that matter, interrogate anyone they summoned to their presence.

There were one hundred Grand Senators in all. By law, the distribution of Grand Senators was based on population – which meant that sixty of the Grand Senators belonged to Earth or the other Core Worlds. Few Inner Worlds had the population to influence election to the Grand Senate, while Outer Worlds and Rim Worlds had none. In theory, five Grand Senators were elected by the Outer Worlds, but in practice those Senators had never been near the worlds they were supposed to represent. And then the seats had effectively become hereditary. To all intents and purposes, the Outer Worlds had no representation in the Grand Senate.

"Please, be seated," the Speaker said. "We are gathered here to discuss weighty matters."

Jeremy nodded as he sat down where the Grand Senators could see him. He had a distinct feeling that deals had been struck even before the formal meeting had been called; several Grand Senators were obviously sitting together, making their alliances clear for all to see. Others were keeping their thoughts well-concealed, leaving Jeremy to wonder just what might have been decided before he'd arrived. Collectively, the Grand Senate was all-powerful. Who knew *what* they might have decided…?

"We shall first hear from Senior Functionary Tiburon," the Speaker said. "He has compiled an exhaustive report for us."

Tiburon was a grey man wearing the traditional grey uniform of the Imperial Civil Service, looking vaguely uncomfortable under the spotlight. His voice was dry, but Jeremy fancied that he could hear nervousness under the droll precise tone. Perhaps it wasn't surprising; it had been centuries since the ICS had been politically neutral. Right now, Tiburon's report could make or break his career. If he didn't tell the Grand Senators what they wanted to hear...

"Overall, seventeen thousand have been confirmed dead or wounded since the rioting in Imperial City," Tiburon said, after a brief outline of the events leading up to the riot. "The injured who do not require immediate medical treatment have been told to return to their apartments and stay there until they can be dealt with, as Earth's medical stockpiles have been largely exhausted. Emergency orders have been placed for additional supplies, but the producers warn that they may be a long time in coming.

"Twelve thousand remain in custody, scattered over various makeshift holding facilities," the bureaucrat continued. "Their ultimate fate has yet to be determined, but legal challenges have already been mounted to their incarceration. A number of injured have also been arrested..."

Jeremy kept his face blank as Tiburon droned on, repeating facts he already knew – and, he was sure, the Grand Senators knew too. He understood the value of ensuring that everyone knew, even if it did mean going over the same facts time and time again, but this was excessive. Perhaps they were just trying to lull him into a false sense of confidence, or maybe the bureaucrats had something they wanted to bury under a mountain of bullshit. Either one seemed to make sense...

"The preliminary investigation has finally been completed," Tiburon said. "Certain issues have yet to be explored thoroughly, but various facts are clear. First, the marchers had access to a number of forbidden weapons, which they used to deadly effect. Second, the forces on hand to respond to the march were utterly insufficient to the task. Third, the Marine force that responded to the crisis used excessive violence and was directly responsible for a number of deaths."

The spotlight fell on Jeremy. "Commandant," the Speaker said. "Would you care to respond to that charge?"

Jeremy had a nasty feeling that he'd been ambushed, but there was no alternative to pressing ahead and hoping for the best.

"It is unfortunately true that a number of rioters died during our attempts to apprehend them," he said. Unlike the Civil Guard, the Marine Corps tried to learn from its mistakes. "However, in almost all cases, the dead were either using lethal weapons themselves or put themselves in deadly positions. One dead rioter was throwing stones from a statue when he was stunned; he lost his grip on the statue and fell to his death. Several others died of being trampled by their fellows as they tried to flee the advancing Marines."

He gritted his teeth, knowing that the Senators wouldn't appreciate what he had to tell them. "The riot was already out of control when we arrived," he reminded them. "Do you think that the death toll would have been any lesser if no Marines had been involved?"

"But the Marine Corps has taken most of the blame," Tiburon said, when the Speaker invited him to continue. "Public opinion believes that the presence of armed Marines on the streets only made a bad situation worse."

Jeremy, who cared little for public opinion and knew that the Senators cared even less, was unimpressed. But it *was* having an effect on the Marines. He'd had to order the few remaining Marines on Earth confined to barracks, if only to prevent fights between them and Civil Guardsmen who believed the crap media talking heads were spewing out about the Corps. Marine Intelligence had wondered if someone had deliberately set out to incriminate the Corps, or provide an excuse for further limiting their activities. It seemed quite likely; after all, the Civil Guard had killed a hell of a lot more protestors.

"This situation needs to be handled with tact, but firmness," Grand Senator Stephen Onge said, when called upon to speak. "I believe that we should start by removing the Marines from Earth."

Jeremy realised, as the Speaker called for a vote, that the issue must have been planned and settled in advance. Onge, for whatever reason, wanted the Marines gone from Earth. Even if they just went to Luna, it would take hours to get back to Earth to respond to a new crisis – if they were allowed to return. Jeremy had wondered why the Grand Senate had called Captain Stalker to face them personally; now, he realised that the

Grand Senate had seen an opportunity to send a company of Marines to the edge of the Empire, well away from Earth.

The motion passed, with only a handful of Grand Senators in opposition.

Stephen allowed himself a cold smile as he watched the Commandant's face. Blaming the Marines for the disaster in Imperial City was completely unfair – even *he* would acknowledge that – but it had provided an opportunity to get the Marines away from Earth. There was a follow-up force assembling to head to Albion; the Earth-based Marines could join it, leaving Earth behind forever.

"Removing the Marines should help quiet local protest," he said, when silence fell in the chamber. It was time to gamble. "However, we must face facts. The security situation on Earth is deteriorating."

He tapped points off on his fingers as he spoke. "The sudden rise in food prices has caused unrest," he continued. "The economic turmoil caused by the destruction of Orbit Station Seven has caused unrest. The response to the student protest has caused unrest. Let us not forget, Honoured Senators, that there was even an assassination attempt on our beloved Prince! We cannot let this go unanswered."

Dramatically, he pulled a piece of paper out of his robe and waved it in the air. "We fund the students as they make their way through Imperial University," he proclaimed. "And what is our reward? Demands! Outrageous demands! Demands that we could not meet, even if we were inclined to try! How many of you believe that we could order all debts to be written off?"

He paused for effect. "And that is the *least* of their demands," he added. "Should we accept their final demand and give them a share in government? Who do they think they are?

"We must respond to this challenge, Honoured Senators, and we must respond to it in a manner that will ensure that it does not rise again," he thundered. "I propose that we declare a full state of emergency and bring additional troops to Earth!"

There was a brief outburst of applause, but he hadn't finished. "In order to lower the unrest, we shall apply both the carrot and the stick," he said. "We shall officially pardon the arrested students, on the condition that they stay out of trouble in future. We shall encourage the algae-farms to expand their production of food supplies to ensure that everyone has enough to eat; we shall provide subsidies to encourage the importation of new food supplies from the Inner Worlds. But we will also put more troops on the streets."

He lowered his voice. "A terrorist group turned a protest march into a riot," he said, "and attempted to assassinate Prince Roland. We will hunt those terrorists down like the dogs they are! We will show them that terrorism cannot force us to bow our heads in submission!"

Sitting down, he waited for the vote. Some of his allies had been carefully primed to speak in favour of his motion, others had been pushing for a harsher response to the crisis ever since the student riot. Between the vote – and the backroom deliberations – he knew he would get what he wanted out of the affair, the power to take control of the Empire.

Catching the terrorists wouldn't pose a problem – after all, Bode led them and he knew how to find Bode – but that wasn't the true objective. Radicals of all stripes could be rounded up under the guise of searching for terrorists, while undirected riots could be quickly and brutally crushed. But not too quickly. If the situation seemed to worsen, the Grand Senate would rally around the man who promised to deliver them from chaos. They wouldn't see the knife in his hand until it was too late.

The vote passed, almost without objection.

Jeremy would have freely shown his rage and frustration if there had been any point. The Grand Senate had avoided the issue of bringing charges against specific Marines, but they'd made it clear that all Marines had to leave Earth. In some ways, it would be a relief to take his men out of a dangerously unstable situation, yet abandoning Earth wasn't an option. It was the one world that humanity could not afford to let slip into chaos.

But if it did…the entire Marine Corps might not be able to make a difference.

He planned all this, Jeremy thought, looking at Onge. The Grand Senator had not only proposed his carrot-and-stick approach, he'd apparently already started to gather troops for deployment on Earth. Oh, he'd been careful to make it look like a coincidence, but Jeremy knew to be suspicious of convenient coincidences. Nothing he'd done – at least nothing that Jeremy actually knew about – was illegal, at least not for a Grand Senator. And yet it left Jeremy smelling a rat.

Marines weren't really intended for crowd control, but they did have far more training and discipline than the Civil Guard, let alone the near-mercenaries that the Grand Senate wanted to bring in to reinforce the Guardsmen. Jeremy couldn't see anything other than disaster coming out of the new deployment, a disaster that might be difficult to deal with. But what could he do? The Grand Senate had made up its mind.

There's always Safehouse, he thought, grimly. It had seemed an unnecessary precaution when he'd inherited it from his predecessor. Now, it seemed like their only hope. Maybe something could be salvaged from the coming apocalypse.

There was one bright spot to the disaster, he told himself, as the Grand Senate pushed through one security measure after another. He'd intended to chew Specialist Lawson out for swearing an oath to Prince Roland. It wasn't technically against regulations, but only because no one had considered it a serious possibility. Marines weren't meant to serve specific Emperors – let alone Princes. But being Prince Roland's liegeman would automatically override her position as a Marine, meaning she wouldn't have to leave Earth. At least the Prince would be in good hands.

For what it's worth, he thought, numbly. Prince Roland would be better off grabbing what he could, changing his name and running for the Rim. He was little more than a rubberstamp for the Grand Senate, at best. The population would blame him for whatever steps the Grand Senate took to restore order. But there was nothing Jeremy could do about it.

The next proposal concerned businesses. In order to prevent a sudden surge in unemployment, businesses would be forbidden to lay anyone off until the crisis came to an end. Jeremy had never been a businessman, but even *he* could see the problem with that. If a business was so frail as to need to lay people off, how could it survive if it had to keep paying wages? If there was a subsidy from the Grand Senate...for the moment, they could keep the system going by moving money from one pocket to another. But it wouldn't last.

What will happen, he asked himself silently, *when the money runs out for good?*

He couldn't help feeling that the Empire had fallen too far to be saved.

Chapter Twenty-Four

One relatively simple demand was for debt relief. On paper, it seemed ideal; if the debts were cancelled, the indebted would have more money to spend on other things and jump-start the economy. However, if the debts were cancelled, the banks holding the debts would themselves fold. This would cripple what remained of the Empire's economy and wipe out the savings of billions of people, as well as rendering millions more unemployed.

- Professor Leo Caesius, The End of Empire.

"You *all* have to go?"

Belinda didn't believe in coincidences; the timing of the Grand Senate's decision was odd enough to suggest that it was no coincidence. She'd taken control of the Palace's security only yesterday, but her plan to bring in two platoons of Marines to serve as Roland's bodyguard had been ruined. If it had been deliberate...

"Every active Marine on the planet has been ordered to leave," the Commandant informed her. "That includes the HQ staff and myself; we're going to be moving to Armstrong Base, at least at first. The base on Earth will be sealed."

"Right," Belinda said. She'd had support cut off before in the middle of a mission, but this was particularly annoying – and dangerous. Roland needed an experienced close-protection detail that could be trusted. "There's no way you can get an exemption?"

"I doubt it," the Commandant said. He looked older than he had the last time Belinda had seen him, as if some great weight was finally crushing him. "You're the only active Marine who will be left on Earth – and only because you're Roland's liegeman. The rest are already on their way to orbit."

Belinda gritted her teeth. If it had been up to her, Roland would have left the planet by now – but it wasn't her choice. Or even his, really. Perhaps they could just stay in the Summer Palace and hope that the assassins weren't organised enough to attack a heavily-defended building. But then, the Grand Senate would expect Roland to keep making speeches and rubber-stamping their decrees. They wouldn't allow him to become a hermit. Hell, they'd probably expect him to continue patronising the Arena...

A thought struck her and she smiled. "I'll take care of the problem, sir," she assured the Commandant. "You just take care of yourself."

The Commandant eyed her for a long moment, then clearly held himself back from asking questions. He'd served long enough to know that there some answers would simply upset the questioner.

"Let's hope so," he said. "I'm sending you a secure datachip by courier. If the shit hits the fan, you can access it – and then do as you see fit."

His image vanished from the display. Belinda let out a long breath and then scowled, before logging back on to the Marine network. There was no such thing as an ex-Marine and, if a retired Marine happened to live on a given world, he would register with the local Marine network so that he could stay in touch with his brethren. The contact details for the twenty-seven retired Marines on Earth – nineteen of them working for the Arena – glowed in front of her mind. It was unlikely that the Grand Senate had intended to include them in the order to leave Earth.

They're clearing the decks for something big, she thought, as she prepared a message for the retired Marines. Roland had access to a surprisingly large expense account – it had shocked her to realise that it was peanuts compared to the seemingly-limitless wealth of the Grand Senate – and it could be used to hire bodyguards. It would be harder to get the right equipment for them, but her new status might just give her the clout to obtain it. If, of course, she could convince them to return to service.

She scowled as she clicked on to the main media network. The media was making a big song and dance about the prisoners being released, displaying images of young students having their handcuffs removed before walking out of the makeshift prisons. Generally, prisoners *weren't* handcuffed while they were in the cells; it didn't take much experience to recognise that the whole affair was a propaganda coup. But the media was also warning that more Civil Guardsmen were being deployed on Earth and further trouble would not be tolerated.

Belinda wasn't impressed. Much of Earth's surface was covered with cities; keeping them all under control would be an impossible task. Hell, the Civil Guard didn't even *try*. But if the Grand Senate was bringing in more security officers…she couldn't understand what they were planning to achieve. It might well be better, in the long run, to allow Earth to implode – after moving as much as they could off the planet. Earth had become a black hole, sucking in the Empire's resources…

But billions of people would die, she told herself, angrily.

On the other hand, she couldn't see the Grand Senate worrying overlong about mass slaughter. They'd ordered atrocities before…

Her implant buzzed. "Colonel Lawson, we have a request from the Grand Senate," the dispatcher said. "Grand Senator Onge wishes to meet with Prince Roland."

"Clear him for passage through the security network," Belinda ordered, as she stood up. The Prince wasn't being given a *choice*. He had to see the Grand Senator. "And make damn sure that you give him a full check before allowing him to enter the Palace."

Roland was in the next room, running through a series of exercises that Belinda had taught him. It wouldn't be long, she decided, before he could take the exercises to the next level; she'd already taught him how to shoot in the Palace's shooting range. Given time, he might have made a good soldier, even if it was unlikely he would ever have the discipline to become a Marine. The legacy of a childhood filled with luxury and indulgence would never fully fade away.

"Grand Senator Onge is coming to see you," Belinda said. "Are you ready to meet him?"

"Not really," Roland answered, standing up. Sweat was trickling down his face, glistening as it caught the light. "Do I have a choice in the matter?"

"Not really," Belinda pointed out. She checked her implants and discovered that the Senator would be visiting in less than an hour. "Go shower, then get into your formal robes. You may as well look the part."

Roland gave her an odd look. "Are you all right?"

"The plan to get you some Marine bodyguards fell through," Belinda admitted. She briefly outlined what the Grand Senate had ordered – and her own puzzlement. Their decision didn't seem to make any sense and, as she'd been taught in Pathfinder School, that suggested that there was something she didn't know. Just because a decision made no sense to her didn't mean that the person who'd taken it didn't know what they were doing. "I'm trying to find you some retired Marines to serve as additional bodyguards."

"Oh," Roland said. He scowled thoughtfully, then changed the subject. "Does the Grand Senator know about you?"

Belinda honestly didn't know. In theory, only a handful of people knew that she wasn't just Roland's aide – or at least that had been true, before she'd had to assert her authority. She was reasonably sure that neither Hicks nor Singh had bitched to their patrons about her, but it was quite possible that one of their subordinates also had political patrons. The habits of a lifetime – including sharing sensitive information with their political superiors – might not be broken by graphic threats, even from a Marine Pathfinder.

The Grand Senator shouldn't know. But that didn't mean that he *didn't* know.

"Maybe," she replied, finally. She'd just have to monitor the Grand Senator carefully and attempt to determine the truth. "Go shower. We'll find out in an hour."

Stephen refused to show any reaction as the Senate Security team scanned both him and Lindy before allowing them to enter the Summer Palace. Normally, he would have been annoyed at being poked and prodded by the staff, but he had to admit that they had good reason to be on their toes. Twelve of their comrades had died, barely a day ago, and that would be enough to alarm *anyone*, even a security team that had been allowed to grow lax.

The Prince's new aide met them as soon as they were cleared by the security team. She was beautiful, Stephen had to admit, and seemed made of stronger stuff than the last few aides the Prince had gone through. Long blonde hair framed a perfect face and hung down over a tight shirt and a short skirt that revealed a pair of excellent legs. It might have been the product of the body-shops, Stephen reminded himself, but even so he had to admire the Prince's taste. He too had chosen his aides for looks, once upon a time.

"His Highness is waiting for you," the aide said. "If you will come with me, Honoured Senator…"

Stephen allowed her to lead him up the stairs and into the Prince's reception room, where Prince Roland sat on a small throne. The Grand Senate was not impressed by outward displays of power – they knew too much to mistake them for reality – but Stephen felt a cold chill as he realised that Prince Roland looked far more composed than he had expected. It had been months since he'd last met the Prince, yet the change was staggering. The Prince actually looked *healthy*.

He scowled inwardly as he bowed formally to the Prince. Roland had been carefully isolated from the levers of power almost as soon as he had been orphaned and brought up in the Summer Palace. No single Grand Senator had been able to gain and exercise power over the Prince – too much was at stake for the others to allow it – so Roland had effectively been left to drift. It had seemed the best solution at the time; a Prince whose only interest was his own pleasure was unlikely to upset the apple cart. And Roland had shown no signs of growing up into someone who could use his formal position to build a power base of his own.

Now, however…he looked healthier and more determined than anyone had expected. Stephen had heard vague reports, but they hadn't troubled him; in hindsight, perhaps he should have taken a closer look at the young man. Roland had deliberately been kept ignorant and yet…as he looked at the Prince, he thought he saw a certain comprehension in his eyes that had been lacking the last time they'd met.

"Your Highness," he said. "I speak on behalf of the Grand Senate."

"We welcome you," Roland said, in a clear and formal tone. "Your service is appreciated by Us."

Stephen bit down the anger that threatened to overwhelm him. The Empire was poised on the brink between apotheosis and nemesis and this young fop dared to take that tone to him? Roland had been sitting in his palace, wasting away, while Stephen had been making his preparations for one final gambit to save the Empire. If Roland hadn't been part of his plan, Stephen would have stormed out and ensured that the next set of assassins would have succeeded. The Prince was useless for anything, apart from rubber-stamping decrees.

And once he had served his purpose, he would be eliminated.

"The Grand Senate has passed Emergency Bill #23," Stephen said. In over three thousand years only seventy emergency bills had been proposed – and only twenty-two had ever been approved. There were literally *millions* of standard bills, but emergency bills came into effect as soon as the Emperor stamped them into law. "We request that you place your signature to the bill."

The Prince's aide came forward and passed him a datapad. There was a long moment as the Prince scanned the bill, his lips moving as he sounded out some of the longer words. One definite advantage emergency bills had was that they were short, concise and sweeping; a standard bill could be longer than a small novel and read in their entirety by very few people. The old Roland wouldn't have asked questions, Stephen knew, but the new one…he kept his thoughts and feelings under tight control. There was no time to do anything about the Prince now.

"Interesting," Roland said, finally.

Stephen would have rolled his eyes, if he'd felt like it. Was *interesting* all the Prince could say? But then, he probably didn't understand what he was reading, even if the language was clear and blunt. A state of emergency would be declared, a three-man emergency committee would handle law enforcement operations on Earth, the Marines would leave the planet, food and drink prices would be frozen, normal legal rights would be suspended…and Stephen, as the leader of the emergency committee, would be in place to tighten his grip on power. It was a coup, to all intents and purposes, and it was perfectly legal.

"We have no choice but to sign," Roland said, grandly. "However, We must also caution you. Our homeworld is in an unstable state. We do not wish to see it become another Han."

"We will take control to prevent that from happening," Stephen assured him. One day, he promised himself, he would no longer need Roland. And then the Prince could be eliminated. "Our goal is to prevent the complete collapse of law and order."

There was a long pause. Roland eyed him, then nodded slowly and pressed his thumbprint against the datapad.

"Thank you," Stephen said. He wasn't sure what he would have done if Roland had refused to grant his assent. It wasn't needed, technically speaking, but some legalistic asshole would probably have made a fuss. For the moment, the Grand Senate was following him, yet that wouldn't last. The smart ones wouldn't be blind to how much power they'd placed in his hands. "There is, however, another issue that needs to be raised with you."

Roland lifted a single eyebrow, politely.

"You are alone," Stephen said. "The next person in line to the Throne has only a vague claim – and it could be contested. Beyond him, there are seven people with roughly equal claims, all of whom could be used by different factions to tear the Empire apart. It is the wish of the Grand Senate that you marry and produce children."

The Prince looked shaken. No doubt he enjoyed his affair with his aide and wouldn't want to sacrifice it for married life. Not that he had to remain faithful to his wife, once she had given birth to two sons. There was no shortage of Imperial bastards out there, all officially disinherited from taking the Throne. They tended to be given a lump sum and told to go make their fortune along the Rim.

"We have selected you a bride," Stephen continued. "The Honourable Lily of House Sapphire is of good bloodline and in excellent health. You should have no difficulty in producing heirs with her."

Lily Sapphire had other advantages, Stephen knew. She wasn't a close relation to any of the Grand Senators, so the balance of power wouldn't be badly affected. But her family *did* have close ties to Stephen, which was at least partly why he'd put her name forward. She could be relied upon to follow her father's lead – and her father knew which side of the bread Stephen had buttered for him. He would do what he was told.

Roland looked shaken. "She wants to marry me?"

Stephen grinned at him, noticing that the Prince had slipped into first-person. "Who wouldn't want to marry a handsome Prince?"

It didn't matter *what* Lily thought. Her marriage had been arranged by the Grand Senate; if she'd refused to undergo the ceremony, she would be disinherited and thrown out of the upper class. A few days in the Undercity would teach her better manners, assuming she survived. Like most of the upper class children, she had been cosseted and pampered until she had mush between her ears. She *was* fertile, and she *was* pretty, and that was enough for the Grand Senate's purposes.

"I'll have to think about it," Roland stated, slowly. "I have never even *met* the girl."

"Don't think too long," Stephen advised. "Your Highness, these are troubled times for the Empire. Whatever we can do to distract the population from their woes must be done. A Royal Wedding may buy us enough time to save the Empire.

"We shall also see to your security," he added. "I shall have Admiral Valentine arrange more guards for the Summer Palace. The terrorists must not be allowed a clear shot at you."

He bowed and turned to leave. Roland was clearly sharper and more dangerous than he'd realised. It was possible that the shock of nearly being killed had concentrated his mind on something more than pleasure…and if that were the case, he might become a problem. He would have to be dealt with firmly.

"They want me to get married?"

"So it would seem," Belinda said, absently. Most of her mind was considering the provisions of Emergency Bill #23. The Grand Senate might not have realised just how much power they'd handed over to the emergency committee. It had been a long time since the Tyrant Emperor had concentrated a great deal of power in his hands. The next tyrant might not even be of royal blood.

She glanced into the exhaustive files compiled by Marine Intelligence, but there was very little on Lily Sapphire. The girl was barely fourteen years old; the single picture suggested a personality that might have been well-matched with the old Roland. But pictures could present a misleading image.

Belinda shook her head, tiredly. The Grand Senator hadn't shown any sign of realising what she actually was, but if he followed through on his threat to send additional guards the cat would definitely get out of the bag. And then…?

"We'll just have to see what happens," she said, tightly. She had the uncomfortable feeling that a noose was being drawn tight around her neck. Her combat instincts had never failed her before. "And make some contingency plans, just in case."

CHAPTER TWENTY-FIVE

It would be a mistake to believe that the Grand Senators were unaware of the looming disaster. Unlike the civilians, the Grand Senators had access to unmassaged data and knew the truth. However, they faced a dilemma that made it difficult for them to act. If they made sweeping changes to the system, they risked destroying the base of their own power – and provoking rebellion from among their own followers. But if they didn't, their power base would eventually collapse when the Empire itself fell to rubble.

- Professor Leo Caesius, The End of Empire.

"Emergency Bill #23, signed by Prince Roland four days ago, has ordered an immediate freeze in food prices," the talking head said. "It has been declared illegal to raise food prices above an officially-mandated limit or to hoard food supplies in the hopes that the price will start to rise again. A number of shopkeepers have been arrested for failing to follow the new directives and…"

Jacqueline clicked the display off in exasperation. She'd *been* to the shops and discovered that there was hardly any food to be had, apart from the standard algae bars. And *they* were being rationed. Normally, one could buy as many algae bars as one wanted, but no longer. Jacqueline had only been able to buy five bars – enough for a week – and had been cautioned by the shopkeeper that hoarding was thoroughly illegal. What the fuck did they think that she was going to do? Five bars hardly constituted a *hoard*.

She hadn't been to the protest march that had turned into a riot, but she'd seen dozens of injured students and felt the sullen defiance pervading the university. If she had been able to afford it, she would have moved away from the university or simply gone back home, rather than stay in a place that felt as if it were on the verge of exploding. But she didn't have the money to leave, any more than her parents could afford to come and collect her. All she could do was wait and pray that the whole crisis blew over.

No one had seen anything of Amethyst since the riot either. Amethyst's name wasn't on the list of dead students – or on the list of students who had been arrested and held in custody prior to their release. Jacqueline, worried about her friend, had asked around, but no one seemed to know anything. Admittedly, her friend *had* been spending time with a new boyfriend, yet she wasn't even answering her handcom or replying to messages. Surely she could just send back a brief note to tell Jacqueline that she was alive and well.

Jacqueline splashed hot water into a mug, poured in a handful of flavoured granules and slowly stirred it with a plastic spoon. Amethyst's disappearance worried her on more than just one level. They shared the apartment, but if Amethyst stopped paying her share of the rent they would both be evicted. And if that happened…Jacqueline had few illusions about the future. Where the hell would they live? Come to think of it, they wouldn't be able to afford *anywhere*.

She fretted about it as she nibbled one of the algae bars. As always, it tasted like cardboard, even though the sellers swore blind that the bars provided everything a growing human would need. The flavoured bars were much more expensive – and besides, they too had been in short supply over the last month. Only the very basic bars had been available in the stores, even though algae was *easy* to produce. What did *that* mean for the future?

Shaking her head, she picked up the datapad and tried to concentrate on her course notes for art and design. All classes had been cancelled, but she'd been falling behind; she needed to study, if only so she could parrot everything she had read back to the tutor. A few moments later, she gave up in disgust. She just couldn't concentrate.

Absently, she picked up her handcom and sent another message to Amethyst. There was no reply. She swore out loud as she put the handcom down and walked into the bathroom, undressing and stepping into the shower. They'd received all sorts of lectures on saving water when they first moved into the apartment block, but few of the students had taken them seriously at the time. Now, the water seemed lukewarm rather than hot – and several students had received warning notices stating that they would be evicted if they didn't control their usage. Jacqueline had no idea what it meant, but she doubted that it was anything good.

The lights flickered briefly as she washed and dried herself, causing her to swear out loud. *That* had become an increasingly regular occurrence – and it had caused her to panic, the first time it had happened. There were no windows in their little apartment; if the power went out for more than a few seconds they would be plunged into instant darkness. She'd heard rumours that other apartment blocks had lost power completely, each story more horrifying than the last, but she didn't know what to believe. The news media had never reported any such stories.

Jacqueline glanced at the handcom – Amethyst *still* hadn't replied – and stepped into her tiny bedroom. The walls seemed to be closing in on her, the room growing smaller and smaller every day…she knew it was an illusion, but it was proving very difficult to shake. If she'd been able to go outside…but no, half of the student nightclubs had been shut down and besides, she didn't have anyone to go with. And the campus was crawling with university cops and Civil Guardsmen. Maybe she was going crazy. There was no shortage of rumours about other students going mad from the pressure and doing stupid things. She pushed the thought aside, lay down on the bed and closed her eyes. Perhaps the world would look better in the morning.

It felt like no time had passed before she heard the buzzer. Jacqueline shook herself awake and glanced at her handcom; it was two am. Who could be calling at this hour? Amethyst didn't need someone to open the door for her, unless the fingerprint sensor was bust again; who else would want to visit so late at night? Jacqueline was tempted just to stick her head back under the covers and ignore the sound, but what if it *was* Amethyst? She couldn't leave her friend outside for the night. Muttering curses under her breath, she rolled out of bed, pulled a thin nightgown on to cover herself and stepped out into the living room.

Someone was banging on the door, she realised. The metal square seemed to be on the verge of exploding inwards, allowing whoever it was outside to get in. She glanced at the monitor and blinked in surprise as she saw a university cop and three Civil Guardsmen. What were *they* doing outside? She couldn't think of anything she might have done to attract their attention. Perhaps it was just a routine test of their security…she reached for the handle and opened the door. The next moment, she found herself shoved backwards by an immensely strong man.

"What…?"

"Shut up," the man barked, as he pushed her into the wall. Jacqueline was too stunned to offer any resistance, even when her nose was rammed into the metal. He caught her hands and pulled them behind her back, slipping on a pair of handcuffs. "Name?"

It took several moments for Jacqueline to reply. "Jacqueline, sir," she said. They'd been advised to always cooperate with the university cops when they first entered Imperial University, but she'd never heard of the university cops breaking into someone's apartment…the sensation of being handcuffed was eerie, as if she was looking down at herself from outside her body. "I…"

He swung her round and glared at her, his breath smelling faintly unpleasant. "Where is your roommate?"

"I…I don't know," Jacqueline stammered. A small army of Civil Guardsmen seemed to be staring down at her, their eyes flickering over the thin nightgown. She suddenly wished that she'd paid more attention to those rumours. Some of the stories told by the arrested students had been horrific. "I don't know."

"Your roommate is your friend, right?" The man demanded. "And you don't know where she is?"

Jacqueline shook her head mutely.

"Not much of a friend," the man sneered. His hands ran over her body, searching her – although quite what he thought she was hiding in the thin nightgown was beyond her. "Sit here" – he pushed her to the floor as he spoke – "and wait."

Jacqueline sat, barely able to feel her hands because the cuffs were on so tight, and watched in dismay as the Civil Guardsmen searched the tiny apartment. Amethyst's room came in for special attention; everything she had inside was dragged out into the living room and inspected, one by one. Jacqueline couldn't help staring as they went through her friend's clothes, as if they expected to find something hidden inside her undergarments. She'd thought that only happened in bad entertainment flicks. There was a crash as something shattered and she winced. Even if they left without doing any more damage, it would take hours to clean up the apartment.

"That's my room," she protested, as several Guardsmen opened the door and headed inside. "You…"

"Shut up," one of the men barked.

Moments later, they were emptying her possessions out into the living room too. Jacqueline couldn't help blushing as they found her small collection of sexy underwear, including a pair of thongs that her first boyfriend had given to her. He'd spent more credits on them than she'd been able to put aside from her BLA every month, something that had touched her heart before she'd discovered that he was cheating on her. The remarks the Guardsmen made left her feeling helplessly exposed and vulnerable as they pawed their way through her possessions. All they had to do was look at her and they would see most of her secrets.

"Add a charge of hoarding to the list," the man who had cuffed her said, dropping three of the ration bars to the floor in front of her. "Don't you know that stockpiling food is forbidden?"

Jacqueline stared at him, then felt tears welling up inside her. She'd heard rumours…but she'd never really paid close attention, even after so many students had been arrested without charge. There were so many laws, rules and regulations on Earth that it was impossible to keep them all straight; pretty much everyone broke one or more laws every month, without even knowing it. But three ration bars was hardly a large stockpile…

"I…"

She started to cry, great heaving sobs that seemed to wrack her entire body. The Guardsmen stared at her, then returned to searching the apartment. She barely noticed when they put the datapad she'd been issued by the university in an evidence bag, along with a random selection of clothing. The man who'd cuffed her produced a bottle of something from his belt and pushed it gently against her lips. It tasted thin and mildly unpleasant, but she gulped it down gratefully. She was almost grateful for the hand he put on her shoulder, even though she knew it shouldn't have been comforting.

One of the Guardsmen let out a shout of triumph. "I found it!"

Jacqueline blinked. Found what? Amethyst's private collection of dirty pictures? A small stockpile of alcohol and pleasure drugs? She honestly couldn't imagine her friend having anything that might interest the Guardsmen; God knew neither alcohol nor pleasure drugs were actually illegal. Besides, if they'd started arresting students for overindulging themselves they would have to arrest most of the campus.

One of the Guardsmen shoved a book under her nose. "Do you know what this is?"

Jacqueline shuddered in recognition. Richard – the boy who had so impressed Amethyst – had given Amethyst the book. Jacqueline had never read it, but she had a feeling that wouldn't be enough to save her. Richard had *warned* them that the book was thoroughly illegal. But she hadn't even known that Amethyst had kept the book in their apartment.

"The possession of a book on the banned list can earn the possessor exile from Earth," the Guardsman said, softly. "Tell me; where did your friend get the book?"

He shook Jacqueline roughly as she started to cry again. "You can talk to us now or you can talk to us down at the station," he said. "If the latter, you may be charged as an accessory to your friend's crime…"

Jacqueline struggled to think clearly. She was tired and upset and sore – and no matter how much she flexed her hands, she couldn't break the handcuffs. They seemed almost to be getting tighter and tighter. Amethyst was her friend, but Amethyst was gone – and left her to face the Civil Guard. And her parents would be broken-hearted if their daughter was exiled from Earth, if they ever found out what had happened to her. So many students had been lost in the confusion that they might never learn the truth.

"Help me help you," the Guardsman said, gently. "Tell us the truth and you will have nothing to fear."

"There was a boy," Jacqueline confessed, finally. She ran through the whole story, despite the Guardsman's frequent interruptions, concluding with the meeting they'd had at the nightclub and her decision not to go back. The whole affair had seemed thoroughly pointless to her. If half of what Richard had told them was true, what the hell could they do? "I...I don't know anything else."

"Your friend seems to have become a domestic terrorist," the Guardsman informed her. "Did you know what happened to her?"

Jacqueline shook her head, frantically.

"I believe you," the Guardsman said. He stood up. "Stay there," he added. "I need to speak to my superiors."

Jacqueline scowled at his retreating back. Stay there, he'd said. As if she had any choice! Shame welled up within her as she realised that she'd betrayed her friend, but if Amethyst had become a domestic terrorist... what should she have done? She just wanted to be a student...

Sure, part of her mind whispered. *And what hope do you have of finding a job now?*

She felt tears falling on her breasts as she started to sob again. Everyone knew that their records followed them throughout their lives. Even if the Civil Guardsmen didn't charge her with anything – and it dawned on her that they could charge her for not betraying Richard at once – she'd still be recorded as the friend of a known terrorist. The job market would be permanently closed to her.

There was another crash as one of her entertainment devices was dropped on the ground. Normally, it would have outraged her to see the device treated so roughly – they were expensive; hers had been a gift from her parents that had been several years worth of birthday presents rolled into one – but now she found it hard to care. Instead, she just stared down at the floor, wondering if she could just close her eyes and forget the world. Her parents were going to be so disappointed in her...they'd hoped that their daughter would be the first in the family to escape the BLA. But it didn't look as if they were going to get their wish.

"You're going to have to come with us to the station," the Guardsman said, as he returned. "There will be other questions for you."

Jacqueline stared at him in absolute betrayal. He'd pushed her into talking…and he wasn't even upholding his end of the bargain! But then, it had been stupid of her to think that he could just let her go. Even if she wasn't under arrest, she was someone who could identify Richard and Amethyst…and the others she'd seen at the nightclub. Of course he wasn't going to let her go!

"Can…" She started to cough and had to clear her throat before she could speak again. "Can I get dressed first?"

"No time," the Guardsman said, as he helped her to her feet. "I'm afraid we have to leave now."

"But…"

"But nothing," the Guardsman said sharply. His voice hardened. "The first priority is getting you to the station as quickly as possible. You will be provided with clothes there."

Jacqueline swallowed, hard. Everyone was going to see her marched down the corridors and into the Civil Guard aircar, wearing nothing more than a thin nightgown and a pair of handcuffs. She would *never* recover from the embarrassment and humiliation of being under arrest…even if she *wasn't* under arrest, the witnesses would certainly *think* that she was under arrest. They'd probably take photographs and upload them to the university network. If someone could take photos of their girlfriend in the nude and share them, there was no reason why they couldn't share photographs of her. Or videos…it was the middle of the night, but she knew that plenty of students would still be awake. There were no classes, after all.

The Guardsman caught her arm and pushed her towards the door. "Walk slowly," he ordered. His voice was firm, unwilling to tolerate any more arguing. "Don't speak to anyone, apart from me. Keep your eyes lowered…"

Jacqueline barely heard him. Her mind was swimming, as if she were on the verge of fainting. If he hadn't been holding her, part of her mind realised, she might have collapsed…

And her parents were going to be so disappointed in her.

The thought mocked her as she was shoved out of the apartment, leaving everything familiar behind.

CHAPTER
TWENTY-SIX

This was nicely illustrated by the death of Grand Senator Medici. It is difficult to put together the precise details, but it appears that Medici intended to start a program of mild reform in his family's holdings. However, his family refused to tolerate his program and rebelled against him. At first, he was merely stalled in family meetings. Later, as he spoke to other families and tried to get them to join his program, he died in suspicious circumstances.

There was no real investigation. Medici's body was cremated and his ashes were scattered on his family's private vacation world – and his reforms, as minor as they were, undone before the flames had finally died. No one genuinely believed that the death had been an accident and the rest of the Grand Senate took note. In future, reformers would have to be very careful – or die.

- Professor Leo Caesius, *The End of Empire.*

Brent had never considered himself political.

Like most of the students at Imperial University, his life had revolved around enjoying himself as much as possible – and doing as little work as he could get away with. He'd only joined the protest march against rising food prices because a girl he'd been interested in – and her very adventurous girlfriends – had joined the march. None of them had expected the march to turn into a riot – or, after the Marines arrived, to wake up chained to a railing in a disused stadium. The Civil Guard couldn't do that; the students knew their rights. But their rights had been ignored...

Worse had happened. His would-be girlfriend had been mistreated while she was in their custody. Brent didn't know exactly what had happened, but his imagination filled in the details in graphic detail. The girl had been a bubbly outgoing sort, with more boyfriends and girlfriends than anyone else he knew. Now, she shied away from physical contact, particularly with men. The look in her eyes as she'd met his, even from across the room, had sent shivers down his spine. He didn't know for sure, but rape seemed the most likely answer.

She hadn't been the only one to be traumatised – or angry. Brent had become angry; how could someone – anyone – do that to innocent students? The mood of sullen anger and resentment pervading the campus had become rage; Brent had spent hours talking with other angry students, considering what they could do to strike back. They had no weapons, but some students knew where they could get some – or how to make their own. The next time the Civil Guard threw its weight around, they were in for a nasty surprise.

The students had known the moment the Civil Guardsmen entered the apartment block and made their way swiftly to the fifteenth floor. Brent had organised his little group at once, convinced that they were coming for him. Instead, the Guardsmen had headed to an apartment shared by two girls and gone inside. Brent had puzzled over that – as far as he knew, neither of the girls were anyone important – but used the time to get organised. Their only chance was to get in and out as quickly as possible.

He could hear banging and crashing from the raided apartment as his team took up position, but there was no point in trying to go any closer. Most of the students living in the apartment would pay no attention – there were louder noises every night – and those who did were bullied away by the Civil Guardsman standing outside the door. Brent felt a flicker of sympathy for the girls – he knew what it was like to have his room searched without permission – while he waited with his team in an open room just around the corner. Finally, the banging and crashing seemed to come to a halt.

Gambling, he made a show of walking around the corner – and almost stopped in surprise. There was one girl, looking small and pathetic compared to a Civil Guardsman wearing bulky armour, her hands cuffed behind her back. The nightgown she wore was so thin, almost translucent, that he could see her breasts and the patch of hair between her thighs. She looked so helpless that he felt a surge of rage, even as he ducked back around the corner. How could the Civil Guardsmen treat *anyone* like that? No doubt they would entertain themselves with her as they flew back to their barracks…

He motioned to the rest of his group as the Civil Guardsmen came around the corner, the girl in their midst. Few of them had any real experience with aggression, but they all remembered being mistreated during the protest march. There was a moment of hesitation, a moment where it could all have ended right there and then – and then Brent charged forward, screaming a rebel yell as loudly as he could. The Civil Guardsmen had bare seconds to reach for their weapons before the students started attacking them with baseball bats.

Brent knew better than to aim for their armour; the advice passed on by the handful of students with violent experience had been that the armour took a lot of force to crack. Instead, he aimed for their exposed faces and slammed the baseball bat right into their head. One of the students yelped as a Civil Guardsman slammed a fist into his face, but the others kept pushing forward, knocking the Guardsmen down by sheer weight of numbers. Brent found himself staring down at one of the Guardsmen, but he barely saw him. Instead, he saw the look on his would-be girlfriend's face as she'd shied away from him after her period in custody.

"Brent! Snap out of it, damn it!"

He came back to himself in a rush and stared down at what remained of the Civil Guardsman. His baseball bat was dripping with blood; the Guardsman's face had been smashed to a bloody and utterly unrecognisable pulp. They'd taken down *all* of the Guardsmen, although four students had been wounded, one badly. And the girl they'd arrested had fainted dead away.

"Get her cuffs off," he ordered.

He scowled as the students exchanged glances. How did one unlock a pair of cuffs anyway? They looked strong enough to need a molecular debonder to break – and none of the students had access to one. He didn't even know if there was one in the university. Shaking his head, he rolled the girl over – unable to avoid noting that her nightgown had ridden up, exposing a cute ass – and examined the cuffs. There was a fingerprint sensor on the metal cuffs. He smiled as he manoeuvred the closest Civil Guardsman over and pressed his fingertip against the sensor. The cuffs unlocked and he pulled them away from the girl before they could lock themselves again.

"You two, take her to the upper levels," he ordered. Their plans would have to be advanced, he knew; he keyed his handcom, sending a message to the rest of the group. "The rest of you, come with me."

Judy Thornton disliked students intensely. As a rule, they were arrogant bastards and bitches who thought that the sun shone out of their assholes. They all looked down on Judy and her fellow university cops, considering them little better than morons who couldn't even pass the entrance examinations to a very basic university. Given that few students could even *read* – and Judy *could* – it took some nerve to think such dumb thoughts. But most of the students were thoroughly dumb.

She stood in front of the nightclub, scowling at the students as they walked past, ignoring her so blatantly that she *knew* they were trying to annoy her. The sense of growing anger on the campus was easy to sense, but she did her best to ignore it. If it had been up to her, she would have suggested allowing the Civil Guard to take over sole responsibility for policing Imperial University; they'd certainly given the students a nasty fright during the riotous protest march. But her superiors had disagreed. The last thing the university cops needed was to suggest to the bean-counters that the cops were no longer necessary.

Her wristcom buzzed an emergency alert. Judy glanced down at it in surprise and saw a red alert blinking up, an alert that was only used in situations when there was no time to contact their superiors and make a full report. The localiser had already homed in on the signal; it was coming from an apartment block only a few hundred metres from the nightclub. Judy hesitated, then started to run towards the source. If *she* were in trouble, she would want her fellow cops coming to the rescue.

She checked her uniform belt as she ran. Unlike the Civil Guard, university cops weren't allowed to carry anything more dangerous than a stunner and neural whip. It had always grated on her, even though she'd *known* that most students were pussies – at least until the big riot. Now, she wished for something more lethal, but her superiors had refused to authorise it. The beancounters always took years to authorise new equipment, particularly equipment that required vast amounts of paperwork.

The apartment block seemed to have attracted attention from the Civil Guard as well as the university cops. Four Civil Guardsman, wearing armour that could only make Judy fume with envy, were standing outside, talking rapidly with two university cops. Judy slowed as she approached them, blinking in surprise as a second aircar with seven more Civil Guardsmen dropped out of the sky and landed beside the apartment block.

"A Civil Guard snatch squad went inside the building," one of the university cops explained. "Forty minutes later, there was an emergency transmission – and then nothing."

Judy blinked in surprise. What could have happened to the squad? Maybe it was a drill…no, with so much tension on the streets, no one would consider holding a drill. But what else could it be? One Civil Guardsman might be overwhelmed by a bunch of student pussies, but an entire snatch squad? She listened to the rest of the details and shook her head in disbelief. Two girls had overcome an entire squad? That only happened in bad entertainment flicks.

"We're going to move in once the building is secure," a Civil Guardsman called. He appeared to be the highest-ranking officer in the vicinity. "The Civil Guard will take the lead; university cops will back us up."

Judy felt a flicker of annoyance at the calm dismissal in his voice, before deciding that it was probably for the best. The Civil Guard would take the blame for any screw-ups if they happened to be in command – and besides, if the snatch squad *had* run into something it couldn't handle, the Civil Guard was better armed and armoured than the university cops.

It took nearly thirty minutes before the Guard was ready to move into the building. Judy would have preferred to go in at once – it was the quickest way to stop trouble from getting worse – but the Guardsmen seemed to disagree. Anything that could stop an entire snatch squad had to be dangerous. She followed the Guardsmen into the reception hall and stopped in surprise. Normally, the reception halls were crammed with students chatting to their friends or catcalling down from the balconies, but this hall was as dark and silent as the grave. The doorman – a student who made a little extra cash by pretending to be a security guard – was nowhere to be seen.

"We'll take the stairs," the Civil Guard CO muttered. The Guardsmen advanced towards the double doors that permitted entrance to the stairwell, clutching their weapons nervously. "And then…"

Debris started to rain down on them. Judy had barely a moment to realise that the students had concealed themselves on the balcony before a piece of falling rock slammed into her arm. She staggered under the impact, silently grateful for the protection woven into her uniform. It was all that had saved her arm from breaking. The Civil Guardsmen lifted their weapons, just in time to be hit by a wave of bottles from high overhead. A moment later, a powerful stench assailed them and sent the Guardsmen stumbling backwards. Gas! The students had made gas! Other bottles released multicoloured smoke that suddenly made it very hard to see properly.

The Civil Guardsmen started to open fire, before their CO bellowed for them to hold fire and get back out of the building. Judy, her arm aching, was only too glad to obey. A handful of Guardsmen had been badly injured, despite their armour, and had to be dragged out by their comrades. Thankfully, the students didn't bother to harass them as they retreated, although Judy wasn't sure if that was a deliberate decision or sheer luck. Maybe whoever was in charge of the students knew that giving chase would expose them to the men outside the building.

Her wristcom had been smashed, but she heard emergency reports echoing through the wristcoms worn by the other cops. The entire campus seemed to have gone crazy. Mobs of students were pouring out of their apartment blocks and heading for the main buildings, as if they intended to capture or destroy them. She heard the sounds of more rioting in the distance as the Civil Guardsmen attempted to reorganise themselves. In all of her career, she'd never heard the campus sound so…*aggressive*.

And then she turned and saw another mass of students pouring out of a nearby building…

No, there were other students pouring out of *other* buildings. She glanced from side to side, realising that both cops and Guardsmen were doing the same...they were trapped, with an angry mob on all sides. The Guardsmen had their aircars, but Judy knew with a sickening certainty that they wouldn't be able to get off the ground and into the air in time. She saw the faces of the students as they came closer and realised that they were no longer pussies. The Civil Guardsmen might shoot hundreds of them, but there were thousands waiting to join the attack.

"Throw down your weapons," a voice bellowed, from behind them. She turned to see a student standing in the doorway, the same doorway that they'd just been thrown out of. He *had* to be a leader. "Throw down your weapons or die."

Judy hesitated, then obeyed. She hadn't been trained to fight – and she wasn't paid enough to face an angry mob. The Civil Guardsmen followed suit, many of them looking completely terrified. They'd been quite happy to push unarmed civilians around, but when they were challenged...she winced as strong arms grabbed her and removed everything she'd been carrying, before securing her hands with a long roll of duct tape. The others were getting the same treatment before they were hauled into the apartment block.

Dear God, she thought, stunned. Everything had just turned upside down so quickly. *What now?*

Her first thought when she woke up was that the whole affair had been a nightmare caused by eating too many algae bars. Some of the foodstuffs she'd tried at university had given her bad dreams and tummy upsets; she'd never heard of anyone ever suffering after eating an algae bar, but there had to be a first time. But her wrists hurt and her bed felt odd and...

Jacqueline opened her eyes. She was lying on a strange bed, in a strange room, wearing her nightgown. There were nasty marks on her wrists and odd bruises on the rest of her body. She realised, to her horror, that the dream hadn't been a dream at all. They'd come for her, arrested her, and then...

Her memory failed her.

"Hey," an unfamiliar voice said. "You're awake!"

Jacqueline turned her head and saw a dark-skinned girl looking down at her, wearing a white shirt and shorts. "I'm Jo," the girl said, by way of introduction. "How are you feeling?"

"Headachy," Jacqueline said, truthfully. "What…what happened?"

"We attacked the Civil Guardsmen who arrested you," Jo said. "How could you be so stupid as to be caught with a forbidden book?"

"It isn't mine," Jacqueline admitted. If they'd attacked the Civil Guard… she couldn't feel sorry for the Guardsmen, but what was she going to do now? There was no way she could go back home and vanish, not on Earth. Perhaps she should just walk into the indenturing office and surrender herself. It would certainly save time. "What's happening outside?"

"Everyone seems to know, apart from you," Jo said. She smiled, reducing the sting in her words. "We've taken the campus!"

Jacqueline blinked. "Taken the campus?"

"Occupied the university," Jo explained. "And we have some hostages too. This time, they will *have* to listen to our demands."

Jacqueline shook her head slowly, feeling the ache growing stronger. She'd once thought that the universe was fair, but that had been before the riot – and before she'd been arrested. God alone knew what would have happened to her at the station. Now…she was a wanted fugitive – and the Civil Guardsmen always got their man. It was the plot of a thousand entertainment flicks. What the hell could she do now?

She looked down at her wrists again and shuddered. How could she escape?

And it hadn't even been her fault!

"Brent would like you to tell the world about your experience," Jo said, as she passed Jacqueline a glass of water. "They all have to know what happened to you."

"Ok," Jacqueline said, finally. What else could she do? She wanted to run, but there was nowhere to go. All she could do was follow Jo and Brent, whoever they were, until the end. "I'll do my best."

"That's all we ask for, darling," Jo assured her. At least she sounded more comforting than the tutors. "That's all that anyone can do."

CHAPTER TWENTY-SEVEN

Grand Senator Stephen Onge was one of the Senators who was caught between two very different positions. His solution was to attempt to speed up the Empire's collapse, hoping that he could use the first upswings of violence to declare a state of emergency and put himself (and his allies) into a position of supreme power. In effect, they would not attempt to enlarge the Empire's pie, but snatch it all for themselves. The first step in the plan was to covertly create a terrorist group that answered to him personally. That group would take steps that would create the chaos he needed for his plan to succeed.

- Professor Leo Caesius, The End of Empire.

Roland came at Belinda, fist outstretched. Belinda stepped to one side and stuck out a foot. The Prince tripped over her and fell head-first onto the mat.

"You're coming at me too blatantly," she said. It had been *years* since she'd been in Boot Camp, yet she'd done better than that. But then, her father had been a firm believer in the school of hard knocks. "And you're over-committing yourself."

She watched as Roland slowly climbed back to his feet. The Prince was angry; not at her, but at the Grand Senate. His insistence on thinking about the marriage proposal hadn't prevented the Grand Senate from making it official, telling the Empire that Prince Roland would marry Lady Lily Sapphire. It hadn't taken too long for the media to turn a blatant act of political opportunism into a romantic saga to thrill every heart, male and female alike. By now, the entire world believed that Roland had fallen in love with Lily after meeting her eyes across a crowded room. The fact that Roland rarely attended functions hosted by the Grand Senate families had somehow passed them by.

"I want to hurt someone," Roland said, angrily. "Why…?"

"Anger is a poor servant and a terrible master," Belinda said. She'd been taught to push all emotion aside to focus on her appointed task, whatever it was. Anger could come later. But Roland had never been taught the self-discipline he needed to keep himself under control. "You won't be able to think of anything while you're fuming."

She sighed, inwardly. Roland hadn't been able to sleep properly; eventually, he had climbed out of bed and demanded that they go to the mat. If he'd been an experienced Marine, it might have been an interesting challenge; as it was, she had to work hard to stay just ahead of his level of development. Roland wouldn't learn anything if she beat the crap out of him every time. The Drill Instructors, she had decided, were underpaid. Whatever the Corps paid them was too little.

"They just want me as their puppet," Roland said, tartly. "They have even denied me the right to choose the mother of my children. Why should I not be angry?"

"You need to put the anger aside," Belinda said, patiently. "If you're mad at the world, you won't be able to think clearly."

Roland scowled as he rubbed his chin. "Fine," he agreed, grudgingly. "Did your friends find out anything useful?"

Belinda shrugged. She hadn't been able to pull much about Lily Sapphire out of the datanet, so she'd forwarded the question to Marine Intelligence. Colonel Chung Myung-Hee, who had extensive files on every member of the high-ranking families, had filled in the details for Belinda. The files hadn't been very encouraging.

Grand Senator Onge didn't have any *direct* family tie to the girl, at least not without going back at least seven generations. However, he did have strong financial ties to the girl's *parents*, as did several other Grand Senators who might be in his camp. In fact, two of them were serving on the Emergency Committee. It was impossible to escape the impression that Lily would be the Grand Senator's puppet, influencing and controlling her husband – at the very least, she'd certainly be spying on him.

Belinda couldn't blame Roland for being angry. She'd considered the matter carefully and hadn't been able to find any way to get the Prince out of the arranged marriage. If Roland said no, the Grand Senate would blame him for refusing to marry Lily – which would be a public relations disaster. Marine Intelligence had warned that Roland was taking the blame for many of the emergency measures instituted by the Emergency Committee; what would happen, she wondered, if the public felt that they had been denied a Royal Wedding?

Cold logic suggested that a wedding would do nothing to improve the state of the Empire – and would almost certainly make it worse – but cold logic wasn't involved.

Maybe Lily wouldn't be that bad, she thought, before deciding that wasn't likely to be true. Even if she had been the sweetest person in the world, she would still have been forced into a man's bed – and Roland would feel much the same way. Maybe they'd couple long enough to produce children – there were fertility treatments that would guarantee successful conception – and then have nothing more to do with one another. The Imperial Palace was large enough to allow them never to see one another again, if they didn't want to. It would be a very unhappy marriage.

Belinda had never really given much thought to her own marriage. Marines were not allowed to date within the ranks and she had very little in common with non-Marines. Besides, her work kept her busy and her enhancement ensured that she wasn't under any time limit. She'd always planned to marry and have children, perhaps after she retired, but she'd always envisaged choosing her own man. The thought of having a man chosen for her was horrific.

But you are stronger and nastier than most men, Pug's voice seemed to say in her head. He'd always been the joker in the unit. *Who would feel safe being forced into marriage with you?*

Dickhead, Belinda thought.

Her implants sounded the alert before she could say anything. "You have a call from the Grand Senator," she informed him, reluctantly. She knew that it would only upset the Prince. "He wants to talk to you."

Roland pulled his dressing gown on, covering his shorts and sweat-stained shirt. "He probably thought he was going to wake me," he muttered. "I'll try to look thick-headed and see what he has to say."

Unsurprisingly, Roland's communications room included the very latest in holographic display technology. Belinda, who knew that such equipment was desperately needed on the front lines, hadn't been too impressed when she'd seen it, although Roland had admitted that there were some special functions that weren't generally included in military equipment. One of them allowed the user to magnify specific parts of the incoming image to hilarious results.

Roland sat down in front of the console, checked to make sure that Belinda was out of the sensor's reach and tapped a key. The Grand Senator's face appeared in front of them. He looked surprisingly tired, as if he'd been woken up early himself. That was…odd.

"Your Highness," the Grand Senator said. "There has been a…development at Imperial University."

"Oh," Roland said. He studied the Grand Senator for a long moment. "What sort of development?"

"A student uprising," the Grand Senator said. "The Civil Guard has been driven out of Imperial University. Hostages have been taken."

Belinda blinked in surprise, then accessed her implants. The Marine network had been crippled by the departure of most of the HQ Staff, but the channels she had access to as Roland's liegeman confirmed the Grand Senator's words. Mobs of students had seized Imperial University, driven out the tutors…and taken hostages. Upwards of seventy law enforcement personnel seemed to be hostages. How the hell had it happened so quickly?

Planned in advance, the cynical side of her mind suggested.

She skimmed through the details, cursing the officers who seemed to speak in riddles rather than admit that they didn't know. A snatch squad had vanished, student rioters had attacked a back-up force…and Civil Guardsmen had been attacked all over the campus. It certainly *looked* as if someone had planned it all in advance, although there were curiously few weapons. But that wouldn't be a problem now that the Civil Guard had been overcome. Their weapons security was non-existent.

"For the moment, the Civil Guard has cordoned off Imperial University," the Grand Senator continued. "However, the students are starting to spout their own propaganda onto the airwaves. We are unable to stop or jam their transmissions. Their uprising might be just the first in a series of explosions..."

"I understand," Roland said, very calmly. "And what would you like me to do?"

"This requires harsh measures," the Grand Senator said. "I would like you to authorise the Civil Guard to go in with extreme force."

Belinda stared. He *had* to be insane. There were hundreds of thousands of students caught up inside Imperial University and they couldn't *all* be guilty. Sending in the Civil Guard in such force would result in mass slaughter at the very least. The riot the Marines had put down would be a minor headache compared to the coming apocalypse.

Roland seemed to have thought of that for himself. "There are thousands of students in the campus," he reminded him, sharply. "How many of them are you prepared to kill?"

"This is a direct challenge to our authority," the Grand Senator snapped. "We have got to respond harshly before it spreads out of control. I require you to sign a bill authorising extreme measures."

"You don't need me to sign anything," Roland said. His tone hadn't changed. "Emergency Bill #23 gives you the authority to take whatever steps you deem necessary to save the Empire."

"Yes, but it has to be explained to the Empire as well," the Grand Senator said. He was clearly running out of patience. "If the action is clearly supported by the Crown Prince, it will be harder for our dissidents to oppose it."

"You mean you want me to take the blame for the slaughter of thousands of students," Roland said. He glared at the Grand Senator with undisguised loathing, not even *trying* to hide his feelings. "If you feel the urge to crack down, *Senator*, you can do it without my help."

The Grand Senator, for a long moment, showed true surprise. He hadn't expected the uprising, Belinda realised in shock; no wonder his approach to Roland had been terribly clumsy. Given more time to think, he might have come up with an argument that would convince Roland to help him. The student uprising threatened the power base he'd so carefully built up, culminating in Emergency Bill #23. And if he failed to deal with it, the Grand Senate might turn on him.

"You are the Crown Prince of the Empire," the Grand Senator said, finally. "You have an *obligation*" – he stressed the word – "to maintain law and order."

Roland's face darkened. "How could you maintain law and order by slaughtering thousands of students?"

The Grand Senator ignored him. "Life is good for you, Your Highness," he said, lowering his voice until it was a threatening growl. "It can easily get worse."

"Like it will get worse for those students?" Roland demanded. "I do follow the reports, Senator."

"Then you will know that we *cannot* meet their demands," the Grand Senator snapped. "Food supplies cannot be brought into existence with a wave of a magic wand. The algae farms are already pushed to the limit merely keeping the damn population *fed*! As for their other demands… the Empire needs strong leadership. It does not require a *popularity contest*."

He leaned forward until he seemed to be glaring right into Roland's eyes. "The Empire is at stake, Your Highness," he hissed. "I will not permit you to prevent us from doing what needs to be done."

"My coronation oath states that I will protect the citizens of the Empire," Roland hissed back, "even from their own government. I will not allow you to slaughter thousands of students."

The Grand Senator leaned back, very slightly. "And how do you propose to stop us?"

His voice hardened. "You appear to be getting delusions of grandeur," he added, nastily. "You have no authority to override the Grand Senate, nor do you have troops to intervene. Your sole function is to give us your approval for whatever actions we deem necessary, for which we gratefully allow you your palaces and your pleasures. I suggest, *Your Highness*, that you learn to behave. Or I will send my steward to give you a whipping."

Roland ignored the mocking threat. "I will go there myself," he said. "Will you risk having me killed in the crossfire?"

Belinda stared at him in disbelief.

The Grand Senator seemed equally surprised. "You are out of your mind," he said, finally. "If you go there, you will walk right into a firestorm."

"I'm going," Roland said. "I will not be your puppet any longer."

He hit a key and the Grand Senator's image vanished.

"That...was unwise," Belinda said. "There is no *way* that I am going to let you go into that maelstrom."

"You swore loyalty to me," Roland reminded her. "You *have* to let me go."

"I swore loyalty, not blind obedience," Belinda snapped. Somehow, she'd come to like Roland enough to want to see him live for more reasons than professionalism. "No halfwit from the Civil Guard would risk allowing their primary to go into such a nightmare willingly. It would be impossible to guarantee your safety even with a company of Marines surrounding you."

"There's one of me," Roland pointed out, "and thousands of them. Is my life more important than theirs?"

Belinda gritted her teeth. He couldn't have picked a more inconvenient time to learn about self-sacrifice. She knew that Marine COs often hated having to remain behind while their Marines went to war, but...she shook her head firmly. Roland could not be allowed to put himself into danger like that.

"Your death would destabilise the Empire further," she pointed out, finally.

"If I stay here, the Grand Senate will just tell everyone that I back their actions," Roland said. "They might even create an illusion of me ordering the Civil Guard into action. And then thousands of people will die! I can't stay here and let it happen. If I was there, they couldn't risk killing me..."

Belinda scowled at him. He had a point. If the Civil Guard killed an important hostage, they could expect to be severely punished for it, even if it wasn't their fault. Roland wouldn't be a hostage – she assumed – but his death would still be disastrous. The fact that Roland had gone there of his own free will wouldn't be taken into account. None of the Grand

Senate would lose any sleep over the hostages already there, but if the Crown Prince died…

…If nothing else, they'd have to struggle over who should inherit the throne.

"And if you do go," she said, as calmly as she could, "what will you do? Just sit there and stare at the Civil Guard?"

Roland hesitated; Belinda pushed ahead.

"The problem with hostage situations," she explained, "is that the hostage-takers are trapped. They know that they cannot escape – and they know that the only thing keeping them alive is the presence of the hostages. Their only hope is to negotiate a way out that leaves them alive and free – and that isn't easy. They have to suspect that the Grand Senate will go back on any bargain once the hostages are safe."

She scowled. No matter how she looked at the situation, it seemed nightmarish. The Grand Senator might have already written the hostages – and the students – off completely. It would even make sense; Imperial University had long ago stopped producing anything but graduates with a huge sense of entitlement and very few prospects. A slaughter that left most of the students dead and the remainder on one-way tickets out to the Rim might suit them very well. Few voices would oppose shutting down the university after such a tragedy.

"I can write them a formal pardon," Roland insisted. "I checked; I have the authority to write pardons. They have to be confirmed by the Emperor – and I will be Emperor in a few months. I think they would be legally binding…"

"The Grand Senate might disagree," Belinda said, tiredly. On the other hand, the Grand Senate might realise the dangers inherent in overriding their puppet so publically. They might grit their teeth and accept it, particularly if the hostage situation came to an end. "Roland, I…"

"I have to go," Roland said. There was a pleading note in his voice, but also underlying determination – and strength. She'd helped put it there. "It is my duty. Even if you don't come, I have to go. If nothing else, it is the best chance I am likely to get to break free of their control."

"I should tie you up," Belinda said, exasperatedly. "Or whip you myself."

But he was right. This *was* his best chance to break free…and save thousands of students into the bargain. The coming bloodbath had to be prevented; if there was even the slightest possibility it could be prevented, she had to try.

And she *had* sworn an oath to serve and defend the citizens of the Empire. And the students, as stupid as many of them were, were citizens of the Empire. She was obliged to defend them with all the weapons at her disposal.

"Very well," she agreed, wearily. The Commandant was going to court-martial her. She'd been required to study past court martial proceedings at the Slaughterhouse; offhand, she couldn't recall any as…*controversial* as her own was likely to prove. "I shall organise our transport immediately."

Chapter Twenty-Eight

Unfortunately, matters started to spiral out of control. Each action he took – the deliberate provocation of a riot and the harsh response by the authorities – proceeded to have significant unintended consequences. The punishment handed out to the students, for example, illustrated the true nature of their position far better than any agitator could hope for. It also helped to radicalise their parents, who grew worried about the safety of their children.

- Professor Leo Caesius, The End of Empire.

Stephen rarely allowed himself to become angry.

It was a luxury he could not afford, not in his position. The time he'd caught his son molesting one of the bodyguards? He'd been mad then, with good reason. His son's sexual leanings were of no concern, but trying to force a bodyguard into his bed? It had been *insane*. He'd disowned his son, stripped him out of the line of succession and exiled him to a world along the Rim. The family could not afford such a madman so close to the top.

But Roland had managed to get under his skin. The Crown Prince had almost no power – and Stephen *knew* that he had almost no power. He was no ignorant citizen to be impressed by pomp, circumstance and arrogance; he knew that the Crown Prince's job was to look good, help convince the masses to obey and little else. Did Roland really think that he could impress a Grand Senator?

And yet Roland had managed, accidentally or otherwise, to threaten his position.

Cold rage burned through his mind as he contemplated the ruination of his plans. Earth – and the solar system – was the one place in the Empire where outright violence could not be condoned easily. Earth was the core of the Empire, home to the bureaucrats who kept the system running – many of whom had children in Imperial University. He'd worked hard to provoke the riot that had provided the excuse to take control of the government – to all intents and purposes – but now it seemed that matters were slipping out of control. The students believed that they could take hostages and get away with it.

Stephen hadn't expected such a violent uprising. It shouldn't have been possible. Everyone *knew* that the inhabitants of Imperial City were sheep, that the only thing the university cops had to worry about was someone drunk or stoned out of his mind – and the Civil Guard should not have been involved at all. Stephen's agents had had to work hard to produce the riot, in the process rubbing the students' collective faces in their own powerlessness. And now the students had turned violent.

He glared down at the latest report from Admiral Valentine. The students didn't seem to have too many weapons, but there was no way the Civil Guard could crush the uprising without causing massive slaughter. Roland had been right, damn him. Stephen briefly considered negotiation before dismissing the thought. The Empire did not negotiate with terrorists. It was a cardinal rule. Besides, giving the students what they wanted – or even enough of what they wanted to satisfy them – would weaken the Empire's bargaining position in future.

Everyone wanted something, he knew. There were just too many factions in the Empire who would start their own uprisings if they believed that the Empire would fold rather than fight. God alone knew how much damage they would do, given half a chance. The Empire *needed* to stop the student uprising in its tracks, *before* it encouraged other uprisings. And the students were somehow getting the word out over the datanet. There was little hope of containing the situation quietly. It would only get worse if the Crown Prince arrived as a voluntary human shield.

Damn you, Roland, Stephen thought.

Years ago, he'd had a genealogist look into the question of who, after Roland, was the Heir to the throne. The Royal Family had been careful, too careful; there were several possible heirs, but none of them had a very strong connection to the Throne. Not that it would matter in the end; Roland's successor would be approved after a great deal of political horse-trading by the Grand Senators, regardless of which of them had the best claim to the Throne. It would be a political struggle at the worst possible time.

The Emergency Committee hadn't expected to go unchallenged indefinitely, but the student uprising would ensure that the challenges started sooner, rather than later. Stephen had planned to quietly establish an iron grip on Earth and the solar system *before* they were challenged openly, but events were being pushed forward far faster than he'd dared fear. If Roland did something utterly idiotic, the rest of the Grand Senate would happily use it against the Emergency Committee.

We should have taken him into protective custody from the start, Stephen thought, coldly. *Who would have thought that he would actually develop a spine?*

He'd believed Roland to be stupid and useless, just like so many children from the Grand Families. They were raised in the height of luxury, without so many of the woes that afflicted so many people on Earth. And they turned into useless human beings, spoiled so badly that they literally turned spoilt. Some of them were incapable of doing something as simple as dressing without assistance. He'd thought that Roland was just as pathetic.

But if he'd been aware of his true position all along...

Stephen shook his head. It could not be tolerated – or risked. The Empire had enough problems without the Crown Prince trying to carve out a role for himself.

He keyed his wristcom. "Connect me to Colonel Jamey," he ordered. There was only one thing to do now. "I have a job for him."

"I think they were searching your apartment," Richard said, quietly.

Amethyst stared at him. They'd spent the last several days in the same apartment, doing nothing apart from having sex – and it had started to grow a little tedious. She would have felt better, she suspected, if she had been able to get out of the box-like room, but Richard had forbidden her to leave. The Civil Guard was on the alert and if she had been identified…

The old her would have been horrified at the thought of violent students occupying Imperial University. But the person she had become found it delightful, in a strange way. She'd done too much to go back now; the only hope, as she'd learned from the Professor's book, was to push onwards and pray that they could bring the Grand Senate down. She'd wanted to go to the University, taking as many weapons as she could with her, but Richard had forbidden that too. Getting from their apartment to the University would have been incredibly dangerous.

She found her voice. "*My* apartment?"

"Your apartment," Richard confirmed. He had a handful of friends in the middle of the uprising, he'd said, friends who were keeping him updated. "It was searched just before the uprising broke out. I think they hauled your friend off in chains."

"*Jacqueline*? But she wasn't involved…"

Richard laughed at her. "I think you should know by now that guilt or innocence doesn't matter too much to the Civil Guard," he reminded her derisively. "But in any case, they found your copy of the Professor's book."

"But I hid it really well," Amethyst protested. "I…"

"The Civil Guard is very experienced in searching apartments," Richard said. He gave her a sharp look. "What do you think you might have thought of that wasn't thought of by countless people before you? Besides, Jacqueline *did* attend the first meeting. That alone would be enough to condemn her."

Amethyst blanched. She'd barely given a thought to her friend since she'd joined Richard's little group. God knew that she didn't dare risk returning to her apartment, but she could have tried to warn Jacqueline… what would the Civil Guard do to her?

"Exile is the standard punishment," Richard answered when she asked. "However, it seems that Jacqueline was freed by other students. Right now, she may be in more danger."

"We have to go there," Amethyst said. "We could help…"

"There is absolutely nothing to be gained by throwing our lives away," Richard said. He ignored her stunned expression. "Every student on campus is trapped; if we go there, we will be trapped too. And we *cannot* stand up to the massed firepower of the Civil Guard. The uprising *will* be crushed and most of the students caught up in the fighting will be killed."

"I thought the idea was to force the Grand Senate to change," Amethyst protested. She felt hot tears stinging her eyes as she pushed onwards. "Letting them kill thousands of students…"

Richard spoke calmly, as if he were speaking to a child. "Our sole advantage is being difficult to find," he told her, flatly. "If we go to the University, we will lose that advantage – and gain nothing from it. The students in the University are marked for capture or death. Those who survive capture will be exiled as indentured colonists. There is nothing we can do to stop it."

Amethyst stared at him. Richard had been a young student; idealistic, brave…and hot. She had found him attractive – and charismatic – right from the start. But, just for a moment, she saw something else, something cold and merciless, hidden under his smile. It was gone a second later, but she could never forget it. Who – what – was Richard, really?

She had no idea where to find any weapons. Imperial City forbade the private possession of weapons; even buying a knife for cutting food could result in bureaucratically-mandated harsh questions. Hell, the population been told that weapons were dangerous and evil since they'd been born. But Richard knew where to find weapons…and not just any weapons, but military-grade weapons. Amethyst looked at him and wondered what kind of student would have that knowledge. The military had little to do with Imperial University.

Until now, she thought, bitterly.

But she didn't dare ask him, not after what she'd just seen.

"There has to be something else that we can do," she said. She needed some time alone to think, but he couldn't leave the apartment either. "Maybe we can cause a distraction somewhere else."

Richard smiled at her. "Maybe we can," he allowed. He stood up and helped her to her feet. "I'll certainly see what the others want to do. For the moment, however, I think there's only one thing we can do."

Sex was the last thing Amethyst wanted right now, but she suspected that refusing would only make him suspicious. God knew that she'd gone along with him so far in everything, from politics to sex. And yet…

Just what was Richard, really?

Belinda studied the replacement aircar with a jaundiced eye. She'd ordered a new one directly from the industrial nodes orbiting Earth, but the speciality design she'd wanted hadn't been completed yet. Instead, she'd been forced to hire a team of engineers to modify the spare aircar so that it would provide much more protection to the Prince. More armour, more countermeasures…even some weapons, controlled directly through her implants. It was tough, but it was still vulnerable. And the terrorists, who'd shot down the last – identical – aircraft, would know it.

Don't be an ass, Doug's voice mocked her. *You've flown in far more dangerous aircraft.*

"But I didn't have the Prince with me," Belinda said, out loud. The doctors had wondered if she was suffering from some form of PTSD, although it was surprisingly rare among the Marine Corps. Hearing the voices of her dead teammates probably wasn't a good sign. "And I was expendable."

She linked into the aircar's systems with her implants and ran a full check. The mechanics who worked at the Summer Palace seemed to be competent, thankfully, but caution had been battered into her head at the Slaughterhouse. Imperial Army maintenance was a very mixed bag – Belinda had fought alongside units that kept their equipment in perfect working order and units that were lucky their vehicles didn't fail on the battlefield – and the less said about the Civil Guard's maintenance habits the better, yet whoever had drawn Roland's mechanics from the Imperial Army had chosen well. The extra pay probably helped. Everything seemed to check out fine, but she wasn't entirely happy.

You're flying into what is effectively a war zone with the Prince in tow, she told herself, sharply. *That court-martial record is looking more and more awesome all the time.*

She seriously considered – again – carrying out her threat to tie the Prince up to prevent him from going. It wasn't as if he could resist her – and the rest of the staff wouldn't interfere. But it would destroy the fragile trust they'd built up...and he might just be right. If they went to the University, their presence might prevent a bloodbath long enough for calmer heads to think of a solution. Roland's pardon would provide a convenient fig-leaf for burying the whole incident under the rug and forgetting about it.

Standing up, she walked back to Roland's suite and scowled at him. "The aircar is ready," she said, crossly. "And so are the escorts."

Roland had wanted to go without escort vehicles, claiming that the students would be much more likely to accept them if they weren't surrounded by armed men. Belinda had squashed *that* thought, pointing out that he wasn't exactly free of enemies. Besides, they didn't know if the students would even accept them. It was quite possible that their leadership would try to take Roland hostage before he had a chance to talk.

"Good," he said. He seemed to have grown up overnight. "Do I have to wear this suit of armour?"

Belinda snorted. She'd had a uniform prepared for him, based on the standard Marine uniform. It would provide some protection from bullets or knives, but not enough to guarantee his safety, particularly if a sniper aimed for his exposed head. Besides, the material was very far from perfect. She would have preferred to put him in a heavy combat suit, but the students would not have been willing to talk to him if he'd been armoured. And the suits had to be matched to their individual wearer and there was no time to produce one.

"Yes," she said, flatly. "And it will *not* provide complete protection, so *don't* get cocky."

She led the way back down to the landing pad and motioned for Roland to get into the aircar while she ran a final check. The pilot eyed her nervously – she'd searched him the moment he'd reached the landing pad, then told him to sit in the cockpit until the Prince was ready to depart – as she ran through the checks. Once they were completed, she ordered him to prepare for takeoff and sat down next to Roland. The Prince was skimming through the reports from the Civil Guard.

The aircar lurched as it took off, the armed gunships falling into formation around it. Belinda watched them grimly, remembering what had happened to the last formation of gunships. Maybe she'd underestimated Senate Security, she told herself; they didn't seem to allow disasters and assassination attempts to slow them down. But then, Senate Security was responsible for protecting the Senators. The Grand Senate wouldn't stint on their own protection.

Roland caught her arm. "Did you tell the Civil Guard that we were coming?"

Belinda laughed at him, not unkindly. "You only just thought of that now?"

Roland flushed a bright red. "It never occurred to me," he admitted. "But you were saying that airspace over a combat zone is tightly controlled…"

"I told them that we were coming," Belinda said. "They shouldn't shoot us down."

The Civil Guard *had* established an exclusion zone over Imperial University, but some of the more adventurous reporters had been trying to sneak in anyway. God alone knew what they were thinking; it wasn't likely that their superiors would allow any stories that disagreed with the official line to be printed. Maybe they just wanted to be real reporters for once. It would certainly be more impressive than their normal behaviour.

She glanced up sharply as a small convoy of aircraft appeared on the live feed from the aircar's sensors, heading right towards them. Belinda glanced at the IFF signals and muttered a curse under her breath. They appeared to be Civil Guard aircraft, but judging from the precise codes they actually belonged to the troops the Emergency Committee had brought in to maintain order. The troops that had been suspiciously ready to move to Earth as soon as the emergency bill had passed through the Grand Senate.

"We may have a problem," she informed him, grimly.

Briefly, she considered trying to evade the newcomers, but it would be difficult to outrun military-grade craft. Besides, they were badly outgunned. She outlined the problem for Roland, considering all possible options. They didn't seem to have very many.

"They're hailing us," she said. *That* wasn't a surprise. If the newcomers wanted Roland dead, they would have opened fire by now. They certainly had the firepower to blow Roland's aircar and its escorts out of the sky. "Listen."

She tapped a switch, allowing Roland to hear the message. "...Is Colonel Jamey of the Civil Guard," an unfamiliar voice said. The accent didn't suggest Earth, or anywhere within the solar system. "We are here to take Prince Roland into protective custody. The Prince's aircar is to land at once so that he can be transferred to our vehicle; other aircars are to return to the Summer Palace. Comply at once."

Or die, Belinda filled in, silently.

Roland stared at her. "What do we do?"

"There's no choice," Belinda said. The newcomers could force them down, given time. It would be risky, but it could be done. "We have to land and surrender."

CHAPTER TWENTY-NINE

Historians have tended to look at the events surrounding Crown Prince Roland as decisive in the rapidly-accelerating collapse. Certainly, Roland's defiance snatched a tool out of the Grand Senator's hands. However, in the long run, Roland was essentially irrelevant. The damage to the Empire was done centuries before Roland became the last Crown Prince.

- Professor Leo Caesius, The End of Empire.

"Don't do anything stupid," Belinda ordered, as the aircar settled to the roof of the nearest CityBlock. "We have to play for time."

Roland stared at her. "I'm not going to let them take me," he said. "They..."

Belinda caught his arm. "If we fight now, we die," she said. "We have to cooperate long enough to find another way out of this mess."

She scowled as she watched their gunships backing off, the newcomers moving into position to cover them. A large assault shuttle – an older design, now rarely seen away from the Rim – landed nearby, its hatches opening to reveal a handful of armed men. They wore Civil Guard uniforms, but Belinda could tell that they weren't Civil Guard. For one, they looked a hell of a lot more professional than Earth's Civil Guard.

"Please leave the aircar, Prince Roland," Colonel Jamey said. "I assure you that no harm will come to you – or your aide."

Belinda motioned for Roland to obey, running through the files in her implants to see if she could locate Colonel Jamey. The connection to Earth's datanets had been severed by the jamming. Her implants had copies of files on all the important or well-connected officers, but there was nothing that seemed to be related to a Colonel Jamey. Belinda guessed that he was either a private security officer or one of the soldiers the Emergency Committee had brought in to maintain order.

The air smelled unpleasant as she stepped out of the aircar, careful to keep her hands in sight. Jamey had referred to her as an aide, which suggested that he didn't know what she really was. It was something she had used to her advantage before, back when she had been part of Team Six. As long as they didn't do a full body-scan, they'd never have a clue that she wasn't anything more than a slightly frightened aide, at least until it was too late.

"Prince Roland," the leader began. He was a tall, remarkably pale man, without a trace of facial hair. The crow-black hair and inhumanly dark eyes marked him as a native of Nightshade, a inhabited world that orbited an unusual distance from its primary star, forcing the settlers to use genetic enhancement to improve their eyesight and hearing. "You will come with us."

Roland didn't move. "Am I under arrest?"

"We are taking you into protective custody," Colonel Jamey said. "Of *course* you're not under arrest."

"You cannot kidnap the Crown Prince from his own aircar," Roland said tartly. "There isn't a person on the planet who can give you orders to take me into anything…"

"It is for your own good, Your Highness," Colonel Jamey said. His voice hardened. "My superiors will provide full explanations. For the moment, I suggest that you accompany us – or we will be forced to carry you."

Belinda silently hoped that Roland would have the sense to stop arguing. Colonel Jamey didn't *look* as though he was prepared to recognise Roland as having any authority – and besides, Nightshade was one of Grand Senator Onge's client worlds. Jamey would have been raised to be loyal to the Grand Senator, even if it meant going against the rest of the Empire.

"That would be touching the royal person," Roland said. "You do realise that is treason?"

Jamey sighed and removed a stunner from his belt. "I would prefer to take you willingly, but I do have permission to stun you if necessary," he said. "You'll wake up several hours from now nursing a colossal headache. And it would be a shame if *something* happened to your lovely aide."

Roland scowled at him, clearly understanding the threat. Belinda felt a moment of sympathy; Roland had never allowed himself true friends because he understood that they could be used against him. Part of the reason he'd been unpleasant to the staff was to stop them developing ties to him – or, for that matter, to stop him from developing ties to them. He'd formed a friendship with Belinda, only to discover that it made him vulnerable.

She wanted to reassure him. But that would have been out of character.

"Come," Jamey said.

He nodded to one of his men, who ran a sensor over Roland's body and removed the pistol Belinda had given him. The sensor wasn't a very good one, Belinda noted with some relief; it shouldn't be able to uncover her true nature. She braced herself as she was scanned. They wouldn't expect an aide to be carrying weapons near the Crown Prince, but if they grew suspicious…a moment passed, then the sensor was withdrawn. No one seemed alarmed.

Roland was gently pushed into the assault shuttle and ordered to sit down on one side of the compartment. Belinda almost smiled at his expression; there were no seats in an assault shuttle, certainly not one that wasn't expected to take the lead in a planetary assault. Soldiers would sit along the bulkheads, ready to jump up and abandon ship if the shit hit the fan. Belinda had done it herself, during training. She wondered, absently, just how ready for an emergency the Grand Senator's private soldiers actually were.

"Place your hands behind your back," Jamey ordered, one hand holding a plastic tie.

An aide wouldn't comply at once, so Belinda didn't, forcing him to grab her hands and wrap the tie around them. Roland gave her an odd glance as she was pushed down to sit next to him. They hadn't tied *his* hands…all she could do was pray that he didn't do something stupid. Did they really think that a plastic tie would be enough to secure her?

They don't know what you are, Pug reminded her. *Get ready to teach them a lesson.*

The fake Civil Guardsmen seemed professional, but they also seemed vaguely inexperienced, Belinda decided. They relaxed as soon as the two prisoners were seated, even though Roland wasn't tied; they didn't even keep a sharp eye on them. A standard prisoner transport craft would have a partition between the prisoner compartment and the cockpit, just to ensure that escape and hijacking wasn't an option, but the assault shuttle hadn't been designed for transporting prisoners. But then, they were at least *trying* to pretend that they weren't arresting Roland.

Her implants were still being hit by jamming – they must have assumed that Roland had implants, or they would have known that she was more than she seemed – but she managed to link into the assault shuttle's processor node. Most of the active functions had been carefully isolated, she discovered a moment later. Someone didn't want prisoners – or anyone else, for that matter – hacking into the system and taking control. Belinda wasn't too surprised; it was an open secret that there were command overrides built into most Imperial-designed systems and removing them was an obvious step.

She skimmed though the system as the shuttle rose into the air, trying to determine where they were going. Assuming a straight-line flight, it seemed likely that they were heading directly *away* from Imperial City, back towards the Summer Palace. That seemed unlikely, so Belinda skimmed through the massive download on Earth she'd been given when she'd taken up her new post. There *was* a military base, largely disused until the Emergency Committee had taken power, not too far away from the Summer Palace. It would be a perfect place to hide Roland until his views could be *corrected*.

Belinda started preparing for action as the shuttle started to pick up speed. She couldn't risk allowing Roland to be kept prisoner. Roland was tougher than he looked, but a few weeks of conditioning would have him doing whatever the Grand Senate wanted. Certainly, there would be outrage if the truth came out, but she had a feeling that the Grand Senator was well past caring. Alternatively, they could keep him under wraps and produce a computer-generated substitute, although that would be tricky.

The rest of the Grand Senate would eventually demand to see the flesh-and-blood Roland.

Bracing herself, Belinda boosted – and snapped the plastic tie as if it had been made of paper. Jamey had no time to react before she was on him, moving with inhuman speed. His expression barely changed before Belinda's fist punched through his nose and shattered his skull. The other soldiers hesitated, unable to quite comprehend what was happening as Belinda hurled herself into their midst. The handful of blows that landed on her were easily shrugged off as she tore through them, each blow placed in just the right spot. After so long, it felt good to just fight…

A slight reduction in speed, Doug's voice stated. *You've slipped, girl.*

Shut up, Belinda thought, as she sprang towards the pilot. He was reaching desperately for his weapon, rather than trying to signal for help; her hand slammed into his neck as his hands closed around the handle of his pistol. She felt it break under the blow; she pulled his body out of the chair and dumped it on the deck before it had even stopped twitching. It had been nearly a year since she had flown an assault shuttle – and she'd never flown one of this model – but the cockpit was almost identical to newer designs. She had never thought that she would bless the unimaginative designers the Imperial Navy hired…

"My God," Roland said. His voice seemed to crawl in her ears; the boost was still burning through her system. "I…what *are* you?"

Belinda purged the boost from her bloodstream. It was an astonishing rush, but it could also be very dangerous – and addictive. Marines weren't supposed to be able to become addicted to anything – recruits had been kicked out of Boot Camp for bringing drugs with them when they arrived – yet boost had been known to break that rule. Those who used it felt superhuman as long as the boost empowered them. The aftermath was often far from pleasant.

"Pathfinder," Belinda said. Her body was starting to shake; even as augmented and enhanced as she was, the boost took a toll. She fought to control it; there was no time to allow the shakes to fade away naturally. "And don't you forget it."

She saw the horror in Roland's eyes and winced, inwardly. Most humans didn't react well to people with extreme genetic modifications, particularly those who lived on high-gravity worlds. A Pathfinder looked more mundane, until they went into action – Roland had just seen her become a blur, tearing through their captors as if they were made of paper. He would never look at her in the same way again.

"Right," Roland said. His voice sounded as shaky as Belinda felt. "What are we doing now?"

Belinda scowled. "This tub doesn't have the power to make orbit – it should have, but it doesn't," she said. "If we go back to the Summer Palace…"

"We might as well paint targeting crosshairs on our bodies," Roland finished. "So where do we go?"

For once, Belinda honestly didn't know. There were no other Marines left on the surface – apart from the retired ones at the Arena. But getting to them would be difficult – she *did* have the codes to get into Marine HQ, even if it was sealed up, but getting there would be harder still. The Grand Senator had gambled when he'd tried to get Roland into 'protective' custody; he could hardly back down now. If he had troops on the surface…

"I think we were being taken to Scorpio Base," she said, slowly. Perhaps they could storm the base…no, she was being absurd. A full team of Pathfinders or a company of Marines would be able to go through the base, but there was just one of her – and she had to keep Roland safe. "We don't really want to get there."

She checked the display and scowled. Three gunships were providing escort – and she would have bet good money that substantial reinforcements had been held in reserve. After all, if one Grand Senator could plot the effective kidnap of the Crown Prince, why not another? And Prince Roland might have hired more guards for himself…

"We need to get away from our escort," she said, as she checked the weapons panel. The shuttle had most of its original weapons load, although the refitting crew seemed to have stripped out some of the advanced sensors before selling the shuttle to commercial interests. A civilian might not have cared about losing the sensors, provided they had the weapons. How much military training did the Grand Senator have?

"Good thought," Roland said. "And then…?"

"Run to the Arena," Belinda said. She couldn't think of anywhere, apart from the Imperial Palace and Senate Hall, more likely to cause an explosion if the Grand Senator's private army went in heavy-handed. "Sit down and strap yourself in."

She brought the weapons online and grinned to herself. Most threat receivers depended on picking up active sensor sweeps, but there was no need to use military-grade sensors to target her missiles when the targets were so close. She programmed the firing sequence into the missiles, then fired them in a single salvo. Two of the escorting gunships were blown out of the air before they had a chance to do anything more than realise that they were dead; the third heeled over and started to fall out of the sky.

"All right," she said, as she yanked the shuttle around. "Here we go."

The Grand Senator had, thankfully, given his private army IFF codes that would allow them to move unmolested by Traffic Control. Belinda had no idea how well they would hold up after she'd shot down three other shuttles, but she had a feeling that the Grand Senator would have done something to ensure that Traffic Control paid as little attention as possible. After all, if he intended to use his army to cope with his political enemies, he wouldn't want to attract the forces of law and order. The thought made her smirk as she gleefully broke several traffic control regulations, flying by the seat of her pants. If they could outrun any pursuit…

She swore as new icons popped up on the display. The shuttle's IFF processor insisted that they were friendly, but Belinda had no difficulty in recognising the same codes her own shuttle was using. God alone knew what was going through their heads – or the head of their master – but they knew they had to stop her before it was too late.

"Crap," Roland said, when she filled him in. "What are they going to do to us?"

"They're locking weapons on now," Belinda said. Their shuttle didn't have very good defensive systems, she realised. "They may feel that they can force us down…"

An alarm sounded as the enemy opened fire, launching four missiles towards their shuttle. Belinda cut the antigravity system for a brief second and the shuttle dropped like a stone, confusing one of the missiles long enough for it to go haywire. She barely noticed the sick expression on

Roland's face as she yanked the shuttle through a tight turn, then skimmed so close to a CityBlock that two missiles slammed into the building rather than going after the shuttle. The fourth missile fell to the handful of countermeasures built into the shuttle.

Belinda keyed a command into the console, returning fire. The enemy shuttles would probably manage to evade the missiles, but it would buy them a few extra seconds…she pulled the shuttle around a corner and saw an enemy shuttle racing towards her. *Shit*, she thought, as she hastily tried to evade. They must have had more support than she'd realised…

"Brace," she snapped, as the enemy shuttle opened fire. A missile rocketed towards them and detonated, far too close for comfort. Alarms sounded, warning her that the shuttle was badly damaged. The bastards might want to take Roland alive, but they were pushing it – or maybe the Grand Senator had decided to write Roland off after all. He might think he could take power without Roland's unwilling help.

Belinda gritted her teeth. Their power was failing, there were at least seven enemy shuttles hunting them – and they were rapidly running out of options. Right now, she doubted the shuttle would last long enough to reach Imperial City, let alone the Arena. If they fell out of the sky, they'd fall right into the Undercity.

A shudder ran through the shuttle as one of the power cores died. They were going down. Belinda tried to steer the shuttle, but it was starting to act more and more like a flying brick, falling faster and faster as the power died. She tried to send a distress signal to the Marine network, only to discover that the jamming was still active. Not that it would have mattered much, she reminded herself. There were no other active Marines on Earth.

"I'm sorry," she said. Perhaps it would have been better if she'd let Jamey take them to the base instead. Roland might not have been conditioned – and there might have been a chance to break free. "We're going down."

The shuttle plummeted out of the sky. Belinda conserved what power she could, then threw it all into the antigravity nodes. They screamed in protest, but held just long enough to slow their fall. She prayed that it was enough to keep them alive…

…As they crashed headlong down towards the Undercity.

CHAPTER THIRTY

Perhaps the greatest danger lay in the poor infrastructure of Earth – and, to some extent, the entire solar system and the core worlds beyond. Earth's vast cities required obscene levels of maintenance, very little of which was forthcoming. As the Empire's funds dried up, so did their maintenance crews – and the decay started to mount up. Eventually, something had to break.
- Professor Leo Caesius, *The End of Empire.*

Earth's population, Jolo Lafarge had been told when he'd finally found a job in an algae plant, was colossal. The official population alone was nearly ten times the size of Terra Nova's population – and Terra Nova, humanity's first extra-solar colony world, had been settled for over five *thousand* years. No one knew for sure just how large the population actually was, but Jolo had heard estimates that ranged from seventy billion to well over a *hundred* billion. It seemed impossible that any single planet, no matter how advanced, could support so many people.

He looked down at the bubbling algae in the vats and shivered. Algae grew and multiplied at astonishing speed, even before the geneticists had gone to work. The massive vat below him was capable of turning out a new crop of algae ready for processing every four hours, enough to feed thousands of people for several weeks. Once ready, the algae was processed into ration bars and distributed to the hungry. It might taste like shit – the geneticists couldn't or wouldn't improve the algae's natural flavour – but it kept them alive. A man could live on algae alone.

But he wouldn't be living for much longer, Jolo knew, as he stood up and headed towards the manager's office. Very few people *wanted* to spend the rest of their lives in an algae plant, but Jolo was one of them. He'd fallen in love with the whole concept the day he'd been shown how the system worked and, as he had nothing in the way of qualifications, it had seemed like a good career. It even paid better than many other jobs – after all, it was *important*. Jolo had worked his way up through the ranks until he had been promoted to Floor Supervisor. The positions above supervisor required qualifications that had nothing to do with the job, qualifications that Jolo lacked. It had rarely bothered him; his superiors didn't do more than issue a handful of useless orders and then stay in their offices, pretending to work. At least they stayed out of his hair.

He stepped into the manager's office and nodded politely to the little man sitting behind the desk. Manager McNulty wanted every inch of paperwork to be filled out perfectly – Jolo had never bothered with paperwork since he'd become Supervisor, which was part of the reason his section was way ahead of the others – and proper respect from his subordinates. And yet he wasn't the worst manager the plant had seen. There had been the one who'd gotten drunk and thought that it would be safe to take a swim in the largest vat...

"Supervisor," McNulty said. He had a thin nasal voice, as if he was permanently sneering at the world. Like the other managers, he never actually socialised with the workers outside of office hours – not that they cared, of course. If anything, they were grateful. "What can I do for you."

"I need to shut down the vats," Jolo stated, bluntly. "All of them. The entire production run needs to be sterilised."

McNulty blinked at him. "Shut down *all* of the vats?"

"Yes," Jolo said. He'd learned that the best way to get along with his nominal superiors was never to give them any ground. "There are...problems with the current production run."

The system for producing algae was surprisingly basic, so much so that every newcomer eventually started offering suggestions for expanding production. But the system that had been worked out over centuries was stable, while altering the process could have unexpected side effects. Now, with a demand for increased production from the Grand Senate, some of the vats had been imperfectly cleaned between production cycles. Jolo had yelled at the workers responsible, but the damage had been done. Parts of the production run in the vats right now were decaying. Already.

McNulty didn't ask for technical details. That was odd; normally, he insisted being given every last detail. Instead, he just looked as if he was weighing some very difficult choices.

"Problems," he repeated, finally. "Disregard them and carry on."

Jolo stared at him. "Manager," he said, "the production run is *contaminated*!"

"We have strict orders from the very highest levels to ensure that production continues at this expanded rate indefinitely," McNulty informed him. "We are to disregard all problems."

"If the algae is released onto the market," Jolo said, "people will *die*!"

McNulty looked back at him. "I was under the impression that all ration bars were treated to prevent them actually harming people," he said. "Was I, in fact, incorrect?"

"Right now," Jolo answered tightly, "we have algae from at least two different batches mixed up together in the vaults. The production life cycle is destabilising – a problem made worse by the insistence that we speed up production as much as possible. I do not know if it is *possible* to process the bars properly – or if they will be safe for human consumption in any case. We need to ditch the current production run and clean the bloody equipment thoroughly!"

"That is impossible," McNulty said. "The production speed must be maintained."

Jolo took a breath. "The equipment is designed to endure a standard production cycle," he said. "By speeding the cycle up, you are stressing the equipment and pushing it past its design parameters. Sooner or later, something else is going to break – and when it does, the entire production line will go with it."

He forced himself to calm down. Maybe McNulty could be reasoned with. "We just need to ditch this production run and do some maintenance," he offered. "We can catch up later."

"If we don't meet our quota, there will be consequences," McNulty said.

"We *can't* meet our quota," Jolo insisted. He didn't know who had dreamed up the quota, but it was clear that they knew nothing about algae farming. "It isn't physically possible!"

"Make it possible," McNulty snapped.

Jolo stared at him for a long moment, a dozen retorts flashing through his head. He could quit; he could tell McNulty that he wouldn't share any responsibility, no matter how small, for a mass poisoning. But he had a wife and two children and if he quit…the Emergency Committee's new rules stated that anyone who quit his job willingly would not be able to claim the BLA. And if he were fired…he didn't know. It would all have to be sorted out by the courts and that would take years, at the very least. His family would have starved to death by the time the courts came to a decision.

He saw no way out of the trap. Do what he was told, and bear some responsibility for a mass poisoning, or resign and watch his family starve. He wanted to tell McNulty precisely what he thought of him…but then, it wasn't really McNulty's fault. The orders had come from far higher up the food chain; no one would be punished, he knew from long experience, as long as they obeyed orders. Common sense was never allowed a look-in.

If he'd been on his own, he told himself, he would have had the determination to resign rather than take any responsibility. But he wasn't on his own.

"Yes, sir," he said. At least he could oversee the cleaners when the current batch was finished and make sure it didn't happen again. "I'll see to it personally."

Four hours, he thought numbly as he left the office. One more hour to complete production; two hours to bake the algae into ration bars and a final hour to insert them into the distribution chain. And then lethal ration bars would be on the streets, waiting to strike down the unwary.

He thought wistfully of the power outages they'd been having in the apartment block, power outrages that had been blamed on the student revolutionaries. Maybe one of them would take down the algae plant's power and they'd have to dump the entire production run as it spoiled...

But nothing happened.

"Well, you useless slut," a voice barked. "How much did you make this morning?"

Bella barely opened her eyes from where she lay on the bed. Seventeen men, four of them sadists who couldn't get hard unless they heard a woman *scream*...after the last had gone, she'd pressed an injector tab to her neck and allowed the drug to overcome her. The pain in her body faded away into insignificance as she relaxed into the high, even though she knew it wouldn't last. She'd been using Calm for so long that it rarely affected her for longer than ten minutes.

"God, you're useless," Ravi, her pimp, said angrily. His face twisted with disgust as he stared down at her naked body. "Or have you been holding back on me again?"

"No," Bella slurred. Fear was driving the drug's effect out of her mind. The one time she had tried to hold back a tip, Ravi had somehow known what she'd done – and beaten her to within an inch of her life. She'd healed, with a little help from an underground doctor, but the scars on her mind had never faded. Ravi *owned* her, body and soul. Escape was impossible. "Nothing..."

"Then one of them must have stiffed you," Ravi sneered. He caught her arm, pulled her upright and glared into her eyes. "You dumb slut! Why didn't you get the money *first*?"

"I...I did," Bella protested. His grip was hurting her, but she knew better than to protest out loud, or even show any sign that it bothered her. "I was just trying to take as many customers as possible."

"God knows why they want you," Ravi snapped, as he let go of her. She fell back onto the bed, arms and legs flailing helplessly. "You're a fucking mess, barely even worth your room and board."

He was right, Bella knew. Once, she had been moderately attractive, attractive enough to land a man who would take her out of the very lowest level of Rowdy Yates Block. She *had* found a man, but Ravi's seduction had masked a darker motive. The slip into prostitution had started gradually; by the time she'd realised Ravi's true nature, it had been far too late. Even if she ran, she had nowhere to go. He'd gleefully pointed it out to her the first time she had tried to stand up for herself.

Whores didn't last long in the very lowest levels. A few months of servicing random men took its toll – and as her beauty declined, so did the quality of her customers. Some of them were diseased, she was sure, but Ravi hadn't allowed her to refuse anyone. Bella was seventeen years old; she looked forty, at least. It wouldn't be long before Ravi threw her out completely and left her to fend for herself. She'd wind up dead, either through murder or simple starvation.

"And don't cry," Ravi added. "You know I hate that."

He caught her legs and held them upwards, then started slapping the backs of her thighs. Not hard enough to cause permanent damage, but hard enough to remind her of her place. If she was so careless again, it would be worse; Ravi was a past master at hurting her and his other whores without leaving any proper bruises. He certainly wouldn't pay for her to visit the doctor again.

"Your next client will be here in an hour," he said, as he let go of her legs and dropped something onto the bed. "Clean yourself up, put on a gown and be *ready* for him. He won't want to wait for you."

Bella watched as he stalked out of the room, then reached for the item he'd dropped on the bed. A ration bar, newly produced; she shocked herself by how quickly she tore at the packet and exposed the brown-coloured bar inside. It smelt faintly unpleasant, but she ignored it. Surprisingly, the taste was better than usual. But almost anything would have been better than usual.

Moving carefully, she pulled herself to her feet. The back of her legs hurt where he'd slapped her; her chest hurt from where her last client had poked her when she didn't do as he wanted fast enough. It blurred into the aches and pains that affected her every day, the legacy of countless brutal couplings…she was seventeen and she already knew that she was not going to reach eighteen. And even if she did, what of it? She would still be trapped, still be a whore…where could she go?

Ravi had placed a mirror in the bathroom; she stood in front of it and stared at herself. He was right; she did look a mess. Her straggly hair – Ravi refused to allow her to cut it – hung down past her ass, while her bones showed up clearly against her skin. She had a feeling that she was actually too thin, that the pains she felt might be more than just the result of nasty clients and her pimp, but what could she do? Her eyes were pale and worn.

She should get ready for her client, she knew, but it seemed too much effort. Instead, she just collapsed on the floor and lay there.

The stomach pains started moments later.

Everyone who thought of the Undercity – at least everyone who happened to live in the Inner City – thought of it as dark and grimy. And, Dennis, would have happily conceded, there were plenty of parts of it that *were* dark and grimy. But it wasn't *all* like that, particularly for those with power.

Dennis had started young; when he'd been seven, he'd started running errands for the gang lords in the massive CityBlock. It had taught him the true nature of power – and just how far one could go, if one had the power and the will to use it. By seventeen, he had wormed his way into a minor gang lord's good graces and served as his personal enforcer. It had only taken him two years to learn everything he could from his master and then kill him. After that…

There was no shortage of people in the upper reaches of the city – and the entire planet – who wanted something from the Undercity. Instead of fighting other gang lords to carve out territory, Dennis had inched his way upwards, forming links with others in the upper levels. By the time his rivals had realised that he was more powerful than them, it had already been too late. Their enforcers had been exiled to the colonies, the gang lords had been killed and their daughters had become his slaves. Admittedly, the girls were so dosed up on Sparkle Dust that they would obey anyone who gave them orders, but nothing was perfect. It wasn't a bad achievement for the son of a whore.

Still, his little empire needed maintenance. And something very worrying was going on.

"Ninety-seven of our people have died, my lord," Rufus said. "Nineteen of them were Ravi's whores. The others were small fry; rat-runners and dogsbodies, mainly. It appears to be poison."

Dennis frowned. There was never any shortage of whores, or young boys ready to indenture themselves to the all-powerful gangs, but still… losing so many of them was annoying. Ravi specialised in squeezing the last few credits out of whores shambling towards their deathbeds; his losses would affect his position within the gang. He might even do something stupid to his fellow gangsters, convinced that one of them had poisoned his bitches. Dennis wouldn't have cared – he encouraged a certain amount of infighting – but if it *wasn't* one of the others, he needed his gang reasonably united.

And the fact that others had died suggested that it was no simple poisoning.

"Have Doctor Stockwell take a look at the bodies," he ordered, finally. The good Doctor had been lucky to escape to the Undercity when the Civil Guard had come looking for him. If Dennis had been a more moral man, he might just have executed the Doctor himself and saved the government the trouble. As it was, a man with the Doctor's weaknesses – and his desires – could be useful. "And then let me know what he has to say."

He considered the problem briefly. Poison had never been his weapon of choice – it was much more impressive to kill with one's bare hands – but he *had* used it on a few of his victims, when naked force wasn't necessary. Simple logic pointed out that anyone who died of poison had to have drunk it – and someone who didn't die hadn't actually drunk it. There *were* poisons that could be tailored to one person, or rendered harmless by a previously-taken antidote, but it seemed unlikely that anyone would go to all that trouble and expense to kill a few whores.

And if it was poison, what had all the victims had in common? It wasn't as if they had all shared a single drinking fountain or something else that would be instantly recognisable.

Shaking his head, he tapped the bell and called his secretary. When he arrived, Dennis issued orders; the enforcers were to investigate all of the poisonings thoroughly. He'd spent enough time explaining the importance of intelligence to them that it had become thoroughly stuck in their heads. Given enough of it, Dennis might just be able to figure out who had attacked his gang…

…And then he could make them pay.

CHAPTER THIRTY-ONE

It should not have been surprising that the first major disaster – the first one that affected a significant percentage of Earth's vast population – involved algae. Even before the fall of Orbit Station Seven, the algae vats had been starting to break down through lack of maintenance. When the Grand Senate insisted that production levels be massively increased, the result was a series of minor failures that added up to a major disaster.
- Professor Leo Caesius, *The End of Empire.*

The compensator field held just long enough to save their lives.

Belinda hung on for dear life as the shuttle crashed through a rooftop and into the darkness, silently relieved that the shuttle was so heavily armoured. Roland let out a yelp as there was a final series of crashes, followed by absolute silence. The shuttle's power died seconds later, plunging them into darkness. Belinda unstrapped herself from the pilot's chair and stood up, her eyes adapting instantly to the gloom. God alone knew where they were, but they couldn't stay there. The enemy would be coming after them.

Roland looked scratched and bruised, but largely intact. Belinda grinned at him – his eyes might not have any augments, but his enhanced eyesight would adapt reasonably quickly - and inspected the shuttle's hull. They'd come down hard; the shuttle would never fly again, even though it had saved their lives. She tried to ping the shuttle's processor with her implants, but there was no response. The hulk was completely powerless. A quick check revealed that there were no other processor nodes within range. She couldn't even reach the Marine network.

She glanced over as Roland stood up. The Prince looked oddly excited, the same sort of excitement that Belinda had felt after completing her first mission after graduation. He looked a little unsteady too – the shuttle's deck was tilted, making it harder for him to find his footing – but otherwise he looked intact. They'd been luckier, Belinda decided, than they deserved. But if the Grand Senator had been willing to use force to capture or kill the Crown Prince, it was unlikely that they would have been left alone in the Summer Palace for much longer.

Roland found his voice. "Where are we?"

"The Undercity," Belinda said. She accessed her implants and reviewed their records, but it wasn't as useful as she'd hoped. The desperate flight had taken them closer to the Arena, yet they were still at least fifty miles away – and they'd crashed into the Undercity. There were no proper maps of the Undercity in existence. "Finding our way out might be tricky."

That, she told herself, was definitely an understatement. The Undercity was nightmarish; massive city blocks piled on city blocks, entire communities buried so far underground that they never saw the light. There were all sorts of horror stories about strange creatures running through the very lowest levels, each one a reflection of the unknown. Far too much of humanity's history had simply been buried under the endless city blocks. Even if they got back up to the light, they were still going to be in deep trouble. It wasn't as if they could call for help.

"Tricky," Roland repeated. He probably knew enough to be concerned. "Can they find us down here?"

Belinda considered it as she found the emergency packs and tossed one of them to Roland, then stripped down one of the bodies for the armour. "I don't know," she admitted, finally. The enemy shuttles would have tracked their fall, surely, but sending troops into the Undercity would be difficult. They'd have to be prepared to fight the locals as well as operate in a strange environment. "We can't stay here."

She passed the bloodstained armour to Roland, then checked for any other supplies while the Prince reluctantly donned the armour. Marines tended to be a little superstitious about using equipment that belonged to the dead, but Civil Guardsmen weren't given a choice. Their budgets just weren't large enough to provide new equipment for every recruit. *Roland* couldn't be given a choice either. Her mission was still to protect him, even if it had suddenly become a whole lot harder.

Once the Prince was armed and armoured, Belinda inspected the airlock. The power cells had failed, forcing her to crank it open manually. At least it *was* possible to open it by hand, she told herself; there were civilian designs that turned into inescapable traps when the power failed. There was a brief hiss of air as the airlock opened, allowing the Undercity atmosphere to seep into the shuttle. Belinda couldn't help recoiling at the stench.

Roland gagged and swallowed hard, trying to keep from vomiting. "You said people *live* here," he said, his face green. "How is that even possible?"

"You can get used to anything, if you endure it long enough," Belinda said. Even without any enhancement, Roland would adapt to the stench if he stayed there for hours and stopped noticing it. "Stay here."

Belinda slipped out of the shuttle and looked around. They had crashed through a concrete roof and fallen into a strange building, illuminated only by a faint glow from high overhead. There was no sign of any humans, but she could see bats and spiders lurking in the shadows, daring her to come closer. She looked at a network of tubes and half-filled vats in the shadows and decided that she was looking at a production plant of some kind. The dust lay so thick that it might be completely impossible to remove. She shook her head in silent awe. The chamber had to have been disused and deserted for hundreds of years. By now, it had developed its own ecology.

She closed her eyes and pushed her augmentations to the limit, trying to pull what information she could from her surroundings. There was a faint buzzing sound in the distance, reminding her of the insects that had infested parts of the Slaughterhouse, the noises they made blurring into one ever-present drone. Maybe it *was* insects, she decided, as red alerts flashed up in front of her retina. The environment was contaminated, they warned, but her implants hadn't been able to identify the contaminant. Something in the air…

"Get a facemask," she ordered, as she opened her eyes. They'd have to wear them – and pray that between the masks and their enhancements, they would be able to cope with whatever was in the air. Thankfully, it didn't appear to be radioactive. "And then we'd better start walking."

Roland still looked green as he clambered out of the shuttle. "What's causing the light?"

Belinda frowned. "Lichen, I think," she said. "It thrives everywhere."

The breed had been genetically engineered to provide natural lighting; she vaguely remembered something about a religion that had believed in abandoning technology and returning to the basics of life. They'd bred a number of useful plants to help create their utopia; the fact that they'd needed technology to do that had evidently escaped them. Most of their worlds had fallen from the path within three hundred years, as the children of the believers started to ask just why their parents had abandoned technology in the first place. At least one of them had fallen down into civil war.

She pushed the thought aside as she started to walk away from the shuttle. "Time to start walking," she said, dryly. "There's a long way to go."

Roland blinked at her. "You know the way?"

"No," Belinda admitted. She'd hoped he wouldn't ask that question, but he was smarter than most people had realised. "All we can really do is keep heading upwards."

The darkness closed in around them as they found a passageway leading out of the vast chamber and walked up it. Belinda hadn't known that Roland was claustrophobic, although it wasn't something that was likely to be obvious in the Summer Palace. Or maybe it was just nerves. At Boot Camp, recruits had had to find their way through tunnel systems – and several had simply refused to enter, unable to face the thought of crawling through the tunnels. Belinda had had problems coping at first. The vast open spaces of her homeworld hadn't prepared her for the tunnels.

"Damn it," Roland breathed, as a small swarm of spiders rushed past them. "Do you think they're poisonous?"

"You should be safe," Belinda assured him. Roland's ancestors had spliced all kinds of protections into their genes, according to the files. It would take a very strong poison to discomfit him. "And yes, they probably are poisonous."

And they didn't show any fear of humans, she noted. On her homeworld, animals that lived near human settlements kept their distance;

they'd learned just what humans could do with the power of the gun. The ones who lived on the untouched continent didn't flee when they sensed humans approaching. It suggested that there were few humans still living so far underground.

Or that they're not the dominant life form, Belinda thought. She kept *that* thought to herself. There were researchers who had proposed uplifting animal life forms to sentience, but the Empire had always banned the practice. And yet there were always rumours from the Rim and the hidden colony worlds beyond. Who knew *what* would happen if the Empire's authority collapsed completely?

They stopped as they saw a metal plaque pushed against one wall. It was rusty, but Belinda managed to pick out a handful of words. DEPT... TRAVEL...ROGERS. She puzzled over them for a long moment before deciding that the mystery was probably insolvable – and besides, it didn't matter. Knowing what the building had once been wouldn't help them now.

The walls seemed to change as they stepped through a door, heading upwards. Belinda had a feeling that they'd moved out of one building and into another, although it was difficult to be sure. The oldest parts of the city had been buried under the newest parts, after all. She couldn't help wondering just what that meant for the city's structural integrity; if the CityBlocks had been built on older buildings, did that mean that their foundations were unstable? Just for a moment, she wished for an Engineer, even one from the Civil Guard. He might be able to answer her question.

CityBlocks were built out of Rearden Cement and Hullmetal, if she recalled correctly. Both materials were tough; Rearden Cement had been known to withstand and redirect nuclear blasts in the past, during humanity's nastier wars. But what would happen if their foundations collapsed? Belinda had a vision of entire CityBlocks falling, the shock shattering parts of their internal integrity...she pushed the thought aside, grimly. If the city decided to collapse on them, they would die before they knew what had hit them.

They rested, long enough for Roland to catch his breath, and then continued upwards. Most of the spiders and insects appeared to have vanished, although there were traces that suggested the presence of larger animals. She caught sight of a cockroach and rolled her eyes inwardly; cockroaches, rats and rabbits were epidemic on almost every world humanity had colonised, defying every attempt man had made to eradicate them. Even asteroid colonies had problems with unwelcome residents. She said as much to Roland, who wondered if the Undercity dwellers were actually farming them. It definitely seemed possible.

She froze as she heard a moan in the distance. Her audio-discrimination program, operating at the very limits of its capabilities, insisted that it was a human sound. Belinda exchanged a long glance with Roland, then headed towards the source of the sound, every sense alert for signs of an ambush. Using distress calls to suck people in was a favourite terrorist trick.

Her implants reported trace elements of several illegal drugs hanging in the air as she moved forward, enough to disorient anyone who didn't have enhancements designed to cope with it. Belinda ignored it as they peered around a corner and saw a long room, illuminated only by more of the eerie lichen. Inside, several men and women lay on the ground, one of them groaning constantly. The others appeared to be dead, their bodies still cooling. Whatever had killed them had done so very recently.

"Stay here," Belinda hissed. Drug addicts had been known to accidentally overdose themselves and die, but she doubted that so many of them would do it at the same time. "And watch your back."

The groaning form was a woman, she realised, as she knelt down beside her. It was hard to be sure; what little she could see of the woman's body suggested that she was almost inhumanly thin, so thin that her breasts were practically non-existent. One hand was clutching her stomach, as if she was trying to beat pain out of it; the other was torn and broken. Belinda touched the woman lightly on the forehead and felt her flinch back in shock. A moment later, there was a final convulsive shudder and she died.

Roland stepped over to where he could peer down at the body. "What happened to her?"

"I thought I told you to stay there," Belinda snapped at him. "And I don't know *what* killed her."

A proper autopsy would reveal the truth, she knew, but she didn't have the equipment or time to carry one out. She examined the woman's body quickly and concluded that she'd been starving to death, but that didn't explain the convulsions – or why so many had dropped dead at the same time. Several of the other bodies had vomited before they died… poison? Perhaps their food, wherever it came from, was poisonous. Or maybe there was a darker explanation.

"Could be a new disease," she said, thoughtfully. The Undercity struck her as a very good place for such a disease to appear. It was unlikely that anyone born there would have any enhancements, even the basic disease resistance treatments handed out in school. But there would probably have been some seepage anyway. "Or maybe a recurrence of a very old one."

Roland gave her an inquiring look. "I heard a story from a Marine who was stationed on New Boswell," Belinda explained, reluctantly. "They had trouble with a minor insurgency, so the government requested backup from the Empire – and they got a Civil Guard regiment from a nearby world instead of anything useful. The CO wasn't a bad sort, but he was so determined to do well that he set up camp away from the settlements – and forgot the importance of basic hygiene. Two weeks later, his entire regiment was down with the galloping shits."

Roland snickered. "And you say that this CO wasn't a bad guy?"

"Standards are low," Belinda admitted. "He wasn't stealing his men's pay, he wasn't taking bribes…compared to many of his fellows, he was a paragon of military leadership. And he *did* lead his men into battle."

She shrugged. "Point is; these people are thin and wasted. If they caught something, their ability to resist it would be low."

Roland seemed oddly thoughtful as they walked away from the chamber and headed upwards. Belinda could guess what he was thinking; someone had to do something about the poor bastards living in the Undercity. She could sympathise with him, but she knew that it was impossible to do anything. The vast resources of the Empire couldn't help more than a relative handful of Earth's population, not in any meaningful way.

Maybe we should have used something to prevent them from breeding, she thought, coldly. But it was now far too late. Besides, using such treatments was taboo in the Empire; they had been used by an unscrupulous planetary development corporation to carry out a soft genocide. Even the Grand Senate, no strangers to committing atrocities in the name of profit and power, had been shocked.

She stopped as her implants picked up the unmistakable sounds of someone trying to not make a sound. There were at least three people ahead of them, she realised; this time, they were definitely lying in ambush. Someone without implants would probably have missed their presence until it was too late. She hesitated, wishing that Roland knew the sign language Marines used to communicate when they couldn't speak out loud, then pulled him close to her so she could whisper in his ear. At least she could practically subvocalise to him.

"Stay here," she ordered, once she'd told him what was ahead of them. "I'll deal with our new friends."

She walked right into the next chamber, doing her best to project an image of a fat and happy victim walking blindly into the trap. It must have worked; three young men wearing scavenged clothing stepped into view, leering at her. Their faces suggested, part of Belinda's mind noted, that they were the products of centuries of inbreeding, perhaps even outright incest. Was it actually possible for a human settlement to devolve?

"You're trespassing," one of them said. His accent was thick, but understandable. "And we don't *like* trespassers."

Belinda pretended to look nervous while she evaluated them. The leader carried a neural whip, but her implants suggested that it might not be charged up. His two followers carried nothing more dangerous than metal clubs, which they balanced on their shoulders as if they were rifles. There was no sign of any actual firearms at all.

"Get your shorts down and bend over and we might just forgive you – afterwards," another one said. "And we might even find you a new job."

Belinda didn't bother to draw on the boost. The day she couldn't deal with three untrained and overconfident thugs was the day she would be kicked out of the Pathfinders for gross incompetence. None of them had the slightest idea of her true nature.

"I have a better idea," she told them, as she surged forward. None of them had time to react before she smacked all three of them down, knocking out the two thugs completely. A quick check revealed that the neural whip wasn't just powerless; it was broken. She picked the leader off the floor and glared into his eyes, sneering at him. "Why don't you take me to your boss?"

CHAPTER
THIRTY-TWO

Post-collapse scholars have wondered why – actually, the words they use were ruder – the bureaucrats did nothing to solve the Algae Crisis. Put simply, the problem was that they were attempting to do the impossible. They needed to raise food supplies on Earth; at the same time, they needed to carry out maintenance – which would reduce the amount of time spent producing more food. Earth was already suffering a significant shortfall when contaminated algae bars began to appear on the planet.

- Professor Leo Caesius, *The End of Empire.*

"You *lost* him?"

Stephen stared at Colonel Jamey's second-in-command, unable to believe what he'd just heard. Colonel Jamey hadn't had a very difficult task. All he'd had to do was secure the Prince and move him to somewhere where his attitudes could be adjusted. Given the firepower he'd brought with him, it should have been easy to deal with the Prince's bodyguards if they put up a fight. Instead, they'd taken the Prince and his aide without a fight and then...

He shook his head in disbelief. "How did the Prince manage to overcome so many armed men?"

"I don't know, sir," Lieutenant Addis admitted. The young man stood ramrod straight, as if he knew perfectly well that his superior would be looking for scapegoats. Addis hadn't had anything to do with the planning, let alone the first part of the operation, but that wouldn't save him if the Grand Senator wanted someone to blame. "The first I knew of anything going wrong was when the hijacked shuttle started to open fire."

Stephen scowled. Roland hadn't had any combat training, at least as far as he could determine. He did have an enhanced body – and a number of implants – but that didn't automatically make someone a lethal fighter. Colonel Jamey should have had no difficulty subduing him; at worst, the Captain had had authority to stun the Prince. Instead...

Far too many people had seen the brief, but violent clash in the skies of Earth. The Emergency Committee still controlled most of the media, yet rumours were flying freely – not helped by the students in the university broadcasting their messages to everyone who might listen. No one seemed to know the real story, not yet, but some of the rumours were even more disconcerting. The brief battle had actually been a military coup that had failed, according to one rumour; a second suggested that terrorists had actually infiltrated the Civil Guard and turned on their erstwhile comrades. And a third even had the nerve to suggest that the Civil Guard was turning against the Grand Senate.

He met Addis's eyes. "Did the Prince survive the crash?"

"Unknown," Addis said. "The shuttle was lost somewhere within the Undercity; I didn't have the manpower to go after the Prince directly. However, those shuttles are designed for hard impacts. It is quite possible that he survived."

And if he didn't, Stephen thought, *his body might be intact.*

That would be worrying. If the body was eaten in the Undercity – there were persistent rumours of cannibalism – that would be gruesome, but acceptable. But if the body was recovered by one of Stephen's rivals, they could use it against Stephen himself, starting by questioning just what had happened to cost Roland his life. Did the Emergency Committee have the authority to detain the Prince or take him into protective custody against his will? The answer, naturally, would depend on the situation rather than the fine print...

"Roland didn't know how to fight," Stephen said. But he'd underestimated the Prince before; what if he'd underestimated him all along? "Have you secured the Summer Palace?"

"Yes, sir," Addis said. "Everyone who was there has been taken into custody."

"Good," Stephen said. At least Addis had done one thing right. "You are hereby promoted to Captain and command of Unit Nine. Put together a team to find the shuttle and recover the Prince's body, if possible. Also, interrogate everyone at the Summer Palace. I want to know what *really* happened there over the last few years."

"Yes, sir," Addis said. He didn't sound too happy at the promotion, but it *was* something of a poisoned chalice, even if it did come with a larger salary. "I shall see to it at once."

He withdrew, leaving Stephen alone to contemplate the disruption Prince Roland had caused to his plans. The Civil Guard had taken up positions around Imperial University, ready to move in and crush the rebels, but it might already be too late. There were reports of problems at a thousand different government buildings, where parents had realised that their children were in danger. This wasn't a riot; this was a threatened massacre. Stephen suspected that every hour they hesitated, the situation was just going to get worse and worse – but there might be even more trouble if the Civil Guard crushed the uprising. Maybe they could just starve the students out.

Roland might have been right, he thought sourly. *Damn him.*

It was nearly an hour before Lindy requested permission to enter his office. "I have the reports from the interrogation team," she said. "Prince Roland's new aide is more than she seems."

"She would have to be," Stephen muttered. The last few aides had been driven away by the Prince's sexual harassment. It wasn't a good way to ensure loyalty. "What is she?"

"It took some time to get Colonel Hicks to talk," Lindy admitted. "He belongs to Grand Senator Devers – we had to threaten to use intensive interrogation methods just to get him to open his mouth. The official record states that Belinda Lawson is just another aide, hired from a recruiting agency. Unofficially, she was inserted into the palace by the Marine Corps."

Stephen stared at her. It had taken years of careful manoeuvring to separate the Marines from the Prince, citing the need to keep as many

Marines on the front lines as possible. The Corps still had a legal right to have their own people there, but it had been generally understood that they wouldn't use it. And they'd slipped someone in without his people even *noticing*.

"And Hicks didn't tell *anyone*?" He asked. "Why...?"

"He told his mistress," Lindy said. "The Grand Senator just didn't see fit to pass the information onwards."

Stephen growled wordlessly. Grand Senator Devers was *not* one of his supporters; she had too many ambitions of her own to tamely accept anyone holding power over her. Even the Emergency Committee couldn't push her around easily. She'd known about the Marine's presence – and she'd kept it to herself. No doubt she'd thought it could be used for her own advantage later on.

"Damn it," he said. A single Marine would not have been a problem if they'd known what she was. But Stephen had assumed that she was just Prince Roland's latest sexual toy and hadn't looked any further. "What *kind* of Marine?"

"Unknown," Lindy said.

The Marines kept some details to themselves, Stephen knew – and even a Grand Senator had trouble finding out what they might be hiding. A standard Marine wouldn't operate alone, but there were Marine Pathfinders and Green Lights...there was even a rumour of something called the Marine Corpse that existed in the shadows. There was no way to know. Only one thing was clear; Belinda Lawson had to be someone very special.

"I take it you checked their records," he said, finally. "Did you find anything?"

"Nothing," Lindy said. "But you know what happens with Marine records."

Stephen nodded, sourly. A recruit who reached the Slaughterhouse could have his records sealed or wiped, if he wanted to start a new life. It was impossible to be sure how many recruits had gone to the Slaughterhouse, or what might have happened to them afterwards, once they started active service. Maybe there *was* a record for Belinda Lawson out there – it was hard to bury *everything* – but it wouldn't be accurate. The Marines kept their secrets close.

"Assume the worst," he ordered, tightly. "What was she doing with the Prince?"

"Physical training, apparently," Lindy said. She made an odd face. "The maids didn't have to be pushed to talk. They were quite impressed by how the Prince had stopped molesting them…he used to pull them into his arms quite frequently. And some of them even said that he was *polite*."

"I see," Stephen said, remembering his own son. Roland had clearly learned a few lessons from the Marine – and better than Stephen's son, if what the maids said was true. But then, the maids hadn't really had anywhere to go. If they'd been sacked, they would have gone straight into the Undercity. "So he grew up a bit."

"Yes, sir," Lindy confirmed.

"We have to find him," Stephen asserted, flatly. "Let me know the moment Captain Addis reports back."

Two hours later, he knew the worst.

"The shuttle was clearly abandoned, sir," Captain Addis said, calling in from where the shuttle had crashed. "The Prince and his aide are missing, but the capture team are dead. Most of the evidence was badly damaged by the fall…"

"Get to the point," Stephen growled.

"The capture team appear to have been killed by an augmented human," Addis said. "There was also a snapped plastic tie on the deck. I think we're hunting for someone with top-of-the-range enhancements."

"So it seems," Stephen agreed, quietly. A Pathfinder, then; regular Marines didn't have so much augmentation. And they hadn't even realised that she was there. "Can you track them?"

"I don't think so, sir," Addis said. "We're not outfitted for a long crawl through the Undercity."

"Understood," Stephen said. He shook his head, minutely. Given a few hours, he suspected that the Prince and his bodyguard could lose themselves in the Undercity – or get murdered by its inhabitants. "Get back up here and put together a team with proper equipment, then wait for my command to go back down. I have another card I want to play."

He closed the channel and keyed a command into his private processor. Maybe the Civil Guard couldn't find someone in the Undercity, not if they didn't want to be found and the locals objected to Guardsmen crashing around in their territory. But there were other options. It was time to speak to Bode.

"I have to go meet with a supplier," Richard said. "Do *not* leave the apartment for any reason."

"Right," Amethyst answered, crossly. She couldn't help feeling trapped, even when she pushed her doubts about Richard aside. Just what could she do in the tiny box-like apartment? She didn't even have a handcom. "I'll stay here."

"I mean it," Richard insisted. "Or do I have to tie you up to make sure you stay put?"

He wasn't joking, Amethyst realised. "No," she replied, tightly. How *dare* he treat her like that? But it wasn't as if she had anywhere to go. "I'll stay here."

Richard gave her a long searching look, then headed out the door. Amethyst heard the lock click and shook her head in disbelief. Just what had she gotten into, really?

They'd started a riot. They'd fired on the Crown Prince. But Richard had refused to do *anything* about the uprising at Imperial University, pointing out that it would just get them killed for nothing if they got involved. Amethyst worried endlessly about her friends; Richard didn't seem to care. Instead, he'd just insisted that they spend most of their time in bed. It had long since lost its allure.

But where could she go? They knew who she was now; the raid on their flat proved it beyond a shadow of a doubt. If they hadn't already had her details – and every civilian was supposed to be registered with the government from birth – they'd have them now, along with proof that she'd owned a banned book. And if they'd connected her to the assassination attempt on Prince Roland…the media had promised that those responsible would be caught and killed, before falling silent on the whole issue. Richard had told her that meant that they didn't want to admit that they hadn't found the assassins, but they could easily bring it up again. If they caught her, it wouldn't be exile. She'd be executed.

Shaking her head, she stood up and looked around for Richard's bag. He'd left it under the bed, warning her not to touch it. Amethyst had obeyed, but now she wanted to take a proper look; she tried to pull it out and blinked in surprise. It was *heavy*! She'd complained about the weight she'd had to carry, back when they'd been preparing to fire on Roland's aircar, but Richard was carrying a far greater weight without complaint. Carefully, she dragged it out and opened the zip on the top. A faint smell of metal and oil rose to her nose as she peered inside.

There were five guns, two of which she recognised as being similar to the ones he'd taught her to use. The other three were beyond her ability to identify, although one of them struck her as looking rather like an oversized pistol. She touched it gingerly and discovered that it was surprisingly heavy. Below the weapons, there were a handful of ammunition clips, a set of credit chips and a stack of weird-smelling bars. Her first thought was that they were ration bars – they smelt vaguely of marzipan, something she'd only tasted once when she'd been very young – but they felt odd to the touch. Putting them back, she examined the credit chips thoughtfully. They were unmarked – thus illegal – and very difficult to obtain.

Hidden at the bottom of the bag, she found several tools she didn't recognise, a couple of unmarked datachips and a reader. She hesitated, then pushed one of the chips into the reader and turned it on. The reader demanded a password. Amethyst cursed – she should have thought of that, but passwords were officially forbidden on university-issued equipment – and removed the chip, returning it to its hiding place. She returned everything to the bag, sealed it up and pushed it back under the bed. Richard had more weapons than she had expected, but nothing else. Nothing that would tell her what he really was.

But having the weapons alone would be enough to condemn him, Amethyst thought, grimly. *If he were caught with any weapon, let alone so many…*

She made sure that the bag was hidden and then lay down on the bed, trying to get some sleep. It wasn't easy; she kept thinking of Jacqueline…

and of the moment where she'd seen something else lurking under Richard's handsome features. And then the door opened.

"Grab your clothes," Richard ordered, shortly. "We have to move."

Amethyst blinked. "They're coming for us?"

"I don't think so," Richard said. "We have a job to do."

"Oh," Amethyst said. "What sort of job?"

Richard's face flickered – for a long chilling moment – with rage. "There is someone we have to find," he said, as he caught her hand and pulled her to her feet effortlessly. Perhaps he wouldn't have any trouble with the bag at all. "Now, get dressed or I will have to…encourage you."

Amethyst hesitated, then obeyed before he could carry out his threat. Richard seemed more intense than usual, almost nervous…what could be bothering him? She pulled on the clothes she'd obtained – the drab unimaginative outfit of a bureaucratic drone – as he opened his bag and removed one of the strange bars and a small pen-shaped device.

"We won't be coming back here," he informed her, unpleasantly. "They'll track the room down eventually – and then they'll be in for a shock."

"Good," Amethyst said. What *were* those bars? Greatly daring, she asked. "What are those things?"

"Explosive," Richard replied, without looking up. He missed the shock that passed across her face. "We can't do much to the Reardon Cement that binds this place together, but we can sure mess up any investigators when they try to enter the apartment. Should make them a little more careful in future."

He looked her up and down, then nodded slowly. "Take your bag," he ordered, shortly. "Then you can wait outside."

Amethyst nodded and obeyed, fighting down the urge to shake helplessly. What would have happened if she'd *eaten* one of the bars? Would it have exploded in her stomach? Outside, there was almost no one in the corridor; the worker drones had gone to work and most of their children would be in school. She pushed herself against the wall, wondering just what the other unmarked metal doors hid. It wasn't as if they'd had a chance to get to know their neighbours.

"Done," Richard announced, as he pulled the door firmly closed. "The next person who opens that door is going to get a nasty surprise."

He strode off down the corridor, forcing her to run to keep up. "Where are we going?"

"First, to meet up with the others," Richard said. "And then…we're going to the Undercity. We have someone to find."

Amethyst caught his arm, forcing him to turn and face her. "Who?"

"You're asking a lot of questions today," Richard observed unpleasantly. He'd warned her that the less she knew, the better. What she didn't know she couldn't betray. "Is there a reason for that?"

"I'm worried about my friend," Amethyst said. It was easy to look pitiful in the garment, her hair tied up into a bun. She was ruefully aware that she looked at least thirty years old. "Will this help her…?"

"It might," Richard said. His face twisted into an odd sneer. "The person we're looking for is Prince Roland."

He grinned at her expression, then turned and started to walk again. Amethyst stared after him in disbelief. Prince Roland? What was *he* doing in the Undercity?

"Come on," Richard snapped, as he reached the stairwell. "We're not the only ones looking for him."

CHAPTER THIRTY-THREE

A further problem was that the bureaucrats (and many of the other workers) were locked into their positions. Failure to meet the Grand Senate's wishes would result in personal disaster; they preferred to keep their jobs and pray that everything went well. Those who did realise that there was a problem were ordered to keep silent to avoid upsetting the situation further. The outcome was inevitable. Through selfish inaction – and moral cowardice – the bureaucrats condemned millions of people to death. They did not go quietly.
- Professor Leo Caesius, *The End of Empire.*

"What the hell is this place?"

"Gang lair," Belinda explained, quietly. They might have been on Earth, rather than Han or one of the other battlefields she'd seen, but the basic principles were universal. There would be a leader, who might be a subordinate of someone higher up, and a lieutenant who would serve as the principal enforcer. The others would jostle for their positions, often stabbing their fellows in the back to gain an advantage. "Stay quiet."

The gang lair wasn't very elegant. Most of the gangsters seemed to sleep in a large room, their weapons by their sides. They eyed Belinda with some alarm; the gangster escorting them had explained to the guards that she'd knocked out his two friends and was clearly very dangerous. Belinda rolled her eyes, inwardly. The gangsters, knowing nothing of true discipline, would only knuckle under to a display of strength. Half of them seemed to be drugged up already, creating a potential nightmare. She pretended to be completely unconcerned as they led her deeper into the lair, all too aware that several gangsters were trying to block their line of retreat.

She refused to show any expression as they walked past a room where several naked girls lay, their eyes dull and hopeless. The gang's women, protected from the Undercity, but forced to service the gangsters as they saw fit. It was always heartbreaking to see so much potential simply wasted, particularly on Earth; they could have been educated or even allowed to leave and head to a colony world. But they had no hope and never would. How was it *just* or *right* that being enslaved to the gang was perhaps the best thing that could happen to them?

But the universe is not just or right, nor is it fair, Doug's voice whispered. *Don't you know that?*

Belinda ignored it as they passed the girls. She wanted to do something to help them, but what? The Empire couldn't do anything to give them a better life; the Empire could barely take care of the citizens in the upper cities. Even if they tried, they wouldn't be able to reach more than a tiny percentage of the vulnerable population. The rest would just be given false hope. On other worlds, the Marines had managed to help some of the victims, if only by arranging for them to have a second chance at life. Earth's population was too far gone.

She smiled humourlessly as she was shown into the gang leader's office. Unsurprisingly, it was finer than the rest of the lair; the gang leader had to show off his wealth and power, just to remind everyone that he was in charge. It also provoked envy from his subordinates, who would certainly plot to kill him and take his place. If they succeeded, a new gang leader would arise.

"You're a very strange person," the gang leader said. He was trying to sound sophisticated, but not quite succeeding. "And you were trespassing in my territory."

Belinda studied him for a long moment. Like many of his fellows, the leader looked to be the product of inbreeding, with a thick neck, slovenly face and dark eyes. His visible skin was covered in tattoos, each one an exercise in raw intimidation; in the Undercity, tattoos were administered without the benefit of anaesthetic. Just having so many testified to his ability to resist pain.

Bastard, Belinda thought, coldly. He might have been the product of his environment, but he was still a bastard. Besides, if he wanted to show he could handle pain, he should go through the Slaughterhouse. Except he'd probably never even complete Boot Camp.

"We're not interested in your territory, or you," Belinda said. She sensed the hidden relief in the gang leader's stance and smiled inwardly. "Might I have the pleasure of knowing who I am talking to?"

The gang leader stared at her for a long cold moment. "You may call me Bat," he said. "And why are you here, if you are not interested in my territory?"

Belinda had given the matter some thought. She had no idea how the Undercity was structured; if she lied about where they came from, Bat might know it. There was no way that he would know anything about Belinda, but it was quite possible that he would have heard of Prince Roland, maybe even seen a picture. For all she knew, the Grand Senate was putting out alerts right now. And there would certainly be a hefty reward for Roland being captured and returned, alive.

But what kind of explanation could she give that wouldn't make them a different sort of target?

"We're looking for new contacts," she said, finally. It was a lousy explanation, but everything else was worse. "Do I assume that you might be interested in talking with us?"

Bat gave her a surprised look. "And there I was thinking that you might have something to do with the crashed shuttle," he said, dryly. "Silly me."

Belinda cursed, inwardly. They'd been caught in a lie.

"Quite a few odd things have happened," Bat added. His eyes were scanning Belinda's face, as if they were trying to sort truth from fiction. "Did you know that an armed team of Guardsmen followed the shuttle down, eventually? They don't normally bother. And then they were withdrawn."

"Oh," Belinda said, mildly.

"So tell me," Bat said, with a hand signal to his goons. "Just who are you? Because I'm sure that there are others up among the toffs who would be happy to pay for you…"

He allowed his voice to trail off suggestively. The bastard was right, Belinda knew; the Grand Senator would happily pay a large ransom to have Roland handed over to him. But he wouldn't want Belinda herself, even if he still thought that she was just an aide hired more for her looks than experience. And if he knew who she was…

"I think that we could pay you more to hide us," she said, carefully. They *could* fight their way out, but that would send shockwaves through the entire city. She dared not assume that the Grand Senator's hunting party – and she was sure that one would be dispatched – would be unprepared for her tricks. "And there might be other advantages."

"Indeed?" Bat asked. He leered at her, his gaze leaving her no doubt what sort of advantages he had in mind. "And those would be…"

Belinda looked up at Bat's enforcer. He was a giant of a man, easy large enough to pass for an artilleryman; he wore nothing apart from a loincloth, the better to show off his muscles. Belinda would have mistaken him for a heavy-world genie if she hadn't been sure he came from Earth. What sort of genie would want to live on humanity's ruined homeworld?

"This," she said.

She lunged out with augmented strength and punched the enforcer in the throat, before he could even see her coming. Her fist went right through his skin and broke his neck, sending him tumbling to the ground as soon as she withdrew her fist and wiped it on her shirt. The gangsters stared at her, unable to quite wrap their minds around what they'd seen. They'd grown up in an environment where women were – at best – third-class citizens. Most of them would not expect a woman to be able to fight, let alone kill a man with a single blow…

She'd seen it before, on several of the more traditional worlds. But it never ceased to amuse her. What sort of idiot lowered his guard just because he saw a pair of breasts?

"Hide us, help us get on our way and you will be rewarded," Belinda offered, smoothly. The gang leader hadn't shown any reaction at all, at least not to his men. Belinda could see his pulse rate increasing as he thought rapidly. "The alternative is…death."

She hoped that Bat saw sense. Unless he was completely stupid – or ignorant – he had to guess that she'd been augmented, even if he didn't know about the boost. Trying to drag her down would be costly – and Belinda knew that she could tear through most of his men before they could pile on her. Hell, given the nature of her augmentation, she might well survive fighting the whole gang. He had to be worried…and yet she'd embarrassed him, perhaps humiliated him, in front of his men. His pride might not let him accept her offer.

"Very good," Bat agreed, finally. "How much are you offering in exchange for our help?"

Belinda scowled, inwardly. She had access to some credit accounts run covertly by the Marine Corps, but she had no easy way of getting to them until they reached the Arena. Roland would have access to his own accounts, yet she would have been astonished if they hadn't been blocked by now. Denying Roland access to money would be a simple way to control him.

"I can get you unmarked credit chips when we get to the Inner City," she said, shortly. "Maybe around twenty thousand credits."

Bat smiled. "Maybe so," he said. "And we need someone to look at a puzzle. Solve it for us and you will have my aid."

He stood up and led the way out of a different door, deeper into the complex. Belinda followed, aware that the other guards were keeping their distance. It wouldn't be long before the entire gang had heard that she'd killed their enforcer effortlessly – and they'd be too scared of her to cross her. Or so she hoped. She wouldn't put it past Bat to try to play both ends against the middle.

Roland looked pale but stable as they entered a long room. The smell was worse than in the lower levels, the stench of too many ill people in one room. She grimaced as she saw nineteen men and women lying on the floor, sweating and shivering; several of them had thrown up or lost control of their bowels. Roland stopped on the edge of the room and hung back. Belinda couldn't blame him, even as she adjusted her implants to filter out the smell. This would be a very poor time to show weakness.

Two girls were moving from person to person, working desperately to try to keep them alive. It was immediately obvious to Belinda that the girls either didn't know what they were doing or weren't allowed to use what they knew. Even the Civil Guard wouldn't have kept its wounded in such a disgusting makeshift hospital.

"We don't know what made them ill," Bat said. "We suspect poisoning."

"Or bad food," Belinda retorted, coldly. The women were nude, their bodies clearly starved – and bruised badly. Given their condition, it would be months before they healed properly – if they were ever allowed to heal. It was much more likely that they'd simply be pushed out to die. "What were they eating?"

"Just ration bars," one of the girls said. There was a pitiful look in her eye and she avoided looking directly at Bat. The scars on her legs told their own story. "And water, which we boiled."

"Give them plenty of water to drink," Belinda advised. "And clean this place up. Even if they don't die of whatever it was they ate, they might catch something else from the filth."

She looked over at the other girl. "Find me one of those ration bars," she ordered. "And then some water."

"I thought the bars were healthy," Bat protested, crossly. "Are you saying that someone *poisoned* the ration bars and killed my bitches?"

Belinda had to fight down the urge to rip off his head. A single blow would kill him; she could take out the other guards and then…cold logic and the dictates of survival asserted themselves. She might take out the entire gang, but they'd still have to find their way to the Arena. And even there, they might not find help. Absently, she triggered her implants and pinged for a processor node. Nothing responded.

"It's possible," she admitted, tightly. One of the girls returned and thrust a ration bar into her hand. "Let's have a look."

The bar itself was unmarked, apart from a single line – STANDARD BAR: FOUR SERVINGS. Belinda shuddered, remembering her first experience with one of them, during a brief visit to a Civil Guard camp. The best that could be said of the bars had been that they only had to eat a little to keep themselves alive. She turned the bar over and over in her hand, looking for anything that might identify the source. But there was nothing.

She knew that something was wrong the moment she opened the bar. Normally, ration bars could last indefinitely, at least as long as they were left sealed. They were odourless, almost tasteless...this one stank. She'd heard that the algae processing system ensured that the bars couldn't decay, but something had clearly gone wrong. And, judging from the dead bodies they'd seen earlier, the whole process might be lethal.

"The bars are decaying," she explained, out loud. "Anyone who ate some of the rotten food would get a stomach ache at the very least."

"They came to us from the government," Bat said. "Do you think they gave them to us deliberately?"

Belinda shrugged. She could easily see some of the Grand Senators shipping poisoned food into the Undercity, but they'd chosen a remarkably inefficient method. And, given that there was no visible difference between one set of bars and another, the bars might well make their way into the more important parts of the planet's population. If poisoning had been intended, why not use something that took longer to take effect?

It isn't deliberate, she realised, in a flash of insight. *The production system is breaking down.*

"They put them out on the streets," she realised, in horror. "They must have known that there was something wrong and they put them out anyway."

She'd seen Logistics Officers standing by regulations and refusing to issue ammunition and supplies, even to hard-pressed military units, until all the paperwork was properly filed away. Why would the bureaucrats in charge of the production plants stop production when they couldn't be held responsible for the results? And, in fact, when they would be punished for doing the right thing?

The picture unfolded in her mind. Each plant produced millions of ration bars per day. The bars were all identical, without any clue on the wrapping about which plant they came from. If there was only one contaminated plant, the bars would still kill millions of people – and if there was more than one, that figure was going to rise sharply. And the ration bars were all that kept Earth fed. If people were dying now...

"I'll have to tell the master," Bat said, when she'd explained – briefly – what had happened. "Will these...victims get better?"

Belinda had no idea. Food poisoning could be lethal – and the victims would never get the right level of medical care they needed to survive. If

Earth's system had had problems coping with the wounded from the student riot, it would collapse completely under the new influx. It was hard to imagine even a fraction of the ill getting any treatment at all.

"Perhaps," she said. If she'd said no, Bat might well have just shoved all the ill out of the lair, even the men. "Make sure they get water and uncontaminated food."

"I will," Bat promised. "And you will have the best room while we try and negotiate passage through other territories. Where precisely do you want to go?"

"The Inner City," Belinda said. "And I want to leave as soon as possible."

"You will," Bat assured her. "I do, however, have to barter for your safe passage first. Until then, you may sleep here."

Belinda scowled. She didn't want to spend *any* time in the lair, but it was quite likely that he was right. Bat was a very minor gang leader in the grand scheme of things – and even a major one would not control enough territory to let them walk directly to the Arena.

"I should warn you," she said, as he beckoned for them to follow him, "that I am a very light sleeper." It was true – and it had been true even before she'd been augmented. "Don't allow anyone to come into our room without knocking."

She said nothing else until they reached the room and the door was firmly closed. If it was the best room, she would have hated to see the worst. A tiny bathroom, a faint smell of rotting food…at least it wasn't the worst place she'd had to sleep. She checked around and found no surveillance devices, but a handful of peepholes that could be used to spy on the inhabitants. Once she'd pointed them out to Roland, she blocked them up and pointed to the bed.

"Get some sleep," she ordered. She could go on for several days if necessary, even though she would eventually start losing her edge. They'd been warned never to depend upon the drugs if it could be avoided. "We might need to leave at any time."

"Awful place," Roland muttered quietly.

"I've seen worse," Belinda said briskly. "And believe me; this is going to get a hell of a lot worse than all of them."

CHAPTER THIRTY-FOUR

The first anyone knew of the risk was when people started to die. Given the random distribution of the bars, the deaths were likewise random; some families would lose one or two members, while others would be either completely wiped out or untouched. At first, there was panic – and then, when it became clear that the media was lying about the whole crisis, panic turned to rage.
- Professor Leo Caesius, *The End of Empire.*

"Help me!"

Amethyst saw the woman as they came out of the stairwell. She was screaming and battering at doors, tears streaming down her face as she demanded help. Richard gave her an oddly contemptuous look as he saw her, but she started to plead with them as soon as they came into view. Amethyst hesitated, then allowed herself to step inside the woman's apartment. Richard, shaking his head in some irritation, followed her.

"My children," the women pleaded. She seemed half out of her mind with grief and terror. "Please save my babies."

The two children lay on the bed, both pale and shivering despite the warm air. Their clothes were badly stained with vomit; Amethyst recoiled at the stench as they drew near. She wasn't a doctor and knew nothing about medicine – and few on Earth would help someone, for fear of being blamed for any failure – and she knew that there was nothing she could do. She still felt bitter helplessness as she realised that the two boys – the youngest couldn't have been more than four – were going to die.

"They've eaten something bad," Richard said. He sounded impatient. "Give them plenty to drink and make sure it keeps going through their system. If anything can help them, that will."

Amethyst blinked at him. "Can't she take them to a medical centre?"

"I have a feeling that the medical centre is a little overwhelmed," Richard said. "And besides, she just isn't very important."

The poor woman's children weren't the only ones affected by the bad food – or whatever it was. As they made their way down the corridors, they saw several other dead or seriously ill people, their families fretting over what to do with them. Death stalked the CityBlock, striking at random; some families only had one person affected, others lost all but one member. Amethyst didn't have the slightest idea what could do anything like that.

Richard seemed to have become interested in the puzzle, even as they were still making their way down to the very lowest levels. "I think it was the ration bars," he remarked to a young man who'd just lost his partner. "They smell funny, don't you think?"

"The ration bars?" Amethyst repeated. The man seemed oddly familiar, but she couldn't remember where she'd seen him. "What happened to them?"

"If something went wrong at the algae plant, no one would notice until it was far too late," Richard pointed out, mildly. "And then the poisoned bars would be impossible to separate from the safe bars. The only thing they could do would be to round up every bar and destroy it – and that would be impossible."

The man stared at them. "Why didn't they tell us?"

Richard snorted. "They didn't want you to know?"

Amethyst gave him a sharp look at the callous expression on his face. Richard honestly didn't *care* about the victims, even though he seemed to have regarded the whole issue as an interesting puzzle to solve. So many deaths – if they'd seen at least nineteen, there had to be many more that they hadn't seen – didn't seem to affect him at all.

"My partner is dead," the man said. "I don't want to live anymore."

"Then go eat one of the ration bars," Richard replied, dryly.

"No," the man said. A new – and ugly – determination had entered his eyes. "I will warn everyone else about the dangers."

Amethyst sucked in her breath, suddenly remembering where she'd seen the man before. Dillon-Dillon was a newsreader, someone who read out the news – the officially-cleared news, according to the Professor's book – for billions of viewers. If he chose to tell everyone that the ration bars were poisoned and the Grand Senate had refused to do anything about it…there would be trouble. But would he even be allowed to finish telling the world before they took him off the air?

"Good luck," she said, quietly.

Richard caught her arm and pulled her out of the apartment and further down the corridor, towards the sound of raised voices and cries of fear. They turned the corner and saw a pair of young men threatening several older men with makeshift weapons, angrily demanding food and drink. One of them was eying a girl with naked lust in his eye, clearly contemplating rape as well as theft and murder.

"Give us all of your bars," one of the young men ordered. His victims were clearly terrified. "Now!"

Amethyst found her gun in her hand before she quite realised what she was doing. She wasn't a very good shot with the pistol, but she shot the first thug through the head before he even realised that she was there. The second one gaped at her, dropped his weapon and fled; Richard sighed, produced a weapon of his own and shot the retreating thug in the leg. He crashed to the ground and lay still.

Their victims stared at the gun in Amethyst's hand, then fled.

"Sheep," Richard said. He sounded amused. "One sight of a gun and their legs turn to jelly."

"They were being robbed," Amethyst protested. "And that one wanted to hurt the girls…"

Richard started to laugh, derisively. "Did you really think that civilisation would endure indefinitely?"

His voice grew colder. "Civilisation is a thin veneer painted over the beast at the heart of the human soul," he lectured. "When civilisation is damaged, that veneer grows ever thinner – until it finally breaks and the beast emerges. The forces of law and order have been weakened for so long that there truly is very little of the veneer left, even here. Right now, it's every man for himself.

"If civilisation collapses, it will be the rule of the strong. How many men would rape if they thought they could get away with it? Plenty of men find themselves touched by the impulse – what happens if civilisation is so decayed that they give it free rein? Or steal, taking from those who have, but cannot defend what they have? In the future, all that will matter is brute strength. The strong will rule, taking whatever they want; the weak will obey or die. And then the strong will age and be replaced by someone else…it took thousands of years to build up civilisation. How long will it take to do it again?"

Amethyst stared at him. "But humanity doesn't behave like that…"

Richard's laugh became a snicker. "You *students*," he said, making the word a curse. "You suck in the crap your tutors feed you, all the brilliant little intellectual theories that make you feel so clever when you finally understand them – and so superior to those who don't – and you never realise that the real world simply doesn't work that way. Civilisation is an endless struggle to maintain the balance between the permissible and the forbidden – and yet none of you really understand that.

"Do you know why the Undercity fell so badly? People like you, acting from the best possible motives, forbade the forces of law and order from dealing with problems before they became serious. People who did bad things could not be arrested or punished because theists claimed that it wasn't really their fault that they were bad. Teachers in schools were not allowed to enforce discipline, or even to grade properly. The students could learn nothing and still pass. And you had the bright idea of distributing free food to the poor, without realising that it would just boost the number of hungry mouths. Look around you when we go into the Undercity. It is the end result of millions of ignorant fools like yourself.

"You were protected and cosseted within a secure bubble maintained by people you despised, never seeing what they actually did to protect you. Instead, you turned on them, demanding endless cuts to the military and law enforcement – and never realising that you were setting yourself up for the chopping block. Right now, Earth is already unstable – and it will get worse as news of the poisoned bars spreads. There will be an uprising – and the military force left on the planet will be unable to stop it from spreading. And you and your fellow students will find yourselves in deep shit. The living will truly envy the dead."

He snickered again and ended his diatribe. "Look upon your works, ye insignificant and ignorant, and *despair*."

Amethyst was still staring at him in horror as they found the hatch that led down into the Undercity and headed further downwards. What *was* he?

The Empire had a law that guaranteed freedom of speech. Dillon had read about it while he'd been in Imperial University – and about the endless series of regulations that were intended to ensure that media outlets never actually offended anyone. It was difficult, almost impossible, to do anything without violating one of the regulations, which was at least partly why Truth News pre-recorded everything and then ran it past the lawyers first, before putting it out on the datanet. The only exception to that rule was news pieces handed down from the Grand Senate's press team. *They* could be read out on the air without any interruption.

He'd wanted to be a great reporter when he'd been a student, but it hadn't taken him long to realise that the media was firmly under control. Hell, his first mentor freely admitted that he'd only taken Dillon on because she thought that he was attractive, not because of any qualifications he might have obtained from Imperial University. In fact, true investigative reporters no longer existed, not really. Someone could come to Truth News with a story that the Grand Senate would find embarrassing, but it would never see the light of day. The successful reporters were the ones who did as they were told.

It was easy to be cynical, particularly when one had been chosen for his looks. Dillon's job was to read the news; his appearance, apparently, appealed to a certain kind of demographic. His co-anchor, Amber, appealed to another; she wore a very tight shirt, a very short skirt and no panties, allowing her to flash the audience from time to time. The news itself might have been bland and uninformative, but no one cared. They didn't tune in to listen when Amber was on the air.

Dillon had played ball. He'd risen up in the ranks, even if he still couldn't afford to move into a better CityBlock. Now, though, he no longer cared. They could sack him or arrest him and it wouldn't matter, because his partner was dead. His life had revolved around coming home to Alfred and now Alfred was gone, poisoned by the ration bars. It hadn't taken much sniffing around the news office – the smallest department in the building – to establish that Alfred was far from the only victim. There were *thousands* dead, maybe many more. How many had not been reported?

He stuck his head into the monitoring room and smiled to himself. The ration bars had actually made themselves helpful, ironically; the Civil Servant who monitored the transmission hadn't reported into work. Normally, someone else would have been sent to replace him at once, but this was not a normal day. In the confusion, no one had actually decided to shut down operations. Instead, they were going to broadcast live for the first time in centuries.

There was no sign of Amber when he walked onto the set. A gofer passed him a datapad containing the news – it had been passed down by the Grand Senate – and muttered a quick explanation. Amber simply hadn't shown up for work at all. Dillon couldn't help wondering if she'd been struck down by the ration bars or caught up in one of the riots that had broken out in several CityBlocks. In the end, it didn't matter. At least she would be out of the line of fire.

He skimmed through the news bulletin, pretending to commit it to memory. The Grand Senate's Public Relations Division – the Propaganda Division, the media staff called it when they thought they couldn't be overhead – had prepared a statement that was blander than usual, saying very little about the ration bars. Instead, they'd talked about 'dissidents' spreading rumours to undermine the Empire and little else. He felt cold anger burning through his chest as he realised just how little they cared about the population. There wasn't even a suggestion that the newer ration bars should be destroyed.

"We're live in ten," the producer called. "Get ready!"

Thankfully, he didn't have the authority to actually cut the transmission, not when the speech had been written by the Grand Senate's servants. For once, bureaucratic ineptitude would work in Dillon's favour. The producer might not dare cut the transmission even when it became clear that the speech he was reading was not the one he'd been given. Dillon took a breath and settled back in his chair, pasting the Very Serious expression he'd been trained to use on his face. By now, it was second nature.

"Good day," he began, as the countdown reached zero. "I'm Dillon-Dillon, speaking for Truth News. A grave crisis has struck our Empire, a crisis caused by the bureaucrats the Grand Senate has allowed to remain in power. The ration bars that feed our people have become contaminated."

He'd taken a look at the raw information sent in to Truth News and had a good idea of just how the crisis had actually begun. There were laws to protect whistleblowers, none of which would actually *save* one under normal circumstances. After all, it was relatively easy to track down the whistleblower and sack them – or worse. Now, however, it might be difficult. For once, the general public would be thoroughly enraged.

"The Grand Senate demanded a massive increase in algae production to feed the planet," Dillon continued. "However, the ancient machinery that produces algae was unable to cope with the demand and the bars became contaminated. By now, there are millions of contaminated bars, utterly inseparable from the safe bars, out on the streets. The bureaucrats knew that the bars were contaminated and they sent them out anyway. By now, hundreds of thousands of people are dead or ill and the hospitals are overflowing."

He braced himself and went on. "My partner Alfred is dead. Many of my co-workers are dead or missing. How many other vitally important departments have lost some of their best men? How many others…"

The light went out. Someone had finally pulled the plug.

"I'll have your head for this," the producer bellowed, as he stormed onto the set. "Do you know what that will cost us in fees?"

Dillon glared at him, no longer bothering to hide his opinion. The producer had been given his position through nepotism – and he would have been better at it if he hadn't spent so much time luring the female staff into his bed. His only virtue in the eyes of senior management, as far as Dillon could tell, was a slavish adherence to the rules. At least it had worked out in Dillon's favour for once.

"It doesn't matter," he snapped. "All that matters is that people are *dying*."

"Out," the producer snapped. "You're fucking fired!"

"Thank you," Dillon replied, mischievously. "I can claim the BLA now."

———

"The ration bars are perfectly safe, I assure you."

Lieutenant John Foster, Civil Guard, glared at the bureaucrat. Hardly anyone liked logistics officers at the best of times – and now, after hearing about the contaminated bars, his entire unit was on the verge of mutiny. Privately, part of him wanted to mutiny too.

"Right," he said, flatly. Dillon-Dillon hadn't said anything *useful*, like how to separate out the good ration bars from the bad, but John had a few ideas of his own. "I want you to try the bars before we start serving them to the men."

There was a dull rumble of agreement from his troopers. John hadn't spent as much time with them as he should – the NCOs were meant to provide a barrier between the enlisted and the officers – but they'd all had to bed down together while they waited outside Imperial University. It had allowed him to realise that his men had their own thoughts and feelings – and that they were terrified that their food had turned poisonous. The Civil Guard drew their rations from the same production plants as the civilians…they knew they might find themselves becoming the next victims. It was not helping morale.

"I can't," the bureaucrat protested. "I…"

John pulled his pistol out of the holster and held it against the bureaucrat's head. "Open the bar and take a bite," he ordered, coldly. "Or die."

The bureaucrat started to splutter, a splutter that died away as John met his eyes, trying to convey an absolute certainty that he would shoot, if the bureaucrat failed to obey. Reluctantly, the little man's fingers went to work, tearing open the bar and exposing the brown mass inside. Normal ration bars lasted for years, but John had been careful to ensure that the bureaucrat tested one of the new ones. The smell wasn't as bad as he'd expected, yet it shouldn't have been there at all.

"Poison," one of his men said.

The bureaucrat stared in horror at him, suddenly aware of his own vulnerability. He'd lorded it over the enlisted men ever since he'd joined Logistics; like the rest of his kind, he'd forced the officers to fill out endless reams of paperwork and hampered training by refusing to issue ammunition and equipment in sufficient quantities. Now, all of the bonds that had held the Civil Guard together were gone…

John looked him in the eye, smiled once – and pulled the trigger.

CHAPTER
THIRTY-FIVE

No one had known what would happen if Earth's population rose up in a body, but the Grand Senate had always been worried about the possibility. Now, faced with that fear becoming reality, the Emergency Committee attempted to lock the planet down hard. It was already too late. The students at the university had become irrelevant.

- Professor Leo Caesius, The End of Empire.

Admiral Valentine looked worried. In fact, the malicious part of Stephen's mind noted, he looked like a man who was afraid that he was going to be blamed for something.

"The Civil Guard is revolting," he said, quickly. "We've lost control of a dozen units so far!"

Stephen stared at him. "Start at the beginning," he ordered, finally. "Tell me exactly what happened."

"The Guardsmen were listening to the broadcast from Truth News," Valentine admitted. "They heard about the ration bars – some of them had even seen people who had eaten the damned things. Some of them saw the ration bars they'd been issued and thought that they'd die if they ate them. So they demanded that the logistics officers nibble them first…"

He caught himself. "Right now, roughly nine *thousand* men are openly mutinous and plenty of others are leaning that way," he added. "The barricade around Imperial University has been effectively broken; mutinous Civil Guardsmen and students are fraternising openly. A number of officers have been shot for daring to restrain their men; hell, junior officers have actually *joined* the mutiny. This is *disastrous!*"

For once, Stephen considered, the Admiral might actually have a point. Normally, Civil Guard units were kept under tight control – and they still sometimes mutinied. When that happened, the Army or the Marines had to be called in to crush the mutiny. Now, however, there were no Marines left on Earth and most of the Imperial Army would be in a similar state. The contaminated ration bars had undermined the entire establishment.

"Most of the...ah, *special* forces are still loyal; we supplied their rations from out-system," the Admiral said. "But the Civil Guard can no longer be considered reliable. And enough of the officers have mutinied to make it quite likely that others will follow."

Stephen rubbed his forehead. The Civil Guardsmen received very limited training, certainly nothing as rounded as soldiers or the Marines. Even their officers were carefully focused on the tactical part of their jobs; they were never expected to serve as strategic planners or overall commanders. If multiple units were involved, an Army officer would take command. In theory, a unit that mutinied could be isolated very quickly – and without control over its own logistics, would rapidly grind to a halt.

But if so many units had mutinied on *Earth*, they were very close to the supply depots...and, for that matter, Senate Hall. What would happen if they decided to march there, or on the Imperial Palace? If they believed that they had been poisoned, either through deliberate malice or simple bureaucratic carelessness, why not? What did they have to lose?

Silently, Stephen cursed the bureaucrats under his breath. If someone had had the wit to halt deliveries, they might have been able to nip this fresh crisis in the bud. Instead, the contaminated bars had been distributed to the public...and, just to complicate matters, it had taken hours for the bureaucrats to put the information together and realise the true scale of the crisis. Each CityBlock had a medical centre, but the doctors hadn't reported the problem at first, unaware that it was more serious than it seemed. By the time word had finally reached the Emergency Committee, millions of people were seriously ill – or dead.

We should make an example out of everyone in that damned plant, he thought, coldly. It would have to be something more dramatic than a public execution. Maybe they could be shoved out onto the Arena sands and fed to the man-eating monsters the staff had been saving for Roland's coronation. But they needed those workers to produce more algae bars… they couldn't be killed, simply because there were no replacements. He'd just have to kill the bureaucrats instead.

"Very well," he said, finally. "Is there anything we can do about the mutinous units?"

"Not…quickly," Valentine hesitatingly said. "With all due respect, Grand Senator…"

"Spit it out," Stephen growled.

"The problems are not limited to the Imperial University or the Civil Guard," Valentine said. "A vast number of workers have simply not come into work. That damned broadcast was only allowed to go on as long as it did because the censor was absent, for example, but he wasn't the only one. The orbital towers are reporting that vast numbers of workers have not shown up for duty."

Stephen scowled. What was the problem with just spitting out the news? "Yeah, so?"

"So bringing additional units from the Imperial Army – or the Mars Civil Guard – to Earth is going to be tricky," Valentine said. "We simply don't have that many spacecraft capable of landing on Earth; we rely on the orbital towers if we need to move large amounts of men and equipment. Even if we commandeered every shuttle in the solar system, our logistics would still be very bad."

Stephen stared at him. Was Valentine trying to hide his own incompetence? "I happen to know," he said tightly, "that entire occupation forces have been landed on hostile worlds before."

"Yes, they have," Valentine agreed. "But the shuttles and heavy landing pods we use for that are not based on Earth. It was simply never anticipated that we might have to land troops on Earth – and if we did have to reinforce the Civil Guard, we would simply use the orbital towers. Now, however, the towers are going to be operating a reduced service for the foreseeable future."

"So get those landing craft back to Earth," Stephen snapped.

"I had my staff look at it," Valentine said. "It would take upwards of two months to get the craft here – and that assumes that everything went perfectly, which it wouldn't. My staff figured that three months would be a more likely estimate. The best option would be to try to get one of the orbital towers back to full functionality and then ship the troops down via the tower."

Stephen looked down at the table. He'd never really considered the effects of absenteeism before, if only because he was careful to pay his retainers and private army enough to make them loyal to him – and to put their families on his client worlds, rather than a place as unsafe as Earth. But if it took ten workers to make something work – and five of them stopped working – that something would stop working with them. And *that* meant...

The orbital towers were no longer functioning properly. That meant that shipments of foodstuffs from out-systems were going to be delayed, which meant in turn that many of those shipments were simply going to perish before they could reach their intended recipients. And supplies of HE3 and other vital tech components to keep Earth going would also be delayed, which meant that the planet's infrastructure would start failing.

And what if the power technicians walked off the job? Earth *depended* on the fusion power plants that produced the planet's power supply; if they stopped working, either through a shortfall of fuel or simple absenteeism, large parts of the planet would simply be plunged into darkness. Stephen had a nightmarish vision of entire CityBlocks dying as the air circulation and filtration systems failed for want of power. Or, even if the emergency systems held true, the population panicking and tearing itself apart.

For want of a nail, he thought. The Commandant had been fond of quoting that rhyme, but Stephen had never truly understood it until now. *For want of a nail, a shoe was lost; for want of a shoe, a horse was lost; for want of a horse, a message was lost; for want of a message, a battle was lost; for want of a battle, a campaign was lost; for want of a campaign, a war was lost; for want of a war, a kingdom was lost...*

...Or an Empire, he added silently.

"There is one option," Admiral Valentine pointed out, reluctantly. "You *could* order KEW strikes on Imperial University."

Stephen considered it for a long moment before shaking his head. "It would only make the whole situation worse," he said. "Besides, using KEWs in Imperial City would send the wrong message."

He looked down at his hands, then back up at the Admiral. "Start making preparations to transfer as many troops as you can to Earth," he ordered. "I don't care how you do it, just *do* it. And make damn sure that those troops draw their rations from Luna or Mars. We don't want *them* fed contaminated bars too."

"Yes, sir," the Admiral said. "May I make a suggestion?"

Stephen would have preferred not to hear the Admiral's voice any longer, but he nodded reluctantly. "There are far too many people skiving off their jobs," the Admiral said. "Perhaps you could offer to forgive them if they return to work tomorrow – one of your PR officials could make it sound good. There are simply too many people involved to punish as they deserve."

That *was* a good suggestion, Stephen decided. Far too good to have come from the Butcher of Han. One of his subordinates was clearly a more original thinker than Valentine could ever hope to be. Maybe he should identify the young officer and have him promoted. He could hardly do a worse job. Besides, he admitted to himself, part of the reason the crisis had exploded so badly was that loyalists had been promoted over the heads of more competent officials.

Still, it wouldn't be entirely *his* decision.

"I'll bring it up with the Emergency Committee," he said. The Committee would have to take immediate steps to maintain their power, if only because it wouldn't be too long before the rest of the Grand Senate started pushing against them. "Just get as many troops as you can to Earth."

Jacqueline rubbed her eyes as dusk fell over Imperial City. It had been a long, crazy day; first, she'd been arrested, then freed…and then she'd found herself the mouthpiece of the student rebellion. She'd told her story time and time again, ensuring that the entire university knew what had happened to her. The students who enjoyed trying to hack the datanet had even managed to get a recorded version of her interview out to the wider world, even though the security officers kept trying to wipe it. She'd done her best to forget that they were surrounded by the Civil Guard and effectively trapped. A handful of students had fled the university since the uprising began, but it hadn't been long before anyone leaving the campus was immediately arrested. No one knew what had happened to them since then.

Probably nothing good, she thought, as she flipped through the pages of Amethyst's book. She'd known that her friend had had it; why hadn't she read it before? It was an eye-opener; they'd never truly realised just how carefully the truth was hidden from them until someone had pointed it out. Other copies were floating around the campus, with several students actually *reading* them to their fellows. No tutor had ever enjoyed such an attentive audience.

It was the Civil Guard that had been the big surprise. Jacqueline had never given them much thought until a snatch squad had tried to arrest her. After that, she'd been scared of them...and astonished when some of them actually came over to the students. Who would have expected the Grand Senate to feed its own soldiers poisoned ration bars? Maybe it had been an accident, but very few people believed it. The Grand Senate was capable of anything.

"Jacqueline," Laura called. "The media just announced that there is going to be a world-wide announcement from the Emergency Committee in twenty minutes. Come and see it."

Jacqueline sighed, marked her place in the book and stood up. Ever since Dillon-Dillon had been knocked off the air, the media had been more circumspect and bland than usual – and quite a few channels had disappeared altogether. Thankfully, the censors were having problems removing the recordings of the broadcast from the datanet. It did have the correct authorisation codes for universal distribution, after all. Not that it really mattered any longer; rumours, each one crazier than the last, were spreading at terrifying speed. There were so many dead that the Grand Senate could not hope to hide the scale of the crisis.

The office had once belonged to the University's Grandmaster, a political appointee who – as far as Jacqueline had been able to tell – had done nothing beyond collecting a hefty paycheck and signing expulsion orders for students who went too far. It was grand, far larger than the apartment she'd shared with her parents and siblings, decorated in a style that suggested that the Grandmaster had had no sense of taste. No one knew what had happened to him; the general conclusion was that he'd fled Earth after the unauthorised protest march, if only to escape the wrath of his political masters. They'd put him in his position to control the students and he'd failed spectacularly. It was, Jacqueline had decided, as good a theory as any.

"They're putting it out on all channels," Brent said, waving to her to sit down next to him. "You want to bet that it isn't anything important?"

A dark-skinned man wearing a Civil Guard uniform sat down beside her, his face twisted with worry. It was funny how she'd never thought of the Civil Guard – or soldiers in general – as *human* before; the Professor's book had pointed out that they'd been carefully conditioned to be both contemptuous and frightened of the military right from the start. If Earth's population shunned violence, whatever the situation, they wouldn't be able to fight the Grand Senate. Or so the Professor had believed.

She caught herself staring and looked away, back towards the display. It was showing the Grand Senate's emblem and a countdown ticking down to zero. They'd picked a good time, she realised; ten o'clock in the evening was normally when the population would be sitting back and watching the hugely popular *Five People In A Glass Dome Show*. The series featured a random selection of people who were forced to live together – and, just to make it exciting, the producers invented tasks for them to complete. Some of the tasks had been downright disgusting – one contestant Jacqueline remembered had been ordered to rape a female contestant – but her parents had loved the show. They would still be trying to watch it, even with the CityBlock dissolving into chaos around them.

The display cleared as soon as the countdown reach zero, showing a single woman standing in front of a podium. Constance Nightingale, Jacqueline realised; the Empire's leading anchorwoman. She was tall, dignified rather than blatantly sexual; her patrician features framed by long white hair. It was impossible not to take her seriously, even when she was reading out regurgitated crap written by propaganda departments. The Professor had had a lot to say about that too.

"The Empire is in crisis," Constance said. Her voice was calm, but firm. "Through an attempt to produce additional food, Algae Farm Nineteen accidentally introduced contaminated algae bars onto the streets. Those bars have since sickened or killed several hundred people. Precise figures are not available, owing to trouble-causers exaggerating the figures."

Jacqueline was mildly surprised that they hadn't sought to come up with a cover story, rather than admit that the bars were contaminated, but someone had evidently had an attack of common sense. There was no point in trying to conceal the truth, not now that word was spreading through the datanet as well as the rumour mill. Instead, they'd minimised the danger and dismissed the more outrageous death tolls as lies. As a damage-limitation exercise, it wouldn't have been too bad – if the news hadn't spread too far already.

"The people responsible for this crisis have been arrested and sentenced to death," Constance continued. "Their executions will take place at the Arena, where they will be thrown to the man-eating monsters. Tickets for the event will be sold at standard rates, but a special reduced rate will be available for anyone who has lost family to the contaminated algae bars. The event itself, of course, will be broadcast live from the Arena."

Her voice hardened. "However, faced with such a crisis, the Emergency Committee has declared a full lockdown on planet Earth. All citizens without employment are under curfew from this moment. They are ordered to remain in their homes until the lockdown is lifted. Citizens *with* employment are allowed to make their way to and from their homes, but not to travel anywhere else. Anyone caught violating this instruction will be detained indefinitely.

"Furthermore, a number of misguided citizens have absented themselves from their place of employment," Constance concluded. "The Grand Senate has decreed that every citizen who returns to work tomorrow will be pardoned; they cannot be blamed for believing lies spread by agitators. However, those who *fail* to return to work tomorrow will be marked down for arrest and exile from Earth."

She looked up, straight into the camera. "These are hard times for Earth," she said. "But we will overcome. We will emerge stronger than ever before. And those who try to stop us will pay."

"Really," Brent said. He grinned at Jacqueline, mischievously. "Not a word about us, or the mutinies. You want to bet that we're still marked for death?"

"No bet," the Civil Guardsman said. He seemed to have drawn new resolve from the broadcast. "It won't be long before they come for us."

CHAPTER THIRTY-SIX

As the Emergency Committee panicked, others started to react. The Grand Senate was, in effect, a power-sharing exercise; the Grand Senators had been reluctant to cede so much power to the Emergency Committee, regardless of their worries about the future. Their natural reaction was to try to take the power back. But by then, the Emergency Committee was desperate. Failure would mean absolute disaster.

- Professor Leo Caesius, *The End of Empire.*

"I'm afraid the news is true," Chung said. "The Civil Guard is mutinying."

"Revolting, you mean," Jeremy clarified, deadpan. Discipline was largely a joke among some of the Earth-based Guardsmen, but even the most disciplined unit would have probably mutinied if it believed that it had been deliberately poisoned. "How many are lost to the Emergency Committee?"

"It's hard to be sure," Chung admitted. "Thirteen units seemed to have either gone over to the students or simply dissolved into chaos. Plenty of others are sitting on their hands, waiting to see what will happen. I'm not sure if any of them can be considered loyalist."

Jeremy nodded. Standard practice when dealing with a unit that might be disloyal was to isolate it from any other mutinous unit and then disarm the soldiers – at gunpoint, if necessary. But the remaining loyalists – or the units that the Emergency Committee had raised to support them – might not be capable of carrying out such a mission. He was mildly surprised that the Grand Senator hadn't ordered orbital bombardment to settle the matter…

But then, Earth was hardly Han. Even a precisely-targeted KEW strike could cause minor earthquakes; on Earth, the shockwaves might start weakening the foundations of Imperial City. The hullmetal and Rearden Cement that lined the CityBlocks might be difficult to break, but the rest of the structures weren't so solid. Earthquakes might start bringing the entire city down. And besides, the bureaucrats who kept the Empire going had to be protected. If the Grand Senate destroyed Earth, it would take years to rebuild.

If they *could* rebuild. The reports from the Core Worlds were not encouraging. Earth had lost Orbit Station Seven, which meant that there was a smaller market for foodstuffs from the Core Worlds on Earth. Demand might not have fallen – *that* was unlikely to happen – but the amount of material that could be transported to the planet most definitely *had*. The trickle-down economic effects were crippling the Inner Worlds, as well as threatening even the larger shipping lines with financial trouble. After Terra Nova's bankers had seized a dozen independent freighters in lieu of debts, many independent shippers had simply vanished into the underground community or headed out to the Rim. Their absence would only weaken the local economies further.

Few people really understood the true size of the Empire. If it took four days in Phase Space to reach Terra Nova – the closest inhabited system – it could take upwards of a month to get a message from Earth to the Inner Worlds. Assuming that everything went well, it took at least two months to get a message to the Inner Worlds and receive a reply. The Grand Senate might not have realised it, but the information they received was already outdated by the time they received it. A threatened uprising on Clarke might have become an outright rebellion, complete with a declaration of independence, by the time the Grand Senate even knew that it was a possibility.

They hadn't really realised it because it had never truly mattered before. The Empire was *colossal*. Local problems rarely became sector-wide problems before the Grand Senate could slam the lid on tight, if only because local Imperial Navy detachments could at least prevent problems from spreading. But now problems would spread faster than the Grand Senate could issue orders to control them, let alone compromise with rebellious factions.

"So they can't stop the mutinies," he said, dragging his attention back to the here and now. "What else can they call on?"

"Imperial Army detachments from Mars Training Ground," Chung said. "Or Civil Guardsmen from Mars and Luna...and there are a couple of platoons of Marines left in the solar system, based on the *Chesty Puller*. We actually picked up a request from Admiral Valentine for the *Billy Butcher*."

Jeremy blinked. It had been hard enough to keep the Marine Transport Fleet active, given all the cuts the Grand Senate had instituted over the last two decades. *Billy Butcher* didn't even have any Marines embarked, merely an auxiliary crew who were preparing to transport a number of vital supplies to Safehouse. She couldn't do anything to support the Civil Guard.

"The Admiral appeared to believe that she still had her assault boats," Chung explained, when he asked. "He seems to be trying to collect all the atmosphere-capable shuttles in the solar system."

It took Jeremy a moment to figure out the reasoning. "He wants to move troops to Earth," he said, finally. He doubted that it would work, at least not quickly enough to matter. "How much luck is he having?"

"Not much," Chung admitted. "The independent shippers are clearing out of the system as fast as they can go."

"And the corporate-operated starships rarely carry their own shuttles," Jeremy said. He shook his head, bitterly. "And to think that they insisted on chasing us *out* of the system."

"I don't think we could do anything," Chung admitted. "The disaster on Earth has gone too far to stop."

Jeremy would have preferred to believe otherwise, but he'd been taught never to indulge in self-deception.

"So it would seem," he said. "And Specialist Lawson?"

"We've lost all trace of her and Prince Roland," Chung said, ruefully. "The Summer Palace was apparently occupied and searched by the Grand Senator's personal guards and then abandoned. If Specialist Lawson is still alive, chances are that she's a prisoner."

Jeremy grimaced. The reports had suggested that Roland had finally been starting to man up, but it was too late – and in reality, it had been too late long before Roland had been born. He had never been anything more than a puppet. Even if they did manage to escape – assuming that the Grand Senator's personal guard hadn't managed to kill Lawson – they couldn't save the Empire.

"Keep watching for her anyway," he said. "And keep moving supplies out of Luna Base. We won't be staying here much longer."

The intercom chimed. "Commandant, we picked up a message from Grand Senator Devers," the dispatcher said. "Her personal yacht is approaching Luna Base; she wishes to speak with you personally."

Jeremy exchanged a glance with Chung. "Understood," he said, finally. "Clear her to land, but warn her to leave her security team behind."

Chung snorted. "She won't like that," she said.

"I don't care," Jeremy admitted. "Right now, the Grand Senate is losing control. The Empire is doomed."

It was unusual to have a female Grand Senator – a fact that Margaret's male cousins had pointed out to her time and time again as she grew up. She might have been her father's only legitimate child, but she was a girl…and could therefore expect to be traded off in a marriage alliance, rather than allowed a chance to reach for power. They hadn't realised just how formidable Margaret would become or how determined her father had been to pass his chair on to a child of his own body. By the time he had resigned and gone into retirement on Summer Isle, Margaret had controlled enough of the family's holdings to make resistance futile.

She smiled coldly as she saw her reflection in the dark metal walls. As a young girl, she had been stunning; her gene-engineered beauty yet another weapon to use against her rivals. Now, she was old enough to allow her hair to grey, to give the appearance of age without the weaknesses. She'd said that her own children were not yet ready to take her chair, but the truth was that she enjoyed exercising power too much to give it up. Besides, she was still the sharpest mind in the family. If her sons managed to unseat her, they'd be fine heirs.

But now she was coming to Luna Base as a supplicant. The thought gnawed at her, reminding her of all the mistakes the Grand Senate had made, all the mistakes that had seemed right and logical at the time. She hadn't realised the dangers either, even though she'd hedged her bets as much as she could. The Emergency Committee had seemed a good idea at the time. And yet, the Committee members had pulled a fast one. They'd managed to secure far more power than she'd considered possible.

That alone would have been bad enough. Given time, the Emergency Committee might have forced the remaining Grand Senators into permanent subordination, although absolute control would have been impossible. But now Earth was dissolving into chaos. If the Emergency Committee lost control of Earth, they would soon lose control of the rest of the Empire. And then chaos would sweep across the stars. All of her family's holdings would be destroyed.

Perhaps my son was right, she thought, as she was ushered into the Commandant's office. *I have been a Grand Senator for too long.*

The Commandant smiled at her, although – with the experience of a practiced politician – Margaret could tell that he was more surprised than pleased to see her. She'd never quite trusted the Marines; everyone said that they were incorruptible, but in Margaret's experience everyone had their price. And there *had* been a handful of rogue Marines over the years.

"Grand Senator," he said, as he rose to his feet. "What can I do for you?"

Normally, Margaret would have made small talk first – but her patience was limited and the Commandant would be unimpressed with bullshit. Instead, she went straight to the point.

"The current situation on Earth is intolerable," she stated, flatly. "It is the considered opinion of a majority of the Grand Senate that the Emergency Committee has gone too far."

"I would not disagree with that," the Commandant assented, calmly. "Why have you not acted to strip the Committee of its powers?"

Margaret pressed her lips together. Her father had taught her that admitting weakness was always a bad idea, particularly in front of men. They might help, but they would also never forget that she had *needed* that help. Men could be very stupid that way.

"I think you know as well as I do that the Emergency Committee holds most of the reins of power on Earth," she said, tartly. "The Civil Guard is either mutinous or under its direct control; the Imperial Army has been subverted…and they have their own troops as well. They have effectively launched a coup and taken control of Earth."

"And your liberty died with your thunderous applause," the Commandant said. It sounded like a quote from somewhere, but Margaret didn't recognise it. "And to think that it was all perfectly legal."

"We need their control broken before the situation grows worse," Margaret said, pressing onwards. It was also important, her father had said, never to become discouraged. The ones who won were the ones who refused to just give up at the first hurdle. "The problem is that we cannot meet in sufficient numbers to make a quorum."

The Commandant looked blank, so she explained. By tradition, all Grand Senate meetings had to be attended in person; she couldn't cast her vote over the datanet. It was also traditional that all important debates had to be held in the Imperial Palace or the Senate Hall, but neither one was realistically possible with at least a third of the Grand Senators off-world. There was no law preventing them from meeting on a starship, yet it was quite possible that the Emergency Committee would refuse to recognise it as a legal meeting – and as they controlled most of the power, their opinion counted.

"It seems to be very complicated," the Commandant pointed out, when she'd finished. "I would not dare to suggest which way the lawyers would jump."

"The lawyers would come up with an answer that suited the winners," Margaret snapped. His bland attitude was irritating; if she hadn't needed his help, she would have stormed out by now. "And we would be the winners."

"So you might," the Commandant agreed. "However, I am not a legal expert. What does all of this have to do with me?"

Margaret suspected he already knew – he *wasn't* stupid – but was pretending not to understand what she wanted. Fine; she'd be as blunt as possible.

"A quorum of the Grand Senate wishes the Marine Corps to remove the Emergency Committee from power," she explained, cuttingly. "You are to assault the Imperial Palace and capture or kill the Emergency Committee and their supporters. Their placed men in the military and the Civil Service are to be arrested and replaced by loyal officers."

"It sounds," the Commandant said, "as if you want me to launch a coup on your behalf."

"On behalf of the Empire," Margaret snapped. "How long will it be before the Emergency Committee disposes of the rest of the Grand Senate – and yourselves? There is already a bill before the Grand Senate to thoroughly investigate the supplies you draw from the Logistics Corps. What happens if they use that to shut you down completely?"

"They could not do that without agreement from the Emperor," the Commandant pointed out.

"The Emergency Committee has the Prince under their control," Margaret said. "How long do you think it will be before they turn him into even more of a puppet? It isn't as if he has the bloody-mindedness of one of your Marines. Maybe he has implants intended to keep his thoughts from being forcibly rewritten, but there are plenty of ways to break someone without rewiring his brain."

"True enough," the Commandant agreed.

"So do it," Margaret ordered. "You have clearance from the Grand Senate…"

"I could claim that the clearance was not actually legal," the Commandant said, interrupting her. "By law, an Enemy of the Empire must be formally *declared* an Enemy of the Empire by the Grand Senate. The vote must be open and the results declared to the entire system – and the target has to be given a chance to respond. You cannot pass judgement on anyone in secret session."

"And exactly how often," Margaret demanded, "has that rule been honoured?"

"But in any case, it doesn't matter," the Commandant said. "You see – the mission is impossible."

Margaret stared at him, honestly shaken. "*Impossible?*"

"Yes," the Commandant said.

He explained before she could say anything. "Counting myself, there are currently thirty-one Marines in the solar system," he told her, flatly. "If we bend procedure and include auxiliaries, I would have seventy – most of which would not have proper armour or weapons. That is nowhere near enough to hit the Imperial Palace, even assuming that the Imperial Navy or Earth's orbital defences refuse to get involved. The Emergency Committee has – effectively –two divisions committed to protecting the Imperial Palace and the Senate Hall. A forced landing against such a heavily-armed target would be suicide."

Margaret took a long breath. "And how," she demanded, "would you go about it?"

The Commandant smiled. "I wouldn't," he said. "You see; Earth is simply too heavily defended to be hit, even by a full Marine division. The high orbitals are controlled by the Imperial Navy and Earth's defence forces. We would need to clear the way, either through taking those defences out or subverting them – and we can do neither."

He looked her right in the eye. "You agreed to send the Marines off Earth, after the Grand Senate blamed us for a crisis some of your number deliberately created," he said. "But that wasn't the start of it. You starved us of funds and backing we desperately needed to keep in fighting trim. Bases and regiments we needed desperately have been closed down or disbanded. The results were inevitable.

"Right now, the Marine Corps can do nothing to solve your problem – or save the Empire."

Margaret wanted to look away, but he somehow held her attention. "The Civil Guard was allowed to become utterly corrupt," he said. "You controlled promotion in the Imperial Army, ensuring that your lickspittles were put into command positions regardless of their competence – and then you started wondering why your tools broke in your hand or turned on you. Those you stepped on grew to resent it; now that the Empire is weakened, some of them will make their own bids for power."

"No," Margaret said.

"You cannot hold your position," the Commandant told her, simply. "Your only chance is to flee Earth with as much as you can carry. The Grand Senate has neglected the planet so much that it is unsalvageable."

"You *must* be able to do *something*," Margaret protested.

The Commandant laughed. For the first time, Margaret looked at him – and wondered just how long he'd wanted to say that to one of his superiors.

"You don't understand," he explained. "We might be able to pull in troops from the Slaughterhouse – that's where the closest division is based. Maybe we could get through Earth's defences and take out the Emergency Committee. But it wouldn't matter. Whatever you do cannot repair the damage caused by centuries of neglect. Earth is completely unsalvageable."

Margaret stared at him for a long moment, then bowed stiffly.

"I was told that you were always honourable men," she said, as she rose to her feet. "And here you are, forsaking the Empire you swore to serve."

"The Empire is doomed," the Commandant said. "I have spent *years* trying to shore it up, watching good men and women die to protect their civilisation, only to see my best efforts ruined by my lords and masters. There is no longer anything I can do.

"The Empire is doomed," he repeated, quietly. "And so are you."

CHAPTER
THIRTY-SEVEN

The simplest way to understand the permanent power balance between the Grand Senate families is to view the Empire as being made up of vital locations that had to be fought over for control. The Imperial Navy was one such location, as was Luna Naval Yard, Civil Guard HQ and the Imperial Palace. Each of the families attempted to place their own people in positions of power there, so they could manipulate the location to their own advantage. (For example, an Imperial Navy starship might carry out a technically unauthorised mission on behalf of the Captain's patrons.)

- Professor Leo Caesius, *The End of Empire.*

"Don't draw your weapon unless I do," Richard muttered. "And don't show any sign of fear."

Amethyst made a face. She was terrified; terrified of the darkness surrounding them, terrified of what she'd seen on the upper levels of the block…and terrified of the man beside her. The Undercity lay in shadow, barely illuminated by flickering lights and glowing lichen; *anything* could be out there, hiding in the darkness. Her imagination populated the shadows with monsters in human form, just like the thug she'd shot. Or *real* monsters. God knew that there were plenty of rumours of what had escaped from the Arena over the years.

The passageway came to an end, revealing a dimly-lit dome covering a number of small buildings. Amethyst realised in astonishment that the dome had been erected over the buildings, then the megacities had been built on top of the dome. The buildings looked quaint, almost like something from a drama set on one of the more rustic colony worlds, yet there was a sense of age around them that almost overpowered her. She was looking at buildings that might well have been older than the Empire.

"There was a time when they wanted to preserve this place," Richard muttered. "So they domed it and built the Rowdy Yates CityBlock on top of the dome. And then they forgot all about it."

Amethyst nodded. The Professor's book had explained that the Empire had deliberately sought to erase its own history. Few people truly realised that Earth had once been as green and blue as any of the colony worlds, rather than covered in megacities and pollution. Even the students had never understood the truth. Given the level of indoctrination and outright lies they were subjected to from birth, how could they have? It had taken someone born outside Earth to start the Professor questioning his own assumptions.

Four men carrying guns appeared out of one of the buildings. "Keep your hands where we can see them," one ordered. "Who are you?"

"We wish to speak to Dennis," Richard said. "And you may call me Culp."

There was a long pause. "The boss will probably want to speak with you," the leader said, slowly. "We will take your weapons and escort you to him."

Richard nodded. "Give him your guns," he ordered Amethyst as the men closed in. "Don't worry about it."

Amethyst scowled as the man took her gun, then ran his hands over her shapeless uniform to search for more weapons. He pulled her datapad out of her belt and examined it briefly, then passed it to one of his friends and continued to search her. Another man searched Richard, removing several weapons and devices that Amethyst didn't recognise. Richard didn't seem too bothered when they were finally finished; instead, he seemed almost amused.

"Follow us," the leader ordered. "You will have your weapons and equipment back when you leave – if you leave."

The strange buildings seemed eerie, almost haunted, as they came closer and walked through a large front door. Inside, it was a whole different picture; it was clean, warm and brightly lit, bright enough to force Amethyst to cover her eyes against the glare. A set of young women, completely naked, were carrying trays of food and drink through the corridors. Amethyst couldn't help shivering at the strange expressions – half-vapid, half-ecstatic – on their faces, or the lustful glances fired at them by the escorts.

"Sparkle Dust addicts," Richard said, when he saw her staring at the girls. "By now, they won't have any real free will left for themselves. They'll go do whatever they are told, no matter who is issuing the orders – and it will *please* them to obey."

He seemed rather amused at the whole concept. Amethyst just shivered. She'd never used Sparkle Dust herself, but several of her first-year girlfriends had insisted that it was a fantastic rush. How many of them had gone on to become addicts? She couldn't understand why *anyone* would do that willingly, if it turned you into an helpless slave. Maybe the girls had started out, like so many other addicts, convinced that they could control their addiction. Or maybe they'd simply been fed the drug by force until it had taken effect...

"Drugs are a good way to control people," Richard muttered. "There are entire communities – even planets – where the population is addicted to a specific drug. As long as they behave, they get their fix; if they start causing trouble, they are left to die. How do you think many of the gang lords keep their pawns under control?"

Amethyst had no answer as they were ushered into a large office. A man sat behind a desk, studying a datapad; he looked up as they entered and nodded briefly. Amethyst met his eyes for a long moment and saw an absolute ruthlessness, a complete lack of scruples, that scared her to death. She had never believed that such people could exist, despite all the evidence; she had never truly grasped the concept of evil. Now, she saw it everywhere she looked. The man – Dennis, perhaps – was a monster. And so was Richard...

"Culp," Dennis said. "It has been a long time since I heard that name."

"Yeah," Richard agreed. "It has."

He smiled, rather dryly. "I won't mince words," he added. "Two people are missing within the Undercity, within your territory. We need to find them both or recover their bodies. If you assist us, we are prepared to pay heavily."

Dennis stared at him, coldly. "You are aware, no doubt, that we were fed poisoned ration bars," he said. "Tell me, *Culp*; why should I do *anything* for you?"

"Because in the future, if not right now, you are going to need support from my patron," Richard stated, sharply. "If you help us find the missing fugitives, you will be rewarded beyond your wildest dreams. Money, weapons…it would not be impossible to give you your own colony world to run, if you thought it might not be a good idea to stay on Earth. But you only get the reward if you help us."

"No doubt," Dennis said, dryly. "Who are these people?"

"I'm afraid your men took my datapad," Richard said, "so I cannot give you their details. However, I can tell you that they're wanted on charges of high treason; the Grand Senate Emergency Committee wants them, dead or alive. They must be found."

Amethyst kept her expression as blank as she could. It defied belief that Dennis wouldn't recognise Prince Roland on sight…or did it? Everyone who'd seen Roland on the datanet had seen a teenager in fine robes, wearing a small crown on his head. He might look quite different in real life, enough to make him unrecognisable if someone passed him in the streets. The gangsters might never realise who they'd caught.

"And you believe them to be alive," Dennis said. He placed his fingertips together and leaned back. "What makes you think that they have survived so far?"

"The woman is a trained survivalist," Richard said, tightly. "We know she survived the landing – and I doubt that the Undercity could kill her."

"You make her sound dangerous," Dennis mocked. "Maybe I should keep my men out of her way."

Richard grinned. "And miss your chance to set up on your own world?"

The gang leader smiled. "Very well," he said. "As it happens, I might just be able to find your friends for you."

Amethyst shivered.

"Excellent," Richard said. "And there are some precautions that you will have to take…"

It was several hours, by Belinda's internal clock, when Bat knocked on the door. She used her implants to listen for the heartbeats of anyone near him, but as far as she could tell the gang leader was completely alone. Nodding to Roland to stay alert, she opened the door and beckoned Bat into the room. The gangster looked tired, but relieved.

"I have spoken with my superior," he said, bluntly. "He is prepared to grant you safe passage, in exchange for a large amount of cash. The cash is to be transferred to an unmarked cash-chip once you reach the Inner City and handed over to me. I will see to its distribution."

Taking a small amount for yourself, of course, Belinda thought, silently. It was always the same, on Earth or a far-distant colony world. Corruption begat corruption. Everyone in a position to skim a little for themselves did so – and why not? They knew perfectly well that everyone *else* did it. But she could hardly complain as long as it got them out of the Undercity. The longer they stayed in one place, the greater the chance of someone else tracking them down.

"Good," she said. "Will you be escorting us alone?"

"Four of my soldiers will be accompanying me," Bat informed them. "I do not want to go unprotected."

Belinda snickered. "I suppose not," she said. "We'll be ready to go in five minutes."

Roland stood up, looking disgustingly fresh. He'd slept; Belinda hadn't dared, even though they should have been safe. The Prince's enhancements had never really been tested until Belinda had started to push him into self-development, she knew; it was a relief to see that they worked properly. Given enough time, maybe Roland *would* have made it as a Marine after all.

The Prince rubbed his tummy. "Is there anything to eat?"

"There are some stocks we saved for emergencies," Bat said. "They should be healthy, but…"

"Bring some anyway," Belinda ordered. They were both enhanced; contaminated ration bars shouldn't be able to do much damage. Besides, her implants should be able to detect something dangerous before she swallowed it. "We can pay for that as well."

Bat nodded and left the room.

"This isn't going to be fun," Belinda warned Roland, as the Prince headed into the bathroom. Oddly – or perhaps it wasn't odd after all – the Prince seemed almost cheerful. "The Undercity is a very dangerous place."

"Gangsters fighting over power and pushing the weak around," Roland's voice drifted back. "Why, it's just like the Grand Senate."

Belinda had to laugh.

Bat stepped back into the room, carrying a pair of ration bars. "The escorts are ready now," he said, as Belinda opened the first bar and inspected it. "They're ready to go."

"We're on our way," Belinda said. The first bar seemed to be fine, so she passed it to Roland and opened the second bar. As always, it tasted like cardboard, but at least it was edible. "How far do we have to walk?"

"Several miles," Bat said. "I'm afraid that there's a state of emergency up top. If you go straight up into Rowdy Yates, you might be arrested. We've lost several rat-runners that way; the Civil Guard stunned them and carted the poor bastards away. We don't know what happened to them after that."

Belinda could guess, but said nothing as she pocketed the rest of the ration bar and motioned for Bat to lead them out of the room. Outside, there were fewer gangsters than before; Bat probably didn't want them to see him treating Belinda and Roland as honoured guests. Her lips twitched in bitter amusement. The merest suggestion that Bat was *scared* of the crazy super-strong bitch who'd killed his enforcer would undermine his position like nothing else. Any of his subordinates might decide that he could be killed at leisure...

She wasn't entirely sure what Bat *did*. A simple protection racket might not work very well so far below the megacities; the inhabitants had very little to offer the gangsters. Drugs or women might work, she decided; there might be little money in offering girls to the poor, but there was no shortage of civilians from high overhead who would want to visit a brothel. And those brothels might offer services forbidden even to the Grand Senate. She shuddered as she remembered what some of the insurgents on Han had done to raise money to continue the fight. God knew the Undercity dwellers would have even fewer scruples about doing whatever they had to do to survive.

"Anything that tends towards survival is moral," the History and Moral Philosophy tutor had said, back at the Slaughterhouse. "How many of you would be appalled by the thought of selling one of your sisters into prostitution to raise money? All of you? Good – but that is a measure of your situation rather than any universal morality. If you had no choice but to do so, you would find yourself rationalising it to yourself – and defending it to any outsider.

"It's easy to say that you would sooner die than sell your sister into slavery," he'd added. "It's much harder to avoid doing it when you are actually confronted with the need…"

Belinda scowled as she pushed the memory aside. The Undercity bred nothing but survivalists, every one of them out for themselves and no one else. If it would help keep them alive, they would think nothing of selling their sisters into slavery – and many other horrors beside. There was no shortage of girls and boys who could be sold into brothels, all under the legal age of consent – and the hell of it was that many of them would consider it an improvement in their lives. It was shocking, it was disgusting… and the Empire just didn't care.

But what could they do? The Civil Guard could do its duty and arrest the paedophiles who visited such brothels – and even send the children to a colony world where they could grow up away from Earth - but it wouldn't be anything more than a drop in the ocean. There was never any shortage of victims or people willing to prey on them. She could do nothing to stop it. And it never stopped gnawing at her.

Bat's guards met them as they reached the edge of his lair. "We have to move quietly," Bat explained, as they checked their weapons. Bat himself carried an outdated pistol; the others carried nothing more dangerous than makeshift clubs and swords. A trained Engineer – either from the Marines or the Imperial Army – could have produced better from the junk lying around the Undercity. "We are going to be moving through disputed territory."

Though enemy lines, Belinda thought, wryly. Moving around without being seen was what Pathfinders *did*. Roland's joke about the gangsters being exactly like the Grand Senate was more accurate than he realised. The gang lords controlled territory and skirmished with their rivals, trying to push them back and eventually occupy their possessions. But if there were so many gangs, there would be an uneasy balance of power...

She followed Bat as he led the way out of the lair, every sensor stepped up and watching for trouble. The passageways seemed largely empty at first, until they reached a wider corridor that seemed to have once been part of a mass-transport system. A number of people were lying in the grooves, trying to stay out of sight. Belinda felt her heart twist in bitter guilt – there was nothing she could do for them, any more than she could help any of the others – until she looked away.

There seemed to be more life in the Undercity than she had expected. One long low room included a marketplace, where people were buying and selling items from high overhead. Several sellers were loudly proclaiming that their food was free of all contamination, although as they were selling sealed ration bars it was hard to tell. Several gangsters moved through the market, others flinching away from them as they passed, keeping the peace as best as they could. Roland had definitely been right; swap the gangsters for the Civil Guard and the market could be in the Inner City.

They walked past a group of young men, one of whom reached out to grab Belinda's ass. Without looking back, she caught his hand and squeezed with augmented force, crushing his bones into paper. Her companions roared with laughter as he screamed in pain. Belinda regretted her overreaction a moment later – she'd effectively crippled him for life, which wouldn't be very long in the Undercity – before she pushed the thought aside. If he was prepared to try to molest a girl escorted by five gangsters, what would he do to a girl without any protection at all?

Bat led them out of the market and into another series of tunnels and large rooms. There were dozens of people scattered around, many of them clearly having marked out their own territory. The larger gangs seemed to give the smaller ones a wide berth, something that puzzled Belinda until she realised that squashing them could be costly; the smaller gang might be exterminated, but the larger gang might be crippled. She caught sight of a handful of children and shivered at the cold hard expressions on their faces. They were barely seven and yet they were already monsters by civilised standards. But what else could they do to survive?

The sense of *threat* grew stronger as they walked into a larger room. Belinda tensed, unsure of what she was sensing; her instincts were telling her that something was wrong. But her implants couldn't pick up anything at all…and then it struck her that was what was wrong…

And then something fell on her from high overhead.

CHAPTER
THIRTY-EIGHT

What the Emergency Committee had done (with remarkable speed, suggesting a considerable level of pre-planning) was to remove a number of officers and replace them with their clients. It gave them, at least on paper, control over both Home Fleet and the considerable armed forces stationed on Sol's inhabited planets – which gave them a formidable advantage. In theory, the Grand Senate could cancel their charter; in practice, the Emergency Committee held the guns.

- Professor Leo Caesius, *The End of Empire.*

Amethyst couldn't help feeling a little impressed by how easy it had been. Once Dennis had been convinced to help them, he'd admitted that two strangers – one of them matching the descriptions Richard had provided – had forced their way into a lair belonging to one of his subordinates. The subordinate had then gone to Dennis and requested safe passage through Dennis's territory for his unwanted guests, claiming that they'd offered the gang a vast sum of money in exchange. Dennis and Richard had planned the ambush carefully, without telling the subordinate anything. Prince Roland and his bodyguard had walked right into the trap.

Dennis had been surprised – and then annoyed – when Richard had insisted on using the capture net. It made the whole affair much more complicated, he'd complained, even though the report from Bat's lair stated that the bodyguard had killed one of his enforcers with a single punch. But Richard had prevailed…and the net had worked, catching the bodyguard before she could run or fight. And now…

———

Belinda swore out loud as the net fell around her. Someone had been thinking ahead; if they'd seen the carnage she'd left behind in the shuttle, they would have realised that she was heavily augmented at the very least. And if they'd given her time to run, she could have grabbed Roland, boosted and fled far faster than they could hope to follow. Using the net was clever and…

She heard the crackle a split second before the net discharged a colossal electric pulse into her body. Alarms flashed up in front of her eyes as her implants struggled to mitigate and counteract the pulse; even with her enhancements, that had *hurt*. Warning messages followed the alarms, alerting her to damage to a number of vital components. The neural link she used to access computer networks failed; if she'd been linked to anything at the time, she would have been lucky to avoid brain damage at the very least. Several other components died as she staggered and fell to the floor, the net powering up for a second pulse. Repeated strikes would kill her, or leave her so badly injured that she would not be able to survive for long.

Bracing herself, she yanked at the edge of the net, trying to pull it away from the floor. They'd thought of that too; it was magnetised, almost immovable even with enhanced strength. The metal plating covering the floor held her helpless and trapped. They might even take Roland and leave her there, knowing that eventually the net would kill her. It could not be allowed. And yet…

She noticed, through the haze, Bat's body hitting the ground, followed rapidly by his men. Someone had shot them and she hadn't even heard the shots! And he'd led them into a trap…but he hadn't *known* it was a trap. Someone had told him precisely what route to take, without bothering to mention that he and his men were expendable. No doubt Bat was a liability to his superior; he'd have to be wondering what deals Bat might have struck with Belinda and Roland.

Roland howled, lifted his weapon and fired towards the source of the shots. Belinda couldn't tell if he'd hit anything by the time he ran out of ammunition, but it didn't matter. A man emerged from the shadows – well away from where Roland had been aiming – and advanced towards him, moving with the easy confidence of the combat veteran. Roland turned and tried to fight, but this man wasn't holding back. He shrugged off Roland's punch and hit him in the stomach, hard enough to force the Prince to double over, clutching his chest. A second blow sent him falling to the ground.

"Your Highness," the man whispered, as he rolled Roland over. "Welcome to the end of the line."

He shot a triumphant glance at Belinda, who realised in horror just what sort of person the Grand Senator had sent after them. A sociopath, almost certainly; a man incapable of feeling any real emotion, certainly not capable of feeling anything for anyone else. Such a person would have fitted in well among pirate society, or even in the Grand Senate, but they would be a liability in the military. But he'd clearly been a soldier at one time.

"I'd have fun with you," he hissed, "but I think I'll leave you here instead."

Belinda gritted her teeth. Desperately, her fingers reached down to where she had hidden the monofilament knife. No one knew she had it, even Roland. She twisted her body, stumbling face-forward to the floor, as she grasped the hilt and withdrew it. The net was starting to crackle with power; it wouldn't be more than a few seconds before it shocked her again, stunning her long enough for the newcomer to carry Roland back to the Grand Senator. She flicked the switch, activating the knife, and cut right through the net. Sparks flashed around the blade as it sliced though, but she was free.

She threw herself forward, out of the net, and advanced towards the newcomer. He jumped backwards as she stabbed at him with the knife, his eyes glinting with a savage chilling amusement. An augment, she realised grimly; no ordinary person could have avoided her thrust. And her own augments were damaged…now she was out of the net, her neural processor was starting to attempt to repair her systems, those that *could* be repaired. The remainder…it had taken months for the full series of augmentations to be implanted and then matched with her body. How long would it take to repair the damaged systems?

"What an *inspired* hiding place," the newcomer leered. "Did you learn *that* at the Slaughterhouse?"

Belinda ignored his taunt. Her battle analysis subroutines were damaged, but she didn't need them. The way the newcomer was moving suggested that he'd come from the Imperial Army, rather than the Marines; there was a brutal directness in his motions that didn't quite match basic Marine training. And his augmentation didn't seem to be quite up to Pathfinder standards…at least as far as she could tell. Augmentation was such a useful tool that the Grand Senate would hardly have allowed the Marines to keep a monopoly.

He stepped forward, moving with boosted speed, and lashed out at her. Belinda nipped back, then threw back a punch of her own, hoping that he would expose himself long enough to allow her to land the killing blow. Instead, he side-stepped it and darted backwards, putting Roland's prone form between them. Belinda took a moment to boost herself, then lunged forward again. He threw up an augmented hand to block her punch, then threw a wicked kick at her. She barely managed to twist in time to avoid it.

"You seem to be slipping," he observed, mildly. He was *taunting* her during the fight! What sort of training encouraged such recklessness? "A Pathfinder should have beaten me by now."

Belinda ignored the taunt, even though he was right. Even with the boost, she was barely matching him.

"Who are you?" She asked, as she studied him for weaknesses. "What do you want?"

"My name is Bode," the newcomer said. He sounded as if he were bragging. "You may have heard of me."

Belinda stared at him in disbelief. It *could* be a coincidence, merely a case of two people sharing the same blackened name, but she doubted it. Captain Bode had been the CO of a small counter-insurgency team on the corporate-dominated Jitter's World, she recalled. He'd been given *carte blanche* to deal with the insurgency in any way he saw fit…and his methods had shocked even the hardened Bloody Blades, one of the most ruthless detachments of the Imperial Army. The Marines had joked, bitterly, that you had to be a sociopath to join the Blades. In this case, Bode had been arrested, dishonourably discharged from the Imperial Army and sentenced to a lifetime on Hellhole. No one ever got off the world once they were dumped there.

And now he was here, on Earth. And augmented.

"The Grand Senator," she said, slowly. She'd researched the Grand Senator's holdings after it had become clear that he wanted to be Roland's puppet-master – and his corporation had controlled Jitter's World. "You never went to Hellhole, did you?"

"Of course not," Bode retorted, dryly. "A person as…useful as myself is never thrown away to rot. Don't you know that?"

Belinda nodded, coldly. She'd seen too many atrocities committed in the name of the Grand Senate to doubt that someone like Bode would be seen as a useful tool. Why bother manipulating events to exterminate a settlement or enslave a colony when you had someone who would do it without batting an eyelid? And Bode had gone too far even for the Bloody Blades to stomach. He would be a *very* useful tool.

"Yes, I do," she admitted. "What have you been doing on Earth?"

Bode snickered. "Are you trying to delay me? You do realise that I hold all the cards?"

Belinda met his eyes. "Really?"

"Really," Bode assured her. "An armoured recovery team is already on the way. Even if you manage to beat me - which you won't – you can't get away any longer. The armoured goons will take Roland to the Grand Senator – and kill you. You're just too dangerous to keep around."

His eyes glittered. "Do you know that it was I who started the first riot? Or faked an assassination attempt on Roland? And now the Grand Senator rules the Empire."

Of course, Belinda thought. Part of his career had involved provoking uprisings to give his corporate masters an excuse to stamp on them – and if anyone innocent got crushed along with the rebels…well, it was no skin off their noses. Everyone knew that those who harboured rebels were effectively rebels themselves. Why, the rules on counter-insurgency had been signed into law by the Grand Senate itself!

Now, it was clear. The Grand Senator had manipulated everyone in order to put himself into power. Given enough time, he could marginalise or destroy the other Grand Senators and declare himself Emperor. But it was too late. Maybe he could have saved the Empire, if he'd started a century ago; now…

It would have been easy to manipulate the students. God knew Belinda had seen extremists succeed in manipulating people who had far more life experience than the students of Imperial University. Besides, all he'd had to do was cause a riot and the Civil Guard would do the rest. None of them would ever realise the truth.

"The Grand Senator's house of cards is tumbling down," she informed him, tiredly. The dominos were already falling, one by one. She doubted that the Grand Senator could arrest the process, even if there was no further resistance. The contaminated ration bars would cause riots far greater than any the planet had yet seen. "What's the *point* in taking Roland to him?"

"Power," Bode said, simply. "I shall be rewarded with power beyond my wildest dreams."

"I doubt that," Belinda said. The Grand Senator might be an evil bastard, but he wasn't stupid. "A tool like you will be destroyed once it is no longer useful. Besides, you know too much to be allowed to live."

Bode laughed. "Why doth treason never prosper?"

"Because if it does, none dare call it treason," Belinda said. She drew on the boost, bracing herself. "But it doesn't matter. The Empire is tottering. It won't be long before it falls…"

She sprang at him, without warning. He jerked back, then threw a blow at her. Part of Belinda's mind noted that he'd expected trouble, even if she'd moved too fast for him to see the tells that she intended to move; the rest of her mind concentrated on the fight. They were both boosted, moving at inhuman speeds…and neither of them could land a killing blow. Belinda lashed out with her knife, then threw it at him in a calculated gamble. Bode threw himself right across the room instead of trying to take advantage of the opening she'd offered him.

Damn, she thought. The knife had gone too far to be retrieved before he hit her in the back. Whoever had trained Bode had done a good job.

Too good. For once, the Imperial Army had shown remarkable competence...at precisely the wrong moment for everyone. But then, that was just a Marine conceit. There were plenty of units in the Army that were reasonably competent, even though they were not up to Marine standards.

"There really is no chance for you to win," Bode informed her. "Why not just leave? I'll tell the Senator that you vanished somewhere within the Undercity, all very regretful and so on."

Belinda smiled, inwardly. He must be weakening. The boost was wearing away at her, all the worse for having her augmentation badly damaged, but Bode would be suffering too. Perhaps the battle would be won by the one who managed to stay boosted for longer, assuming they didn't collapse together. His augmentation was undamaged...but she had no idea of its precise specifications. The Bloody Blades had kept the exact details of their augmentation to themselves.

He would have been stripped of his augmentation before he was dumped on Hellhole, she thought, quickly. *Could it be that the Grand Senator gave him something special – or was he pulled out of the penal system before he could be disarmed?*

"I have a better idea," she told him. "You fuck off and tell the Senator that you couldn't find either of us. It's a big place down here. You could spend *years* searching for someone in the Undercity. He isn't going to question a few days spent larking away down here."

"That isn't an option," Bode said. "You see, I want my reward."

He started to inch closer to her, talking rapidly. Belinda watched him warily, bracing herself as best as she could. Her vision was starting to blur, a sure sign that the boost was starting to damage her body. Bode didn't seem to be showing any side-effects himself, but there was no way to be sure. She'd have to assume the worst – and finish the struggle as quickly as possible.

"Your hands are twitching," Bode observed. "Having a little trouble with the boost, are we?"

Belinda swallowed a curse. The side-effects would keep growing worse as long as she drew on the boost – and yet without it, she wouldn't have a chance. She gathered herself, knowing that it was likely to be her last stand...

Shots rang out from the distance, aimed right at Bode. They missed, but for an instant he was distracted…just long enough for Belinda to lunge forward and slam her fist into the side of his head with augmented force. He would have light armour protecting his skull, just like Belinda herself, but the blow would have stunned him. Belinda watched him fall, then stamped on his head as hard as she could. It took several blows to crush it utterly. A moment later, his body burst into towering white flame, burning brilliantly in the semi-darkness…and revealing a girl holding a pistol. She looked too clean to have come from the Undercity…

Belinda shivered as she came off the boost, flushing it from her system as quickly as possible. More alerts blinked up in front of her, warning that she'd damaged a number of vital organs – despite implants intended to limit the damage. The net had crippled more of her augmentation than she'd realised. Once the boost was gone, tiredness fell on her like a lead weight. Somehow, she kept herself upright as Roland stumbled to his feet.

The Prince stared at the girl. "Who are you?"

"Amethyst," the girl said. "He…he controlled us. He turned us into monsters."

During one of the Slaughterhouse exercises, the recruits had been ordered to walk ten miles – only to be told, when they reached the end, that they had to walk another ten miles. And then another, and another… those who passed had to have the endurance to keep going anyway, no matter what, as long as it was humanly possible. Belinda had been drained, almost completely, when the exercise had finally ended, but now…now, she felt worse.

But she couldn't stop, not now. Bode had said that reinforcements were on the way.

"Come here," she ordered.

The girl, trembling, did as she was told. Belinda reached into her pocket, pulled out the roll of duct tape she'd carried out of habit, and used it to lash the girl's hands behind her back. It was far from polite, or decent, but she knew nothing about the girl – or where her loyalties lay. She couldn't be trusted, even if she had helped defeat Bode.

Roland blinked at her. "Is that necessary?"

"Yes," Belinda said, shortly. "Take the gun and be ready to use it."

There had been other gangsters nearby, but they'd fled. Belinda chose a passageway at random, hoping and praying that they were heading away from gang territory, and started to walk, nibbling at the remains of the ration bar as she moved. Her body needed a rest as well as food, but there was no time. They would just have to keep going until they found somewhere out of the danger zone…

If there was such a place left on Earth.

CHAPTER
THIRTY-NINE

However, no purge could eliminate all of the officers who had patrons from outside the Emergency Committee. Grand Senator Devers might have lost part of her network, but other parts remained intact, giving her an unexpected advantage. However, this advantage was not sufficient to assume control of enough firepower to force a stalemate.

- Professor Leo Caesius, The End of Empire.

EARTHCOM ONE was a single massive orbital battlestation, armed and armoured enough to go toe-to-toe with a battleship and survive. Commander Tsonga had been told, when he'd been assigned to the Earth Defence Force, that normal tactical doctrine simply didn't apply when the orbital defences were powerful enough. A stationary target was easy to hit, doctrine stated – but EARTHCOM ONE had enough firepower to make anyone who wanted to take out the station pay a heavy price for their efforts. And its sensors were capable of tracking and eliminating unpowered missiles launched beyond its engagement range…

…Not, Tsonga admitted, as he made his way down to the armoury, that they had ever been tested. Earth hadn't been attacked since the Unification Wars; the worst the solar system had seen in thousands of years was the occasional pirate attack, hardly anything to exercise Home Fleet. The defence planners regularly scoffed at the idea of someone attacking Earth. Everyone *knew* that humanity's homeworld was impregnable.

Normally, their confidence would be fully justified. Almost every orbital battlestation, industrial hub, habitation settlement and asteroid in orbit around Earth was tied into the main defence network, their sensors locked into one vast system that maintained an ever-present watch over the Earth-Moon system. *Nothing*, not even a cloaked ship, could enter Earth's space without being detected – and most of the orbital facilities were armed, even the civilian ones. Earth was so heavily defended that Home Fleet, the most powerful formation – at least on paper – in the Imperial Navy would bleed itself white trying to break through. There was good reason to assume that Earth was safe.

But the current situation was far from normal. Tsonga was surprised that he hadn't been reassigned after the destruction of Orbit Station Seven and the Emergency Committee's rise to power. He could only guess that the Emergency Committee – which had just happened to reassign officers that weren't part of its client network – hadn't realised that he belonged to Grand Senator Devers. Or maybe they'd just concentrated on the senior officers and ignored the juniors, perhaps assuming that they would obey orders without question. It was an assumption that was going to explode in their face.

He smiled to himself as he stepped out of the stairwell and walked down towards the armoury. There were no guards outside the armoured hatch; it was simply impossible to open without the proper codes. Even a debonder wouldn't work, he'd been told – and *using* one would certainly set off a whole series of alarms. But it didn't matter. He'd been given the code by one of the Grand Senator's other clients, who'd also added his biometric signature to the security system. As far as the armoury was concerned, he was a legitimate visitor.

The security panel felt cold against his fingertips as he pressed them against the sensor, then keyed in the code. If the newcomers *had* realised that there was a hole in their security, he was about to be arrested, interrogated and then thrown out into space…there was a long moment when he feared that something had gone wrong, then the hatch opened smoothly, revealing a large compartment crammed with weapons. He stepped inside, looking around for familiar rifles and pistols. His weapons training at Luna Base had been very limited.

"You got in," Ensign Sandra Higgs said. She was another person who had enjoyed the Grand Senator's patronage; in her case, it had saved her from having to use her body to graduate from basic training. It was lucky for her that she *had* been offered patronage; as pretty as she was, it wouldn't have been long before the instructors or upperclassmen came sniffing around. "Grab the rifles and let's go."

The other three arrived as Tsonga started passing out the weapons and armour. He took a small selection of security tools, suspecting that they might come in handy, as well as a pair of stunners. There was no point in pretending that he was going to defy the Grand Senator – no one would trust him if he betrayed his patron – yet he did want to avoid killing if possible. The new CO and his cronies wouldn't be missed, but everyone else was, at the very least, his workmate. They didn't deserve to die.

"All right," he said, as he closed the armoury and code-locked it. No one else should be able to get inside now, at least as long as the CO didn't override his commands. Thankfully, it was impossible to do that without actually visiting the armoury. "You know what to do. As soon as the elevator opens in Command Central, Joe and I will stun everyone. Everyone else hang back unless they start shooting at us."

He checked the stunner as they stepped into the elevator, then used the security tools he'd taken to override the system's protocols, allowing them to go directly to Command Central. It shouldn't alarm anyone, if only because the CO had given his cronies full access rights – and people had been getting used to them swaggering around the station. By the time the command staff realised that they *weren't* friendly, it would be far too late.

"Here we go," he said, as the elevator neared Command Central. His mouth was suddenly very dry. It had seemed easy when he'd planned it, but actually carrying it out was going to be much harder than he'd thought. "Don't fuck up."

The elevator doors hissed open. Command Central was massive, easily the size of a football pitch, crammed with consoles operated by pale-faced men and women trying to keep track of what was going on near Earth. With so many independent and even small corporate shippers fleeing the solar system, their task had suddenly become a great deal harder. Who knew if one of those freighters wouldn't decide to try to take out another orbital station? It was a very real possibility.

He pressed down on the trigger and started to spray stun pulses towards his targets. One advantage of stunners was that they didn't actually damage anything they hit; he could fire the stunner into a console for hours and not damage it at all. Several operators glanced towards him as they heard the stunners, but it was far too late. They dropped where they stood before they could do anything. The CO was still reaching for the pistol he wore at his belt when he was hit and sent falling to the deck. It barely took thirty seconds to sweep the entire compartment.

"Check them all," he ordered. It was just possible that some of them could be faking it, if they'd had the presence of mind to drop to the deck when they'd started shooting. "Hurry!"

He ran over to the CO's chair and slipped a pre-prepared datachip into the console. A competent CO could control most of the station's internal functions from his console, if he knew what he was doing; within moments, the entire station was under his control. Quickly, he activated the security overrides, putting most of the station into lockdown. The remainder, believing that there was a genuine emergency, should follow orders from Command Central without question.

Not, in the end, that it would matter.

The Grand Senator's orders had been clear. First, take control of EARTHCOM ONE. Second, engage as many Emergency Committee-controlled orbital defences as possible, before they realised that something had gone badly wrong. He wasn't the only one, he'd been told; if he failed to carry out his orders, he would be dooming others to failure. Tsonga hesitated, considering the danger of what he was about to do, then started to set up the firing solutions. Everything within reach of EARTHCOM ONE had to be considered a legitimate target.

Seven minutes later, he pushed down on the firing key and the civil war began.

The first Stephen heard of the emergency was when the Imperial Palace's alarms started to howl. A moment later, the floor fell away and the chair he was sitting on fell down an antigravity chute and into a secure bunker underneath the palace. He was still trying to recover from the shock when the display in front of him lit up with an emergency communication from Admiral Valentine. What the hell was going on?

"We have a mutiny on several stations," Admiral Valentine said. He looked badly shocked. "Earth's defence network has fragmented! A number of battlestations are firing on their own kin!"

Stephen stared at him, unable to grasp the magnitude of the disaster. "Why?"

"Unknown," Admiral Valentine admitted. "The first we knew of it was when EARTHCOM ONE opened fire, but the command network was hammered beforehand. We don't know how many stations have remained loyal and how many are being overwhelmed with mutinies and how many are just sitting on the fence…"

"Get a grip on yourself, man," Stephen barked at him. Rage would drive away fear – he hoped. What would happen if someone hostile to the Emergency Committee took control of the high orbitals? "What is the exact situation?"

Admiral Valentine pulled himself to attention, slowly. "Seven orbital defence stations – led by EARTHCOM ONE – have opened fire on other orbital defence stations, mainly the ones that were completely under our control. All of them were caught by surprise and took heavy damage. At the same time, the unified command network has been fragmented, even subverted. We don't know who is on what side."

Stephen took a moment to put it all together. "So if we fired on the wrong station, we might create additional enemies," he said.

"*Yes*," Admiral Valentine averred. "The best we can do is tactical analysis; we think that six of the seven stations are working together, but we don't know for sure. And then we don't know what the seventh is doing either!"

Devers, Stephen thought, coldly. Perhaps it would have been better to offer the bitch a seat on the Emergency Committee, rather than leaving her in the cold, but he'd wanted a number of her assets for himself. And besides, she would hardly have accepted his direction as tamely as some of the others. *She* knew better than to allow someone into a position of near-absolute power.

And she'd been to see the Marine Commandant. Were they planning something together? Stephen had worked hard to get as many Marines off-Earth and out of the system as possible, but the Marines had a habit of doing more with less. It was unlike them to take sides in political struggles, yet this struggle risked everything. Couldn't they see that he was doing it for the Empire? He would have stabilised it, made it strong again...the fact that he would have boosted his own power beyond all recognition was merely the icing on the cake.

But it isn't too late, he thought, grimly. *And we took out most of her network when we purged the solar system.*

"Get the Imperial Navy into the act," he ordered. "I want those hostile stations taken out!"

"Your Excellency," Admiral Valentine said carefully, "if we use heavier warheads, we will rain debris down on Earth."

"So?" Stephen demanded. "It will just burn up in the planet's atmosphere!"

"Grand Senator, Orbit Station Seven's destruction threw thousands of pieces of debris into the atmosphere," Admiral Valentine said. "But anything large enough to hit the ground was blasted into fragments by the orbital defence network. Right now, that orbital defence network is in *tatters*! If we start destroying entire stations, chunks of debris *will* get through, they *will* hit the ground and they *will* cause damage!"

He took a breath. "Your Excellency, this isn't a KEW strike," he warned. "This is something that could shake the entire planet. A large chunk of rock hitting Earth would kill billions! If it hit the water, it would throw tidal waves in all directions..."

Stephen stared at him coldly until his voice died away. "You seem to have forgotten your place," he said. "I put you in command of Earth's defences to ensure that there was no trouble that might threaten our grip on Earth. I gave you a defence network that had been purged of other patronage networks. I made you what you are."

His eyes narrowed. "Now tell me, *Admiral*, are you no longer willing to obey orders?"

"That isn't what I said," Admiral Valentine stammered. "I just..."

"Then use the heavier weapons," Stephen ordered. "This problem *cannot* be allowed to spread. And once the stations have been taken out, prepare to deploy KEWs against targets on the ground. The food rioters have gone too far. We can rebuild after the dust stops falling."

"Yes, Your Excellency," Admiral Valentine said. "I will issue the orders at once."

"See that you do," Stephen ordered. "And don't contact me again until you are ready to proceed with ground-strikes."

He cut the connection and stood up, looking around the Emperor's bunker to find the main display. From what the staff had told him, when the Grand Senate had taken over the Palace, the Emperor had kept a private network that was responsive only to people with the right bloodline, something that Stephen had intended to use Roland to circumvent. There was little point in being Emperor when he could rule behind the scenes – and control Roland's child as soon as he was born. Hell, he didn't even *need* Lady Lily any longer. Roland could marry one of his daughters and die as soon as the Heir was born. Having a child-ruler had been very helpful...

Bode was still searching for Roland, he knew, along with a team of soldiers from his personal guard. Communications systems just didn't work well down in the Undercity; it might be hours before Bode checked in with him, even if he had only failure to report. With a skilled and experienced Marine protecting Roland, finding him would be difficult. And yet there was no time to wait for results. If Roland appeared to be in command, the more mutinous units would hesitate...surely.

And what, a cold voice at the back of his mind asked, *if they don't?*

There were already food riots tearing through thousands of CityBlocks. Each one was stretching the loyalists to the limit; in fact, he'd had to order the Civil Guard withdrawn from large parts of the planet, just to keep them from being overwhelmed...when they hadn't joined the rebels in mutiny. At least his own soldiers were still loyal. *Their* food came from his private stockpile – and besides, they knew better than to expect mercy if he lost...

And yet, the voice of doubt mocked, *what if you lose control completely?*

He pushed the thought aside and linked into his own communications network. Devers had managed to catch him by surprise, he admitted to himself, and given him a nasty few moments, but she hadn't managed to gain an overwhelming advantage. Certainly not enough of one to force him to surrender, or share power with her. And he had a few surprises of his own. The bitch had been paranoid, with very good reason, yet he'd managed to slip one of his people into her patronage network. How could she find a spy who didn't *know* that he was a spy?

But spying wasn't what he'd really had in mind for that particular agent…

Grinning, he sent a signal into the communications network and then settled down to wait. He was still in control. Whatever happened next, he would still come out on top.

Commodore Levine had been an experienced tactical officer in the Imperial Navy when he'd been offered a chance to transfer to Grand Senator Devers's personal staff. It had been a hell of an opportunity; the Grand Senator paid well and actually *listened* to tactical advice. Levine had helped plan her counterattack on the Emergency Committee, even though he'd warned her that the odds of success were not high. But he'd had to agree with her that the only other alternative was kowtowing to the Emergency Committee and hoping that they'd let her keep a few scraps of her once-vast holdings.

He opened the message that blinked up in front of him…and died, his personality shattering beyond hope of recovery. In its place, a new personality – created by a neural link, then buried at the back of his mind – came forward and took control. It had been stripped down to bare essentials – it certainly couldn't pretend to be Levine for very long – but it would last long enough to carry out its mission. Levine's body stood up, one hand fingering the pistol at his belt, and walked into the next compartment. The Grand Senator was seated in front of a holographic tactical display, monitoring the battle. She'd been advised to head for the Phase Limit, just in case, but she'd been too stubborn to run. Not, in the end, that it would have mattered.

The part of the buried personality that served as a tactical analyst noted that there was no one in position to defend its target. There were no armed bodyguards, merely a handful of systems operators who were unused to actually firing the pistols on their belts. Devers had *trusted* her people, using it as a tool to gain loyalty – and she had been right; Levine had been loyal to her. But Levine was no longer in control of his own body.

'Levine' drew the pistol, pointed it at her head, and pulled the trigger. By the time anyone realised what had happened, it was far too late. The Grand Senator was dead.

CHAPTER FORTY

What this meant, even before Grand Senator Devers was assassinated, was that neither side would win a quick victory. Consequently, the civil war would not only rage out of control – as neither side could back down – but Earth's massive orbital infrastructure would be degraded and destroyed in the crossfire. And all of this was visible down on Earth.
- Professor Leo Caesius, *The End of Empire.*

Amethyst couldn't help wondering if she was in a state of shock. She felt almost as if she were drifting through life, even though she was being pushed through the corridors by Prince Roland's bodyguard, a grim-faced woman who looked almost inhuman to Amethyst's eyes. And yet, she'd matched Richard…Amethyst still couldn't believe what he'd been, or how easily she'd been manipulated. Or, for that matter, that she'd fired on Richard. By now, all she wanted to do was sit down and rest.

But that wasn't an option. They were in the *Undercity* – and they were being hunted. Richard – Bode, he'd called himself – had said that there were others after them…and she wasn't the only person he'd recruited. For all she knew, there could be hundreds of people searching the Undercity for Prince Roland. God alone knew what they'd do if they caught her, after what she'd done. She truly had nowhere to go.

The darkened corridors and passageways seemed empty, but she could hear people in the distance. Shouts, screams of rage and horror… all sending chills running down her spine. She wanted to be a long way away from whoever was making those sounds, but it was impossible to tell where they were coming from. Instead, she just kept walking onwards, glancing around nervously. One room seemed to be crammed with dead bodies, all showing the same symptoms as the dead people in the upper parts of the block. How far had the poisonous ration bars spread?

She winced as the Prince's bodyguard propelled her into a darkened chamber, then pushed her face-first against one wall. "Stay there," a cold voice snarled in her ear. Amethyst was too terrified to do anything but obey. Richard had been frightening, when she'd seen his mask drop; the Prince's bodyguard was a thousand times worse. She had never *dreamed* that such people existed before becoming involved with Richard. And to think that she'd willingly taken him into her bed.

But he wouldn't have taken no for an answer, she thought, numbly. Had he kept her around for sexual pleasure, rather than the planned revolution? God! How stupid had she been? Would she have eventually become a whore, just like the girls in the Undercity, or would he have eventually dumped her to face the music alone? And had he been the one who'd betrayed Jacqueline to the Civil Guard, therefore ensuring that Amethyst had no place to go? It seemed far too possible.

Silently, she tested the duct tape binding her hands. It was too strong to snap; escape was futile. She would just have to hope that Prince Roland wasn't feeling vengeful, even though she'd helped save his life. She'd certainly had a hand in endangering it as well. If not her, it would have been someone else…but somehow she doubted that argument would impress anyone, least of all the woman who protected the Prince. What *was* she? No normal human could move like that, right?

Strong hands caught her and spun her around, then pulled the duct tape away from her mouth. Amethyst yelped in pain as it came free, taking some of her skin with it, then looked up into cold blue eyes. The Prince's bodyguard looked battered, her clothes were in rags – and yet somehow she managed to look thoroughly intimidating. Amethyst couldn't meet her eyes for long; she had to look away as the woman studied her. She couldn't help wondering if she was about to have her neck effortlessly snapped and her body left to rot in the Undercity. No one would pay attention to another dead body.

"All right," the woman growled, as she pressed her fingertips against Amethyst's neck. "I can read your body's responses. The first time you lie to me, I will hurt you; the second time, I will start breaking bones. If you still try to lie, I will kill you. Do you understand me?"

Amethyst nodded frantically.

"Good," the woman said. "Now, start talking. What were you doing with Bode?"

"And why," Prince Roland added, "did you turn on him?"

Amethyst looked from one to the other, then started to talk.

Belinda wrinkled her nose as a faint smell of urine reached her nostrils. The girl had wet herself. It wasn't an uncommon reaction when someone was scared to death – it had been known to happen to soldiers having their first taste of combat – and it was even useful, but it was still distasteful. The girl might not even have noticed that she'd lost control of her bladder.

"My name is Amethyst," the girl said. "I thought I was rebelling..."

The whole story came tumbling out, piece by piece. Belinda listened, asking the occasional question from time to time, shaking her head in disbelief. How could *anyone* have been so stupid? But it was far from unusual. Extremists, terrorists, rebels and criminals had managed to trick innocent – and ignorant – people into doing stupid things before and would be doing it until the very end of time. Amethyst had been used, which didn't make her any less guilty. A smarter or more experienced person might have asked how the students actually benefited from starting a riot. Or, for that matter, from trying to shoot down Prince Roland.

It would have been easy to snap Amethyst's neck. She was a rebel, a terrorist and a traitor; Bode hadn't had put a gun to her head to force her to do anything. There was a point beyond which ignorance could not be used as an excuse. If Belinda had handed her over to the authorities, Amethyst would be executed. There would be no new colony world or even penal dumping ground for her. She'd simply gone too far.

But she'd also saved Belinda's life.

Belinda scowled as the girl finally stopped babbling, thinking hard. Amethyst had apparently had doubts after the first few weeks, but it had been too late to escape – or to save herself, if the authorities caught up with her. That wasn't unusual either; criminal gangs and terrorists both wanted new recruits compromised as soon as possible. It was harder to switch sides if the authorities knew that one was to blame for a terrorist atrocity. And besides, she'd seen enough of Bode to be terrified of what he might do to her. She'd actually been very lucky. If half the stories she'd heard about Bode were true, she would have suffered terribly before she died.

"I couldn't let him kill the Prince," the girl had said. "I…I was stupid."

Yes, Belinda thought, coldly. *You were stupid.*

"Tell me what's happening up top," she ordered, grimly. "We've been in the Undercity for too long."

Roland stepped forward. "And what happened to the University?"

"They declared full lockdown," Amethyst said. "People were dying – or rioting. I don't know *what* happened to the University."

"You saved us," Roland stated, bluntly.

Belinda caught his arm and pulled him away from the girl. She stared after them, aware that they were going to decide her fate – and that she was unable to escape. Belinda had seen people like that before, people who had simply endured too much to be able to care about what was happening to them. Maybe snapping her neck would be the kindest thing they could do for her. And it was quite possible that she would be a liability…

"She saved our lives," Roland hissed, barely loudly enough to be heard. "We can't just kill her."

"Yeah," Belinda said, slowly. "But do we have to take her with us?"

"You can't leave her tied like that here," Roland snapped. "She wouldn't get a mile before they caught her."

Belinda hesitated. Part of her wanted to cut the girl's bonds and tell her to run; part of her admitted that the girl might be useful in the future. *And* Amethyst had saved their lives; in truth, Belinda knew herself to have been badly injured. Parts of her augmentation had simply died – and she was vulnerable. Roland might need more help in the future.

"I can pardon her," Roland insisted. "We *owe* her."

"I suppose we do," Belinda agreed. She turned and walked back to the frightened girl. "You have a choice."

Amethyst looked up at her, unable to speak.

"You can come with us as we try to get somewhere safe," Belinda said. Right now, she didn't have the faintest idea of where to go. The plan to head for the Arena might have been scuttled by the food riots – and there were going to be riots. Even if only a tiny handful of ration bars had been contaminated, mass hysteria and panic would do the rest. "If you do, you will have to obey orders – and if you try to betray us, I will kill you."

She lowered her voice. "The alternative is that we free you, then allow you to make your own way out of the Undercity," she added. "You will be free, as long as you don't try to come after us. Make your choice."

"I'll...I'll go with you," Amethyst said. She sounded terrified, but at the same time there was a faint hint of hope in her voice. "Please..."

"Good choice," Belinda said, dryly. She pulled the monofilament blade out of her pocket, spun Amethyst around and sliced away the duct tape binding her hands. "I just hope that I don't come to regret it. Now, how did you get into the Undercity?"

"Through Rowdy Yates Block," Amethyst said, as she rubbed her wrists. The duct tape had taken more skin with it when Belinda pulled it free. "There was a passageway there..."

"Not too surprising, I guess," Belinda mused. "The Undercity has been inching upwards for centuries."

Amethyst stared at her. "But I never knew..."

"It seems there is a great deal that you never knew," Belinda pointed out rather sarcastically. "You've been a fucking fool. Try and do better in future."

She leaned back, then beckoned for Amethyst and the Prince to follow her. "We'll get up through Rowdy Yates ourselves, then try and link into the Marine network," she added. If they could, she reminded herself. Half of her implants had been fried. There *were* ways to get into the network through the civilian datanet, but if there was a full lockdown in process the datanet would have been disabled. "That should tell us what is going on."

Prince Roland gave her a sharp look. "And what do we do then?"

"What seems best at the time," Belinda said. She had *no* idea what they would have to do; they just didn't know enough to make even vague plans. Perhaps they should try to reach the orbital towers and climb up to orbit. Or the military spaceport… "We'll find out what's going on and then we will decide what to do."

They started to make their way up towards the entrance to Rowdy Yates CityBlock, every one of Belinda's remaining sensors scanning for trouble. No one moved to block their path, or even demand a toll for moving through their territory, something that Belinda couldn't help finding ominous. The crime lord Amethyst had told her about, the one who had been working with Bode, would have lost face in front of his rivals by how they'd escaped the first ambush. Logically, he should have tried to stop them before they could get up into the Inner City…but nothing materialised. Belinda puzzled over it as they climbed up a half-ruined set of stairs and through a large compartment that stank faintly of diesel. A handful of rusty vehicles lay in one corner, buried deep under the megacities.

Pug would have loved it, she thought, grimly. Her teammate had had a gift for driving and repairing all sorts of vehicles, to the point where his superiors had tried to talk him out of Pathfinder training. But he'd been too stubborn to take their gentle hints as orders and passed through the training with flying colours. And now he was dead.

The level of pollution in the air seemed to be rising rapidly, according to her implants, although they were having problems in identifying the specific pollutants. A nerve gas warning flashed up in front of her eyes for a brief moment and she almost grabbed Roland to carry him backwards, before realising that the warning had to be a false alarm. *She* had immunities worked into her body; Roland and Amethyst would have dropped dead by now, if the nerve gas had been real. The alert vanished a second later, to be replaced by a warning about dangerous chemicals from an industrial plant. Someone had been dumping them into the Undercity.

No one was guarding the stairwell that led up to Rowdy Yates. Belinda clutched her knife in one hand and inched up the stairs, her remaining sensors picking up sounds of screaming and fighting from high overhead. A handful of bodies lay near the access point, three of them wearing Civil Guard uniforms. Judging by their condition, they had been battered to death when the gang had surged up from the Undercity. The other bodies had been shot, but there were no weapons lying on the ground. Someone had to have taken them to use against their former owners.

"Come on up," she said, grimly.

Roland appeared, one hand holding his pistol so tightly that his knuckles were turning white. His face, already pale, seemed to pall further as he looked at the devastation. "What happened?"

"The Undercity is rising up," Belinda said. No *wonder* no one had sought to bar their path. With their food supplies contaminated, the gangsters had decided to attack the Inner City…and if every gang had made the same decision, the lid was well and truly off. "I think we're in deep shit."

She attempted to ping the nearest network node, but there was no response. Ordinarily, she would have been able to tell if there was no node or if it was simply not responding to her, but her implants were so badly damaged that it was impossible to be sure what was happening. A wide-band scan picked up countless alerts on the civilian emergency frequency, all hysterical and none of them very informative. As far as she could tell, there were no Civil Guard or Marine transmissions at all.

It would be a long walk from Rowdy Yates to the Arena – if that was truly the best place to go – and the streets were in chaos. They'd have to be incredibly lucky if they avoided having to fight. And yet, where could they find an aircar? If there was a lockdown underway, they'd all be grounded; registered aircars had transponders that deactivated them on government command. An unregistered aircar would risk attracting unwanted attention from the Civil Guard…

"There should be emergency vehicles in the loading bay," Amethyst said, when Belinda had explained the problem. "By law, they're supposed to be there."

Belinda nodded, ruefully. That *was* true…assuming that someone on the Block Committee hadn't decided to cut corners by not buying the vehicles after all. "It's our best chance to avoid having to walk," she agreed, shortly. "Let's go."

Han had been bad, a nightmare – and Belinda had missed the worst of it. Earth seemed to be rapidly becoming worse; every level they passed through brought new horrors. Men mutilated and then murdered; women and children raped and then left to die...the savagery of the Undercity had finally burst upwards, completely out of control. Some of the bodies even seemed to have been gnawed...Belinda saw Amethyst looking sick and felt a touch of sympathy for the girl. She'd never really understood what was happening until it was far too late.

One room had been a teenage community centre; by law, every teenager was supposed to spend at least two hours a day socialising with his or her fellow students. From what Belinda had heard, it was one of those laws passed by people who thought they knew what was best for Young Children and Teenagers...and it didn't work as well as they'd expected. Now, the community centre had been ripped apart; bodies lay everywhere, many savagely mutilated. A middle-aged woman, probably the supervisor, had been tied to a chair and forced to watch, before someone had mercifully cut her throat. God alone knew what she'd done to deserve it, if anything. The savage uprising wasn't really under anyone's control.

The emergency section had been sealed and the power had failed. Belinda couldn't tell if that was a security precaution or another case of poor maintenance finally catching up with them, but it hardly mattered. She had to jigger a power cell from a food dispenser and use it to unlock the hatch, something that would have been beyond anyone from the Undercity – or Imperial University, for that matter. Maybe it was a case of fridge brilliance after all...

"There's an aircar," Amethyst said, relieved. The aircar was ancient, but it looked serviceable. "But where *is* everyone?"

"Good question," Belinda mused. She checked the aircar thoroughly; as far as she could tell, it was fully functional. "Get inside. I'll open the hatch."

It wasn't difficult to crank open the hatch, allowing her to stare out over the megacity. Smoke was rising from hundreds of different places, far too many for the emergency services to handle. High overhead, chunks of debris seemed to be falling through the planet's atmosphere...what was going on up there? Her implants reported high-energy discharges in low orbit...

She turned and walked to the emergency lockers, searching for something she could use. Most of the equipment had been taken, but she managed to find a datanet terminal and several tools. Pocketing them all, she walked back to the aircar and joined the other two.

"Time to go," she told them, quietly.

CHAPTER FORTY-ONE

Combined with the food shortages, this was the final straw for Earth's population. Starving and angry, the population rose up and attacked the government. But by then it was far too late. Even if the Emergency Committee had folded quickly, Earth had fallen too far to be saved. The lid had come off a pot that had been simmering for generations.

— Professor Leo Caesius, *The End of Empire.*

Earth's Traffic Control System was the envy of the Empire, at least according to the government's propaganda. The happy owner of an aircar – barely one in a million citizens – could set the destination, then sit back and relax as the TCS guided the aircar through the air, avoiding all danger of a collision with either another aircar or one of the CityBlocks. In practice, Belinda knew, it was just another example of the government treating the population like children. The novel idea of actually allowing people to take responsibility for themselves had never crossed their minds.

The system had been breaking down even before the crisis had begun. Belinda had reviewed its safety record when planning Roland's expeditions outside the Summer Palace and discovered that there was at least one accident nearly every day. Aircars would fly into buildings, or ram other aircars, killing everyone on board. She couldn't imagine ever boarding an aircar that didn't have a manual override, but the citizens of Earth had just tamely accepted it. Now, the TCS was completely down. How many aircar owners could even fly their cars?

She stared out the window as the aircar flew away from Rowdy Yates CityBlock and headed towards Imperial City. Normally, she would have taken the aircar higher up, but she didn't dare. The orbital defence network seemed to be in the middle of a civil war – either that or Earth was under direct attack – and one side or the other might start shooting at aircars. And then there were whatever forces the Emergency Committee had in place to defend the Imperial Palace.

The smoke seemed to be growing thicker as they headed northwards. Down below, hundreds of thousands of people swarmed through the streets, smashing away at everything they could touch and destroy. The Undercity was rising up…and so were the poorer parts of Earth's population, the parts that had borne the brunt of bureaucratic mismanagement for so long. Now, with safe food supplies running out, they no longer had anything to lose. Why *not* take it out on the government?

She banked the aircar to avoid a CityBlock, wincing in horror as she saw people spilling out of the windows and falling down towards the streets far below. Running from the rebels or just overcome with hysteria…it hardly mattered. They were falling to their deaths. How many of them were going to die before it all ended, if it could end…she glanced up sharply as something raced through the atmosphere, high overhead. It looked large enough to do real damage when it struck the ground.

"Crap," Roland said lightly.

Belinda sucked in her breath as the Arena came into view. The entire structure seemed to be blazing as howling mobs tore through the complex, hunting down and killing everyone they could catch. They'd loved the gladiators, but they'd hated and envied them too; now, with civilisation collapsing around them, the population had turned on the Arena that had been used to distract them from the truth. Belinda saw a handful of monsters from various worlds – all bred to be extremely dangerous – escaping from the Arena and heading out into the city. If Earth survived, they were going to have to be hunted down before they could breed. No doubt it had seemed to make sense, at one time, to bring breeding pairs to Earth. Now…

"Crap indeed," she said. The plan for getting help from the Arena security staff seemed to have collapsed before it had even fairly begun. "Now what?"

She guided the aircar over to a rooftop and landed gently. "Keep an eye out for trouble," she ordered, as she picked up the datanet terminal and examined it thoughtfully. "I'll see what I can get out of this piece of junk."

The terminal took several tries to link into *any* datanet node, but at least it had found something, unlike her implants. Belinda accessed functions that few of Earth's citizens even knew existed and pulled up an outline of the network's current status. It wasn't good; a third of the nodes seemed to be completely offline, while the civilian network had been put into lockdown. In theory, that should have cleared the network for military traffic, but in practice the network seemed to be on the verge of complete collapse. The fighting in orbit had taken out a number of critical processors.

"Damn it," she muttered, as she tried to hook into the Marine network. Even with the emergency codes the Commandant had given her, it was a long time before she could pull a full emergency briefing off the net. Normally, the download would take less than a second. She hadn't seen such poor transmission rates in her entire life. "What the hell is going on?"

The download finally completed. Belinda opened it and skimmed through it quickly, cursing the long delay. Her implants had spoiled her. There was fighting almost everywhere on Earth, all four orbital towers had turned into warzones…and Earth's defence network was tearing itself apart. Home Fleet seemed to have fragmented; outright mutiny seemed to have broken out on hundreds of starships. Her lips twitched in bitter amusement. The Grand Senate had ordered the Marines off the ships, before the crisis had *really* exploded in their collective face. No doubt they were regretting their decision now.

"They didn't go after Imperial University," she said, in some astonishment. Reading onwards, she discovered that part of the Civil Guard had mutinied and *joined* the students, while the rest of the Guard seemed to be on the verge of mutiny. The Emergency Committee had been trying to bring additional troops down to the surface, but the fighting in orbit had put paid to that. "The rebels are still there."

"We could go there," Roland said, seriously. "And…"

"And then what?" Belinda demanded. "Earth is simply too far gone to be saved."

Her duty was to protect Roland. The fighting in orbit almost certainly meant that Earth was going to be bombarded by debris, as well as overrun by starving rioters intent on doing as much damage as they could before they starved to death. Staying on Earth meant almost certain death. She had to get Roland off the planet.

But how?

She paged through the report quickly, thinking hard. The orbital towers were warzones – and, in any case, no one would be docking there in a hurry. There *was* the spaceport, but it was heavily guarded – and it was quite possible that most of the shuttles were gone. And then...

There wasn't anything. The aircar they'd stolen couldn't get into orbit; the very thought was laughable. Marine HQ might have survived – it would have taken a nuke or precisely-targeted KEW to damage the building – but there were no shuttles there. If she'd been able to contact the Commandant, perhaps he could have arranged a pick-up...a quick test proved that the network wasn't accepting messages, even with her override codes. The entire system was on the verge of collapse.

And the Emergency Committee was *still* trying to manage the disaster.

Belinda almost laughed with bitter frustration. Didn't they *see*? No matter what they did, no matter how many troops they deployed, Earth was *finished*! The riots would destroy what remained of Earth's infrastructure, including the bureaucrats who kept it functioning; even if the orbital fighting came to an end before something large enough to shake the entire planet fell out of orbit, Earth was thoroughly screwed. Now, all they could do was flee.

"We need to take those bastards out," Roland said, when she'd finished explaining. "If we could kill them..."

"I can't disagree," Belinda said, tartly. "But you do realise that they have a large force dug in around the Imperial Palace? There are three of us..."

"So we find help," Roland said. "Can't you call the Marines?"

"I can't get through to the Commandant," Belinda reminded him. "Even if I could, I doubt he would agree to send reinforcements. I don't even know if he *has* reinforcements."

Another piece of debris tore through the air, leaving a fiery trail to mark its passage. Belinda silently calculated that it would come down somewhere thousands of miles to the south; it certainly *looked* large enough to survive re-entry. And everyone underneath it when it came down would die.

"Excuse me," Amethyst said, holding up her hand. "I have an idea."

Amethyst swallowed as Belinda turned to face her. Having the idea had been the easy part; suggesting it out loud seemed to be far harder. She'd half-expected the Marine to simply abandon her once they'd seen the chaos spreading through the megacity – and the complete absence of anyone trying to maintain law and order.

"The students have some help from the Civil Guard," she said, carefully. "And they're already in Imperial City, not too far from the Imperial Palace. Can't we ask *them* to help?"

"That's brilliant," Prince Roland said. He gave her a smile that made her legs melt. "They have weapons; they could help us get into the Imperial Palace..."

"There's enough firepower camped out around the Imperial Palace to deal with a small army," Belinda pointed out, coldly. "And believe me, most of the Civil Guard are not worth whatever they're paid by the government. Even if they did attack the Imperial Palace, they'd be quickly slaughtered."

"But they don't have to actually *take* the Palace," Roland said. "They just have to cause a distraction."

"A distraction," Belinda repeated coldly.

"A distraction," Roland confirmed. "They keep the defences busy while we sneak in through the tunnels."

Belinda frowned. "And how exactly do we get into the tunnels?"

Roland held up his right hand. "The Imperial Palace is controlled by a computer network installed by the First Emperor, my ancestor," he said. "It couldn't have been removed or reprogrammed without completely ruining the Palace. And it responds to those with the Imperial Bloodline. Why do you *think* they left me at the Summer Palace?"

He smiled, brilliantly. "They might have limited access rights while they live there," he added, "but I can override them. We can get in and kill the bastards, then take the spacer that is supposed to be buried in an emergency hangar…"

"We might be shot down by the orbital defences," Belinda said, carefully. "But if we took out the Emergency Committee, we might be able to convince them to stop firing and stand down. It still wouldn't save Earth."

She looked over at Amethyst. "You do realise that plenty of your student friends are going to die?"

Amethyst nodded, reluctantly. The chaos sweeping the streets would eventually overwhelm Imperial University, even if it *was* guarded by armed students. And then everyone she'd ever known and loved would die. God alone knew what had happened to her parents…their CityBlock might have been overwhelmed by now. There was no way to know. And it struck her, as Belinda's eyes bored into her skull, that she might *never* know.

"It's a fucking crazy plan," Belinda said, as she turned back to Roland. "But it seems to be the best we have…are you sure you want to go through with it?"

Roland waved a hand towards the chaos outside the aircar. There was a brilliant flash of light in the distance, followed by a rumbling sound that sent shivers running through the entire CityBlock. Most of the structures were built to be invulnerable, Richard had told Amethyst, but they were built on weaker foundations. Some of them might topple over as they lost their stability, or suffer internal collapses. Eventually, they might become nothing more than hollow shells.

"If we can stop this," he said, "even long enough to evacuate people from Earth…"

"We can't," Belinda said. "You could gather every starship in the Empire and you still couldn't take more than a fraction of Earth's population."

"But we have to try," Roland said. "And besides, that shuttle is our only way off the planet."

"Very well," Belinda said, after a long moment. "The Imperial University it is."

Amethyst felt a cold shiver running down her spine as the aircar took off again. Belinda set a course that skirted the edges of Imperial City, rather than flying over the heart of the Empire. The riots didn't seem to have reached Imperial City yet, but it was clear that trouble was brewing. Despite the lockdown, despite orders from the Emergency Committee, there were crowds gathering on the streets below. There was no way to know what was going on inside the residency blocks, but Amethyst would have been surprised to hear that they weren't suffering the same problems as the rest of the world.

Imperial University – a towering white building – came into view. Belinda took the aircar lower, reminding them that there might be loyalists watching for people trying to aid the students – and the students might mistake them for loyalists – and headed towards the first barricade. It had been put together from junk, Amethyst saw; Belinda snorted rudely and commented that it wouldn't stand up to a tank for more than a few seconds, if that. The armed students on the barricades pointed rifles towards the aircar as it dropped to the ground. Amethyst couldn't help feeling that they'd landed on the wrong side…

"Go talk to them," Belinda ordered, as the door hissed open. "Tell them that we want to be taken to their leaders. And make sure that you keep your hands in sight."

Amethyst shivered as she stepped out of the aircar and walked towards the barricade. After everything she'd done, being shot by a nervous student holding an unfamiliar weapon would be the height of irony. She held her hands up as she reached the barricade and halted, realising that Belinda had been right. The barricade really was pretty flimsy.

"All right," a voice drawled. Amethyst looked up to see a male student, posing like a hero from one of the entertainment flicks where the bad guys were very bad and the good guys always won, if only because the bad guys were also stupid. "Stop right there and identify yourself."

"My name is Amethyst," Amethyst said, carefully. She'd heard that Jacqueline was one of the leaders of the uprising – certainly its public face – but what if she blamed Amethyst for what had happened to her? Now she was staring at a student with a gun, the whole idea seemed more than a little insane. "I need to speak to Jacqueline."

"Ye Gods," the student said. "I heard they'd arrested you!"

Amethyst had to smile. "Rumours of my death…"

"Yes, I saw that flick too," the student said. "I can…"

"We don't know *what* she's doing here," another voice said, from behind the barricade. "She might be under their control."

"Or she might have escaped from them," the first student said. "We should call Jacqueline and ask her to tell us what to do."

"I thought the point of this was learning to think for ourselves," a third voice said. It was impossible to tell if the voice was male or female. "We don't know *what* happened to her…"

"Call Jacqueline," Amethyst said, as patiently as she could. The students sounded like members of the debating club, which had been more interesting *before* she'd realised that the debates were slanted in the officially-approved direction. It was astonishing what sort of nonsense could be drawn from data that was also nonsense. "I think that she will recognise me."

"We will," the first student said. He gestured with his gun towards the aircar. "And who exactly are your friends?"

"Allies," Amethyst said, shortly. She wasn't sure that she should mention names yet, at least until she knew what sort of reception she was going to get. "I need to explain to Jacqueline first."

She had to wait nearly ten minutes before she heard the sound of someone scrambling up the other side of the barricade. Jacqueline's dark face appeared and stared down at her in complete astonishment, before her friend jumped down and landed neatly in front of her. Amethyst was still staring when Jacqueline wrapped her up in a hug and squeezed her tightly.

"What happened to you?" Jacqueline asked. It had been weeks since they'd last seen each other, before the first riot had torn apart the trust between students and the government. "And who are your friends?"

"It's a long story," Amethyst said. "But they *are* friends."

"They'll have to face the Committee," Jacqueline said, as Amethyst beckoned for Belinda and Roland to join them. "Who…"

Her voice broke off as she stared at Roland. "*Prince* Roland?"

"Pleased to meet you," Roland said, with a formal bow. "I would have been here sooner, but the Grand Senate…delayed me."

Jacqueline shook her head. "A long story, you say?"

She smiled in disbelief. "You'll have to tell it to the Committee," she warned. "All hell has been breaking loose out on the streets. We don't know what to do."

Amethyst nodded, no longer trusting herself to speak. Seeing Jacqueline again reminded her of just how far she'd fallen since she'd first met Richard - Bode. Her friend might have ended up helping to run a revolution, but she was still *innocent*. Amethyst had lost her innocence the day she'd allowed Bode to manipulate her into becoming a monster. Whatever she could do to make up for it, she would.

But Belinda was right. Far too many students were going to die.

CHAPTER FORTY-TWO

Furthermore, as the Grand Senate had systematically neutralised all other centres of power, the uprising was utterly uncontrolled. Blood ran through the corridors of CityBlocks as the Undercity exploded upwards, its denizens intent on killing as many 'toffs' as they could before they died. We will never know how many citizens, unprepared for such violence and incapable of defending themselves, were raped and murdered as the uprising raged onwards. They were nothing more than collateral damage as the Empire fell.
- Professor Leo Caesius, *The End of Empire.*

If it hadn't been for Prince Roland's presence, Jacqueline would have refused to believe the story that Amethyst told them. Her friend couldn't have helped to start a riot, or launched missiles at Prince Roland's aircar… or played a role in creating the conditions that had allowed the Emergency Committee to take power. It was impossible. But there was no denying Roland's presence, or the scars she could see on her friend's soul.

"Right now, the Civil Guard is either dissolving or coming over to our side," Brent said, when Amethyst had finished. "Why should we not sit tight here and wait for victory?"

"Because you don't have time," the Prince's bodyguard – a strangely-frightening woman who had been introduced simply as *Belinda* – said. "You can see the fighting outside Imperial City and the fighting up in orbit. If the mobs break into Imperial City, you will simply be overwhelmed and destroyed. Or, if too much debris falls into the planet's atmosphere, Earth's biosphere will be ruined – and you will all die."

Her voice hardened. "And the Emergency Committee might win the fighting in orbit," she added. "If they do, you can rest assured that they will use orbital bombardment to bring the mobs under control. And Imperial University will be their first target. A single KEW will wipe all of you out of existence."

Jacqueline shivered.

"I saw…I saw what was happening in the uprising," Amethyst added. "Looting, rape, murder…all sorts of horrible sights. The mobs will come here, eventually. We couldn't hold out indefinitely."

"But if we can take out the Emergency Committee, we might be able to stop it," Roland said, softly. "You're all that's left to try."

John Foster, the ex-Civil Guard officer, frowned. "There aren't *that* many of us," he pointed out, "and some of our units have been having discipline problems."

"Mutiny is habit-forming," Belinda observed wryly.

Foster shot her a sharp look, then continued. "We might be able to lay siege to the Imperial Palace or the Senate Hall, but I don't know if we have the firepower to break in," he said. "It could be disastrous if we try and fail."

"You don't have to break in," Roland said. "All you have to do is provide a distraction. Keep them looking at you, rather than at us."

"Thank you for your time," Brent said, before an argument could break out. "We'll discuss your proposal and come to a decision as quickly as possible."

Roland looked astonished that they weren't just going to agree with him, but his bodyguard helped escort him out. Jacqueline watched him go and then looked back at the small group. They had authority, of a sort, but it was very limited. Foster might have controlled most of the Civil Guard, yet the Guardsmen were forming their own revolutionary committees and debating each and every order. Jacqueline had been puzzled by the whole affair – surely, democracy was a good thing – until Foster had pointed out that there was often no time to debate in wartime. And they were very definitely at war.

"I've been picking up reports from uninvolved units," Foster admitted, as soon as the door was shut. "There are scenes of bloody savagery from all of the megacities. It won't be long before the tidal wave rolls over Imperial City."

Brent frowned. "We can't stop them?"

"We'd run out of ammunition in an hour," Foster said. "All we have is what was either issued to us or stored in the nearby dumps, which we emptied before coming here. And ammunition is produced in the orbital factories, some of which have already been destroyed. Once we run out, there will be no resupply. And then we die. Unpleasantly."

Jacqueline nodded. Ammunition wasn't the only thing in short supply. Imperial University had had a large stockpile of food for the students, but there were so many people in the independent zone that it was being depleted rapidly. The committee had managed to ration food, yet by her calculations they had barely more than a week before they started to suffer major shortages. Several of the committee had wondered openly if the government just intended to blockade them inside the University campus and then wait for them to starve.

And she wasn't sure she trusted the water either.

None of them had any experience living without power or fresh running water – or, for that matter, toilets. The government's decision to cut off power and water supplies to the university had been a stroke of genius; despite the best the committee could do, sanitation was starting to become a major problem. And no one wanted to volunteer to shovel shit.

Brent looked around the room. "We gamble," he said. "But what happens if we lose?"

"We die," Foster said. "But I think we have to face facts. If we cannot get some help, we're going to die anyway. So I cast my vote in favour of attacking the Imperial Palace. At least then we'd have a chance."

"I have a different idea," one of the other committee members said. "Why don't we seize one of the orbital towers and use it to escape…?"

Foster laughed at her. "It's two hundred miles from here to the nearest tower," he pointed out sarcastically. "Two hundred miles, infested by rioters…we couldn't even get there, even if we went in a body. And then we would have to actually take the tower and put it to work. Do any of us know how to do it? And even if we got that far, where would we go?"

The committee member flushed, darkly. "I......"

Brent held up a hand. "We vote," he said. "I cast my vote in favour."

———

War is a democracy, Doug's voice whispered. *The enemy gets a vote.*

I know that, Belinda thought. It was an old piece of wisdom, passed down from Marine to Marine. *But I didn't know that my friends get a vote too.*

She sat in the waiting room, trying to avoid the urge to stand up and join Roland in fruitless pacing. The Prince had never learned the value of patience...but Belinda *had*, over years of training and experience. Losing that knack now was worrying; she'd never been in such a tight spot, yet she should not have lost her composure. Was it possible that her damaged implants had actually caused brain damage?

It should have been impossible. Centuries of experience had gone into producing the implants, including safety precautions intended to prevent sudden power surges from harming their user. If they hadn't been reasonably safe – and isolated, to prevent outsiders from using them to turn their user into a puppet – they wouldn't have been used at all. And yet...she found it hard to avoid the thought. What if she wasn't in as tight control of herself as she should have been?

She ran a series of self-diagnostics through the remaining implants, but it was impossible to know if they were working properly. If the diagnostic programs themselves were crippled, they might make mistakes – and she had no other way to test her implants. Most of their results appeared to be genuine, yet she had no way to be sure. What if she had a spasm at the worst possible moment and started lashing around with augmented strength?

The primary neural link was gone. So were the four backups built into her body. That wasn't too surprising; given that they linked directly into her brain, the systems always erred on the side of safety. The tactical processor that helped to enhance her ability to act, react and plan ahead seemed to be working fine, but some of its results were a little odd. Her body monitoring system was definitely broken; it was claiming that she had a broken leg and a cracked jaw. In reality she was intact, if battered. The boost dispenser was reporting that it was low and needed a resupply. There was barely enough left for one more battle.

Damn it, she thought. Her augmented strength seemed to be largely intact, but the processor governing it was flaky. She would have to be very careful – yet without the boost, she might not manage to react in time to prevent disaster. Her implanted weapons seemed to be largely intact, apart from one poison injector that had broken; thankfully, she was immune to her own poisons. All in all, she should seek medical help. And probably a psychologist.

And there isn't any time, she told herself. *We have to move now.*

She busied herself with a handcom one of the student guards had loaned her, using a sonic screwdriver to fiddle with it. Most of Earth's population thought of handcoms and terminals as solid-state objects; they never realised that they could be modified by their user, if they were willing to disconnect the safeguards built into the devices. But then, they'd been denied practical training for hundreds of years. And then the Grand Senate wondered what had happened to the Empire's technological progress.

Roland stopped pacing and turned to look at her. "Any luck?"

"Not enough," Belinda growled. "I can't reach the Commandant at all."

She glared down at the device. Boosting the signal through the terminal she'd taken earlier had given the handcom more range – and using her all-access codes had prevented the remains of the datanet from locking her out – but there was still no response from Luna HQ. She couldn't imagine the Commandant simply abandoning the base…but if Home Fleet was partly under the Emergency Committee's control, they might have nuked it. By now, the Emergency Committee had to be desperate.

Instead, there was a constant series of alerts, blurring into mindless babble. Mutinies on starships and orbital installations. Rioting across the solar system. Several starships reversing course and heading away from Earth, directly towards the Phase Limit. A major atmospheric leak in Tranquillity City; Sin Crater destroyed, apparently by a terrorist strike. Cloudscoop staff on strike, demanding better working conditions; the

Grand Senate had finally pushed them too far. RockRats declaring exclusion zones around their territory, stating that any Imperial Navy starship that entered would be fired upon without warning...piece by piece, the Empire was coming apart at the seams.

There were fewer transmissions from Earth itself. Driven by a morbid curiosity – and a desperate attempt to stave off her fears – Belinda scanned through signals from Earth. One by one, the desperate voices of Civil Guardsmen or private cops or even emergency service workers stilled as the tidal waves of violence washed over them. A series of final desperate reports – buildings collapsing into rubble, entire CityBlocks consumed by fire – echoed out over the airwaves, then nothing. It had taken thousands of years to build the megacities that housed much of Earth's population, piling CityBlock on CityBlock in a desperate attempt to provide living space and occupation for the inhabitants. Now...

How long would it be, she asked herself, before Earth's population destroyed itself?

Other reports were darker. Debris had struck the Earth in dozens of places, a handful of pieces large enough to do real damage. One report warned of a tidal wave before cutting off in mid-sentence. Another, from East-Meg Two, reported a debris strike that had flattened half the city, a massive strike that had sent entire CityBlocks crumbling as if they were made of paper. The death toll was unimaginably high, utterly beyond calculation. No one even knew for sure how many had lived in East-Meg Two before the debris fell.

Dominos falling, one by one, she thought.

It was impossible to escape the feeling of darkness rushing across the land, heading towards the final patch of light surrounding Imperial City. An illusion, Belinda knew, no more real than the sensation of falling in outer space that separated the spacers from the groundhogs, and yet just as persistent. Maybe they should just find a place to hide and wait for the end of the world. She'd never come close to giving up before, yet now... what was the point of struggling if it was all futile?

She looked up at Amethyst and smiled, inwardly. At least the girl had realised her mistake in time to save their lives. And, judging by the glances she kept shooting at Roland, she'd even developed a crush on him.

Normally, Belinda would *not* have approved; whatever her motives, whatever she'd thought she was doing, Amethyst was a known terrorist. Now, however, it was hard to care. Perhaps she should point them towards a bedroom...no, she was being silly.

Very silly, Doug's voice mocked her.

But quite practical, McQueen offered. *It's the end of the world as we know it. How better to spend it than fucking?*

"Shut up," Belinda subvocalised. "You're dead."

Are you sure, Pug asked, *that you're not going mad yourself?*

"I was hearing voices before my implants were damaged," Belinda snapped. She realised, a moment too late, that she'd said it out loud. Roland and Amethyst turned to give her surprised looks. She scowled at them and then closed her eyes, trying to concentrate on subvocalising. "You're all dead."

Matter of opinion, Pug jeered.

Belinda opened her eyes, silently willing the voices to go away. Surprisingly, they did.

Roland walked over to sit next to her. "Are you all right?"

"I'm not sure," Belinda admitted. Her pride insisted that she was fine, but practicality suggested something else. "The electric pulses did more damage than I had thought."

Roland placed his hand on her shoulder. "Is there anything we can do to help?"

"I don't think so," Belinda said, after a moment's thought. If there had been other Pathfinders – or even Marines – around, she would have reported to the medics and asked for a full examination. They might well have taken her off the duty roster...no, who was she kidding? They would definitely have taken her off the duty roster. Hearing voices was *never* a good sign, particularly when they belonged to the dead.

Roland eyed her for a long moment, then looked away. Belinda sighed inwardly; he might have been the Crown Prince, but he didn't know very much about her implants – or why he should be worried at the prospect of her collapsing into madness. He trusted her...it was funny how that thought warmed her, even though she should have known better than to get too close to him. Or to let him get too close to her.

"Hey," Roland said, changing the subject. "Did you *really* hide that knife up your…"

"Yes," Belinda said. She couldn't help laughing at his expression. "Caught him by surprise, didn't it?"

Roland looked up as Jacqueline walked back into the room, followed by Foster and Brent. "We decided to attack the Imperial Palace and Senate Hall," she told them, flatly. "I just hope that you are right."

Me too, Belinda thought. *Me too.*

"Mummy!"

Gayle screamed as the emergency staff bundled her into the shelter. She wanted her mummy; she *needed* her mummy. The noises echoing through their home on Asteroid Nine were so terrifying; thuds and crashes and alarms she knew were never used, except when it was serious. She kicked and bit the man carrying her, screaming right into his ear, but he ignored her. He wasn't her mummy. Her mummy always took care of her daughter.

"Sit down," the man snapped, thrusting her into a chair. He wasn't giving her any choice; before she could start to struggle again, he had wrapped a belt around her chest, binding her to the chair. She knew from experience that she couldn't escape until someone let her go. "And stay there!"

The noises grew louder. Gayle heard kids screaming as adults, themselves on the verge of panic, buckled them into chairs. There was no sign of her mother; the only person she recognised was fat Mrs Rogers, who taught all of the children on the asteroid. Gayle thought she smelled, and that the tutor treated her as if she was still six years old when she was a *very* mature seven, but for once she was glad to see her. And yet Mrs Rogers was clearly panicking too…

"Incoming," someone yelled. It was louder than her mother had ever shouted, even when Gayle had gone exploring and ended up in the docking complex at one end of the asteroid. She had been grounded for *weeks* afterwards. "Impact imminent…"

"Stop it," Mrs Rogers screamed. "Can't you see…?"

A long dull rumble echoed through the emergency chamber, rapidly growing louder and louder until it drowned out the screams from the children. Gayle pressed her hands against her ears as the rumble became a screech…and was then joined by the hiss of escaping air. They'd all been told to listen to that sound and report it to an adult if they heard it, but none of their training sessions had made it sound so loud. And then she saw a crack appear in the far bulkhead…

She stared as she saw the stars shining outside – and, in the foreground, the dull grey-blue orb of Earth. The screams died away, leaving an eerie quiet in their place. Gayle felt the chair shake, then shatter as she started gasping for air, sending her spinning towards the crack…

And then the whole world just faded away into darkness.

CHAPTER
FORTY-THREE

So, too, were everyone else caught up in the fighting. The inhabitants of the orbital settlements, safe – they thought – from the madness on Earth; millions died as Earth's defences turned on one another. Those who had found safety – or so they thought – in the orbital towers, hoping and praying for escape; they died when missiles eventually struck the towers, inflicting horrific damage. And those who were dependent upon the flow of HE3 from the gas giants... they too suffered and died as the flow was reduced, or eliminated altogether.
- Professor Leo Caesius, *The End of Empire.*

"Asteroid Settlement Nine took a direct hit," the operator said. "She's breaking up."

Stephen watched the chaos, unable to escape the feeling that events might be slipping completely out of control. Grand Senator Devers was dead, but her allies were still fighting as if they knew they could no longer surrender...which they couldn't, he admitted privately to himself. Missiles were flying everywhere, including one that had struck an asteroid settlement and damaged it badly enough for the spin to finish the task of ripping it apart and scattering thousands of pieces of debris into space. Most of them would eventually be drawn in by Earth's atmosphere and fall towards the planet below.

Admiral Valentine had gone off the air. The Grand Senate's communications staff couldn't tell if he was dead, or if communications links were so badly disrupted that the messages simply couldn't get through, but it hardly mattered. No one seemed to be in command of Home

Fleet any longer; if half the reports the staff were picking up were accurate, the entire fleet seemed to be mutinying against its commanders. Desperate gunfights were raging through the hulls as underpaid junior officers and enlisted men rose up against their superiors, or ambitious officers plotted their own break from the Empire. Stephen had once held enough power to make someone jump on the other side of the galaxy, if he'd issued the order. Now, he doubted he controlled much beyond the Imperial Palace.

I may have made a mistake, he admitted, to himself. But what could he have done? Every step he'd taken had seemed logical at the time; even in hindsight, they *still* seemed logical. And yet the wheels were coming off; Earth seemed to be shaking itself to pieces. It would be decades before the Grand Senate managed to regain control. The other challenges to its rule had been outside the solar system, outside the very core of the Empire. This was different.

He pushed the thought aside and forced himself to concentrate on the here-and-now. There was no time to waste. Earth was already being hit by chunks of debris – and, sooner or later, one of them would be big enough to inflict real damage or simply come down on top of the Imperial City. He couldn't stay on Earth, or in the solar system; his holdings in the Inner Worlds should have remained untouched. All he had to do was reach them and then he could start rebuilding his power base while Earth burned.

"Start making preparations for departure," he ordered Captain Yaquis. "We'll take the shuttle to high orbit, then transfer to my personal starship."

He'd had to promote Yaquis; his last Security Officer had vanished in the Undercity while searching for Prince Roland. No one knew what had happened to him or the Prince, but with the Undercity pouring up into the Inner City, it was easy to guess. Besides, Prince Roland had become irrelevant. Chances were he'd been killed and eaten by now, even if he *did* have a very capable bodyguard. And the same went for Bode.

"Yes, sir," Yaquis said. He looked more relieved than Stephen was prepared to tolerate – he didn't like officers who showed their doubts openly – but right now it didn't matter. "The shuttle will have to be flash-woken. It will require nine minutes."

"Do it," Stephen ordered. He should have ensured that the shuttle was powered up already, but he hadn't wanted to even *consider* the possibility of retreat. Abandoning Earth...? His ancestors would be turning in their graves. "And do it as quickly as you can."

An alarm rang, distracting him. "Sir, the students are on the march," another operator reported. "They're heading towards the Imperial Palace."

Stephen turned to stare at the display. He'd largely forgotten about the students in Imperial University; they might have induced parts of the Civil Guard to mutiny, but they weren't going to be a problem for much longer. The uprising from the Undercity would eventually destroy them, if they didn't starve to death or get wiped out by KEW strikes first. Besides, it wasn't as though they had any heavy weapons. Cold logic told him that they couldn't break into either the Imperial Palace or the Senate Hall.

Cold hatred, shockingly intense, flared through his mind. The damned students; the damned ignorant little shits who had never understood the true nature of the Empire. They'd rioted and revolted and they'd cost him everything. If they hadn't rioted, he wouldn't have become the leader of the Emergency Committee...he'd tried to use them as tools, but the tool had twisted in his hand.

"Deploy the guards," he ordered. "I want those little shits wiped out."

Captain Yaquis stared at him. "Your Excellency, they can't break into the Imperial Palace..."

"I don't care," Stephen hissed. "I want them *dead*."

"...Yes, sir," Captain Yaquis said, finally.

Stephen watched him go, wondering if his hesitation was a sign of disloyalty. He was surrounded by traitors, from the officers and men who should have served him to his fellow Grand Senators, all working to undermine him while he struggled to save the Empire. The students would die soon in any case, but this way they would get precisely what they deserved. They would *not* live to regret their imprudence.

John Foster – acclaimed Captain by majority vote – couldn't help feeling uneasy as the mixed force made its way down the Avenue of Truth and Understanding, the long road that led from the Imperial University towards the Imperial Palace. He'd never been anything more than a glorified paramilitary officer, without experience of commanding in large-scale troop movements. He hadn't realised how ignorant he was until he actually had to try to take command of an army and deploy it against a specific target. Coordinating seven thousand people was a nightmare even when they were trained soldiers. *His* army included far too many students as well as Guardsmen.

And they were questioning his orders. He'd been elected Captain, he'd been given command...and yet many of his followers were debating his orders before carrying them out. It shouldn't have surprised him, he knew; he'd certainly seen what happened to commanding officers who demanded unquestioning obedience. But it was irritating.

There were no guards on the streets as the army advanced forward. Most of the Civil Guard had fled or joined the students; the Grand Senator's personal soldiers had better things to do than guard the bureaucrats who lived in the heart of Imperial City. His scouts had reported that most of the Grand Senate residences were under heavy guard, even if the Grand Senators themselves were trying to flee. Anyone would think that their lives were in danger.

He would have preferred to attack the Imperial Palace by hitting it from all sides, but his force barely had the training or coordination to move in a straight line. Half of the armed students didn't have the slightest idea what they were doing; they'd had to be given clubs rather than actual guns, just to give them the illusion that they were doing something useful. The original Guardsmen had been warned to fire as carefully as possible. Once they ran out of ammunition, there would be no resupply.

Bracing himself, he keyed his radio, wincing at the burst of static that echoed over the link. They'd tested the radios as best as they could and concluded that they were still useable for short-range transmissions, even if there *was* a shitload of disruption caused by the fighting in orbit. The radios would be detectable by the enemy, he knew, but there was no choice. If he didn't use them, coordination would be impossible.

"All right," he said, as they reached the turning onto the Avenue of Imperial Harmony. "Group One will head towards the Imperial Palace.

Group Two will head towards the Senate Hall. Remember to watch your ammunition – and if they try to surrender, let them."

He suspected that his final words had fallen on deaf ears. Too many students had family in East-Meg Two, Sino-Cit or one of the other megacities that had been hammered by falling debris. The death toll was already in the billions and still climbing; they wanted revenge, even if it meant their own deaths. And those who hadn't lost anyone still wanted to tear the Grand Senate apart.

This may be completely futile, he thought. The Marine had told him to distract everyone, rather than actually trying to *take* the buildings…but he knew that might well have been lost on his subordinates too. If it had been entirely up to him, he would have advanced with just the remains of his former unit…

He smiled. At least this time he was fighting on the right side.

"Mortar teams," he ordered. He'd positioned them before the main body of the army started to move. "You may fire at will."

The Imperial Palace was, at base, a massive blocky structure that seemed to have been merged with a fairy tale castle. Jacqueline found herself staring as the army advanced towards the railings surrounding the Palace, unable to quite believe her eyes. The planet was coming apart at the seams, debris was falling down from high overhead…and yet the Imperial Palace looked almost beautiful against the rising sun. There was no sign of any guards, but the gates were shut; they would have to batter them down to get inside.

This is just a diversion, she reminded herself. Most of the students behind her seemed to have missed that point. *We don't want to break down the doors.*

It was funny how she was no longer afraid. She'd been terrified when the Civil Guard had tried to arrest her, then frightened when she'd realised just how vulnerable the student-controlled university actually was…and yet now, she no longer felt fear. They might be going to their deaths – hell, they *were* going to die soon anyway – but she felt calm. Maybe she'd just seen too much to be afraid any longer.

There was a dull thump in the distance, followed by...*something*...hitting the Palace's walls. An explosion crackled out, leaving a nasty scar on the walls when it faded away. She couldn't tell if it had done any real damage – the Palace was supposed to be made out of hullmetal, the hardest artificial substance known to mankind – but she was sure that everyone inside had *felt* it. Other shells followed as the mortar team kept firing, peppering the building with direct hits. And yet none of them seemed to inflict any real damage.

"Stop shooting," she snapped at one of her students, who had started to fire on the Palace with his rifle. If mortar shells couldn't get through the hullmetal, what did he think ordinary bullets would do? "Wait for the order to shoot!"

The student glared at her, but obeyed. Brent had insisted that the Committee take the lead when they'd advanced towards the Palace, if only to show the students and Civil Guardsmen that *they* were not going to be cowering in the rear when the fighting began. Jacqueline hadn't argued; the students seemed to have turned her into their inspiration, even though she really hadn't wanted *any* sort of fame. She couldn't let them down now.

Something fell down in the midst of her students. Jacqueline's first thought was that one of the mortar crews had made a horrific mistake, then she realised that a high explosive shell would have blown them all to bloody chunks before she even knew that there had been a deadly accident. Several students had been killed by the impact, but others seemed unwounded...and then she saw the white gas cloud billowing up. Students started to push and kick at one another as they scattered, trying to get away from the gas. Foster had warned them that the different gasses were colour-coded; white gas disoriented anyone who took a deep breath.

"Masks," Jacqueline snapped. They'd all been issued masks from the Civil Guard armoury they'd overrun in the early hours of the uprising, but no one had put them on during the march. Some students were already staggering around like drunken idiots as the gas took effect. "Hurry!"

She pulled her own mask up and over her face, silently grateful that Foster had forced them to practice putting them on. Breathing through the mask was unpleasant, but better than the alternative. At least the gas wasn't absorbed through the skin. Brent had asked Foster about that and

Foster had admitted that most Civil Guard units were barely capable of fighting in masks, let alone full protective gear.

Far too many students had been affected, she realised, as she surveyed the situation. Dozens were on the ground, rubbing frantically at their steaming eyes, or stumbling around in disorientation. The ones who did have their masks on seemed to be nervous, although it was hard to tell. Their masks hid almost all of their expressions from her view.

A screech echoed over the street as the Palace doors finally began to open, revealing a line of men wearing body armour and carrying weapons. Jacqueline was no military expert, but she didn't have to be to realise what was happening. The Palace Guard had used the gas to soften up the students and were now preparing to finish the job. She waved frantically to the rest of the masked students as she lifted her weapon, ready to fight. If they could kill the guards, they might just be able to break into the Palace…

She never saw the sniper who fired the shot that killed her.

———

Foster swore out loud as the Grand Senator's personal guard attacked with a staggering level of ruthlessness, thrusting out of both the Palace and Senate Hall to slash into the students. Several of them were even using flamethrowers, terrifying the students who had maintained the presence of mind to don their masks when the gas shells had landed amongst them. Unsurprisingly, the students were falling back; they'd never really *imagined* such violence, even after everything that had happened over the last few months.

But he still had his Guardsmen.

"New orders," he said, switching channels. "Section One; advance and cut the bastards off. Mortar teams, drop shells on their heads…"

———

"No, *don't* run," Amethyst shouted, as her section panicked. She'd volunteered to accompany Prince Roland and Belinda, but Brent had insisted that she stayed with the rest of the students and fought beside them. "Pull your masks on and fight!"

She pointed her rifle at the advancing soldiers, visible through the gassy haze, and fired at their heads. Bode – she couldn't think of him as *Richard* any longer – had told her that body armour was very good, but it rarely protected *everywhere*. A shot in the face was almost always lethal, particularly if the target was not wearing an armoured helmet. She had the satisfaction of seeing one of the oncoming troopers falling to the ground before someone grabbed her and dragged her away from the battle.

"We can't run," she protested. The student pulling her was too strong to easily resist. "This…"

"We'll die if we stay here," the student hissed. Behind them, the troopers were still advancing. They seemed to be pushing the students back everywhere. "We get into the residency block, hide there until they get past us and then slip out again."

Amethyst swallowed the argument that came to mind as they slipped into the residency block. It was fancier than the one she'd grown up in; certainly much fancier than the ones Bode had used as hiding places… was this where the bureaucrats lived when they weren't working? She looked around as the doors closed, cutting off the noise from outside. It was definitely better than her old home…

And then she heard the screams.

They exchanged puzzled glances. What was making the screams? No, what was making the *people* scream? This was a high-class CityBlock with good security…but the security was gone. A door crashed open, revealing a gang of men carrying makeshift weapons and half-crazed faces. They might have come from the Undercity, through the tunnels that illicitly linked Imperial City to the Undercity, or they might have been former bureaucrats, losing their minds as they lost their Empire. It hardly mattered.

But we fought for them, Amethyst thought. *We wanted to make their lives better.*

The newcomers didn't care. They spread out and began to advance, their faces becoming nightmarish combinations of hunger and lust. Blood stained their clothes; not their blood, she realised in horror. Perhaps the rumours of cannibalism were true after all. She lifted her rifle and pointed it at them, but they were too far gone to care. And when she pulled the trigger, it just clicked uselessly. She'd run out of ammunition.

She threw the gun at them and turned to run, but she barely made it a few steps before they caught her and shoved her to the ground. Hands tore at her clothes, ripping away the mask and leaving her exposed; she caught sight of some of the newcomers actually *chewing* at the other student, ripping away his flesh and stuffing it into their mouths. Cannibals…

Mercifully, she fainted dead away.

CHAPTER FORTY-FOUR

There were those who tried to put an end to the crisis at source. A scratch force of revolutionary students, mutinous Civil Guardsmen and others, led by none other than Prince Roland, attempted to storm the Senate Hall and the Imperial Palace, seeking to destroy the Emergency Committee – while, knowing that all was lost, the Emergency Committee prepared its final fallback position.

- Professor Leo Caesius, *The End of Empire.*

"It's big," Roland said.

Belinda nodded, not trusting herself to speak. Once, Marine HQ had been the linchpin of the Empire, the very core of the Terran Marine Corps that guarded humanity's unity. But it had declined over the years as the Grand Senate whittled away at the Marines, until all that was left was a locked and abandoned building in the heart of the city. The Emergency Committee hadn't even allowed the Commandant to leave a guard.

She touched the globe and anchor insignia on the solid metal door, feeling oddly melancholy as she remembered her history. The Marines had *always* stood up and fought for what was right, with honour towards all and malice to none; there truly was no better friend or no worse enemy than a Terran Marine. And yet all of that history was fading away into nothingness, along with the Empire the Marines had protected for thousands of years. If the Empire died, who would remember the Marines?

"Belinda?"

Belinda nodded sourly as Roland's voice brought her back to reality. In the distance, she could hear the sound of gunfire; either the students had begun their attack or the last remnants of the city's defenders were trying to keep the Undercity from breaking in. It didn't matter; time was *not* on their side. Quickly, she pressed her fingertips against the globe symbol and smiled in relief as it fell away, revealing a biometric sensor. A moment later, the door unlocked, allowing them to enter the building.

She looked around as the lights came on, powered by the emergency generator the Marines had installed, deep under the complex. *They* had considered the dangers of losing the city's power grid, even if no one else had. She led the way towards the nearest access point, thinking hard. Her implants should have automatically linked into the network and downloaded a full update – if there *was* a full update. Without them, she was dependent on terminals and datapads, just like everyone else. At least she should still have full clearance for data access.

"This building is spooky," Roland said, as he followed her. "It feels *abandoned*."

"Thousands of years of history are looking down at you," Belinda commented dryly.

She found an access point and pushed her fingers against the sensor, activating it. There was a brief update from the Commandant, addressed to the retired Marines in the city, informing them that the Marine transports would leave the system in two days – if they wanted to come, they had to get up to orbit and signal for pickup. Beyond that, there was nothing. Quickly, she noted the location of the tunnel access point and shut down the terminal. Maybe, just maybe, one of the retired Marines *would* reach Marine HQ. It might just manage to ride out the coming apocalypse.

"Let's go," she said. God alone knew how long it would be before the students were driven away from the Imperial Palace. "Hurry."

The First Emperor had fancied himself a designer of buildings as well as Empires – which explained the ugly Imperial Palace, Belinda couldn't help thinking. He'd had a hand in designing most of the buildings in Imperial City and taken advantage of the opportunity to link them all to a secret tunnel complex that ran between the different buildings. Very few people knew about the tunnels – Belinda had only been told when she'd been assigned to serve as Roland's bodyguard – and almost none of them could use them. The Emperor, the Commandant, the Grand Admiral, the Grand Senators...everyone else was simply denied access. Surprisingly, given how easy it was to leak information, almost nothing had gotten out to the media.

But no doubt the Grand Senators saw the wisdom in keeping it to themselves, she thought, sourly. *They could use the tunnels too.*

She'd hoped to pull weapons from the armoury, but the Commandant had ordered almost everything removed when the Marines left Earth, perhaps for the final time. There were no suits of armour or even basic protective gear. Belinda shook her head, unable to hold back a smile. The Civil Guard would have left behind enough weapons to outfit a small army. If the Marines had been less efficient...

The lowest level of the HQ had been off-limits the last time Belinda had visited Earth, even to relatively senior Marines. Some of the Marines she'd served with had placed bets on just what was hidden there, some claiming that there was an additional armoury or even a stasis tube holding the still-living body of the First Emperor concealed within the compartment, but it was disappointingly empty when Belinda stepped inside. She couldn't help glancing around – she'd played the guessing game too – yet she saw nothing apart from the bare wall and a single light set within the ceiling. Shaking her head, she walked over to the far wall and pressed her hand against a hidden sensor. There was a dull click, followed by a hiss as the door opened, revealing steps leading down into a darkened tunnel.

"My ancestor was a very paranoid man," Roland commented, as Belinda stepped inside. A single light came on, illuminating their position, but the remainder of the tunnel was still shrouded in darkness. "What was he thinking?"

"If he'd been less paranoid, the Empire might not be in this mess," Belinda said quietly. "Maybe the Grand Senate wouldn't have gained such a stranglehold on power if the Emperor had been more trusting of his own subjects."

There were no signs inside the tunnel to tell them which way to go. Belinda had memorised the chart, but she still found it difficult to navigate their way through an endless series of unmarked passageways. There was no sound at all, apart from their footsteps and a faint hum from the lights as they came on to illuminate each new section. Belinda couldn't help feeling trapped as they walked further, knowing just how difficult it would be to escape if the lights failed altogether. She no longer trusted her implants to let her see in the dark.

"Here," she said as they stopped in front of a solid metal hatch. If her calculations were correct, it led directly into the Imperial Palace. "After you, Your Highness."

Roland gave her a sharp look, then pressed his fingers against the sensor. The First Emperor had been *very* paranoid; no one could use the tunnels to get into the Imperial Palace without his direct permission, or that of his blood descendants. It was hard enough to break into the tunnels – sneaking into any of the buildings that had a link would be difficult – but even so, he hadn't wanted anyone to slip into the Imperial Palace without one of his family to escort them. There was a click as the sensor recognised Roland, then opened the hatch. Belinda slipped through, weapon at the ready.

"Clear," she reported, keeping her voice low. "Get up here now."

She glanced around, looking for potential threats. They were in enemy territory, like it or not. But no one was guarding their end of the tunnel. She couldn't tell if the Senator had been careless and assumed that Roland was dead, or if he simply hadn't known where to place the guards. Even a full scanning team, she'd been told, would have problems finding the door. Even so, Belinda would have placed guards on the lower levels or scattered sensor nodes around to watch for intruders. Maybe the Grand Senator was running out of men.

"I used to think that my Palace would be splendid," Roland said, as he closed the hatch. "This room is...*bare*."

Belinda elbowed him. "This is the access point to the tunnel network," she said. "It isn't where your family would entertain guests."

She motioned for him to remain quiet, then slipped into the next room. It was a security office, she realised in some surprise, but it had been completely abandoned and the computers and data terminals shut down. Judging from the dust it had been shut down for years, well before the current crisis had begun. Belinda puzzled over it for a moment, then realised that the Grand Senate hadn't bothered to leave the guard in place when they'd taken over the Imperial Palace after Roland's father had died. If they didn't know about the tunnel, they might not have seen the need to leave a guard in place.

And the guards wouldn't have talked, she thought, as she checked the consoles. *Having a secrecy implant would have been a precondition of their employment.*

"Come inside," she muttered to Roland. The files she'd been given as his liegeman suggested that the Royal Family's overrides would apply to *all* of their computers. "See if you can turn these computers on."

Roland pushed his fingertip against the sensor. There was a brief pause, long enough for Belinda to wonder if the Grand Senate had used a very basic method to disable the system, then the console came to life. The network the First Emperor had created was still in command of the palace. Roland sat down in front of the system and began to tap away at it, looking for information. Belinda rolled her eyes, regretting – once again – the loss of her neural link. With it, she could have pulled everything she wanted from the network in bare seconds.

The Prince knew very little about computers, even about the network that was specifically keyed to his family. Belinda suspected that most of the secrets were passed down from Emperor to Crown Prince, but Roland's father had died before he could tell his son anything. And the First Emperor had been so paranoid that no one else could use the system, even once it had been unlocked by a blood relative. She had to stand behind Roland and offer advice as he tried to pull information out of the system.

"They seem to have installed their own system," she said, slowly. It made sense; no one would be happy using a network that had overrides built into it by the nominal owner. "It isn't linked to the main network."

"They're still using the Palace's systems," Roland pointed out. "I can crash them..."

Belinda grinned. "Do it," she ordered.

Stephen had never given way to bloodlust in his entire life. He'd ordered deaths in the past, he'd ordered horrific atrocities to clear the way for his own plans, but he'd never enjoyed the task. It was just something he had to do to accomplish his ends. But now, staring at the students and traitorous Civil Guardsmen as they scattered, he felt himself overwhelmed by a desire to make them *hurt*. They could be killed, they could be tortured, they could be raped…they deserved each and every second of pain for what they had done. He wanted them to *suffer*.

"Your Excellency," Captain Yaquis said. "The shuttle is ready for you to depart…"

"Quiet," Stephen hissed. A young student was being beaten to death by three of his men; another, a girl who had obviously breathed in too much of the gas, was choking on the ground, unable even to clear her throat. Maybe there would be enough damage to Earth's biosphere that it would finally collapse, leaving the population to die like the vermin they were. "I want to watch."

"We need to clear our way through the orbital defences," Captain Yaquis said. "Sir, we cannot guarantee maintaining even a laser link to the stations in orbit for much longer."

Stephen ignored him. A pair of students – boyfriend and girlfriend, he guessed – were being made to undress at gunpoint. They both looked absolutely terrified; where, he wondered nastily, was their arrogance now? His men knew that they could do whatever they liked to the students…

"*Sir*," Captain Yaquis insisted. "We have to go now!"

"All right," Stephen agreed, tiredly. Cold logic told him that the Captain was right – there was hundreds of thousands of tons of debris falling on Earth, as well as a colossal uprising from the Undercity – and he could watch the recordings later on his ship, with a drink in his hand. "I'll deal with the defences myself…"

He used his implants to link into the network and send orders for them to avoid firing on the shuttle. Not all of the network would obey – and there were parts that wouldn't get the order at all – but it would give them a chance to survive. And once they were on his ship, they could get away from Earth and head directly to his client worlds, where he could start rebuilding while the Empire fell into chaos.

And then the Imperial Palace's network crashed.

Yaquis swore out loud, clearly rattled. The Imperial Palace had two separate generators and plenty of stored power held in reserve. It was impossible to cut the power from the outside. The only way it could be done was...

Stephen sucked in a breath. "Roland!"

The Prince had *survived*? How *could* he have survived the Undercity? His bodyguard might be good, but was she *that* good? But he had to have survived; the Royal Family were the only people with complete access to the Palace's datanet. No one else, even a liegeman, could simply have shut it down.

He stood up. "We have to get to the shuttle," he asserted, grimly. "Bring all of the bodyguards...and give them specific orders. If they see the Prince, he is to be captured and brought with us."

"Yes, sir," Yaquis said.

Stephen allowed the bodyguards to hurry him out of the room. One way or another, he wouldn't be coming back. When he restored his control over Earth, he would have the Imperial Palace blasted from orbit, just to make damn sure that the previous Royal Family's legacy was completely gone. In fact, he'd turn the entire surface of Earth into dust and then terraform the planet. If the Emperor had to live on Earth, Earth would damn well be a proper home for him.

And if the entire ungrateful population died out, Stephen wouldn't shed a single tear.

"The network is down," Roland said. He glanced outside. "Most of the lighting is gone too."

"They'll head for the hangar bay," Belinda said. Maybe they wouldn't be able to take off without the computer network, but she knew better than to count on it. If *she'd* had even a vague idea of what the Imperial Palace's network could do, she wouldn't have relied on it at all. "Come on!"

The darkened passageways were completely deserted. Belinda guessed that most of the staff had been told to stay in their quarters as soon as the emergency began and not to come out for any reason at all. It *was* standard procedure. The staff would end up dead as the Palace started to collapse around them, but there was nothing she could do for them. Perhaps the collapsed network would give them a chance to leave the Palace...

Sure, Pug's voice mocked. *And go where?*

The hangar bay was surprisingly similar to a starship's shuttlebay, Belinda saw as they ran into the chamber. The Grand Senator was standing in front of the shuttle, turning to stare at them – at *Roland* – with an expression of absolute fury pasted over his face. He almost seemed to be on the verge of madness as his bodyguards ran forward, most of them running straight at Belinda herself. She cursed out loud as she realised that they were augmented too and braced herself. Even if they weren't up to Pathfinder standards, *she* wasn't up to Pathfinder standards either. This wasn't going to be pretty.

Just remember your training, Doug reminded her. *And don't panic.*

Belinda threw herself forward, calling on the last of her reserves. The first bodyguard moved quickly by human standards, but terrifyingly slow by the standards of the boost. She slammed a fist into his throat and crushed it, even though it was augmented enough to prevent her from simply taking off his head. His body twitched and fell to the ground, but Belinda hardly noticed. She tore on to the next one as he took a swing at her and tried to dodge. This time, she was too slow and his blow landed on her upper back. It hurt more than it should have done.

Four more bodyguards lunged at Roland, grabbing him. Belinda tried to get over to help him, but two of her attackers landed on top of her, knocking her to the ground. She twisted, elbowed one of them in the jaw and broke free long enough to pull up her legs, kicking out at the other's face with augmented strength. His head seemed to explode into bloody chunks of flesh, just as his friend grabbed hold of Belinda from behind and started to try to strangle her. She slammed her head back, ramming it into his jaw. He grunted in pain, the distraction lasting long enough for her to grab hold of his hands and rip them away from her.

She barely heard him scream as she tore herself free and jumped back to her feet.

But she was too late. Roland had been dragged onto the shuttle and it was taking off. Desperately, gathering all of her remaining strength and determination, Belinda ran forward and jumped, landing on the shuttle's wing...

...As it rose up above the Imperial Palace and headed towards the safety of outer space.

CHAPTER FORTY-FIVE

But for all their bravery, for all the determination shown by a Prince many had considered a useless fop, the odds were vastly against them...and even though they succeeded in destroying the Emergency Committee's control, it was already too late to save the Empire. The Emergency Committee was not the cause of the disease, but a symptom. Even its destruction could not prevent the final collapse.

- Professor Leo Caesius, *The End of Empire.*

"Well, *Your Highness*," Stephen said. "Your Empire is at an end."

Roland glared at him. Two bodyguards were holding him tightly, while a third prepared to strap the Prince down so he couldn't move, but he still managed to look defiant. Clearly, Stephen noted, he'd underestimated the Prince all along. Or, perhaps, he'd underestimated the Marine's ability to make a man of the foppish Prince. Not that it really mattered, he decided, as his bodyguard wrenched Roland's hands behind his back and slipped on the cuffs. Roland was his prisoner now...to be used or discarded as Stephen saw fit.

"There is no longer any throne for you to inherit," Stephen added. "Lady Lily will not be your wife. The wealth your ancestors gathered is gone. Your Summer Palace was burned down by the mob. Everything you once owned or would inherit is gone. Your very survival depends upon me."

The Prince just kept glaring at him, without saying a word.

"I rather confess that I cannot think of any use for you," Stephen said, keeping his voice as light as possible. "Maybe you can be put on trial for your crimes – after all, most of the Empire relies on the media to do its thinking for it. They were quite happy to believe you a useless fool, weren't they? Or perhaps you'll just be dumped out of the airlock while we're in Phase Space; they say that Phase Space is haunted by the ghosts of all who died while they were in transit. Do you think you might join them?"

Roland leaned forward and spat.

"Charming," Stephen said, as he wiped it off his shirt. "And futile. You are completely in my power, *Your Highness*; you are completely alone. Your bodyguard is long gone."

He turned to take his seat, then looked back. "And even if you did escape," he added, "where would you go?"

Belinda forced herself forward as the shuttle picked up speed, feeling the airflow threatening to push her off the wing if she lost her grip. Only the implants built into her hands gave her a chance of holding on – and not all of them were working properly. She inched forward, seeing red alarms blinking up in front of her eyes; the shuttle was already passing through the upper atmosphere. Soon, she would be in airless vacuum. It wouldn't have been a problem if she'd been fully-functional, but without all of her implants...

The shuttle's hull felt smooth against her fingers as she clung on, as close to the hatch as she could. By Imperial Law, all shuttle and starship airlocks had to be accessible while the ship was in vacuum, just in case someone developed a problem with their spacesuit. She had no idea if that was true of the Emperor's private shuttle, but there was no other hope. Her monofilament knife wouldn't be able to cut through the hullmetal that made up the outer hull.

WARNING, her implants said. *AIR PRESSURE DROPPING.*

Belinda gritted her teeth and banished the warning. It wasn't helping. Instead, she waited until the air pressure dropped to zero and then inched forward to the hatch access control. Her implants flashed up new alerts, reporting everything from targeting sensors to emergency beacons in low orbit; she banished those too, knowing that if someone decided to fire on the shuttle she would die before knowing what had hit her.

A laser beam, Pug suggested nastily. *Or perhaps a nuke. They're throwing them around like party favours.*

Her hand pushed against the access control and the airlock opened. Belinda pulled herself inside and smiled in relief as the shuttle's compensator field took effect. The airlock hissed closed behind her, but the inner airlock remained shut. Belinda wasn't too surprised; allowing someone to find shelter in case of emergency was one thing, but granting them free access to the shuttle was another. Moving quickly, she retrieved the monofilament knife from its hiding place and slashed at just the right place, then kicked it with augmented strength. The airlock's inner door shattered inwards.

She jumped through, retrieving her pistol from her belt as she moved. The Emperor's shuttle was larger than the standard Marine assault shuttle; the rear section seemed to be more of a bar than anything else. It was decorated with more luxury than she'd seen during an operation to recover a passenger liner that had been hijacked by pirates, years ago. The shuttle had probably cost more than the entire Pathfinder team had earned in a year.

More like a decade, McQueen said. *But stop worrying about it now.*

Belinda smiled as she saw four men spinning around to stare at her. None of them looked familiar, so she guessed that they were part of the Grand Senator's personal staff. One of them reached for a handcom and Belinda shot him neatly through the head; the others lifted their hands in surrender. Belinda hesitated, then motioned for them to lie down on the deck and put their hands on their heads.

"Stay here," she hissed. Under the circumstances, she could have legally killed them, but she wasn't *that* far gone. "If you move or speak, I'll kill you. Stay here!"

She left them behind and slipped into the next section. It was a small kitchen, she realised, shaking her head in disbelief. The Emperor had *really* liked his comforts. No doubt all his meals tasted better than Civil Guard rations – and *they* were actually worse than Marine rations. It was funny how she'd never believed that until after she'd tasted them both.

The following section was a small communications system. A man was sitting there, wearing a pair of headphones; Belinda guessed he was trying to follow the progress of the battle outside. If they went too close to a hostile station, or even a remote platform that was firing at everything within range, they would die…someone had to try to figure out a safe passage through the combat zone. Belinda had to smile as she leaned forward and smacked the man hard on the head, stunning him. Only a handful of systems were so heavily industrialised and defended to make that a workable concern.

And normally we would clear the way first, she thought, as the man folded over the console. *But the Senator doesn't have that luxury.*

She stepped through the next door and saw two men coming forward, both carrying guns. They stared at her in disbelief – they might have heard the gunshot without realising what it was and resented being ordered to check – and then started to bring up their guns. Belinda shot them both and moved forward, jumping past their bodies before they had even hit the ground. She pushed the curtain ahead of her aside and peeked through. Prince Roland was seated on the deck, his hands out of sight but probably tied. A bodyguard stood next to him, a pistol pointed at his head. The Grand Senator was seated towards the front of the compartment, staring at her. He must not have taken the gunshots seriously either.

"How the hell…?"

He hadn't believed the stories, not really. Oh, he'd known enough to know that properly trained Marines could do astonishing feats, some utterly impossible to untrained civilians, but some of the stories had seemed completely unbelievable. They'd left the bitch down on Earth, Stephen told himself, as he stared at her. She'd been surrounded by bodyguards, all of whom had been augmented…she should be dead! Or at least trapped on a dying world. How could she be on the shuttle?

She was terrifying. Blood ran down her face, contrasting sharply with cold blue eyes that dared Stephen to make a move. Her clothes were ripped and torn, but she didn't look vulnerable, not even slightly. Instead, she seemed almost insane.

And he'd sent two of his bodyguards to find out what had caused the alarm. They should have intercepted her...

"It's over," she said. Even her voice was inhuman. She'd sounded businesslike, almost sweet, the last time they'd met. It was the same woman and yet Stephen couldn't link them together in his mind, even though he *knew* they were the same. One had been polite and deferential, the other was a monster. "Your time is up."

Stephen found his voice. "Not yet," he said. The girl – no, he had to stop thinking of her as anything other than an incredibly dangerous Marine – might be incredibly violent, but he would bet his life that he could outthink her, given time. He *was* betting his life that he could outthink her. She was clearly wounded, perhaps damaged – and he still had some cards to play. "Without me, you will never find anywhere to go."

The Marine gazed at him, unblinkingly. "There's no way out of this, Senator," she said, her voice still utterly inhuman. "You are not going to get the Prince to your starship."

How had she known he had a starship? He cursed himself a moment later; the answer was blinding obvious. The shuttle barely had the range to reach Mars – and Mars was almost as unsafe as Earth right now. No, any fool would know that he had a starship waiting...she'd rattled him, badly. He should have known that right from the start.

"Maybe," he said. "But if you press the issue, the Prince is going to wind up dead."

"I don't matter," Roland said, sharply. "Kill him!"

Stephen flinched. The Marine didn't move.

I should have gagged the little bastard, he thought, bitterly. An oversight...but one that had cost him dearly. How much else had he missed? Maybe he should have held back on purging the military, or offered Devers a seat on the Emergency Committee...or just concentrated on preparing his client worlds for the day the Empire fell. Instead, he'd tried to take it all...and lost. And now he was staring at a Marine who could rip him apart with both hands tied behind her back.

"We can compromise," he said, trying not to sound as though he were pleading. He hated bargaining, even with his fellow Grand Senators. Bargaining with a Marine gnawed at him...but there was no choice. "We can drop you and the Prince off somewhere, maybe on Luna Base. Or we can take you to the Slaughterhouse."

Belinda's tactical analysis programs were almost gone, but she didn't need them to tell that the Grand Senator was being insincere. On a starship he controlled, crewed by his personal lackeys, he would be able to dispose of them. Even a Pathfinder in perfect condition would be vulnerable. Luna Base was a possibility, but the last she'd heard was that chaos was spreading across the moon too. Besides, she *did* have somewhere to go, if she managed to take control of the shuttle.

"You'd kill us on your starship," she said. She ran through her options frantically. The bodyguard holding his gun to Roland's head was the real problem; as far as she could tell, the Senator was both unarmed and unaugmented. Maybe he had managed to get some military augmentation in the past without Marine Intelligence hearing about it, but he didn't *act* like it. "And Luna Base may not be safe now."

"Of course not," the Senator retorted. "Your comrades have deserted you."

Belinda ignored the taunt. She'd known that the Commandant had abandoned Luna Base from the update she'd picked up in Marine HQ. And she also knew that he was lurking in the system for several more hours. If she could get Roland there...

"I have an alternative," she offered. "Surrender to me and I give you my word, as a Marine Pathfinder, that I will not kill you. I can even have you and your men exiled to Summer Isle, rather than Hellhole or another penal colony. God knows that other losers in the political games have gone there and lived out their lives in relative luxury –"

"But without power," the Grand Senator interrupted. "And I am not yet out of cards to play."

Belinda sighed. She'd seen it before, on a dozen different worlds. The duly-appointed leader, the corporate profit-monger or the revolutionary leader who simply couldn't grasp that it was *over*. They kept fighting – or, rather, they kept others fighting for them – until their forces were completely obliterated, whereupon they went into exile rather than paying the price for their crimes. Was it really so hard to give up power?

Your augmentation is a form of power – and it is damaged, Pug's voice said. *Will you tamely accept it being removed from your body, making you merely human, or will you fight to keep what you can?*

"You are wrong," she said, simply. "There's *no* way out of this. Your minion can kill the Prince – I'll kill him a second later. And then I'll kill you. There's no place for you to go any longer."

She allowed her voice to lower until it became a growl. "Maybe you can kill the Prince," she added, "but what will it gain you? Surrender and you will get to keep your life."

———

Stephen forced himself to think, even though it was so hard. He'd never been physically threatened before; he'd always had a small army of bodyguards protecting him from the very first day of his life. But now the bodyguards were gone – save one, who had to keep Roland at gunpoint. Without the Prince as a hostage, he would die.

His thoughts kept spinning around. If he accepted her offer, could he trust it? Life on Summer Isle wouldn't be bad…he'd taken vacations there, back when he'd been a younger man. And she was right; those who lost power games and were exiled got to live out the rest of their lives in peace, provided that they stayed *out* of politics. He could go there…

…But the Empire was crumbling. How long would Summer Isle remain untouched? There was a detachment of the Imperial Navy stationed there, commanded by a loyalist…and yet, he'd seen just how many crews were ready to rebel against their appointed superiors. The Summer Isle might not remain safe for long.

"Maybe," he said. "But you cannot complete your own mission if the Prince dies."

He was right, of course.

Belinda felt her head pounding as she stared at him. A stand-off and a hostage-situation, combined. It was the most likely hostage situation to end in bloodshed and the death of the hostage. And she was on the verge of collapse. Newer warnings, including some she hadn't seen outside of training simulations, were blinking up all the time. Her body was at risk of a catastrophic collapse. If the Senator managed to stretch it out a few more minutes, she was likely to drop dead in front of him. She had to stop him before she crashed to the deck.

Surely the Senator knew how vulnerable he was…but he didn't seem to care.

Roland threw himself to one side. The bodyguard's gun went off, the bullet missing the Prince and ricocheting off the deck. Belinda threw herself at him as he tried frantically to take aim at her, getting off another shot before she rammed her finger into his eye and right through into the brain. The Senator let out an incoherent howl as Belinda spun around and lunged at him, only dimly aware of the blood dripping from her hands. He put up his hands to try to ward her off, but he might as well have tried to use paper as armour.

The Commandant would want him alive, if possible, but there was no time for half-measures. She knocked his hands aside and slammed his head into the bulkhead, feeling his skull shatter. A moment later, she felt a stabbing pain in her head and collapsed to the deck herself. The implant that monitored her brainpan seemed to have failed…

Get up, Doug ordered. Her former commander's voice cut through the haze for a few brief seconds. *Deal with Roland.*

She pulled herself upright, even though her vision was dimming alarmingly. Roland came towards her, blood dripping from a cut to his face. Belinda reached weakly for the tape they'd used to tie his hands and ripped it free, before she collapsed back to the deck.

"Listen," she hissed. She could barely speak. Shaping a single word had suddenly become a near-impossible burden. "Take the pilot, hold him at gunpoint and force him to alter the IFF signal; transmit my name. You should be picked up by the Commandant."

"You're not going to die," Roland said. There was something desperate in his voice as he pulled at her. He should be leaving her and going to the cockpit, but instead he seemed to have a plan. "I won't let you die."

Belinda smiled at him as she felt the rest of her life draining away. Her implants might be able to save her – they were automatically switching over to preservation mode – but she doubted it. She'd taken too much damage. Her eyes closed…and yet, somehow, she saw the rest of her team waiting to welcome her. Beyond them, there were others; those who had died on Earth in the final days of the Empire. And Marines she'd known who had died on active service. And her grandparents…

And then the universe just faded away.

CHAPTER FORTY-SIX

The end, when it came, came swiftly.

Earth's fall destroyed what remained of the centralised Imperial economy; hundreds of billions of credits simply vanished. The shock thrust billions of people out of work and rendered the Empire's money worthless overnight. As news spread from world to world, the economy crumbled in its wake. Economic collapse was followed rapidly by the vanishing of law and order as planetary governments sought independence, or military officers attempted to take power for themselves. To make matters worse, the old grudges that the Empire had suppressed came back into the light and war raged through the newly-independent systems.

And Earth itself? By the time the fighting in orbit came to an end, so much debris had fallen on the planet that it was rendered completely uninhabitable. Uncounted billions died as the megacities crumbled and fell; millions more starved to death as the planet fell into darkness, the end of technology ensuring that they could no longer feed themselves. By the time the successor states returned to Sol to try to claim Earth for themselves, the entire population was dead.

We know almost nothing about their final days. Did they die peacefully? Or were the former inhabitants of the megacities hunted down by the Undercity denizens? Did they really resort to cannibalism in the hope it would prolong their lives? We may never know, but one thing is clear.

They were the Empire's final victims.

Am I responsible, in some small part, for this catastrophe? It was my book, the book that destroyed my career and earned me permanent exile from

Earth, that Bode used to incite the students, the first step in the Emergency Committee's plan. And yet all I did was point out truths that were there for all to see, had they bothered to read the writing on the wall. I cannot logically blame myself for the Fall of Earth. Nor can I blame many of those who were alive at the time; they might have helped to speed the end, but the seeds were sown thousands of years ago. In truth, the Empire committed suicide.

It just took a very long time to die.

- Professor Leo Caesius, *The End of Empire.*

Jeremy looked down at the final report from Earth.

Most of the orbital defences had finally destroyed themselves, bringing the civil war in orbit to an end, but it was too late. Almost all the orbital infrastructure had been destroyed in the crossfire, leaving hundreds of thousands of pieces of debris to fall on the planet below, while the orbital towers were tottering on the verge of collapse. Earth had been struck so many times that the planet was hidden under clouds of atmospheric dust, blocking out the sunlight. Jeremy doubted that anyone could have survived.

His wristcom buzzed. "Commandant," the Captain said, "we are about to cross the Phase Limit."

And then there will be no more reports, the Commandant thought, bitterly. But then, he didn't want to hear any more. Avoiding bad news was a bad habit, yet what good would it do to listen to the endless series of disasters sweeping the solar system?

"Good," he said. "Take us into FTL as soon as we can go."

He scowled down at the datapad, then clicked it off. The Empire was gone…and yet it would be months before the inhabited galaxy knew it. But Jeremy could not allow himself any delusions. The Empire had been crumbling even before Earth destroyed itself in one final orgy of violence and destruction. Now, once the news reached the rest of the human race, the Empire would simply come apart. And that would be the end.

The Slaughterhouse would be a target, he suspected. One or more of the successor states would seek to co-opt or destroy the Marines. He'd sent orders to prepare for evacuation as soon as he'd realised that Earth's collapse had gone too far to be stopped; his Marines should be ready to abandon the world before the news reached the rest of the Empire. Safehouse was unknown to anyone outside the planning team; it should be safe enough, at least long enough for the Marines to regroup and consider their next move. But what would they do without the Empire?

It had been a badge of honour to be a Terran Marine, right from the start. As the Empire decayed, it had meant more and more to the elite who'd made up the Marines. They'd seen themselves as standing for a greater principle, as being honest and incorruptible when all other institutions were becoming obsessed with form over function. But now the Empire was gone. What were the Marines now?

Prince Roland had made it out, thanks to Specialist Lawson – but his Empire was gone. His position as Crown Prince was meaningless, even more than it had been before Earth had collapsed into chaos. It was even risky for him to *keep* his name and title; there would be no shortage of people willing to blame the Prince for the Empire's collapse. Human nature demanded that they find someone to blame and Roland – the *old* Roland – would make a convenient scapegoat. The fact that he'd been a puppet, then a fugitive, would completely pass them by.

"I'm going to record everything," Colonel Myung-Hee had said. "One day, everyone will need to know what happened at the Fall of Earth."

Jeremy couldn't disagree. One of the reasons for the Empire's slow collapse, according to Professor Caesius, was that the Grand Senate had been allowed to bury historical truths under a mountain of bullshit. He didn't envy Chung's attempt to catalogue everything that had taken place in the solar system – and he doubted that anyone would ever have the complete picture – but she had to try. Future generations might learn something from the Empire's end.

Not that we learned anything from the past, he thought. *Why should our successors?*

His wristcom buzzed. "Sir," Doctor Roslyn said, "we're ready to begin surgery now."

"Understood," Jeremy said. "Good luck."

Belinda opened her eyes.

She was lying on a medical bed, staring up at the ceiling. The omnipresent background hum told her that she was on a starship, almost certainly one of the Marine transports fleeing Earth's system. And yet...she was confused. She'd *known* that she was dead.

Automatically, she ordered her implants to run a status check. There was no response.

A face came into view. "Specialist Lawson? Can you hear me?"

Her mouth felt funny and her voice sounded slurred, but she managed to answer. "Yeah..."

"Glad to see you back with us," the face said. "I'm Doctor Roslyn. You took quite a beating, I'm afraid, but it's all over now."

Belinda remembered Roland and shivered. "The...Prince...?"

"Is safe and well," Doctor Roslyn assured her. "Sleep now. There will be plenty of time to catch up later."

She wanted to protest, but he did something to her and she plunged back into blackness. When she next opened her eyes, she was in a different room and two other faces were looking down at her. The Commandant... and Prince Roland. Both of them looked very relieved to see her.

"What...what happened?"

The Commandant gave Prince Roland a droll look. "Blame the Emperor who designed the shuttle," he said, finally. "He had a full medical centre installed; Roland dragged your body into the compartment and dumped you into the tube. The automated doctor put you in stasis while the Prince called for help. Once we picked you up, Doctor Roslyn went to work and saved the rest of your life."

Belinda nodded. Even that motion was hard.

"Thank you," she said, finally.

"Least I could do," Prince Roland said, but his face was grim. "Earth is gone."

"She doesn't need to know that right now," Doctor Roslyn said. He scowled at both of Belinda's visitors. "You've seen that she's alive, now scram. I need to talk to my patient."

He watched them both leave the compartment, then turned to look at Belinda.

"You do know," he asked, "that you are very lucky to be alive?"

"Yes," Belinda said quietly.

"Your implants were badly damaged," the Doctor said. "And you took a beating. Among other things, there was cranial bleeding, the drug-injectors started leaking and you overdosed on the boost. That you managed to keep functioning as long as you did was nothing short of a miracle."

His eyes narrowed. "But there *was* damage," he said. "I thought we were going to lose you for several hours before you finally pulled through. The brain damage...well, we fixed the damage we *could* fix, but brains are tricky things. You might suffer all kinds of side-effects from that alone. And then we had to replace a number of your implants, just to help your body cleanse itself. In the long term...?

"You may feel fine now, but it will be years before you can consider going back on active service," he added. "My honest advice would be to retire."

Belinda stared at him. Her service as a Marine and then a Pathfinder had given her life meaning...it couldn't be gone. Her father had served out his time; *she* could do no less, particularly if she *could* recover.

She found her voice. "My implants?"

"We had to remove most of the damaged ones," Doctor Roslyn said. There was nothing but sympathy in his eyes. "The neural link, in particular, was contributing to your mental problems. I would be reluctant to install a replacement for several years, at the very least – it would almost certainly make your recovery far more complicated. And the boost and suchlike......?"

He shook his head. "Right now, your system couldn't tolerate the boost," he warned her. "It would kill you. Rest...and if you want to return to duty, follow my orders and show a little patience."

Belinda wanted to argue, but she knew he was right. Besides...

She cursed herself for forgetting the obvious question. "Where *are* we?"

"Onboard the *Chesty Puller*, on our way to the Slaughterhouse," Doctor Roslyn explained. "We're in Phase Space right now; we shouldn't be in any danger, so you can relax and do as I tell you. Or we can put you back into stasis until we reach our final destination and you can start your recovery then. But my honest advice is still to retire."

"To find a house, a husband, have children...?" Belinda couldn't help laughing. "Boring!"

"Then work hard," the Doctor advised. "But *don't* push yourself too hard."

It took four days before the Doctor was willing to let her get out of bed. Even when he finally gave her permission to try sitting up, he watched her like a hawk until she swung her legs over the side of the bed and stood up. A moment later, he caught her as she tottered and almost fell backwards; her coordination was shot to hell. She'd been so used to the implants that she would have to relearn how to walk, just like a newborn baby. The feeling of helplessness was so overwhelming that she almost cried, even though she *knew* she would recover. No wonder there were few Pathfinders willing to have their implants removed so they could live on the Inner Worlds.

Once she could walk without toppling over herself, the Doctor prescribed a mild level of physical exercise – and ordered Prince Roland to supervise to make sure that Belinda didn't overexert herself. Belinda couldn't help realising that the Doctor probably had a point; the exercise she was doing daily was less than the Civil Guardsmen were ordered to do every week. She'd done far more at Boot Camp...but then she'd been healthy, at least for a recruit. Now...

She looked over at the Prince as the treadmill came to a halt. He'd been spending most of his time with her, chatting and playing games... Belinda was glad of the company, if only because she didn't want to spend time with other Marines. It would have been too unpleasant a reminder of what she'd lost.

"You never told me," she said. "What happened on the shuttle?"

"I put you in the tube, then held a gun to the pilot's head," Roland said. "We started broadcasting your name, as you ordered, and an hour or so later we were picked up by the *Chesty Puller*. If the Grand Senator's ship was lurking around, it didn't come after us."

"Probably for the best," Belinda said. The Commandant had promised that he would debrief her when she was feeling better; apparently, there was no need to hurry. Standard procedure was to debrief Marines as quickly as possible, but it wasn't as if she could give another team any invaluable pieces of intelligence. "What are you going to do with your life?"

Roland gave her an odd glance. "I honestly don't know," he admitted. "Is it wrong that part of me is a little relieved? I won't be the Crown Prince any longer; there's no prospect of my becoming Emperor…and yet, I feel relieved."

He shook his head. "But there's another part of me that thinks the whole crisis is my fault," he added. "What if I'd refused to grant my assent to Admiral Valentine's appointment? Or…"

Belinda snorted. "There is absolutely no way in which the crisis was your fault," she said. "You were a puppet. If you'd refused, they would have lied and told the universe that you had signed whatever they wanted you to sign."

Roland turned to face her properly. "But it was me who insisted that we went to confront the Emergency Committee," he reminded her. "It was my fault that you were injured…you almost *died*!"

"It wasn't your fault that Bode hit me with a capture net," Belinda said. She shook her head as he looked doubtful. "I knew the job was dangerous when I took it, so…"

"You have the rest of your life ahead of you," she added. "And you don't have to be the Prince any longer. Why not see what else you can do?"

"You definitely made a man out of him," the Commandant observed when he finally came to debrief her. "I think that you should be proud."

Belinda shrugged. "He thinks that what happened to me was his fault."

"At least he's learned to think of others," the Commandant pointed out. "That is a *considerable* improvement on the spoilt brat everyone knew before Earth fell."

He shook his head. "We're going to have to abandon the Slaughterhouse for a few years," he added. "Luckily, we have a few other training facilities. Roland has expressed a wish to try out for the Marines and...well, I thought he deserved a chance. Not everyone can maintain the presence of mind to shove someone into a medical tube, then take control of the shuttle despite being outnumbered. Besides, there are few other options for him."

Belinda nodded. Who would want a Prince whose Empire had fallen? No one...apart from those looking for someone to blame.

"I do have something for you to do, if you want to stay occupied," the Commandant added. "It's a desk job, but it is vitally important – and I'll make sure you have plenty of time for medical treatment and exercise. But I need someone I can trust to know what they're doing in the post."

"Something to do with the Pathfinders?" Belinda guessed.

"And the Corpse," the Commandant said. "And a few other secrets."

Belinda hesitated. She disliked the whole *concept* of a desk job; one of the reasons she'd tried out for the Pathfinders was that there was no prospect of a desk job in the team. But she would need *something* to keep her busy while she waited for her body to recover...and besides, every able-bodied Marine would be needed elsewhere.

And she was curious. All she'd heard about the Corpse had been rumours.

"Sure," she answered, finally. "Why not?"

The Commandant watched her leave the compartment, the hatch hissing shut behind her, and then looked down at the datapad. There was far too much to do, yet he could do nothing apart from planning until they reached the Slaughterhouse. Once they were there...

He looked up at the globe-and-anchor emblazoned on the bulkhead. The Marine Corps stood for tradition; the Marines were expected to honour their ancestors through carrying on the traditions that had stood them in good stead for so long. But the Marine Corps was going to have to change to survive the coming years. It would have to become something different, something new…and that flew in the face of tradition. But there was no choice.

Belinda had fought the good fight; no one would dispute that. And yet it had been a failure, for all that she'd saved Roland's life. The Marines were charged with protecting the Empire and they'd failed. Its decay had simply gone too far to be stopped, no matter what the Marines did. There was no escaping one simple fact. In the end, they'd failed.

For all its faults, the Empire had kept the peace among countless star systems. Now, as news of Earth's fall spread, those systems would go down into civil war. Billions had died on Earth; billions more would die in the future. And how long would it be before a new empire arose from the ashes?

The Empire was gone. If the Marines were to have any hope of shaping the future, they would have to change. And that scared him more than he wanted to admit.

But there was no choice. He'd failed once.

He would not fail again.

The End

AFTERWORD

It is really depressingly easy to make fun of *Atlas Shrugged*.

The book is a massive doorstopper, over 600,000 words long (roughly five times the size of *When the Bough Breaks*.) John Galt spends three hours in-universe lecturing the entire country on the looter creed and his own response (more like five-six hours in real life) when very few people could muster the ability to listen to such a long speech *and* take it all in, even with the best will in the world. Not that he's the only offender, of course; several other characters in the book had the same problem with blathering too much. It isn't hard at all to poke at selected points – including Rand's personal life – and suggest that they invalidate the entire book.

It is, in fact, so easy that it tends to obscure the fact that Rand was basically right.

"Oh," the critics say. "*Really?*"

Rand spent her childhood in Russia, during the early years of the Bolshevik (Communist) Government. Her father's business was taken over by the Communists, who then expected him to run it for them. Later, after going to university in Russia, she was briefly purged along with hundreds of others for being 'bourgeois' – a term that could hardly be said to apply to her then-destitute family – and was only allowed to return after complaints from foreign students. In 1925, she was allowed to leave for America. She never returned to Russia.

Read *Atlas Shrugged* and then study how Russia decayed under the Communists. Businesses were nationalised…production fell sharply and many of the best managers and designers were sent to the Gulag for being unable to perform. Farms were collectivised…Russia never managed to feed itself and even had to import food from the archenemy, the USA.

Schools and universities became more about indoctrination than about teaching students to think…Russia suffered a monumental brain drain that ensured that the Soviet Union would never be able to match the west. There are eerie parallels between Rand's vision and the fall of the Soviet Union.

Oh, the details don't match. Of course they don't. But the general theme is identical.

[If you don't like *Atlas Shrugged*, look up *The Cold Equations* (Ted Godwin). At some point, the effects of stupidity and ignorance become an unstoppable tidal wave heading towards disaster.]

The keyword for this lecture is *maintenance*. According to the Free Online Dictionary, 'maintenance' is:

1. The act of maintaining or the state of being maintained.
2. The work of keeping something in proper condition; upkeep.
3. a. Provision of support or livelihood: took over the maintenance of her family.
   b. Means of support or livelihood: was ordered to pay maintenance for both children.

Let us assume, for the purpose of this discussion, that you own a car. You buy it and take it home and try to pick up girls in it. And everyone lives happily ever after, right?

Well, no. Your car needs fuel; every few days, you have to refill the tank or the car will grind to a halt. And then there's the windscreen wipers; you have to ensure that the tank of water is kept stockpiled or you will run out at the most inconvenient moment. If you let someone else drive your car, you have to readjust the mirrors, seatbelt and seat position every time you take the car back. All of that is just basic, right?

Over the long term, there are other things you have to do to keep your car in full working order. Even without an accident or vandalism, your car is going to start decaying. Everything from the engine and brakes to the rear headlights need to be watched carefully; some problems could get you a ticket from an alert police officer, others could cost you your life. You also have to pay road tax, have your car undergo the MOT test (at least in Britain) and plenty of other things. And if you don't do them, you can get in real trouble.

Oh, there's always a temptation to skimp on maintenance. Self-delusion is always popular – and plenty of people are happy to think that something will never happen to them. But poor maintenance *always* catches up with you. For the car example, you might be fined, you might end up in handcuffs and riding to jail in a police car…or you might be seriously injured or killed.

With me so far?

The difference between *maintenance* and *repair* is that you do maintenance *before* you run into problems. It can be something as simple as refuelling the car or something as complicated as taking a piece of machinery apart, cleaning it out and then putting it back together again. Chances are, repairing something after it breaks down will be harder than maintaining it. It's useful to bear that in mind.

Now, the important point is that just about *everything* needs to be maintained. The streets outside your home? The drains? The telephone network? The railways? Some things require near-constant attention, others take much longer to decay to the point where they develop problems. However, *you cannot get away* with refusing to do maintenance indefinitely.

A good example is the fate of Britain's railways. Once, Britain had the finest railway services in the world; hell, we *invented* the damn things. Now…ask anyone who has to use them regularly and you will almost certainly hear an endless series of complaints. The fares are going upwards and upwards, delays are becoming epidemic, the system cannot cope with bad weather, there have been some nasty crashes…and no one seems to be taking any responsibility. After the railways were privatised, it actually got worse. Why did this happen?

There were a multitude of problems with the whole system, but the core of it was two-fold; first, the rate of preventive maintenance was cut sharply; second, the bosses became disconnected from the realities of their business. Consider, if you will, the traditional ideal; a young man joins a business and works his way up to the top. By the time he reaches the top, he knows exactly how the business works – and what they can get away with when it comes to maintenance. How many modern-day executives reached the top through immersing themselves in the business?

This is not an uncommon problem. You see it in just about every large organisation, from international corporations to the military. Costs are cut…and something vitally important is eliminated in the process. Sometime later, the need for whatever was eliminated comes back, often after the person responsible has moved on, leaving his successors to grapple with the problem. And the problem is normally extremely difficult to fix.

It should come as no surprise (particularly if you read the *No Worse Enemy* afterword, also free on my site) that governments also require maintenance. When the government is not maintained, when the population do not hold it to account, it decays. Instead of complaining again, however, I have decided to attempt to list a series of possible fixes.

I do not claim that these are perfect solutions, nor am I going to defend them. Each of them will cause problems as well as fix them (and detractors will immediately assert that the problems make them unworkable). What you can decide, if you like, is if they are worth trying.

Term Limits
All politicians are to serve for short periods only (say, one five-year term) then leave politics forever.

Family Exclusion/No Nepotism
A person who is directly related to a politician (partner, sibling, child) may not run for election, or take up work in politics – i.e. they cannot work as an assistant to other politicians.

No Legal Exceptions
Politicians may not write laws that do not apply to them; conversely, they may not write laws that only apply to them.

Residency Requirements
All politicians are required to live in their constituencies for at least five years *prior* to running for office.

Anonymous or Public Financing
Political donations are to be collected by a neutral party, then passed on to the political party or politician without any source of origin. Alternatively, all political donations are to be declared openly and the information posted freely online.

Pre-Election Jobs
Politicians may not run for office before a set age (for example, 30 years old) and must have had a non-political job beforehand.

Recall Elections
The local constituents have the right – if they collect enough signatures – to recall their representative and force him to face a general referendum on his conduct. If he loses the vote, he will be sacked and a local election will be held to find a replacement.

The Idea I Forgot
Why not tell me about it?

―――――

I've used this Heinlein quote before, but it still fits:

"[Why should you be politically active?] Because you are needed. Because the task is not hopeless. Democracy is normally in perpetual crisis. It requires

the same constant, alert attention to keep it from going to pot that an automobile does when driven through downtown traffic. If you do not yourself pay attention to the driving, year in and year out, the crooks, or scoundrels, or nincompoops will take over the wheel and drive it in a direction you don't fancy, or wreck it completely.

When you pick yourself up out of the wreckage, you and your wife and your kids, don't talk about what "They" did to you. You did it, compatriot, because you preferred to sit in the back seat and snooze. Because you thought your taxes bought you a bus ticket and a guaranteed safe arrival, when all your taxes bought you was a part ownership in a joint enterprise, on a share-the-cost and share-the-driving plan."

And consider this – just because you take no interest in politics, as a very ancient statesman observed, doesn't mean that politics will take no interest in you.

Christopher Nuttall
Kota Kinabalu, 2013

Printed in Great Britain
by Amazon